I0730435

The Philosopher and the Assassin

by D. A. Baden

Habitat Press

The characters, events, and places in the story are fictional. Any resemblance to real people or events is coincidental.

Cover by Claire Wingfield

Copyright © 2025 by Habitat Press

All rights reserved.

No portion of this book may be reproduced in any form without written permission from the publisher or author, except as permitted by U.K. copyright law.

PRAISE FOR THE PHILOSOPHER AND THE ASSASSIN
'At once a commentary on the looming responsibility of the climate crisis and our ever-shrinking opportunity to enact meaningful change, and a far from conventional whodunnit, the book plays with the notion of what is moral and what is right. Complicit in the book's central sprawling philosophical dilemma, the reader finds themselves judge, jury and executioner in the case of the century. While the novel tackles prescient and troubling themes and poses difficult questions (how far should we go for the greater good?), it does so with a sense of dry humour and a delightful eye for the absurd. Above all, the warmth and resilience of its ineffable protagonist suffuses the narrative and, as the story ends, we struggle to leave her behind. Not only is this a timely, thought-provoking and essential story in an age of urgent, innovative climate action that demands the attention of us all, but it is a thoroughly enjoyable read. Funny, memorable, characterful and original.'

The Literary Studio

'Denise Baden's campus novel/whodunnit is so much more than just an up-to-the-minute academic locked-door mystery, it's a philosophical treatise wrapped in an exposition of the polycrisis, embedded in a love story, threaded through with alternative democracy and grounded in explorations of grief, motivation and drive. Full of sharp ideas, subtle humour and grounded in the harsh realities of our world, you'll come away with a whole new understanding of our world and what it takes to change it!'

Manda Scott, *Any Human Power* and *Boudica* series.

'If facts are ignored, fiction may be our next best hope. With its story-within-a-story, *The Philosopher and the Assassin* cranks up the dramatic tension around whether we will achieve the carbon transition, or not. Ultimately, a surprisingly hopeful read.'

John Elkington, *Tickling Sharks: How We Sold Business on Sustainability*. Co-founder of ENDS, SustainAbility and Volans.

Also by D.A. Baden

Habitat Man

The Assassin

No More Fairy Tales: Stories to Save Our Planet

Murder in the Citizens' Jury (play)

Fidel (musical)

PRAISE FOR D.A. BADEN

'Truly lyrical and a joy to read…. A natural storyteller.'
   Mark Laggatt, author of *Penitent*.

'Inspirational and entertaining.'
   Dr Matt Winning comedian and author of *Hot Mess*.

'Bursting with powerful stories and brilliant ideas.'
   Rachel Trezise, Prize-winning Author.

'*Habitat Man* is both great fun and a delightful reflection on the ways we live – and die! – at a time when more and more people are grappling with today's environmental challenges.'
   Jonathon Porritt.

'A tale of lust, gardening, love and compost: a hilarious page turner.'
   Dave Goulson, author of *The Garden Jungle*.

'A charming romp that makes you think! Mid-life crisis meets environmental awareness in this rom-com for the 21st Century.'
   Michael Jecks, author of the *Templar* series.

'Superbly written romance with a lovely touch of humour'
   Helen Baggott, author of *Posted in the Past*.

Dedication

There is no better company than a bunch of academics arguing down the pub. Whatever the subject, they will discourse with passion, pedantry, rigour and ferocious attention to evidence. No statement will go unchallenged. You may wax lyrical about your new face cream, and next time you meet they will have tried it on one side of their face, not the other, and challenge you to tell the difference. Or it will be questioned why on a drug information leaflet, precise statistics are given on the chances of you suffering from specific side effects but no corresponding data on the probabilities of benefit. Or a thought-provoking proposition that if we'd have discovered the peaceful bonobo apes before the more macho chimpanzees, we'd have gone on to become a matriarchal society. Unconstrained by politics or commerce, they will debate freely the extent to which economic growth is compatible with a finite planet. Some academics are co-opted by industry and induced with flattery and first-class flights to dance to their tune. But most are not, and never have they been so necessary. This book is dedicated to them and to the glorious planet Earth upon whom the whole merry-go-round depends.

Chapter 1

I'm Iris Tate, Professor of Moral Philosophy. I've published extensively in the academic field, but this kind of thing is new to me. I've been told I should start with a bit about myself.

Typically, narrators writing in the first person find an excuse to examine themselves in a mirror and reveal what they see. Usually someone good-looking. If it's a male author writing as female, she may regard her naked body for a bit too.

I present a cheerful exterior. In my previous position at the Business School, some of my colleagues called me Chip. I'm not sure if it was due to my chipper attitude or my toothy chipmunk smile. I'd love Chip to catch on here, but it doesn't count if you suggest it yourself. All the philosophy in the world doesn't protect you from the need to belong. I was looking for my tribe. A bit late in the day at fifty you might think, but a lot's changed in the last year.

One should reveal character, maybe by saving a cat or something. I've done a few of those personality questionnaires – are you introvert, extrovert, etc. I'm always bang in the middle. I seek balance. Someone said it's because I'm a Libra, but I don't believe in any of that nonsense.

How do we judge ourselves, anyway? Many like to identify with some kind of label. But words, categories, identities – they're artificially created boxes. They're frames on meaning. We exist in a boundless universe of everything, and we put a frame around this or that piece of it and call it a table, justice, bisexual, etc. We then juggle these boxes around, hoping we can make sense of them, and if they don't add up, we argue. These are frames around an infinity of connections and meanings, so it's no surprise. They could never add up neatly.

Although if you hope the book will be full of such philosophical ruminations, you will be disappointed as none of that matters now. I've been blasted out of my ivory tower. So, here I am, trying to make sense of it all. My story encompasses murder, mystery, ethical dilemmas and the possible end of humanity as we know it. Part whodunnit, part confession, part moral philosophy. I justify the uncommon structure on the basis that we need to rethink how we do everything anyway. But really, it's because I've spent too much time dithering over how to present this – a memoir, a novel, textbook, a guide to how we can flourish and survive? It's a story, and how much is true would entail a reflection on the nature of truth and we have no time for that because things start to happen. Things happen all the time of course, but the inciting incident, as they call it, occurred when I encountered the dilemma.

*

Staff briefing day in the Business School was a plush affair. We were treated to fresh coffee, comfortable chairs, round tables with jugs of water. In my newly adopted Faculty of Arts and Humanities, we sat in a lecture theatre in tiered, graffiti-marked seats. Some had brought their own flasks. The content, though, was much the same. I'm old enough to feel nostalgic for the days before tuition fees, when they lectured us about innovations in teaching and learning. Now it was metrics and money.

I looked around at my new colleagues and wondered if any of them would become friends. Certainly not the self-important man at the front with the receding hair and suit. His name badge proclaimed him to be Colin, and he was nodding at everything the Dean said. The only familiar faces were my new boss, Jenna, Dean of Arts and Humanities, who stood at the podium; and Percy, Head of English, sat at the end of my row.

I'd met him during my interview. At the time, I'd been so focused on impressing them, I'd taken in very little — other than the suspicious rise of his eyebrow as I listed my credentials. Jenna had interrupted him when he asked why I was so keen to leave the Business School.

I considered them now. Percy's haughty profile spoke of self-assurance and integrity, and the knitted 'V' of his brows indicated a simmering resentment elicited by everything Jenna said. Jenna herself was immaculate. Perfect makeup, glossy hair and colour-coordinated to a degree that indicated either a strong aesthetic sense or an excessive concern with outward appearances. Image over substance, I decided after listening to her a little longer.

On a slide were the criteria every programme had to meet. Jenna sped through the list. 'Interdisciplinarity, critical thinking, sustainable development goals, decolonisation.' She paused at the last item, which was spelled out in bold capitals: 'ENTERTAINING'.

Percy snorted, and I detected a mutter from the colleague sitting next to him – a portly, crumpled man, who, like Percy, had an exasperated air.

'Next on the agenda are trigger warnings,' she continued. 'These should be provided for sensitive or distressing content.'

'Do I need trigger warnings for my music?' asked a solemn-looking woman.

Several staff sniggered.

'Don't be ridiculous, Georgina,' Jenna said, then hesitated. She turned to Colin, who inclined his head. 'Actually, yes, best to be on the safe side.'

Colin took to the podium. 'All those teaching this semester should have their course outline and assignment details posted by now. I've noticed that certain members of staff still haven't done so.' He looked directly at me.

I projected back what I hoped was a reassuring confidence, but inside I was panicking. I'd put off explaining my circumstances to justify my inaction, because I should have done so in my interview. Then again, it's not like one can know in advance that the heady delirium of a job change wouldn't last. 'Sorry, I really believed the crushing feelings of loss wouldn't affect my performance, but it turns out I was wrong.'

Jenna moved on to the National Student Survey – or NSS as we knew it. Student satisfaction scores were the metric we all danced to.

I opened my laptop under the guise of taking notes and tried again to map out my module. My previous course had been built around business ethics dilemmas. Arts and humanities students would expect something different, but what? A session on democracy would be topical with a referendum coming up. It would have moral and constitutional implications, and they probably don't realise how much it matters. My boys certainly didn't. That was more politics than philosophy, but I could claim interdisciplinarity.

I was distracted by an email popping up, marked 'urgent and confidential'. I was surprised to see it was from the Crown Prosecution Service.

I glanced around to check no one could see over my shoulder and opened it.

> *Dear Professor,*
>
> *I was impressed by your innovative work using students on your business ethics class to assist with ethical dilemmas. Would you be available to undertake a similar consultancy job for me?*
>
> *Please keep this correspondence confidential.*
> *Kind regards*
> *Robert Ash*
> *Director of Public Prosecutions*

I replied immediately, asking for details. Within seconds, I received a protected document, closely followed by a separate email with a password: RASH2345#. I checked over my shoulder again, opened the document and leaned forward to read.

> *I am facing a dilemma that warrants a second opinion as the stakes are potentially extremely high. In this case, it's the young people who have most to lose or gain by any decision made, so it's only right that they get a say. But not just anyone. I need those who have received some grounding in ethics. I hesitate to say more at this early stage. If you take it on, we will need to move fast. We have a generous consultancy budget, which I'd place at your*

disposal. If you're interested, please let me know by return.

Young people have most at stake? It will be about climate. And only murder would warrant the attention of the Director of Public Prosecutions? It must be of an important person. No, it would be in the news. Or maybe *by* an important person. But there's no dilemma there. We're all equal under the law.

Lost in my thoughts, I was caught off guard to hear my name and realised the Dean had introduced me. Jenna was going on in embarrassing detail about the money I'd brought into the Business School with my research into ethical dilemmas and trade-offs that had informed algorithms in automated vehicles. 'This is the gold standard we should all aspire to,' she said, finishing at last.

I smiled self-deprecatingly and waved a hand, uncomfortably aware of the hostility emanating from the rest of the staff.

The meeting came to a close. I dashed off an email to the DPP telling him I was in and joined the throng of academics lining up for the exit.

I found myself behind Percy, who was holding forth to his colleagues.

'Trigger warnings!' he sniffed.

'You'd think there'd be a clue in the title of my module – Genocide in the Twentieth Century.' It was the man who'd been sitting next to Percy. From his accent and expansive shrug, I guessed he was French.

I laughed, and he turned around, pleased to have found an appreciative audience.

'Hi. I'm Iris.'

'Ah. The hotshot from the Business School.' The tone was jocular, but his eyes glinted. 'Marcel.'

'I'm GG,' said the woman who'd asked about trigger warnings. 'I teach music.' She looked sweet. Petite and compact, with unruly hair and soulful brown eyes.

'Nice to meet you,' I said, shaking hands all round.

We edged towards the exit.

'I'm moderating your course… when it's up,' said Marcel.

'Business ethics! Ha ha. Oxymoron, eh?' said Percy.

I tried to smile at the familiar joke. 'It will be moral philosophy.'

'Knock over one old man crossing the road or swerve and take out two pedestrians?' Marcel suggested.

'That kind of thing, yes.'

'What should you do?' asked GG.

I shrugged. 'The trouble with these hypothetical scenarios is that when there's no obvious answer, students can give up and decide there's no such thing as right or wrong. Before you know it, notions of truth go the same way. I flirted with postmodernist ideas in my youth, but I had no idea where they'd lead.'

We came to a halt as a row of staff shuffled out before us.

'So, it's you we have to blame for the post-truth society?' Percy frowned.

'Erm, well, I'm trying to turn the tide before it's too late.'

'How's that then?' Marcel asked.

'I want to make moral philosophy relevant to the big challenges, like climate change.'

We reached the exit.

'You can philosophise at an iceberg all you like...' Marcel shrugged. 'It still melts at zero degrees.'

I located my office on the second floor. I fished for the key and opened the door. Piles of books and journals took up the floor and chairs. I sighed. They'd promised to unpack. Then I saw the shelves were crammed with my books. In fairness, HR had suggested I limit myself to five crates. I'd taken boxloads to the charity shop, but they said there was no call for textbooks that were decades old. The drop in salary was one thing, but the tiny room was harder to bear.

I regarded the philosophy books stacked on my chair. Kant, Socrates, Arendt, Wittgenstein. They'd been my companions, my lifeblood, but what use were theory and hypothetical scenarios now? I collected them up in my arms and hesitated. Wittgenstein arched a superior eyebrow from his collected works. He was right, it would be disrespectful to throw them away. This is just a phase, I told myself and lugged them to the windowsill. Soon I'd have a real-life dilemma to get the juices flowing. Something that mattered more than helping AI algorithms drive cars.

I plugged in my laptop and sat down in my new chair to check my emails. There were plenty, but nothing back from the DPP. I fiddled with the chair to get the right height. I tried a spin and yelped as my shins bumped up against a crate under my desk. An email arrived. It was from Colin subject: UPLOAD FULL COURSE OUTLINE.

I rested my chin in my hands and closed my eyes. Last night had been a bad one. I flopped forward onto the desk and laid my head in my arms. I waved away books to create some space, ignoring the thumps as they fell to the floor. The new environment was no protection and within seconds, the usual images, sounds and smells emerged from the depths to haunt me. I wrestled them back into their box and focused my mind on the imminent deadline.

The ding of an email brought me springing back up to my screen. The DPP had replied. I double-clicked eagerly, then had to scrabble back to find the passcode and tried again. My eyes raced across the screen. I was right. A murder had taken place in a closed committee on climate. I skimmed through the reams of information on climate tipping points, the importance of the rule of law and how normally he'd prosecute without a second thought. It was frustratingly short on detail. Every other line reiterated the need for discretion, so maybe the issue was that the decision on the climate policy wouldn't stand if the murder became public. Was it a secret committee? What was the climate policy?

A second document outlined the terms of the consultancy. My eyes widened at the five-figure fee. I jotted down notes rapidly, sighing with relief. Inspiration at last.

Chapter 2

I woke up, nightmares still swirling like wreaths of smoke. Usually, I purged them by sitting under a blanket to watch cosy mysteries. What I liked about them was that no one ever minded when someone died. After that, I'd munch through some cereal while watching a climate documentary and then work out my feelings with some cleaning. I'm not one to dwell, so once Fay was gone, I'd ordered a five-litre carton of white vinegar, bicarbonate of soda and some citric acid following the instructions of an eco-cleaning book I'd got from the library. The house smelled fresh and lemony clean. It helped, but not enough.

Yesterday was the first time I'd left my home for weeks. This morning, I couldn't stay, even for breakfast. I had to share my proposal fast in case the DPP changed his mind.

*

Dear Robert,

I'd be delighted to help. Some variant of the attached module outline would provide students with the ethical toolkit they would need. I can then make their final assignment mirror yours. You need not worry about confidentiality as I use hypothetical but realistic scenarios in all my lectures, so they would have no reason to pick your one out as real.

Kind regards
Iris Tate
Professor of Moral Philosophy

ATTACHMENT: Proposed outline

Lecture 1: Kant and universal moral standards. The idea of the 'Common Good.'

Lecture 2: Rawls' Theory of Justice. This provides an objective, yet deeply personal tool for ethical analysis.

   N.B., I acknowledge that with the order I am already imposing a kind of bias, and I will endeavour to be mindful of that.

Other lectures would include the following:

- Utilitarianism: This follows the principle of the greatest good of the greatest number.

- Cross-cultural and indigenous approaches. Western philosophers are hung up on finding abstract rules that one can follow in all situations. When exposed to just these kinds of thinkers, students can get frustrated with the fuzziness of real-life. Non-Western philosophers tend to be more accepting of how context determines the rightness of decisions.

- Moral Relativism: This lecture is essential to discuss the case for universal values over ethical relativism.

- I will include others such as virtue ethics and possibly discourse theory or eco-feminism.

The DPP's response came within moments. I clicked it open immediately.

> *Dear Professor,*
> *I'm happy to proceed but am concerned about the*
> *timings. Please call me ASAP.*
> *Kind regards*
> *Robert Ash*
> *Director of Public Prosecutions*

His tone was abrupt, which didn't bode well. But I wasn't new to this game. Everyone always wanted results yesterday. The trick is to get them out of their automatic, get-this-done mode of thinking and pause. They'll fight it, but you need to slow them down until they get to a moment of stillness. Only then will they be open to seeing the bigger picture.

I took some deep breaths and rang the number.

'Professor Tate? I—'

'Oh Iris, please.' I projected a beaming smile into my voice. 'Shall I call you Director of—'

'Robert is fine. I appreciate—'

'How did you hear of me?'

'It was an article in the Alumni magazine.'

'Was it the piece about my self-driving car project?'

'Yes. It said you'd moved to arts and humanities to teach moral philosophy.'

'Then you thought, if businesses can crowdsource their ethical dilemmas to students, why not a Director of Public Prosecutions?' I laughed. 'Very clever.'

I swung around in my chair and bumped against a crate on the floor.

'Hmm. Yes, so—'

'We were at the same university?'

'I was the year above and in the law school, so our paths didn't cross, but I remember you from the drama club.'

'Ah, you saw one of my shows?' I settled back in my seat.

'*Jack and the Beanstalk.* You were very good.'

It may have been thirty years ago, but I still thrilled at the compliment.

'I wrote it too. Although perhaps I shouldn't admit that, as the beanstalk was a cannabis plant.'

'You were the customs guard, so that's OK.'

I detected a smile in his voice. We were ready.

'Now Robert, what are your concerns?'

'I need an answer sooner than ten weeks.'

'It takes time to build moral literacy.'

I looked up at a knock at my door. Colin peered at me through the glass pane. I waved my phone at him. He waited.

I wasn't going to speak before Robert responded. A pause was necessary to allow him to process the truth of my statement.

Colin was still there, frowning slightly.

'Could you use last year's students?' Robert asked.

'I was in the Business School then. The curriculum focused on business ethics. You want the right answer surely, not a fast one.'

'What would you do?'

Oh. I'd not expected that. I looked up. Colin had gone.

'What's the climate policy?'

'All I can tell you is that it would be transformative. For several reasons, the UK is the ideal testbed, and if it works here, it could catch on elsewhere.'

'I see.' I was desperate to know more, but I couldn't push it. 'Just to be clear, Robert. You're not asking me if it would be right to murder someone for a climate policy?'

'No. The dilemma is whether I should prosecute.'

'Prosecuting would mean the climate policy wouldn't go through?'

'That's correct.'

'Losing the opportunity to achieve a low-carbon economy before we pass climate tipping points?'

'Potentially, yes.'

'And is the murderer likely to murder again?' I realised I was saying the word "murder" with relish and checked myself.

'Unlikely.'

I ran the situation through the ethical rules of thumb I taught my students, but they arrived at different answers.

'What is your recommendation as a moral philosopher?'

Murder is wrong,' I began. 'But we're not asking anyone to kill one person to prevent more deaths. Just not to prosecute the murderer who seems unlikely to be a repeat offender, and of course it may be thousands, millions, of lives at stake here.'

'Well?'

'It's right to use the students,' I said. 'As you said, they have more at stake.'

'I agree, but how long are we talking?'

'I've not taught arts and humanities students before. I'll set them an early assignment to get a sense of their ethical reasoning skills, then I'll know what I'm dealing with, and get back to you.'

We finished the call. I stood up and teetered slightly, feeling lightheaded. It had been a while since I'd eaten. I found a vending machine at the end of the corridor with drinks and snacks. I hovered undecided, looking for something more nutritious than crisps and chocolate, then just stood there blindly, pondering again the exact nature of Robert's dilemma. A tap on the shoulder made me jump.

I turned around to see Colin.

'Sorry I couldn't talk earlier,' I babbled to cover my half-scream.

'You still haven't posted a module outline.'

'I've been busy following up on a consultancy opportunity. It could bring in a lot of money, which should keep the Dean happy.'

I was surprised by a look of dismay which flashed across his face.

'I had to work on that first as it's time sensitive,' I followed up.

'Then you'd better get your ethics form in.'

I stared at him open-mouthed, realising the implications of his words. How could I have forgotten? I gave up on the snacks and dashed back to my office.

> *Dear Robert,*
>
> *Before I undertake the consultancy, I must get informed consent from the students. They should know that their answers will have real-life consequences. Please call me if this is an issue.*
>
> *Kind regards*
> *Iris Tate*
> *Professor of Moral Philosophy*

The DPP had made the need for confidentiality clear. The

odds were slim he'd accept that. The office grew gloomy as I transferred books from the crate under my desk to the windowsill. Is informed consent absolutely necessary anyway? My business ethics students had been told that their answers would be fed into the data that informs algorithms for self-driving cars. The question is whether it would have mattered if they hadn't. The students wouldn't be obviously harmed by the omission; it may even benefit them as it's less pressure.

I found the Socrates mug Lee had given me. Socrates, that ancient poser of awkward questions, might ask: does it deprive them of the chance to grow as human beings in a sense of responsibility and purpose? It probably does, but that seems so tenuous against the immediate benefit of ethically informed self-driving cars. Kant would ask: what if we all took that approach – what then? Then we'd have a nation of irresponsible short-termers who will lead us to our doom. And Kant would gesture towards our current political and cultural landscape as evidence.

I gazed at the mug, longing suddenly for someone real to talk to. I'd hoped that here I'd find more simpatico colleagues.

I headed to the staff canteen and joined the back of a long queue. Percy, Marcel, and GG were eating at a small table. Marcel let out a shout of laughter at something GG had said. She looked perplexed. Percy looked up and caught my eye, then turned back to the conversation. I checked my phone, not wanting to be caught staring. I saw a notification. The DPP had texted a reply.

Please call me.

I left the queue. The campus grounds had several paths connecting the academic buildings with the student union and staff club. I followed a tiny path that broke off and meandered past trees and hedgerows down to a stream. Ahead was a bench by the water, beneath an overhanging willow. It had a suitably secluded feel.

Robert answered straightaway. 'It's an issue,' he said at once. 'Where does that leave us?'

'I like the "us" because we're on the same side,' I said. 'We both want to do the right thing. The question is how.'

'The students can't know this is a real situation. If it can be passed off as an accidental death, it won't attract attention, but murder!'

'And I must put all consultancy jobs through the ethics committee. They will require informed consent.'

'What if I pay you the consultancy fee privately and it doesn't go through the university?'

'That would be against regulations.'

'Oh.'

'I'm tempted, but if an ethics professor can't keep the rules…'

'Have you come to an answer yourself? Now you've had longer to think about it?'

He sounded desperate.

I stared at the stream, tapping my fingers against my mouth.

'In such situations, context is everything,' I said eventually. 'Are you sure the climate policy wouldn't get through if the murder was discovered?'

'There are vested interests here. That's why it's…. Look, they won't let an opportunity like that go by. They'll kill it stone dead. We're up against the clock—'

'Icebergs are melting, I know. And you're positive the policy would make a significant difference?'

'If you're fishing for more information, you won't get it.'

I sighed.

'It wouldn't help anyway,' he said in a more conciliatory tone. 'So, what do you think?'

I racked my brains again. This was basically a variant of the trolley dilemma. A runaway train is heading down a track towards five unsuspecting workers. No time to warn them, but if you pull a lever, you can divert the train to the other track towards one lone worker. Kill one with a direct action and save five or allow five to be killed by inaction to save one. What would I do if I were really in such a situation?

Five ducks paddled by; their quacks seeming to mock me.

Robert misinterpreted my long pause. 'Is it about the money? Are you worried you won't get the consultancy fee if you answer right now?'

'It's not that. Although I suppose a five-figure fee does seem a lot for ten minutes work.'

'Ten minutes backed up by decades of experience,' he countered.

'That should be my line,' I said.

There was a pregnant pause. In Robert's silence, I sensed a pressure to provide an answer.

'I can't use the students without their knowledge.'

He sighed. 'This is a blow.'

'I know.'

The nervous energy left my body, and I slumped against the bench. 'Sorry.' I hung up before I was tempted to change my mind.

I traipsed back to my tiny office. I pushed aside the books on the floor with my foot and sat at my desk. Eleven more lectures to prepare. I felt myself sinking into the chair and stood up. I paced to and fro, talking myself up. They'd loved me in the Business School - except last year of course. The final lecture of my Corporate Social Responsibility module was legendary. I'd donned a wig and made excessive use of a gavel I'd bought for the occasion and put Corporate Social Responsibility on trial. The charges were that CSR was just a public relations exercise and a distraction from more effective solutions such as changing the business legal form, regulation or union power. I pretended to be the prosecuting counsel and provided evidence to show that businesses don't act in the public interest if it opposes shareholder interests. Then I swapped wigs and played defense. I concluded with a rousing speech for and against. In the early days I'd grappled with the verdict myself, but then it became too obvious to ignore.

My thoughts returned to Robert's question. It's a while since I'd had a juicy dilemma. I was obsessed years ago when Wittgenstein appeared to be claiming that all philosophical debate was no more than arguments over definitions. His statement was frustratingly difficult to disprove, and it preoccupied me for longer than it should.

The trolley dilemma was a staple of ethics courses, but I

hadn't given it proper thought for a reason. Philosophy is full of mind traps and unsolvable logical dilemmas that can drive you mad if you let them get to you. Bertrand Russell was a cautionary tale. He'd been thrown by a paradox in his set theory: does a set that contains all sets not containing themselves, contain itself? If it does, then the set would be bigger than itself, which is a logical impossibility. If it doesn't, then it cannot be the set of all sets.

Wittgenstein claimed to have resolved the paradox in his equation: $F(Ou) . Ou = Fu$.

Understandably, Russell remained unsatisfied. He was thrown into despair. He'd lost too many loved ones at an early age and couldn't believe in a deity. Logic was for Russell the one stable foundation, and when he lost that, everything fell apart. Was it the grief that drove him mad or the paradox?

My phone buzzed – a message on the family group chat. I felt the familiar twist in the gut seeing the family photo come to life. It still had all five of us. It was down to three now, but no one had the stomach to replace the photo.

Tom: Hi mum. Gotta skip games night this week. Martha wants me to go to her work do.

Adam: Fine by me bro. Got a party.

The week before, Adam had cancelled.

Mum: OK x

I went home and sat under a blanket and spent the rest of the day eating cereal and watching reruns of *Murder in Paradise*. Suspects and motives and glorious settings whirled around along with my thoughts. I thought about my boys and why they cancelled. Normal growing away, or did they blame me? I thought about clues and red herrings. Most of all, I thought about the dilemma.

Chapter 3

I arrived early for the first faculty meeting of term. Jenna was at the front with an ex-colleague who'd left the Business School shortly before me. I went over to say hello.

'Hi Nadal. What are you doing here?'

'Chip! I could ask you the same question.'

I smiled at the nickname. 'I moved faculty. What about you?'

'I'm a consultant now. That's where the big bucks are – as you showed. Except you had to hand most of it over to the Business School.'

'Now you get to keep it all.'

'That's right.' He grinned and tapped his pocket.

I hadn't known Nadal well, but it was nice to see a familiar face. We chatted about old times until Colin appeared to tell me to take a seat.

Reluctantly I looked around for somewhere to sit.

I slid into a free space on the back row next to Marcel, Percy and GG.

'You've blocked off our exit,' said Marcel.

'Sorry,' I whispered, unsure if he was joking.

Jenna coughed loudly. Colin leant over and tapped the microphone, and the chatter subsided. Jenna smiled her thanks at him and beamed around the room.

'I'm excited to share with you results from the consultancy team we employed to improve our scores on the National Student Survey.'

A slide popped up on the screen: 'RECORDING OF ALL LECTURES AND CLASSES'. It was greeted by mutters of disapproval.

'A few have been recording lectures already, but not all.'

Someone waved a hand. 'Then even more students won't attend.'

'That's what the students have asked for,' she replied.

'If we don't get enough turning up, we can't make the group assignments work,' Marcel cried.

'It's down to you,' the Dean said airily, 'to make your modules interesting enough that they want to attend.'

Percy raised his hand. 'We resent the implication that the numbers are down because of boring lectures.'

Jenna continued as if he hadn't spoken. 'We need to move with the times, and away from old-fashioned notions of education. We must entertain – edutainment.'

Percy snorted. 'It's not even a word.'

'Look what happened last time we tried to edutain,' sniggered a woman near the front. Everyone looked at GG.

'What was that about?' I muttered to Marcel.

He shook his head and nodded towards GG, who was looking daggers at the woman.

'The second suggestion was a rebrand, and I'll hand you over to Nadal, who led the consultancy team.'

He stepped up to the podium. 'Thank you, Jenna. We surveyed groups of young people of school-leaving age and piloted images to see which they found most appealing. These are the resulting photos we'll be using in our marketing.'

He pressed the clicker and cycled through images of shiny students of mixed ethnicities, mostly female, engaging in various activities: abseiling, yoga, mountain climbing, drinking and laughing.

'We think this rebrand will bring in the students, and then it's up to you to build on that with fantastic mind-blowing content.'

Jenna beamed at him and started clapping. Colin glared around until a few joined in.

'Any questions?' Jenna asked.

'Where's the mountain?' Marcel asked.

'It's a stock photo,' Nadal replied.

'It's Ben Nevis,' said someone, kicking off a jumble of

comments.

'Do we do abseiling?'

'Any pictures of them learning?'

'No, that's Snowdon.'

'It's in Italy.'

I raised a hand. 'Aren't we in danger of creating expectations we can't meet?'

'Trust you to ask the awkward questions, Iris!' Some of the staff looked around, surprised that he knew me.

'That brings us back to Jenna's first point – entertainment. Our focus groups revealed that the more students pay for their degree, the less they're likely to attend.'

He nodded at the murmurs of disbelief. 'Intuitively you'd assume that they'd want to turn up to get their money's worth, but their attitude seems to be, I've paid through the nose for this, so give me good service.'

'Are you saying they think they can pay for a degree?' Percy boomed from the back.

'I'm saying you're competing with a lot of distractions. Social media, online games.'

Nadal spotted me nodding and pointed to me. 'You could do worse than follow Iris's example. Her lectures were exemplary in terms of relevance and entertainment. Sometimes too entertaining, eh Iris?' He laughed then shouted, 'Guilty!'

I jumped then realised he was referencing my final lecture in the Business School. They hadn't spent thousands of pounds on a business degree to be told that multinational corporations were murdering the planet. My new colleagues also looked upset - and puzzled.

Nadal blustered a bit, then continued his spiel about the need to entertain and be relevant. He was winning a few over, but most just looked fed up – it's often the way when faced with unpalatable truths. Still, there's no point standing like King Canute yelling at the tide to halt. Nadal was right. We could do better. The hypothetical scenarios I set were fun but disconnected. It would be more entertaining to link them up to form a coherent story. That would also provide more context. What's crucial is not that students can solve hypothetical dilemmas. No one can. They need to know how to apply moral reasoning to real-life contexts.

'It's a case of adapt or die,' Nadal proclaimed.

Colin nodded solemnly from his position next to Jenna.

Die.

The sounds around me melted away.

I felt a tingling at the back of my neck as everything came together.

Robert's dilemma had all the ingredients. A closed-room murder and high stakes. One person versus the possible extinction of humankind. It would make for a better story if the DPP had something on the line personally. Reading between the lines, I suspected he had. My excitement mounted. The Dean wanted entertainment; the DPP wanted an answer, and I would deliver. Only one thing stood in my way.

Looking around to check no one was watching, I picked up my phone.

Please call me at your earliest convenience.

The phone rang before I'd switched it to vibrate, giving rise to reproving looks from my colleagues. I rushed out, teeth bared in an apologetic smile, phone clasped to my ear.

'What was that?' I whispered into the phone.

'I asked whether you'd come to an answer?'

'I'm afraid not,' I said as I hurried out of the building.

'What then?'

'We must use the students.'

'But what about the confidentiality aspect and informed consent?'

'I won't accept the consultancy money. Then it doesn't need to be passed by the ethics committee.'

'Really? That's generous of you.'

I demurred, but part of me was a little self-congratulatory.

Looking back, I see I was like a ball-bearing in a pinball machine, pinging desperately from one distraction to another.

*

Before I sent it, I dithered again over the title. It was accurate, but wordy. *Murder in the House of Citizens* would be nicely topical considering the proposal to replace the House of Lords with a House of Citizens. I remembered Nadal's caution about entertainment and attendance. It needs to be more dramatic if they are to engage with it. *Murder in the Citizens' Jury?* There's not been a decent jury drama since *Twelve Good Men* and students are already familiar with the idea of juries.

I added a few lines to my reading to include the various terms, changed the title and sent it.

Reading #1 of Murder in the Citizens' Jury:
Sarah

Sarah ticked off the boxes on the official form.: 'Notification of Eligibility to chair a Citizens' Jury. I declare I am free from bias. I have no personal knowledge of the participants. Participants have been selected randomly to represent the general population. I am in a fit state mentally and physically to chair this citizens' jury. Please check off excluding criteria.'

Sarah ticked her way through, then paused at the last one: Loss of a partner through bereavement, divorce or similar. If she ticked yes, they'd invite her to a follow-up appraisal to test her mental state. She knew this because she'd helped to write the rules.

She could imagine the interview. 'You split up two weeks ago.' 'Did you have to move?' 'It must be an upheaval after twelve years.' 'How do you feel?' How long could she keep it together and not give away the anger, the betrayal? She could hear them now. 'We appreciate your expertise, Sarah. The work you've put in to make this happen. Normally we'd let it go, but this is the first citizens' assembly with real power. We can't take any chances.'

The work she'd put in. Understatement. This had been her life. Her PhD had been on citizens' juries in the US. She'd researched citizens' assemblies in Europe. Co-chaired the Republic of Ireland citizens' assembly on same-sex marriage. Even travelled to Cuba to research their popular councils, where citizens fed back their views on proposed policies. She'd presided over numerous climate assemblies, marvelled at how, when given responsibility, people would take it seriously. Citizens from every class, ethnicity, gender, and age would gather together, and – informed by experts – would calmly deliberate upon the best solutions. Then she'd have to sit by helplessly as government after government ignored their recommendations, focused only on the coming election and their own power-mongering antics. Finally, citizens' juries had been granted power, but there was that last-minute amendment to worry about. They'd learned from Brexit and included a trial period. If anything went wrong, it would all be for nothing. There was no way she'd let someone with less experience take control. Anyway, in the citizens' jury, no-one would ask about her personal life. There'd be no triggers, so it wasn't even relevant.

She ticked 'no' and signed the form.

*

Dear Robert,

I have given the students a reading where a character, Sarah, lies on a form. I attach an outline of my lecture which covers the universalist moral position as exemplified in Immanuel Kant. I'll begin by getting the students to practise applying moral philosophy to lesser ethical breaches before progressing to murder. I will track their moral reasoning skills through regular mini-assignments, and the moment they are ready, I will set them the dilemma as far as I understand it.

Kind regards
Iris Tate
Professor of Moral Philosophy

ATTACHMENT: Lecture extract: Kant and Moral Duty

Later we'll be debating whether murder can ever be ethical, but before we raise the stakes so high, let's warm up our moral muscle on a lesser infringement of the rules. Was it right or wrong for Sarah to lie on the form? Can we even talk about right or wrong or is it all relative? We'll cover this in a later session. Does it matter? Yes. Societies with the highest level of trust, ethics and law-abiding behaviour are the most successful. So, a key concept among moral philosophers is the idea of 'the common good.' A well-known philosopher in this tradition is the eighteenth-century German thinker, Immanuel Kant.

He proposed there are universal duties we should abide by derived from basic principles. For example, we have a duty to behave ethically, to be honest, truthful, and so on. Kant also emphasises consistent moral standards. For example, it would be irrational to enjoy living in a safe society where rights to life and property are respected, yet break the law ourselves.

This kind of thinking gave rise to his most famous principle, the Categorical Imperative: 'Act only according to that maxim by which you can at the same time will that it should become a universal law.' In other words, we shouldn't take any action that we wouldn't want others, faced with a similar situation, to take. A rule of thumb is to ask ourselves: what if everyone behaved that way?

Your first assignment is to answer the question: What would Kant have to say about Sarah's decision to lie on the form?

*

I rushed back to my office straight after my lecture – an extended version of what I'd sent the DPP – and started mapping out my characters: a representative mix of ages, genders and ethnicities. They'll all be suspects obviously and one would be the victim. The motives would reveal themselves in due course, I was sure. The plot, well that was obvious. Emails piled up in my inbox as I wrote and chuckled as idea after idea presented itself. The students were going to love it.

CAST OF CHARACTERS

- Director of Public Prosecutions Richard (and family???)
- Andrew: environmental auditor in the Citizens' Jury
- Needles: brought in to do some knitting and create a calm atmosphere
- Jury members:
    ◊ Ben
    ◊ Devanika
    ◊ Josh
    ◊ Naomi
    ◊ Steve

*

Dear Colin

I'm worried we got off to a bad start. I wanted to reassure you I've hit the ground running. I'm writing a whodunnit as a fun way to showcase ethical dilemmas. It will enable in-depth understanding as students learn to apply moral philosophy in a fictional case. I'm sure they will love it and will show their approval by giving us the high NSS scores we need.

Kind regards
Iris Tate
Professor of Moral Philosophy

That done, I skimmed through a flurry of emails from students assigned to the 9 a.m. class, smiling at the variety of reasons why they couldn't possibly attend. Interestingly, none of the 3 p.m. class were burdened with problems. I paused at a particularly tricky one.

> *Dear Professor*
> *I received the class timetable for your Moral Philosophy module and saw I was in the 9am class. I suffer from mental-health issues, so would need to be in the 3pm class with my friend Zoe Jones.*
> *Thank you for your understanding.*
> *Emily*

I tapped my desk and gazed at the email as I contemplated the best way out.

> *Dear Emily,*
> *I'm sorry to hear about your mental-health issues. The later class is already at maximum, but there's space in the 9am class. Perhaps your friend Zoe would like to switch to the early class to join you.*
> *Kind regards*
> *Iris Tate*
> *Professor of Moral Philosophy*

I packed up quickly. I wanted to get home in time for games night with my boys. I hadn't cleaned the place since term started, and I needed to get in some snacks. Colin's response came as I was shutting down my email.

> *Dear Iris*
> *There's been a complaint about insufficient time to prepare. Please ensure you post reading materials at least a week before you reference them in your teaching.*
> *Kind regards*
> *Colin.*

It was 5 p.m. on a Friday. It would take hours to write the

next chapter.

> *Boys. Sorry have to cry off from games night
> tonight. I'm writing a murder mystery for the students –
> yes I know! Sorry. Mum X*

I clapped my hands, feeling empowered for the first time in months. I was no longer the sad sap desperate for any scraps of attention. I was an artist constructing her masterpiece.

*

Murder in the Citizens' Jury #2: Meet the Citizens' Jury

Steve

Steve barely glanced at the summons. He was trying to stop his wife from leaving.

'Ste-efff.' He lingered over the name. Steve and Stef. He'd played on her delight at the alliteration when they'd first started out. He'd not been in the market for an English Major – he was a practical man, but he'd spotted a softness in her. He'd gone with his gut instinct and it had paid off. She was an asset. 'Don't leave.'

'You only think about yourself.' She unfolded the crumpled jury summons. 'You wouldn't dream of attending, would you? Not unless there's something in it for you.'

He was about to protest when his son entered the kitchen, his brother hovering close behind. 'Can we have a lift?'

'For the last time, no!' he roared.

They retreated rapidly into the hall.

Steve saw the emotion leave Stef's eyes and knew he'd just blown it. 'Look, I'll go to the citizen jury thing. I wanted to anyway, but you said I don't spend enough time with you.' He grabbed the summons and signed it.

'Good.' Stef put the form in the Freepost envelope. 'I'll

post it on my way out. It'll provide distraction for you when we've gone.'

Steve glared at his sons as they followed their mother out. He'd thought the organic farm thing had been the tipping point, but it was the bloody kids. It was their fault. He'd worked his way up the hard way, but they hung around, doing nothing, always wanting something. Take me here, take us there. Bloody scroungers, the pair of them, and now he'd committed to the citizens' jury. She was right about one thing, though. He'd find a way to get something out of it.

Devanika

Devanika scrolled through her phone as her husband drove them back from the hospital. The nurse's words rang in her ears. 'It's not your fault,' she'd said. 'We're seeing more fertility issues each year. It's the build-up of toxins in the environment.'

Her husband was talking about trying again, about whether they could afford it, but she tuned him out. First, she needed to know if the nurse was just being kind.

'The nurse was right,' Devanika cut her husband off mid-sentence. 'Environmental toxins are causing decreasing sperm count in men, and more miscarriages in women.'

When they arrived home, she waved away offers of food and turned on her PC. She needed a bigger screen. The take-home message was clear. While each chemical on its own passed safety tests, the little research that existed on the likely combined impact was alarming. Car exhaust, pesticides in food, endocrine disruptors in beauty products, and contamination of water supplies by agricultural run-off. Together, the effects were synergistic, producing a combined effect much greater than the sum of their parts. Her grief turned to fury and then to action.

She wrote to the local council demanding they become pesticide-free, emailed each company whose products contained toxins, harassed her MP asking for greater regulation, but it wasn't enough. When the invitation to the citizens' jury came, she accepted it immediately. Finally, some power.

Josh

Josh enjoyed his weekly outing at the refill shop. He rarely went out these days, but the Rice Up cooperative run by the local Buddhist group was cheap and had a friendly, non-judgemental feel. He filled up his containers with a week's worth of red lentils and brown rice.

He hung back when he heard an angry-sounding lady berate the staff for running out of organic wheat bran. The excuse that they'd lost their supplier was cutting no ice. He felt his anxiety mount and wished she'd go. She was spoiling the vibe. Eventually she went, and it was safe to pay and leave.

Josh detoured home via the house that left home-grown produce out when there was a glut. Today there was a box of onions and peppers, and a note saying please eat these before they go to waste. He packed a few in his backpack, feeling almost a hero for making use of them.

When he got to his bedsit, he boiled the lentils and put on the rice. He chopped the peppers and onions and fried them with some spices. He was dishing up when he heard the letterbox. A brown envelope. He scanned it in a panic, then rang his mum.

'I've got to go to a citizens' jury. I've been summoned.'

'What have you done?' she asked.

'Not like that, the citizens' assembly thing.'

'Oh. Do you have to attend?'

'I dunno.' Josh studied the form. 'There's a lot to read.'

'Maybe you should go. Get out a bit.'

'Shall I sign it, then?'

'Yes, do you good.'

He obediently signed the form.

'Do get extra meds though, babe. We don't want...' she hesitated. 'See what the doc says.'

There was a pause.

'You know my bedsit's really small?' he said.

'Yes.'

'Now you've some more space, can I store—?'

'No.' Her voice was sad.

There was a moment's silence.

Josh ended the call, sat on his bed and wept.

Thirty minutes later, he filled his bong with grass and got himself high. He ate a bowl of lentils and rice, turned on his gaming PC and played Call of Duty for six hours solid.

*

It had taken the whole weekend and Monday morning, but I'd be faster now I'd made a start. I pressed save and uploaded onto the course website. I leaned back in the chair and stretched out my arms above my head. I noticed the time with a shock. An emergency faculty meeting had been scheduled, and it had started thirty minutes ago. I shut down my laptop and dashed off.

When I arrived, the Dean was talking about a hole in the budget and the need for external funding. Colin right next to her as usual. The atmosphere was grim. I stood in the door slightly dazed, still half in my fictional world. It seemed strangely unreal, like a scene in a horror movie with Colin as the ventriloquist's dummy coming magically to life whenever Jenna looked at him. His eyes followed me as I squeezed past those on the end of the row and slid into the seat next to Marcel.

'Teaching is just part of our job. We must also be bringing in money from consultancy and research.' Jenna smiled, her teeth implausibly white against her red lipstick.

I forgot my story and paid attention.

'The dip in student recruitment means less money coming in from fees. We hope the rebranding will help, but that will take time.'

Colin frowned at the murmurs of protest.

Marcel leaned over to me. 'Bet you wish you'd stayed in the Business School.'

Percy rose to his feet, an impressive six feet two of righteous indignation. 'Are you saying that besides being academic scholar, researcher, educator, mental-health therapist, entertainer, and grant writer, I must now add to the list consultant?'

'All for a salary less than my son's girlfriend makes in marketing,' I murmured.

'What was that?' Colin asked.

'Nothing.'

Marcel patted my arm. 'She said, all this for less than her son makes for his job in marketing.'

I cringed at Colin's withering look.

Finally,' Jenna continued, 'Let us congratulate Colin on his promotion to position of Assistant Dean.'

'Position of head up her arse,' Marcel muttered.

I laughed, and he grinned at me.

Colin puffed up at the desultory applause. He went to say something, but people were already getting up to go.

'He'll be even more insufferable now.' Percy stood up and stretched.

'I loved your comment about earning less than your son,' said GG, edging along the row to leave.

'My son's girlfriend,' I corrected.

'Inflammatory,' Percy's tone held a note of respect.

'We misjudged you,' said Marcel. 'We thought you were one of the suits.'

We joined the line for the single coffee machine.

'I was a philosopher among capitalists,' I declared. 'Although that's not entirely fair, they funded my research trip to Cuba.'

'I don't like their music,' GG said.

'But it's so upbeat.' I attempted a mini salsa.

She looked appalled, and I quickly stopped.

'Iris?'

I jumped and turned around to find myself face to face with Colin.

'Your comment was inappropriate, especially after last year's strikes.'

'But it's not a complaint,' I blustered. 'Teaching young minds is a privilege.'

Colin looked sceptical.

'I'm not one of the grumblers who complain that it was better in the old days,' I reassured him. 'It was, but I understand the argument – taxpayers' money and all that. I'm fully embracing the ethos.'

'Did you hear the point about consultancy money, or did you arrive too late?' He spoke loud enough for Jenna to hear.

She walked over. 'Have you secured some money?'

'Another consultancy gig already?' Marcel raised his eyebrows at Percy.

My mouth went dry.

'Er, no.'

'We expect big things from you Iris.' Jenna's smile didn't reach her eyes.

I thought fast. 'I'll erm, yes I'm working on a research paper - Storytelling for Pedagogy – a case study.' I threw my arms out extravagantly. 'It will be a paradigm-changing paper on how a whodunnit can be used to explore ethical dilemmas.'

Jenna seemed somewhat mollified. Colin started edging away.

'I'll record and transcribe all the lectures as asked and use the transcription, summarising the interactive bits. I'll, yes, I'll add notes to the transcribed lectures showing how this approach enables integration of critical thinking, interdisciplinarity, etc. It will be edutainment,' I called after them as they began walking off.

I turned back to my colleagues. They looked at me, disappointed.

'Edutainment!' Percy frowned. 'It was worth going on strike for that alone.'

'Did you strike?' Marcel peered at me with suspicion.

'No, er.'

'What about solidarity?' he asked. 'We got you an extra two percent and a decent pension. You were happy to take that, but you wouldn't stand on the line.'

'GG struggled to pay her rent because of the pay penalty from striking,' Percy said.

GG nodded.

'Our staff work their arses off for nothing while the Dean earns twice what we do,' Marcel said.

'It's just… It's my only chance to teach them about sustainable business and ethics.'

We approached the drinks table.

'Now we have to do twice the work as they cut lecturing staff, while Jenna gets another assistant.' Marcel filled a cardboard cup with weak coffee. 'How ethical is that?'

I'd lost them. A professor from the Business School who didn't strike confirmed all their prejudices.

'I'm doing four courses now.' Marcel waved his cup around. 'Four. I literally have no time for a shit.'

I stepped back to avoid being splashed with coffee. 'Thanks for moderating my course. Did you like the innovative approach?'

'It's brave,' he replied.

'Is it?' This was worrying.

'Students won't like all that reading.'

'Not Emily with her dyslexia,' Percy said, taking his place at the coffee dispenser.

'She has dyslexia?' I asked, opting for a cup of tea.

'Not officially, but she claims it anyway to give her extra time during exams.'

'She's Percy's nemesis,' said GG. 'She brought down his wife.'

'What?'

'Kate teaches in the psychology department,' Percy said. 'Emily objected to her research into gender differences in the brain.'

'What happened?'

'She'd failed the course, and claimed Kate was punishing her for saying her research was sexist. The University upheld Emily's complaint. She passed and Kate was cautioned.' His face was taut with rage.

I told them about my email exchange. 'As a professor of ethics, I take a firm line against those who try to game the system.'

'That will just be the start,' he warned.

I saw the chance to redeem myself.

'Solidarity,' I said.

'What?'

'I'll take on Emily.'

'We'll see.' Percy's face remained grim.

I returned to my office, despondent. Marcel's comment about leaving the Business School rang in my ears. I never thought it would be so hard to be accepted. The requirement to bring in extra income was another shock. This raised the stakes for not declaring the consultancy. But it was an impossible dilemma to solve alone.

Or was it? I stared out of the window. What climate policy would warrant a DPP seeking out an ethics professor and her students? He said it would be transformative and that's what we need. Soon we'd pass tipping points that we couldn't come back from. Maybe we already have. Any delay in climate action, especially now at this crucial time could have existential consequences for humanity itself. We might get around to making effective climate policies in the future, but by that time our other icecap would have melted and there'd be no going back. Of course you'd let one person off rather than risk that.

I lugged more books to the windowsill and the room darkened. I'd been bigging it up as this huge dilemma, but it was bloody obvious.

Kant's epic tome, *Groundwork for the Metaphysics of Morals*, was blocking out the light. I pushed it to the side. His face was stern, and his eyes held mine. He would say that morality isn't a numbers game. But they're not numbers. They're real people. I felt panic rising, then breathed deeply, calming myself as I've learned to do.

A ding of an email brought me back to the present.

> *Dear Professor*
> *My mark for the Kant essay was disappointing.*
> *I don't understand because I wrote in lots about his*
> *philosophy. Why was my mark so low and please can you*
> *put it up?*
> *Emily*

Here we go!

Dear Emily,
You need to apply what you have learned in the
lectures and classes to the scenario given. Anyone can
paraphrase philosophical concepts from AI or Wikipedia.
To get good marks, you must demonstrate that you have
processed and understood the course material enough to
apply the theories to novel situations.
Kind regards
Iris Tate
Professor of Moral Philosophy

Dear Professor
Yes thank you but you didn't respond to my request
to put my mark up. We didn't get much time to prepare
and now you've given me a low mark it will put me behind
right from the start.
Emily

Dear Emily,
Your work got a fair mark and won't be changed.
There's no need to worry as there are five assessments
throughout the course and the first accounts for just 10%.
I noticed you haven't yet downloaded the course readings.
For your next assignment, you should show evidence of
having read the relevant chapters. For those who failed
their dyslexia test, but nonetheless prefer not to read, I've
kept them short!
Kind regards
Iris Tate
Professor of Moral Philosophy

Chapter 4

A figure stands silhouetted against a mountaintop, gazing into the distance. He has the wise, knowing stance of an older brother. Hope swells in my chest. Is it Lee? No, he's too old. Three hundred years too old, dressed in breeches, a brocaded jacket with a white neckcloth and powdered wig. He turns to face me. It's Kant. He's oblivious to the gaggle of students behind him, drinking cocktails and laughing. They have skis on, although there's no snow. He's expecting me to talk to him, but I have to take the students abseiling. I wouldn't understand him anyway. I don't speak German. Wittgenstein pops up to remind me that language is just a device. *Are you saying the end justifies the means?* Kant asks me without moving his lips. We're abseiling down the mountain now along with the students. I worry his wig will fly off. *The duty of a Director of Public Prosecutions is to prosecute.* The students are far below us. I need to keep up, but Kant is holding me back with his steely gaze. *What if we all murdered anyone we thought was standing in the way of a policy we didn't like? Would you will that letting off murderers become a universal law?*

I woke refreshed and jumped out of bed. The answer wasn't obvious at all. Marcel was wrong. I have no regrets. My first week and this dilemma lands in my lap. The juiciest one of all and it's real.

I rushed to work and by the time the coffee shop was open, I'd designed an exciting cover page for my novella. I got a takeaway latte and returned to my office and wrote up the rest of my cast.

Murder in the Citizens' Jury #3: The Rest of the Jurors

Ben

It had been another frantic day. He'd not even had time for a shit. It was a human right, for God's sake! He should visit the bathroom before he set off for work, as there were few opportunities for delivery drivers. Ben checked the clock. He had to sign the anniversary card, put the toys away, and get ready for work before his wife got back.

'Millie, do you have my pen, love?'

'Nope.' She waved a tiny paintbrush at him.

'Put that away before Mummy gets home.'

'Wanna finish my picture.'

He should look at her efforts, but he didn't want the precious moments between his wife coming home and him leaving to be spent clearing up. Since they'd both taken on extra shifts to pay the bills, they barely saw each other. He gazed at a photo of the two of them laughing into the camera, remembering back to the days when she'd come home, he'd remove her nurse's uniform and they'd go giggling straight to bed.

The baby was asleep in the bouncy chair. Perhaps he could get the kids to tidy up and stay out of their hair while they grabbed some time alone.

'Jack!' he shouted at the ceiling. 'Clear up your mess, now!'

There was a thudding of small feet, then the projectile that was his son skidded into the room, knocking the baby's drink over the card and Millie's picture.

Millie shrieked, setting off the baby who joined in.

Ben shoved a dummy in her mouth and mopped up the liquid, but the card was ruined. He chucked it in the bin along with Millie's sodden painting, ignoring her cries.

'Come on, who can put their stuff away fastest?'

It worked. Millie forgot her picture and grabbed her paints and paper and glitter and shoved it all in the cupboard. Jack threw in his football. Ben picked up the baby walker and hesitated – the cupboard already looked precariously full. He heard a car pull up and rammed it in on top of the scooter and shut the door.

A voice came from the hall. 'Hiya lovelies. I'm home.'

The baby was peaceful again, rocking herself back to sleep with one little foot in the bouncy chair. There was still a chance.

'Kids,' Ben hissed. They drew close, intrigued by his air of secrecy. 'Quick, let's play hide and seek. If you hide really well, I bet we can fool Mummy for ages. I'll go upstairs and you hide down here. Let's see who can stay hidden for the longest.'

They nodded, and Ben ran into the hall and shut the door behind him.

'We have ten minutes,' he whispered in her ear.

'We can't!'

'It's our anniversary.'

He watched her, his heart full of love as she considered, then a dimple appeared in her left cheek, and she giggled. 'Come on, then.'

As Ben mounted the stairs, he had a horrible thought.

'Don't open the cupboard door!' he shouted.

Crash!

They ran into the sitting room to find it strewn with a cupboard full of stuff, and Millie crying, rubbing her head where the baby walker had landed.

He bit back a barrage of swear words and allowed Millie to sob on his shoulder while he shushed her.

He didn't know how much longer he could go on like this.

The summons arrived as he was rushing out the door for work. He thrust it in his pocket and read it later while waiting in a traffic jam. He read only as far as 'free childcare provided' before ticking yes.

Naomi

Naomi was on the phone when the doorbell rang. She rushed
down, wireless earbuds in place, continuing the conversation
with her sister as she answered the door.

'It's just some storage boxes.'

She took the packages from the delivery man without
looking at him.

'I know, sis, but I needed to cheer myself up.' Naomi shut
the door and lugged the parcels into a living room, still talking.

'It's not just the breakup. Well, it is obviously, but at least
I've more space now.' She looked around for somewhere to put
the boxes.

'Someone complained to my company about misleading
blurb on our skin care products... I know!... It's not fair. Bloody
customers.' She laughed. 'I suppose it's not the attitude for a
marketing exec!'

Naomi gave up and lugged the parcels upstairs.

'I'd love you to come down and cheer me up, but...' She
opened a bedroom door and shoved the parcel on the bed along
with all the others. 'It's just I haven't sorted out the spare
room yet... OK... yes..., you're not telling me anything I don't
know.'

She tore open the cardboard and pulled out the storage
boxes. They were smaller than they'd looked on screen.

'...It's fine, love. I'm sorry too. I'm just worried about my
job...'

Naomi wandered into her kitchen and poured herself a gin
and tonic, adding ice cubes.

'At least I don't have to put up with any more nagging about
spending.' She noticed a brown envelope partially hidden under
a pile of brochures and opened it. 'No, I am upset. It's such a
pain having to find someone new... I'm so done with dating apps.'
Naomi paused as she took in what she was reading.

'You'll never guess what... I've been invited to be on
a citizens' jury... You think I should?... Might meet some
interesting people... They'd have to give me time off... You're

right, a chance to lie low for a bit.'

Naomi grabbed a ballpoint from a deluxe leather desk pen holder and signed it.

Needles

Needles knitted in the passenger seat as her daughter-in-law drove back from the supermarket.

'Must you keep doing that?'

'The guerrilla knitters are working on covers for the benches in the underground to make it cosy. We're an underground movement.' She cackled at her own joke.

A fly splatted against the windscreen.

Her daughter-in-law tutted and turned on the wipers.

They pulled into the drive. Her grandson jumped out of the car and helped her out of the passenger seat. He was a lovely boy.

'In my day, after each journey, we'd scrape the windscreen clean of insects,' Needles told him.

'Yuck!'

'But I'm worried, love. Insects are part of what holds us all together. It's like the stitches in me knitting. They go, and it all unravels. It's where your food comes from, sweetie.'

He laughed, humouring her, and swung a Tesco shopping bag. 'Food comes from the supermarket, Grandma.'

'I fear for you young people. What do they teach you nowadays?'

'Maths, economics, I'll be doing business studies for my GCSEs.'

'You'd better get on with it then,' said his mum. She turned to Needles. 'The struggles I have getting him to do his homework.'

'It's a waste of time,' declared Needles. 'With the world heating up, you need to learn how to survive, my boy.'

He looked back at her, wide-eyed with fear.

'Don't go scaring him,' snapped her daughter-in-law.

'But if he's got the knowledge and skills, he don't need to be scared. That's the point I'm making, love,' said Needles.

'He needs good exam results. A good job. I don't need you butting in, telling him it's a waste of time.'

'I just want to prepare him for the future.' Needles watched her grandson escape into the house with the shopping. He hated conflict. He was a sweet-natured lad. Not like his mum. Needles would do all she could to help him learn the skills he'd need.

It took a moment for her to take in what her daughter-in-law was saying.

'It's best you don't see him anymore.'

'What? No!'

'You're a bad influence.'

Needles leant against the car in shock. 'I'd do anything to protect that darling boy,' she said in a quavering voice.

Her daughter-in-law's pursed mouth left no room for argument.

'Anything,' Needles repeated.

*

I sat back, satisfied. I'd set up my citizens' jury. A typical citizens' assembly would have ten times that many people but never mind. I gazed at the dusty textbooks on the windowsill. So dull. I'd be the first to fully embrace a new genre-spanning form – edutainment. The forerunner, Iris Tate, Professor of Moral Philosophy. The one everyone referred to when they said, 'this is when it really took off, and students came back to class, when tuition fees were finally deemed to be worth it'. Who knew it would be the arts and humanities that would save the teetering structure that is higher education?

The fragment of sky visible behind my books was darkening. Normally I'd be heading off home now. They used to take the mick when I claimed I had a book in me. I didn't mind because I liked to see them bonding, my brother and Fay...

A curt knock interrupted my thoughts. Colin stood at the door.

I beckoned him in. Now was my chance to redeem myself.

'This is my edutainment idea.' I leaned back and pointed to the screen. 'It's a classic closed-room murder. It's in a citizens' assembly which leads nicely in to an interdisciplinary lecture on democratic processes. I'll draw upon my research in Cuba to weave in decolonisation and sustainability, and of course critical thinking—'

'May I sit?' Colin interrupted, gazing at a chair piled high with ethical consumer magazines.

'Yes, of course.' I jumped up and moved them to the floor.

I willed him to look away from my cluttered office to my screen where *Murder in the Citizens' Jury* stood out in bright red theatrical font.

'There's been a complaint,' he said, sitting down.

'What?'

'From a student. I'm dealing with it while the Dean's away.' He read from his phone. 'She said that your phrasing, "for those who failed the dyslexia test," was insensitive.'

'I only meant to reassure her that the reading wouldn't be too onerous...'

'The student was brave enough to share with me that after years having her self-esteem negatively affected by difficulties due to her dyslexia, to see the terms "fail" and "dyslexia" paired was incredibly triggering.'

I lowered my head in shame. He was right. It had been a snide joke, but it wouldn't be funny to those who struggled with it.

'I'd hate to escalate this to Jenna.'

'I'm genuinely sorry.'

'Are you being sarcastic?' His eyes narrowed.

'What!'

'I know you come from the Business School, but here we care about our students.'

'I care.'

'Is that why you left, or were you asked to leave?'

'I wasn't asked to leave.'

'Because your students didn't like you?'

'They did like me.'

'I just wonder why you'd voluntarily leave the Business

School that's awash with funds to take a pay cut to work in a different faculty.'

When I said nothing, he stood up and surveyed my office. 'I'll leave you to finish tidying up.'

Once he'd left, I considered a crate of textbooks on sustainable business and Corporate Social Responsibility. I put them all on a discard pile, then hovered over one on sustainable business, trying to work out if I'd need it again. I gave up. Thinking about the future was too hard.

It had been risky leaving a department where I'd been so successful. They'd liked me because I enabled them to tick the ethics box. They'd also liked the consultancy fees. I'd had a spate of offers following my appearance in a documentary about using student input into dilemmas facing self-driving cars. The most common question they wanted answered was how much more would people pay for a product labelled as "sustainable." I'd objected to the question itself, and no amount of money could tempt me.

Fay had dismissed my reasons, but I don't have to care what she thinks anymore. The day after the funeral, I handed in my notice at the Business School and went forth to put it all right.

Chapter 5

Dear Iris

Have you had a chance to assess the students yet? I'm keen to know how long you think this might take.

Kind regards

Robert Ash

Director of Public Prosecutions

Dear Robert,

I've marked the assignments on Kant. The level of critical thinking and moral reasoning is rudimentary, but about what I'd expect at this stage. They will improve. I'm more worried about attendance, but I am pulling out all the stops to keep them engaged. Trust me, we will get an answer to your dilemma.

Kind regards

Iris Tate

Professor of Moral Philosophy

*

I walked taller as I approached the lecture theatre, breathing deeply; building nervous energy, just like I used to do before a performance. I had set everything up beforehand, so it was all ready. I twirled an imaginary cape over my shoulder and entered the lecture theatre, an attention-seeking four minutes late. I took my time heading for the lectern. I set out my water, a list of topics and a pen on the tiny desk and scanned the group before me. I estimated about fifty percent attendance – slightly less than last time.

'Shut your eyes!' I commanded the students.

They looked at me in surprise. I pressed *play* on the control panel and an urban soundscape played softly in the background.

'Imagine it's twenty years from now. What is the world like? Not just your personal world, but your community, your country, the planet.'

They gazed at me, perplexed. Some were still on their phones.

'Put down your phones and shut your eyes and imagine.'

The soundtrack played: a murmur of street sounds and light traffic, a hissing coffee machine, car horns and sirens. A distant strimmer, a hubbub of conversation - friendly, then not so friendly.

I surveyed my class satisfied - all except some giggling lads at the back had shut their eyes. Many were frowning.

'Now dream,' I instructed. 'Imagine we have done everything right and the world is as good as it has ever been. Not just your world – *the* world.'

The next track was a nature soundtrack. Nightingales sang. Wood pigeons cooed, leaves rustled in the wind.

Several students were smiling, brows unfurrowed. The lads at the back had finally shut their eyes and seemed to be deep in concentration.

I spoke softly over the sound of a babbling brook. 'Imagine your neighbourhood. What does it look like? How does it feel to walk through it? What are people doing in this flourishing world that we have made?'

The soundscape came to an end. I paused and let the silence hang for a moment, pleased that the students remained with their eyes obediently shut.

'Now open your eyes and quietly rest in the vision you have created.'

They blinked their eyes open and looked around. It had been just five minutes, but the atmosphere was hushed and expectant.

'Now share your vision with your neighbour.'

I wandered up and down the rows listening in. I noted that their ideal world often featured more nature and less traffic. The lads at the back were discussing *Love Island*.

I returned to the front.

'Think of the world you dreamed. Is it possible? Is that where we're heading now? What is the most important thing - the key factor that will affect whether or not that dream is realised? Does anyone have any suggestions?'

The students stared back at me blank-faced. I wasn't worried. It was always like this at the start. I waited it out. After a moment, an anxious-looking girl in the front row put her hand up. I nodded at her encouragingly.

'Is it democracy?' she ventured.

'Not exactly, but a good guess.'

I allowed a moment, but no one else raised a hand.

'It is who makes the decisions and on what basis. That is what determines the fate of the world and your future.'

I began to pace, getting into my stride.

'This is the question that has dominated human thought for millennia - who should govern and on what grounds? In *The Leviathan*, for example, Hobbes argues that without government, there would be constant conflict. Life would be "solitary, poor, nasty, brutish and short". He suggests it is in our interests to sacrifice certain freedoms for the sake of security.'

I stopped abruptly, remembering the requirement to record all lectures. I needed to anyway so I could transcribe it for my research paper. I fiddled around with the controls and started again.

Lecture 2 The Ethics of Democracy

Lecture Transcription with additional notes.

The legitimacy of a political system is based on the idea that it is just, those in charge have a right to govern, and it meets the function of preserving our personal safety. In the past, fears revolved around being held up by bandits. Today, we need to consider what safety means where the warming climate presents an existential threat to humanity. Indeed, one of the arguments against our current representative democracy is that four-year electoral cycles lead to short-term decision-making which leaves existential threats such as climate change unaddressed. *[Ref sustainable development goal – climate]*

In a few months there will be a referendum that will affect our constitution. On the ballot box citizens will be asked to vote yes or no to the proposal to replace the House of Lords with a House of Citizens. *[Ref interdisciplinarity – politics]*

Transcription note. I paused recording for discussion as many of the students looked puzzled. It turned out few were aware of the referendum or what was at stake. In the interests of truth, I admit to being disappointed that not all of the students had taken in the details of citizens' assemblies and how they operate from the reading. It's hard to know how many read it, and those that did assumed as it was in a story it meant it wasn't true. This is something to be mindful of when devising edutainment materials. The feeling was that politics was boring and the politicians weren't to be trusted. I replied that was all the more reason for them to be involved.

If young people all switch off, it leaves the field wide open for the corrupt and power hungry to do what they like.

You had the opportunity to vote in the last election. Did you? Do you feel empowered by your right to vote? Share your experience and feelings with your neighbours.

Transcription note. Recording paused while students discussed the question. There were several camps – those who didn't bother to vote, thinking it was a waste of time, or they didn't know who to believe, and those who did vote, but often not for who they wanted. A few were still discussing Love Island.

Many seemed to think that your vote was irrelevant, and if you voted, it was often to keep out those you didn't like, rather than to vote for who you did. This isn't irrational. For example, a UK study found that if people voted for the policies they prefer, the Green Party would come out the best, whereas in actuality, the Greens have barely any Members of Parliament.

Such studies cast doubt on the claim that our current form of multi-party democracy represents the views of the population. It also raises the worrying question of whether our democracy will ever make the kinds of policies that could avert the climate crisis. *[Trigger alert: eco-anxiety]*

It's been estimated we'd need three planets if we all consumed like those in Western Europe do, and six planets if we all consumed like Americans. Some countries consume less than one planet's worth but also suffer from poor quality of life as measured by the human development index (HDI) which measures education, health and standard of living. Only Cuba scores high on the HDI and yet lives within its planetary means. So, let's consider the ethics of the democratic process from the perspective of the only sustainable country that has been subject to a sixty-year embargo on the basis that it is a non-democratic, authoritarian regime.

The Cuban revolution, led by Fidel Castro and Che Guevara, overthrew a corrupt regime in 1959. Fidel Castro set up a socialist state, which he presided over for fifty-two years. *[Ref interdisciplinarity - history]*. He promised to address inequality and provide health and education for the poorest in society. This he did. He also promised to restore multi-party democracy, which he did not.

When Castro nationalised American companies in Cuba in 1960, the US responded with an embargo on exports to Cuba. This persists today and is the most comprehensive embargo in modern history, resulting in prolonged hardship for the Cuban people. The primary justification for the embargo's continuance is the lack of a multi-party representative democracy and free media in Cuba. Fidel Castro justified not keeping his promise by claiming that democracy was at the mercy of those with control over information.

Transcription note. Some lads at the back had been laughing amongst themselves ever since my summing up of their discussion. I ignored them until a girl at the front told them to be quiet as 'some of us want to learn'. It turned out that my summing up wasn't entirely correct, as many of the students had assumed

I was asking if they'd voted for who would win Love Island.

So! What is the evidence that those with control over information determine the outcome? In reality TV shows, it's the editors who choose what to show us. It's not so different in politics. In the US, special-interest groups pour billions of dollars into political campaigns, meaning that the information and media content the public are exposed to is determined by those with the deepest pockets. It is also the case that elections and referendums have been characterised by misinformation. Brexit campaigners, for example, targeted animal lovers with content on Facebook that linked bullfighting with the Remain campaign, creating the misleading impression that to vote to remain in the EU was to support bullfighting. This was a deciding factor in the outcome. The traditional media is also compromised as it's foremost a business. Despite their vital role in a liberal democracy of holding power to account, media revenue depends upon selling advertising and selling news. The most shocking and ridiculous of pronouncements are avidly reported at the expense of considered, well-informed viewpoints, because they sell. The media in Cuba is predominantly state-owned, which comes with its own problems. But the media in the West isn't free, either. Politicised editors and profit pull the strings.

A key critique of the colonial mindset is the imposing of western values and assumptions upon other countries – an embargo of six decades is a devastating manifestation of this. *[Ref decolonisation]* But what do the Cubans themselves think of their political structures? When I visited Cuba for research, I discovered how a question leads to different answers and interpretations, depending on how it's phrased. When conversations touched upon democracy and free media, it surprised me that few Cubans spoke of a desire for such, although they were happy to critique other aspects of their system, such as burdensome bureaucracy. The reasons became evident when I rephrased to ask if they had opportunities to contribute to government policy. I learned citizens attend local meetings where potential policies are floated, and feedback sought – much like citizens' assemblies in fact. One phrasing of the question leads to answers suggestive of a lack of democratic processes, whereas the question differently phrased leads to an image of Cuba as an ideal prototype of participative democracy. *[Ref interdisciplinarity - politics]*

I don't claim to know the ins and outs of every aspect of Cuban political life, or the extent to which Fidel Castro abused human rights or liberated an oppressed people, but I do know that government policies are scrutinised by ninety percent of the population in their version of citizens' assemblies and that this is no mere paper exercise, as the majority of policies are amended based on their feedback. On the basis of this process, Cuba is the only truly sustainable country.

Question: what aspects of this argument violate the key tenets of critical thinking? *[Ref critical thinking]*

Transcription note. I'm delighted to report that the girl in the front row put her hand up to say that I hadn't justified the implied connection between their political process and their sustainability credentials. A lad at the back suggested an alternative explanation was that the embargo meant they couldn't consume as much. I applauded them for their incisive comments.

*

After the lecture, I detoured via the staff canteen. Today they had a half-price offer on cake. Before, when I was content, well, content-ish, I'd have been tempted. We'd both had a tendency towards over-eating. Now food was fuel.

I sighed impatiently at the person who was holding things up. Trouble with their card or some such thing.

Percy, GG, and Marcel walked past on their way out.

Marcel was gesticulating wildly. 'Bloody multifactor authentication.'

'What's that?' I asked.

They noticed me and walked over.

'Colin's been checking we've all recorded our lectures and

uploaded them,' GG said.

'I can't ever make it work,' Marcel fumed.

Percy rolled his eyes. 'There are other ways to deal with technical issues than flapping your arms around and swearing.'

'Marcel's recordings all begin with him saying, "For fuck's sake!"' GG giggled.

I laughed. 'Do you know how to edit it out?'

'I stand by it.' Marcel paused and looked at me. 'I suppose you record your lectures?'

'I'm only recording so I can transcribe the lectures to show how a story can be used to illustrate a variety of ethical theories, paying due attention to sustainability, critical thinking, interdisciplinarity and decoloniality.'

'Well done. Gold star,' Marcel said.

They began to walk on.

'I've dealt with Emily, and it was no problem at all,' I cried after them.

'Oh?' Percy turned back.

'She wanted me to raise her marks, and I said no, so she knows where she stands now.' I waited for a pat on the back.

'Any complaints about you?' Percy asked.

'Oh, er…' My face fell.

'Never mind. You tried.'

GG looked at my sad sandwich. 'You should join us next time.'

'We lunch every Thursday at twelve thirty,' said Marcel.

'I teach till twelve forty-five.'

'We'll go at one then,' said Percy.

'Cheers.' I grinned and grabbed a slice of lemon drizzle cake and added it to my tray.

*

CLASS: Feedback on Kant

I gave you all individual feedback on your first essay about Kant, but I'll summarise the key points for everyone. Some of you replicated Kant's moral theory without applying it to the particular situation. That's not enough to pass the course. Anyone can spout a theory, but real life is messy - applying it takes considered thought.

Some said Kant wouldn't allow lying and would say we have a duty to be honest because of the universalisation principle that if everyone lied, it wouldn't be a society we'd want to live in. That's a fair argument and shows an awareness of Kant's key precepts.

Some argued that it depended upon whether Sarah's decision to lie on the form was driven by self-interest, such as a desire to advance her career? If so, Kant wouldn't consider this action ethical, regardless of the outcome. If she lied for moral reasons such as the good of society, he might be more forgiving. Whether he would approve is another matter. Any thoughts?

Transcription note. I gave them a few minutes to discuss among themselves, then asked the students to share their views. These were mostly a series of examples where the end justifies the means argument could be used for good and bad, and none were relevant to this context.

A few claimed Kant would approve of Sarah lying by outlining why citizens' juries are good for society. A couple tried to boost this argument by going into detail about how citizens' juries were more representative, less prone to being hijacked by vested interests, better able to think long-term, etc.

[Ref critical thinking] Does the argument that it's ethical for Sarah to lie on the form because citizens' juries are good for society stand up to logical analysis?

An argument is only as strong as its weakest link. It doesn't matter how convincing one particular point is if it has no logical connection to the causal link you are trying to make. This kind of smoke and mirrors is a key tactic of those who spread misinformation. Someone may make a proposition that you agree with. You feel that dopamine buzz of recognition. You warm towards them and what they're saying as it touches upon your personal experience. You feel validated. And then they say something else as if it's causally related to the first point, and in the flood of goodwill you accept it without question. You may fully agree with the oneness of one and heartily concur with the twoness of two, but it doesn't mean that one plus two equals four. Philosophy, dear students, is mathematics in words. Therefore, precision in language is something I encourage you to strive towards. You can all aspire to the razor-sharp reasoning of Sherlock Holmes – it's a question of mental training. Logic by itself can't answer questions of morality and values, but at least you'll be focusing your attention in the right place. So where does this leave us in terms of the question?

Transcription note. I paused, but again there was no response. I hope soon they'll develop more confidence in expressing a view.

Whether citizens' juries are good for society is irrelevant to the question of whether lying on the form is OK. That point rests more on who is best placed to determine her suitability – Sarah herself, despite being in an emotionally volatile state, or an objective panel.

Finally, some of you were kind enough to give your feedback on the story so far. A couple wanted to know why Josh was crying. All will be revealed, as they say. Several wondered who was going to get murdered and who by. So in the next chapter, I shall reveal the victim and introduce you to our detective.

*

I rushed back to my office to write the next chapter. I was distracted from my creative musings by Kant's face, staring at me from the cover of his book. I gave a slight nod in response to the question implicit in his arched eyebrows. OK, yes, Sarah's situation was analogous to my own. I was focusing on the high stakes for humanity to justify not informing the students their decisions would have real consequences.

I could have insisted on running what I'm doing past the ethics committee. The DPP might have agreed rather than lose the consultancy option altogether. I'd assumed the committee would have insisted upon informing the students. I didn't know for sure.

Ridiculous to want absolution from a dead philosopher.

My intentions were good, though.

Kant's eyes looked into mine. His expression gave nothing away.

Murder in the Citizens' Jury #4: Sarah and the DPP

When the file landed on the desk of Richard Beech, Director of Public Prosecutions, he assumed it was a joke. The victim was Steve, reported dead in a citizens' jury, stabbed through the heart with knitting needles. His smile broadened when he read the next line. *The knitter was brought into the citizens' jury to provide an atmosphere of calm.*

He clicked on the link to footage of police interviews with seven suspects. They really had gone to town. He almost felt flattered. He opened file number one, titled 'Sarah, Chair of the Citizens' Jury'. He pressed *play* and sat back, munching his sandwiches to enjoy the joke.

Sarah is in her forties. An earnest-looking woman with cropped brown hair.

Two police officers sit opposite Sarah. One police officer shows Sarah a piece of paper in a clear plastic folder. Sarah looks at it with confusion, and then with horror.

POLICE OFFICER 1: Our search team found this list of names.
    It's in your writing.

SARAH: That's my list of who sits where. It looks like... like
    some have been circled.

*She leans forward to see, but the police officer puts it
away.*

POLICE OFFICER 1: Two names have been circled, over and
    over again. The name of the deceased, and one other.

SARAH: Who?

POLICE OFFICER 2: You don't know?

SARAH: I didn't circle those names.

POLICE OFFICER 1: Then who did?

SARAH: I don't know. I must have put the list down
    somewhere.

*The police officer holds up another evidence bag. Sarah
looks at it, confused.*

SARAH: Is that...

POLICE OFFICER 1: Bits of cabbage. Can you explain why there
    was a cabbage in the jury room, or shall I interview the
    local rabbits?

SARAH: I have no idea.

Cabbage – that was a new one! Richard grinned. This was a
fun story to take back to Marnie. He'd often longed to share
cases with her, but his position made it impossible. It had
created a distance between them. With retirement, all that
could change.

Then he got the phone call.

An hour later and he was looking at the same body in the
mortuary – cold, naked, covered only with a sheet and very
obviously dead.

Chapter 6

Today's faculty meeting was online. Jenna was repeating what she'd said at the last one. A comment from Marcel popped up in the chat box. I was flattered to see I'd been included in a private chat along with GG and Percy.

Marcel: How did Colin manage to get next to Jenna?

I snorted with laughter. Even on screen, his little box was right next to the Dean. Jenna looked around.

GG: MUTE

I muted quickly, then froze. Jenna had just said something about consultancy money and redundancy. I jumped when she mentioned my name.

'Iris brought into the Business School enough consultancy money to fund a junior lecturer for a year. This is what we need to be doing here.'

I tried to hear what she was saying, but everyone was talking at once.

'Just to confirm,' Colin cut across the babble. 'Any staff who fail to bring in money from consultancy or research will be at risk of compulsory redundancy.'

'But I've got extra teaching!'

'That's outrageous!'

'What if your grant application—?'

It suddenly went quiet.

'Allowances may be made in certain circumstances,' Jenna was saying.

I saw a message in the chat.

Percy: Jenna muted everyone.

Marcel: That's how it starts.

Only Jenna and Colin had their cameras on. Jenna was talking, with Colin nodding from his little box beside her.

Marcel: Now she's switched off our cameras.

I turned my camera on and off and saw my face flash up on screen briefly.

Me: No she hasn't.

Marcel: She will if she needs to. Then no one will bother to turn up, we'll just send our avatars.

After a pause, Marcel's initials changed to a cartoon of a grinning dog.

GG: Do you think everyone has their own private chats going like us?

I gazed at the screen and wondered what was going on behind various avatars, photos, and initials. I went to respond, but the chat function had been disabled.

My phone buzzed, then buzzed again straightaway. It was my boys. I turned the volume down and let my initials attend the meeting on my behalf.

Tom: All good for weekly games night?

Adam: 👍

Me: ☺

Adam: monthly now innit?

*

I was still tidying up when Tom and Martha arrived.

'Hi, Mum.' Tom watched his girlfriend as she held out a beautifully wrapped box.

'This is for you,' said Martha.

'Thanks,' I said, opening the packaging. 'But really you didn't need to bring anything.' I took out a tub. 'Hydrating underarm balm?' I read from the label. 'What's that?'

'It's to stop wrinkly armpits,' Martha explained. 'I get free samples as my team are doing the marketing plan.'

'I worry about bags under my eyes. It never occurred to me I should worry about my armpits too.'

'It's ridiculous I know,' she agreed, laughing. 'But I see it as a form of self-care. It gives us a sense of control over getting old and wrinkly. There's a lot of psychology in marketing.'

'She's really good at her job. Honestly, she earns so much it's disgusting.' Tom's eyes shone with pride.

Martha misinterpreted my expression. 'Sorry Iris, I didn't mean to imply you had wrinkly armpits. It's just a freebie. It might not even work, but there's no harm in it.'

I put on my glasses and read the label: *palm oil*. I looked at her. 'Do you know about the environmental impacts of palm oil, Martha?'

'Don't start, Mum.'

'I'm a moral philosophy professor. That's what you get.'

'Deforestation?' she ventured.

'On a mass scale. Greenhouse gas emissions. Loss of habitat and biodiversity.'

'Lots of products use palm oil,' Martha said.

'I know. Its use has risen consistently every year.'

Tom looked around desperately. 'Where's Adam? He's always late.'

'Are you saying they should use another oil instead?'

'That solves one problem by creating another, as then we switch to other plantations that are less productive. The only solution is consuming less.'

'Martha works in marketing,' Tom said.

'Do you know what the word "marketing" means in Cuba?' I asked.

She shook her head.

'It means ensuring everyone gets access to what they need. No one needs this.' I waved the tub of cream, smiling to take the sting out of my words.

There was a knock at the door.

'Thank God.' Tom rushed off to open it. Adam came in laughing and enveloped me in a tall, skinny and slightly smelly hug.

'I hear you're on form tonight, Mum.'

'I don't know what you mean.'

'Tom said you're picking on his gf.'

'Gee Eff?'

'It's fine,' Martha said.

'Drink?' I asked.

'We're on green tea,' Tom said.

'What?' Adam scoffed. 'I bought beer.'

Tom grabbed the tea, then ran a finger along a dusty shelf and held it out to me with raised eyebrows.

'I'm busy writing my novella. I don't have time for housework.'

I waited for someone to comment on this exciting development, but Adam was gazing at Tom with horror.

'You're tidy now?'

'Martha's trained me.' He wiped his finger down his jeans.

After we'd sorted the drinks and snacks, I ushered them into the dining room where I'd laid out the Risk board.

'Do we have to play Risk?' Adam asked. 'Tom always takes ages.'

'We might as well, now we can,' I said.

Tom and Adam went quiet, and we set up the board in silence. Martha looked puzzled. I wondered if Tom had told her about Fay.

Once everyone had laid their troops and checked their missions, the game got going. It slowed down when Martha got her first set and spent some time laying out her army.

Adam fidgeted. He picked up the tub of hydrating underarm balm. 'What's that?'

'Armpit cream,' I said.

He snorted.

'It's not funny.'

He laughed again, but I meant it.

Martha threw the dice. 'Iris, I'm attacking you in Indonesia.'

'Indonesia used to be full of forests.' I glanced towards the armpit balm. 'There's none left now.'

'Mum!' Tom glared at me.

'It's fine.' Martha was trying not to look upset.

I thought about explaining but couldn't face where that

would take us.

'Pass me the dice then. I only have one soldier left. I'll die quietly.'

*

The weekend was spent struggling with my whodunnit. I got to the library just before it shut on Saturday and borrowed all four books on creative writing. Sunday, I plotted out narrative arcs and motivations for my characters and tried to set up my plot points. I lost time brooding over Martha. She was just doing her job, and that was the trouble. It gave me an idea for the next chapter. Plotlines and characters danced around each other in my dreams, making and remaking patterns. A welcome break from the usual nightmares. Back in the office on Monday, I remembered that I must tie all themes into the DPPs dilemma and ethical theories. I had till the end of the day to post my readings. I gave up and just wrote the story.

*

Murder in the Citizens' Jury #5: The DPP and the Case

Richard glared at the screen. This was decidedly no joke. He'd expected to be tying up loose ends, distributing his pot plants and cleaning out his desk, not dealing with a case that could affect the workings of the British constitution. Due to its sensitivity, it had been pushed up to the top, and unfortunately, that still meant him.

He read the witness statements and saw the problem. It wasn't as cut and dried as it had initially seemed. He'd have to interview Sarah, chair of the citizens' jury, himself. He needed to clear this up quickly before the media got hold of it. They'd been on his back since the recent controversies had put him in the public eye. Still, the court of public opinion was one thing – he'd learned to deal with it. It was the family court he worried about. Last night's argument rang in his ears. They still hadn't forgiven him for his previous two cases. He'd protested he'd just been doing his job, but then Laura responded, 'Were the Nazi's just doing their job?' Marnie always used to mediate between them, but this time she'd joined in. Wife and daughter both attacking him, like it was his fault. He'd taken early retirement to spend time with his family. He just hoped it wasn't too late.

*

RECORDED INTERVIEW BETWEEN DPP, RICHARD BEECH AND SARAH

SARAH: I recognise you.

RICHARD: Hmm. Now you-

SARAH: You're the one who decided not to prosecute the Prime Minister for spreading misinformation.

RICHARD: The evidence wouldn't stick in court.

SARAH: And that lovely old environmental protestor. Eighty-two years old, protesting for the sake of his granddaughter. You prosecuted him. He got five years.

RICHARD: Can we focus on this case?

SARAH: Don't worry, I don't hate you like everyone else.

RICHARD: Good. I just did my job. Now-

SARAH: It's down to the sleaze getting off and the good guys being put in jail that we finally got citizens' juries with real power. Although that's in jeopardy now.

RICHARD: I know the significance. That's why you've got me. How were members of the citizens' jury selected?

SARAH: We sent the invites randomly based on a mix of age, gender, education level, and the occupation of the primary breadwinner when they were fourteen.

RICHARD: Could the participants have known each other

67

beforehand?

SARAH: Unlikely.

RICHARD: To confirm, no experts you brought in during the process were around on the day of the murder?

SARAH: No.

RICHARD: That suggests the motivation arose from something that happened within the citizens' jury.

SARAH: It could have been an accident?

He looks at her, eyebrows raised. There's a pause and Richard looks momentarily distracted. He speaks suddenly.

RICHARD: Would you kill Hitler?

SARAH: What?

RICHARD: Imagine it's 1937. You know he's about to be responsible for millions of deaths. If you could kill him then and get away with it, would you?

SARAH: Is this a trick question?

Richard shakes his head, wipes his brow, and looks down at his notes, flustered.

RICHARD: Forget it.

SARAH: Would you?

RICHARD: Of course not. It's against the law.

SARAH: Even though it would save lots of lives?

RICHARD: Once the law breaks down, you get anarchy, vigilantism. Which brings us back to this case. Is there anything you'd like to add to your original witness statement?

SARAH: No.

RICHARD: That's it. For now.

*

I read through my chapter, pleased. I checked my emails, skimming through until I came to one from Robert.

Dear Iris,
Do you have an update on progress? Please will you send me the readings and dilemmas you are using.
Kind regards
Robert Ash
Director of Public Prosecutions

I checked the last reading and hesitated. Richard Beech, Robert Ash. I wish I hadn't made his name so similar now. The bits about the Prime Minister's misinformation and prosecuting an old environmental protestor were based on fact too. I'd wanted the story to mirror reality as closely as possible to give students a sense that their answers mattered, but without giving it away entirely. Robert was unlikely to see it that way though. He'd say I should have checked with him first.

Dear Robert,
The students' critical thinking is coming on nicely. I'm in a rush now to give a lecture so will get back to you later on the rest.
Kind regards
Iris Tate
Professor of Moral Philosophy

I sent the email, uploaded my chapter and turned off my laptop. I realised with a shock my room was now dark. Hopefully Robert wouldn't notice the time the email was sent - he'd be unlikely to believe I was rushing off to a lecture this late.

I turned on the lights and Kant's face jumped out; his eyebrows raised under his curly white wig. I returned his gaze.

Must we always tell the truth? I challenged him. Or is it right to lie when it seems to be for the greater good? Of course, such thinking offers room to rationalise unethical conduct, but isn't that why we need practical wisdom? Praxis, as Aristotle called it, guided by good intention and free from vested interests.

Kant stared back. His expression was grim, reminding me I'd lied to Colin and Jenna about the consultancy too. I nodded, conceding the point. I also owe a duty to my department. They could do with the income. I still had time to make the case to the ethics committee, with some details omitted for confidentiality reasons. But who sits on committees? Are they the kind of people who'd give it proper thought or did they just sit on the committee to get extra hours off teaching and would take the least risky option to cover themselves?

I picked up Kant's *Metaphysics of Morals* and squeezed it onto my bookshelf, leaving him eye to eye with the challenging gaze of Aristotle.

I turned off my lights and left.

In the foyer, I was surprised to see Percy rummaging for his staff card to exit the building.

'You're late,' I commented.

'Jenna changed the marking criteria. If she'd done it a month ago, it would be no issue, but now term has started, it means redoing everything.' He found his card and flashed it at the screen. 'Kate expected me back hours ago.'

The door opened to let us out.

'Er, Percy?'

'Yes?'

'Do you know who sits on the ethics committee?'

'Why?'

I hesitated. Once he knew, I'd be committed.

'Do you want to join?' he asked.

'Maybe, if they're simpatico.'

'There's Sue Masters, blonde hair, a colleague of GG's.'

'What's she like?'

'GG hates her.'

'I know who you mean.' I remembered the woman who'd sniggered when someone mentioned edutainment.

'Then there's Obi Adebayo. Just finished his PhD. He teaches postcolonialism and art.'

I nodded; he sounded promising.

'And Colin chairs it.'

My heart sank. I couldn't risk it.

'Why are you here so late?' he asked.

'Writing my whodunnit.'

'Hmm.'

'It's time-consuming, but fun.' I smiled, but he didn't look amused.

'I appreciate you taking on Emily, but embracing this edutainment rubbish just encourages them.'

'But—'

'We don't all want to work until midnight every night,' Percy said and stalked off.

'It's only ten o'clock,' I shouted after him. He didn't respond. Sod him. I flashed my card and went back into the building. I got some snacks from the vending machine and returned to my office to continue my story.

*

Murder in the Citizens' Jury #6: Day 1 welcome

FOOTAGE FROM CCTV IN CITIZENS' JURY

Sarah enters an empty boardroom. She moves around the room, consulting a list of names, gesturing as she mutters to herself.

SARAH: If he goes here... the knitter here...

Andrew walks in.

ANDREW: Good morning, I'm Andrew, but—

SARAH: Ah yes, the auditor. Thanks for coming.

ANDREW: Yes, the auditor. And...

He looks up at the babble of conversation from next door.

SARAH: Here they come. They've just watched the film about planetary tipping points.

The door opens and the jurors come in all talking at once.

STEVE: How have they calculated those figures?

DEVANIKA: Why aren't we doing anything?

NAOMI: I didn't know.

BEN: What about my children?

NEEDLES: My grandson. He won't cope.

BEN: They'll just run off to their country houses.

NEEDLES: Poor little mite, he got no survival skills.

BEN: Leave us to deal with the mess.

NAOMI: Why haven't they done anything?

DEVANIKA: It falls outside the electoral cycle, that's why.

SARAH: You're right. A limitation of our current system is that it tends towards short-term decision-making, meaning existential risks such as climate change are insufficiently addressed. That's why you have been invited to be part of this citizens' jury. This is your chance to direct policy.

Sarah ushers them towards an oval table, and they take their seats.

SARAH: Welcome, everyone! I'm Sarah and I'll be chairing proceedings, and this is Andrew.

ANDREW: My role is to assess the social, environmental and economic implications of various climate policies discussed, with emphasis on carbon savings.

DEVANIKA: Don't I know you from somewhere?

Andrew says nothing.

SARAH: We also have a special guest to help us keep things running smoothly, and with an air of calm. This is—

NEEDLES: They call me Needles.

Andrew opens his mouth to interrupt but looks at Sarah and decides not to. Needles takes out some knitting.

NEEDLES: I'll be knitting a jumper for my grandson with recycled wool.

SARAH: Let's start with names.

STEVE: I'm Steve. This lovely lady to my right is Naomi and the Indian lady next to her is Dekanovi.

DEVANIKA: South Asian. Devanika.

BEN: I'm Ben.

Josh hasn't volunteered his name, so Sarah prompts.

SARAH: Josh, isn't it?

JOSH: Er yeah, that's me.

SARAH: And what do you do?

JOSH: Er... Nothing.

BEN: How do you live?

STEVE: On taxpayer's money. You and me, Ben, that's how he lives.

Josh looks down at his feet.

NEEDLES: Here, love, have some knitting. Nice and calming.

Needles hands Josh some needles and wool. She shows him how to guide the wool. He knits a row unsteadily with shaking hands.

NEEDLES: Right needle goes into the first stitch. Wind the wool round... there you go.

SARAH: Would anyone else like to share what they do, or what led you to accept the invitation?

BEN: I've three children, me and my wife both work shifts, so mostly I'm looking after kids or delivering parcels. It's them I worry for.

DEVANIKA: I'm here because I wanted to do something. All politicians do is tell us to turn our heating down or take two-minute showers.

NEEDLES: You should try some knitting next, dear.

Josh quickly passes the needles and wool to her. Devanika looks at it, pulls apart what Josh did and starts again. Her fingers fly, knitting furiously.

SARAH: Thank you. Naomi?

NAOMI: Uh... I'm in skin and cosmetics marketing. And actually seventy-eight percent of our customers reported they'd pay more for a sustainable product!

NEEDLES: My mother said her skin and hair were never as lovely as when she had to stop using products during the war. Nature knows best.

DEVANIKA: She's right. Some chemicals in these products are basically hormone disruptors.

Naomi looks at her sharply.

NEEDLES: I don't use a thing on my skin and look at me.

Everyone looks at her lined skin. It's wrinkled, but in a cool kind of way.

SARAH: And you accepted the invitation...

NAOMI: Oh, you know. Take my mind off work. Maybe meet new people.

SARAH: Right. And Steve, what do you do?

STEVE: I'm a farmer. Thought this would be a good opportunity. A good businessman never misses an opportunity. Professional or... personal.

Steve eyes up Naomi.

SARAH: You should have been at the last one. We covered sustainable agriculture.

STEVE: I'd have told you there's no point unless you make it worthwhile. Farmers want to turn a profit like everyone else.

Devanika glares at him. He shrugs.

STEVE: I took over an organic farm, and it didn't pay, so I
    returned to traditional methods.

SARAH: Hedgerows for biodiversity and crop rotation to
    regenerate the soil?

STEVE: Pesticides and artificial fertiliser.

DEVANIKA: For God's sake! I know you want a diverse group,
    but we're looking for climate solutions and this joker
    actively shuts down a working organic farm?

NEEDLES: I worry about my grandson. He won't cope when it
    all goes tits up, that's fer sure. Don't you care about your
    kids?

She points her needles at Steve.

STEVE: They do all right out of me. What about you, ladies?

Devanika shakes her head curtly.

STEVE: I bet you're one of those birth-strike women, refusing
    to breed because of the climate breakdown.

DEVANIKA: None of your business why I don't have children.

SARAH: This citizens' jury is my baby, and it's a climate
    solution in itself. If anything is going to change our
    world, it will be who makes the decisions and on what
    basis. So I'll be making sure it grows up smoothly.

*Sarah flashes a smile around the room, which has a hint of
steel in it when she gets to Steve.*

SARAH: The mission of this citizens' jury is to answer
    the question, what policy proposal do we put to the
    government to implement to ensure that we reduce our
    greenhouse gas emissions in a way that's sufficient to
    address the climate crisis and is fair and just.

STEVE: It depends what you mean by 'just'. If you mean
    everyone being equal, why should people who lounge
    around doing nothing have the same as someone who's
    worked their guts out to get where they are?

*

I picked John Rawls off the bookshelf and gave him a high five. 'You next.' I laid him on the desk, ready for tomorrow.

I let myself out of the dark building and strolled home, my lecture already writing itself in my head. I paused under a streetlight, got out my phone and turned on the voice recorder and muttered into it as I walked on.

'This last chapter sets the students up perfectly for Rawls' Theory of Justice. I'm surprised no one has taught philosophy this way before... Or maybe they have. Make a note to do a literature search to check what has already been done in this space. I wouldn't be the first to think they've been innovative just to find some ancient Greek has already thought of it. Morality plays were a thing for a while. But in those, it was always clear what the right thing to do was. This is special. Rawls would say... He'd say that...' I saved the recording and brooded the rest of the way home.

*

Lecture 3 Rawls' Theory of Justice

The mission of the citizens' jury is, as Sarah claims, to decide what policy proposal the government must implement to ensure that we reduce our greenhouse gas emissions in a way that's sufficient to address the climate crisis and is just. Steve, in response, queries what she means by justice. In your groups, spend a few moments discussing what is 'just.'

Transcription note. Recording paused while class debated and then fed back.

Many said justice was fairness, but that's more of a synonym. So we need another way in that isn't just a question of definitions. Indeed, Wittgenstein in his *Philosophical Investigations* nearly put an end to philosophy by claiming that all philosophical debates were ultimately a question of terminology. Let's prove him wrong and dig a little deeper.

Philosophers have been debating what is justice for millennia. In *The Republic*, written around 375 BCE, Plato equates justice with the 'common good' and fundamental for a stable and flourishing society. 'Injustice causes civil war, hatred, and fighting, while justice brings friendship and a sense of common purpose.'

These ideas continue to influence debates in the present day. In this session, I'll introduce you to John Rawls, a twentieth-century American legal and moral philosopher, who many believe presented the most definitive proposal of what we can consider just. Rawls says that to avoid self-interest biasing your judgement on what's fair, imagine yourself behind a 'veil of ignorance.' If you were a policymaker, for example, what decisions would you make if you didn't know what position you'd take in that society?

Class exercise: Imagine you are floating in the ether awaiting reincarnation and you don't know if you'll come back as a man or woman; gay or straight. You don't know if you'll be born in Africa or Australia, whether you'll be healthy or disabled, neuro-diverse, good at maths or sports or nothing much at all. You don't know what your desires and preferences are, or whether you will be born tomorrow or in twenty years' time. To be accurate, Rawls didn't actually mention reincarnation, LGBTQ+ or neurodiversity or future generations. He stuck to social status, ethnicity, gender and idea of the good life, but you have to move with the times. Under such conditions, what kind of society would you vote for?

Transcription note. Recording paused for discussion. I was gratified to see them debating the topic. I gave them five minutes, then resumed.

Rawls claims that under conditions of uncertainty, you'd play it safe and go for the minimum of inequality consistent with the need to provide incentives towards hard work and innovation.

A chorus of disagreement came from the cocky lads at the back. A transcript of the conversation illustrates a range of positions on the matter.

Mouthy lad: I wouldn't.

Me: Why not?

Mouthy lad: Cos I'm gonna be rich.

Mouthy lad's mate: We're in a band. We're going to make it big.

Music student: You're idiots. I study music and you've got no chance.

The keen girl at the front was checking her phone.

Keen girl: There's a one percent chance you'd be very wealthy against a twenty-three percent chance that you'd live below the poverty line.

Mouthy lad: I'll take it.

Mouthy lad's other mate: You just have to believe.

I recognised the phrase from a popular influencer. There was just enough truth to hook them, but not enough to deliver. I'd have liked to spend more time on this, but had to get on.

I see there are some with a gambling bent who'd go all or nothing and would accept the small chance they'd be very wealthy against the much greater probability they'd live below the poverty line. But if we draw on the economic principles of marginal utility, it's clear that welfare increases with equality. For example, giving a thousand pounds to someone who is broke has greater benefit that giving it to a millionaire.

From this thought experiment, Rawls proposes under a 'veil of ignorance', rational people would abide by two basic moral principles: each person is entitled to the most extensive amount of liberty compatible with an equal amount for others. Second, differences in social power and economic benefits are justified only when they're likely to benefit everyone, especially members of the most disadvantaged groups.

Next, we need to return to our citizens' jury and consider

the proposals being put forward in terms of whether they meet these criteria of justice, and crucially, their likely effectiveness in averting the worst of the climate crisis.

*

After the lecture, I made my way to the staff canteen, wondering if my colleagues had waited for me as promised. Following Percy's outburst, I wasn't sure. They were already queuing for food when I arrived.

'Do you use emojis?' Percy demanded when I joined them.

'I'll add a smile, but that's about it.'

'Percy's upset that GG used emojis in an email to him,' Marcel explained.

GG showed me the offending email on her phone, which finished with an emoji of an enraged face that resembled Percy's current expression.

I repressed a grin.

'Next, we'll be instructed to mark essays written in emojis. Sausages and mash please.' The food attendant jumped to attention. In her panic, she gave him an extra dollop of potatoes.

I smiled sweetly to make up for him and ordered lentil dhal and rice. A small portion but never mind.

We sat down and conversation moved on to the requirements to produce research.

'They can fuck off.' Marcel waved a forkful of pasta in the air. 'We had two members of staff leave over summer and they aren't replacing them. She expects me to pick up the slack. Four modules a semester I'm in charge of and she wants research on top!' I leaned back to avoid a strand of spaghetti that was threatening to fly off into my face.

'What about you, Percy? Do you do any research?' I asked.

'He's known as the grammar police,' Marcel said.

'My monograph on the Oxford comma was cited by thousands,' Percy said. 'But no one cares about grammar these days.'

'Emojis, a new academic language,' Marcel suggested.

Percy glowered at me when I laughed.

'You could look at how terminology affects our values?' I suggested quickly. 'Referring to people as "consumers" for example, implies our value is in what we take from the planet, whereas the term "citizens' stresses what we give back to society.'

'Our language is also very human-centred,' GG said.

'Worry about your own research outputs.' Percy stabbed a sausage with his fork. 'And stop sending me petitions about animal cruelty.'

'Me too,' Marcel said. 'Anyway, how can you campaign to ban caged animals when you got a rabbit for your son?'

'He runs free,' GG said, scooping up some lentil dhal.

'Are you vegetarian?' I asked.

'Vegan.'

'I'm mostly veggie for climate reasons,' I said. 'But when I eat meat or go on a flight, I've got an app where I can offset the carbon emissions.'

'You can't offset the animal's suffering.'

I tried to think of some way I could. Adopting a rescue dog might count. It would make the house feel less empty, but then I'd make it even more miserable if I wasn't around. I could adopt two dogs to keep each other happy, so I could have the odd burger when the urge came upon me.

'How's your edutainment project going?' GG asked before I had a chance to float my idea.

'I'm ticking lots of boxes – interdisciplinarity, sustainability etc. And I'm learning lots myself about citizens' assemblies and climate solutions.'

I felt a shiver down the back of my neck. I looked up to see Colin glowering at me from the lunch queue. He said something to Jenna, who glanced my way.

Percy followed my gaze. 'There's no point sucking up to the management, hoping they'll like you if you dance to their tune.'

'I don't like this "them and us" attitude,' I declared. 'Now I'm researching citizens' assemblies, I realise their key strength is getting us away from the divisive nature of party politics.'

Percy munched his sausage, unimpressed.

'I like to inhabit the bit in the middle of the Venn diagram where there's common ground. I don't know why that's so rare, when it seems like the obvious place to be when one considers all positions. The University must balance the books after all.'

'Edutain—' Percy began.

'Yes, edutainment is a lot of work, as is interdisciplinarity and all that, but it's given me a real insight. I see now that this "them and us" mentality is systemic. Unions vs management. Defence vs prosecution, left vs right. It's affected the architecture of our thoughts and schemas, so now it's increasingly hard to agree on anything.'

I took a glug of water and replaced my glass on the table and waited for comments.

Marcel regarded me, disappointed. 'This is worse than we thought,' he said to Percy.

'Why?' I felt hurt. Yes, I could go off on a professorial rant at the slightest provocation, but I was an academic. It was allowed. Expected even.

'Colin will hate you anyway,' Percy said.

'He's Jenna's chief toady, and doesn't want any competition,' Marcel explained.

I sighed. I'd incorporated everything they'd asked for. But I'd done it for its own sake, not to suck up to the management. Even so, any success I gained as a result would come at the cost of my colleagues' good opinion.

*

Back at my desk, I made a start on my research paper and jotted down some reflections about the process while they were fresh in my mind. Ideas flowed quickly.

Reflections on 'Storytelling for Pedagogy'

I haven't found it remotely difficult to write in ethical dilemmas that serve as a basis for moral philosophy. People dismiss philosophy as irrelevant, but it's the stuff of life. The real challenge is in writing the story. Percy had a point.

Edutainment is a lot to ask of us. It's time-consuming and I suspect few lecturers would have the skills to be both academics and artists. My experience writing pantomime scripts at university was useful, although I found myself slipping between novel and script layout without realising it. As an avid whodunnit reader, I thought it would be relatively easy to knock up – easier certainly than an academic article. But academic articles have set formats. Here, I have too many options. I can write the story with a different point of view character in each scene to give some insights. Or I could write from the point of view of the CCTV recording the proceedings. Or I could foreground our detective and present the story from witness testimonies and interviews with suspects. I must also have some twists and turns as befits a murder mystery.

It's important not to give oneself too hard a time. After all, an innovative pedagogy requires some experimentation. As this is a prototype, I'll experiment and see what goes down best with my readers.

*

Murder in the Citizens' Jury #7 Murder in the Citizens' Jury: Carbon Offsets

'Countries and businesses use carbon offsets to meet their net zero targets,' the expert explained. 'It also works at the individual consumer level.'

'Are you talking a voluntary scheme?' Steve inquired.

'Yes, carbon offsets and credits work in the voluntary markets.'

Steve relaxed back in his chair. They were no threat. He stopped listening and eyed up Naomi instead.

Josh slid his phone out of his pocket and loaded up Candy Crush.

Naomi wondered if it would be appropriate to ask Andrew about his skincare regime. His face was unlined, but his eyes seemed old. Maybe his skin was so smooth due to his calmness – he didn't look like a guy who'd Botox. Steve caught her eye and winked. She gave a half smile and looked away. Unlike Andrew, he was easy to read.

Ben also wasn't listening. He was seething. 'How come he gets to keep his phone?' he burst out suddenly.

'I've got special needs,' said Josh.

'I've got kids, and I wasn't allowed.'

'Josh, please,' Sarah shook her head at him, 'and Ben, if there are any problems, the front desk has instructions to let you know. But if you really need it?'

'No, it's a relief to get away from them, to be honest,' said Ben, happy once Josh put his phone away.

Carbon offset man continued his spiel. 'Cutting down on emissions on its own won't be enough. We must also take carbon out of the atmosphere. Business and governments and individuals have money that we can harness towards carbon sequestration projects.'

'Huh?' Josh looked confused.

'That means removing the excess carbon dioxide that's in the atmosphere, by planting trees, for example.'

Devanika put her hand up. 'So they chop down an irreplaceable old-growth forest to mine a ton of stuff, then plant a monoculture in some remote area just to tick a carbon offset box?'

'We don't deny some of that goes on, but this app is much more rigorous. This is where auditors are crucial.' He nodded towards Andrew. 'We only include carbon offset projects with triple-A accreditation based on key criteria. That is, they don't solve one problem by causing another, and are genuine carbon removal, not just cutting down on emissions.'

Devanika nodded, satisfied.

'Our app brings together those who want to offset their carbon footprint with carbon removal projects that require investment. Your offset money may reforest an area or contribute to direct air carbon capture and storage.'

He passed iPads around the group. 'I preloaded the app, so have a play.'

Needles shook her head when he got to her. 'Don't worry, love, I'm knitting.'

Carbon offset man looked around with satisfaction as the group scrolled down. 'Each carbon credit removes one tonne of carbon from the atmosphere. You can also set up a profile and type in what you consume, and it will let you know how far over your allowable carbon footprint you are.'

'Can you offset travel?' asked Devanika.

'Yes, that's a popular thing to offset. Click on the offset calculator and type in flights.'

Devanika tapped in a flight from London to Dhaka. It was nearly three tonnes. She clicked on the offset button and faced a list of different projects of varying costs, ranging from twenty to eighty pounds. 'How do I know which project is best?'

'You can choose based on your values. Many have additional benefits. We have a peatland restoration project in Indonesia that not only prevents carbon loss but improves biodiversity and the quality of life for indigenous people.'

*

I took a break to get some snacks to keep me going. The building was quiet. The corridor loomed dark before me. Lights came on as if by magic as I made my way to the vending machine.

How much should I make of the fact that Devanika is from South Asia? Her family would be on the front line of the climate crisis. My brother would say ethnicity matters. The Global South bears the brunt of climate change impacts because of the emissions produced mostly by the Global North. Devanika would have family for whom climate justice was more than a term to be bandied about. But this story was about climate, not race. Yes, they overlap, I mentally responded to his comment, but if I make that a thing, it's too easy to write off the need for change by assuming it's something that will happen somewhere else. You don't have to live in a developing country to suffer the consequences of climate change. Lee had to agree to that.

'Ahem.'

I shrieked, then pulled myself together. It was only Colin. He was looking at me strangely. Had I been muttering like a madwoman to myself?

'Hi, er… You're here late?' I babbled.

'And you.' He looked at me accusingly as though I'd been caught stealing from the stationery cupboard. I felt the need to hold out my snacks for approval and then rushed on back to my office to resume my story.

*

'I like this menu tab,' said Steve. 'Say I was on a date with someone like you who'd want me to eat lentils,' he nodded over at Devanika, 'I could still have a steak, plant some trees in Kenya with a quick swipe and be done.'

'I wouldn't go on a date with you,' retorted Devanika.

'Steady on love, I wasn't asking.'

'You can't offset the animal's suffering,' Devanika bit back.

'I can if I'm having a good time. But then I'd have to go with Naomi.' Steve laughed, and nudged Naomi. 'What do you think?'

Naomi thought he was being a dick, although she couldn't help feeling flattered at his attention. He was handsome and clearly well-off. Shame he was so slimy.

'We hope to partner with major supermarkets, retailers, energy providers, etc. so you can do this at the point of each purchase automatically.'

Naomi put her hand up. 'I don't want to sound selfish or anything, but would people offset if they didn't have to?'

The carbon offset man responded quickly, 'We're hoping to create an expectation, a kind of social pressure, like a service charge at a restaurant. You'd look bad if you didn't tip.'

Naomi wasn't convinced. For all her high salary, she'd maxed her credit cards to the limit. She wouldn't pay more than she had to. Not unless someone was watching.

'It's all right for those with money, but we can only afford to go on holiday once every few years,' Ben said.

'I can't afford most of this stuff anyway,' Josh mumbled.

Sarah looked at her watch. 'Let's get to the figures now.'

Before Andrew could stand, carbon offset man bounded up and wrote 300,000,000 on the whiteboard under 'tonnes of

CO_2 saved'.

Andrew raised his eyebrows. 'That's a lot.'

'I know,' he agreed, pleased.

'Based on what assumptions?'

'That we all sign up to the app and offset any carbon emissions over our personalised allowable carbon footprint.'

'All sign up? To the voluntary scheme?' Andrew asked.

'Please don't write them off,' carbon offset man pleaded. 'You saw the figures. The Greenland ice cap is losing ten thousand cubic metres of water per second. It's past its tipping point. If the other one goes too, we're lost.'

'But it's such a nice day outside,' said Naomi, 'it doesn't seem real.'

'California, Canada, half of Southern Europe is literally on fire as we speak. Even the bloody Arctic is on fire!' he cried.

The rest of the room avoided his eyes as he spoke, uncomfortable at his emotion. He was right, but they were all thinking the same. Naomi was the one to say it.

'The thing is I do care, but why should I give up what I like, or pay extra for it, unless everyone else does? It will make almost no difference to the planet but make a lot to me.'

Carbon offset man shrugged helplessly.

Andrew got the eraser and rubbed out four of the eight zeros.

The click-clack of needles accompanied the sad shuffling of papers and click of the door as carbon offset man left the room.

*

Lecture 4 Egoism

Naomi: *The thing is I do care, but why should I give up what I like, or pay extra for it, unless everyone else does? It will make little difference to the planet but make a lot to me.*

To avoid catastrophic climate change, we must stop producing greenhouse gases as a matter of urgency. The excess carbon dioxide in the atmosphere is melting our icecaps and warming our planet. This requires a cessation of fossil fuel production, a switch to renewable energy, and drawdown of carbon through natural means such as tree/seagrass/kelp planting and technical means such as direct carbon capture and storage.

What is our moral responsibility?

Kant is clear – we should act so that if everyone acted that way, it would be for the good of society. There's little argument that we need a mass shift to low-carbon lifestyles. Rawls leads us to the same conclusion but via a different route. If we didn't know who we'll be or when or where we'll live, we would minimise our risks by adopting policies that protect the environment we depend upon. Ethically, therefore, we have a moral obligation to adopt low-carbon practices.

Naomi's position reflects 'egoism', which some thinkers have tried to claim as a moral philosophy. For example, Ayn Rand, in her *Essay on Selfishness*, suggests it's to the benefit of society if we all follow our self-interest. The appeal of this idea is obvious, but it falls apart under scrutiny. A classic example comes from the Prisoners' Dilemma. This thought experiment supposes that two prisoners are kept apart and are told that if they confess, they'll get ten years, but if they don't, and their partner confesses, they'll get twenty. If neither confesses, they will both be let off. In either case, from the self-interest perspective, it's better for the individual prisoner to confess, even though they'd both go free if they both acted altruistically.

An everyday example might be decisions whether to commute by public transport or car. The car may be more convenient, yet if all choose private transport, the roads become congested, and everyone is worse off.

Thus, the claims of ethical egoists contain a paradox. If everyone made decisions based on self-interest, they, and everyone else, would be worse off. It is such paradoxes that support the belief of most philosophers that it is rational to behave morally.

Plato, for example, posits that the human soul comprises

reason, spirit, and appetites/desires. He claims that one can only be at peace when all three aspects of the soul exist in harmony. One can only achieve such harmony by behaving ethically. He argues that if you act selfishly, you will be internally conflicted as your reason and spirit rail against your actions. Plato shares a story about the Ring of Gyges that illustrates this point. The ring makes the wearer invisible, and, in the original story, terrible acts were committed under the cloak of anonymity.

How would you behave if you could become invisible?

Transcription note. I gave the class a few minutes to discuss, then asked them for their thoughts. I ignored the lad at the back who'd shot his hand up amidst laughter and smutty comments from his friends. I caught the eye of another student who'd been deep in serious conversation with her neighbour and nodded at her to speak.

Student: Maybe I'd nick some stuff?

Me: OK...

Student: But only from a big supermarket, not from my local corner shop.

Me: I see hints of a relativist rather than an absolutist position.

Student: Huh?

Me: We'll cover that later. Go on.

Student: Will my trolley be invisible too, or will people see a trolley pushing itself?

Me: (laughing) I assumed you meant a sneaky bar of chocolate!

Student: I might as well make the most of the opportunity.

A debate broke out about whether anything she touched would also be invisible, and if that extended to the individual items in the trolley. The lads at the back fell into fits of laughter at the idea of disembodied goods floating through the aisles. I suspect they were high.

Socrates is an ancient Greek philosopher from about four hundred BCE and many consider him the founder of Western philosophy. No texts by him exist – he preferred wandering around Athens debating with people to writing anything down. His thoughts and arguments reach us mainly through Plato, who wrote the *Socratic Dialogues*. Socrates claims the man who abused the power provided by the magic ring has enslaved himself to his appetites, whereas the person who continues to act morally is happier as he has greater control. So he proposes that a rational person who has no expectation of negative consequences for their immoral behaviour would still act morally.

This argument is replicated in many religions. A key tenet of Buddhism, for example, is that happiness derives from ethical conduct – if you want to be miserable, think about yourself. Psychological studies also show that altruistic behaviours are associated with greater wellbeing, health, and longevity. Although, to be fair, it can be tricky to separate cause and effect. One may have more capacity to be nice if one is well off and in good health.

Based on all this, how do we answer Naomi's question: *Why should I give up what I like, or pay extra for it, unless everyone else does?*

We could argue based on enlightened self-interest that there are good reasons to behave ethically. To act otherwise is to live in shame or denial. The loss to our integrity and our soul may damage us in subtle but powerful ways. In addition, much of our wellbeing comes from feeling socially accepted and operating within the norms of society – we need to belong. High-consuming lifestyles are becoming less socially acceptable. It's just as likely someone will respond with negative judgement to hearing about your holiday in the Maldives or new SUV or patio heater than with approval.

Another alternative is to agree that she's right. If so, we must accept that an insufficient number of people will voluntarily take on extra costs or accept constraints on their consumption for the benefit of 'the planet'. The ecologist, Hardin, in the 1960s described this as the 'Tragedy of the Commons'. He used the example of over-grazing to show how people acting in their short-term self-interest will destroy the resource they depend upon. Other examples are overfishing, pollution, and greenhouse gas emissions. In the absence of sufficiently strong social norms against overconsumption, the only alternative is governance.

The implications of this are we'd need to remove the voluntary element. For example, in wartime, we rationed limited resources to conserve them. The government could similarly impose a carbon ration, or personal carbon allowance. A modified version of this would be to incentivise low-carbon products and behaviours via taxes and subsidies.

[ref inter-disciplinarity] Now we're in the domain of politics. A ration limits free choice but is fair, imposing the same constraint on everyone. Voluntary carbon offsetting allows free choice but is unfair in two ways. Firstly, people are effectively taxed for their green conscience. Second, insufficient people choose ethics over self-interest, which results in great suffering for those affected by climate change.

There are often trade-offs between liberty and equality – free choice versus fairness. With climate change, the stakes for these political positions are higher than they've ever been.

Your essay assignment is to answer Naomi's question for yourself, drawing upon one or more of the ethical theories we have discussed.

*

I joined my colleagues in the queue for lunch. My post-lecture buzz contrasted with GG's air of gloom.

'What's up?' I asked.

'Colin turned down my ethics application.'

So I'd been right to worry about the ethics committee.

'They were concerned about PTSD,' Marcel said.

I expected a smile, but his face was serious.

'I did a musical last year, and I wanted to interview the audience to see if it made any of them vegetarian.'

Marcel gave me a warning look not to ask questions.

'Steak, please,' Percy said when we reached the food.

GG looked at him disappointed and ordered a mushroom risotto.

Marcel and I followed suit in solidarity.

'My module feedback scores were low too,' she said.

'You can't take them seriously so early in the course,' I reassured her.

'Was your feedback that there was too much reading?' Percy raised an eyebrow.

Annoyingly, that had come up. 'I got an average of four point two out of five,' I said, which was also true.

'What about you, Marcel?' I asked once we'd sat down. 'You do genocide, right?'

'Not personally.' He tucked into his risotto.

'After my storytelling project, I may do more on citizens' assemblies and civic engagement, especially if citizens' assemblies get real power.'

'You go on about citizens' assemblies like you invented them, but the French had direct democracy after the revolution two centuries ago,' Marcel said through a mouthful of risotto. 'Each community deciding its own affairs. The *Enragés* proposed a Commune of Communes.'

'Was that like the proposed House of Citizens?' I asked.

'Je ne sais pas.'

'Oh God, he's gone French,' muttered Percy.

'What happened to them?'

'They called them "anarchists"—'

'Wittgenstein would say—'

'They claimed that without central government, they'd all cavort naked and run riot and steal. But...' Marcel waved a finger. 'So what!'

'It's not a good idea to set him off at work,' GG said.

'It was a French anarchist who said property is theft,' Marcel presented his palm to us in anticipation of opposition. 'But it is the law and order that is worse.'

'Any evidence to support your claim?' I inquired. 'Or are you into conspiracy theories and the like?'

'His PhD was in the community response to disasters,' Percy

said.

'Go on,' I said to Marcel.

'When law breaks down, people sort themselves out very well. Four disasters I research.' He counted off his fingers. 'Flood, earthquake, hurricane and bomb. History tells us we cooperate.'

'My friend is a prepper,' GG said. 'She says we'll turn on each other when things go bad.'

'She is wrong,' he declared. 'People self-organise. They look after the vulnerable. Energy is down? They cook up what's in their freezers and share with each other in streets. Street parties with food. Fantastique! Neighbours look out for each other. There are the chancers but mostly they unite. But then…' he leaned forward. 'Then the law and order come. Some idiot spreads rumours about looting. I ask you, what is looting but requisitioning supplies when supply chains have broken down?'

'Hobbes would say—'

'And the media. Oh là là!' He threw up his hands in horror. 'They repeat these rumours and talk of theft and riots. They send in the troops, and then a peaceful community sorting itself out are treated like criminals.'

'It becomes a self-fulfilling belief,' I suggested.

'Exactement.'

'Kate researched that,' Percy interjected. 'She said women who are primed with the stereotype that women are bad at maths will perform worse on a maths test.'

'It's the same in economics,' I said. 'Most economics models assume we're motivated by "rational self-interest". It's false because if we add up all our behaviours, those that are other-serving outweigh those that are self-seeking. Cooperation is much more prevalent than competition.' I paused and thought for a moment. 'Yes… I think I have it.'

'What?' GG asked.

'I have an idea for some research for all three of you,' I declared.

'The great professor we should all learn from.' Marcel's eyes glinted. 'Go on then.'

I turned to Percy. 'The term "rational self-interest" implies that altruism is irrational. This relates to how language shapes our behaviour, because assumptions we make about human nature become self-fulfilling. If people believe it is natural to behave unethically, then that belief will affect how they behave.'

'And?' Marcel spread his hands questioningly.

'Darwin proposed the idea of the survival of the fittest. Nietzsche, the German philosopher, tied it to the idea of the Übermensch, a kind of superior human, influenced also by the composer Wagner – something for you there, GG.'

She looked perplexed.

'I get it,' Marcel said. 'That influenced Nazi thinking, and so the Holocaust.'

'Yes, and one can argue the opposite. For example, the scientist Lovelock—'

'He came up with Gaia, didn't he?' GG ventured.

'Yes, the Gaia hypothesis that all of nature is connected, but he was influenced by another biologist who showed, in contrast to Darwin, that much of animal life was cooperative rather than competitive. And in turn, Gaia gave rise to a whole new level of environmental awareness and a deeper appreciation of our connection to the Earth. So, there we have it. Language, music and genocide.'

I took a bow while Marcel and Percy clapped.

GG remained morose. 'I'm not going to play people Wagner and see if they get murderous.'

'It wouldn't get past the ethics committee,' Percy agreed.

I gave up. 'There's no pleasing some people.'

Chapter 7

Dear Iris,

Are you making progress? The longer I leave it, the greater the risk of word getting out. I need the students to give me their answer as soon as they're ready – but not before. Their answers must be informed and carefully considered. I know I'm giving you mixed messages. Hurry – don't rush! I just wanted to share the urgency of the situation and trust that you'll do your best to help the students deliver their views on the dilemma as soon as they're able to do so. I haven't yet received the readings and dilemmas you're using with your students.

Kind regards
Robert Ash
Director of Public Prosecutions

Dear Robert,

Progress is steady. I've laid out a brisk timetable for the key ethical theories. Some students already show promising signs of insightful reasoning, but they're the minority. We could consider just using the decision of the brightest students, but I'd be reluctant to do so. From my many years of teaching ethics, I can vouch for the lack of a correlation between academic IQ and moral backbone. I appreciate the urgency of the situation and will try to up the pace on the whodunnit and home in on the key issues earlier.

*

Class exercise:

   Lincoln. Gandhi. Malcolm X. John Lennon.
   The world is as it is because the nice guys get assassinated.

Discuss.

I sat back, pleased. A perfect setup and it should engage the class straightaway. Out of habit, I ran it by my brother. I waved away questions about Fay, then after a few moments of silence, the answer came: *Softly, softly, catchee monkey.* Annoyingly predictable. It was what Lee always said when I charged ahead on something.

I mused on his words, then reluctantly deleted it. He was right, as always. I couldn't risk setting the dilemma too soon. It takes time to nurture incisive reasoning and moral literacy. I'd need several assignments to measure their progress, then the moment they were ready, I'd pose the key dilemma.

I checked the family chat group to see if Friday evening would be free. Nothing from the boys. Maybe Adam had meant it when he said games night was now monthly. Chase them when they don't want to come or crack on with my current project of saving the world through education entertainment?

*

Murder in the Citizens' Jury #8: Library of Things

Richard sank into his plush office chair with a groan. It had been a nightmare journey into work. The heat had melted the tarmac, and the usual ten-minute drive to the station had taken an hour. He'd had to get a later train and had missed his chance for a seat.

He loaded up the footage from the day of the murder. The sooner he made a decision, the sooner he could retire. It wouldn't be a moment too soon. His wife was behaving strangely. Marnie had always been a keen gardener, but she hadn't mown the grass for ages. He'd heard of 'no mow May' but it wasn't May – something was going on.

It took a while before Richard could distinguish specific voices as everyone settled down.

FOOTAGE FROM DAY 6

There is a babble of talk and noise of scraping chairs as everyone takes their places at the oval table. The jurors look hot. Sarah looks flustered. Naomi looks troubled. Josh is breathing hard and wiping his brow. Andrew looks on edge.

SARAH: We're running out of time. We must decide!

STEVE: I made my decision.

DEVANIKA: You're not in charge.

Richard stopped the recording. There was no way he could make sense of things by jumping ahead. He needed to observe the dynamics of the group as they developed. He sighed and opened the file from Day 3 instead.

FOOTAGE FROM DAY 3 WITH LIBRARY OF THINGS EXPERT

The group sits around the oval table, debating. Naomi is knitting.

BEN: How does it work? Can you borrow what you want for free, like a library?

LIBRARY LADY: There are several models. Some Libraries of Things have per-item fees, but some go for a subscription model.

JOSH: A Spotify of stuff?

LIBRARY LADY: Exactly.

JOSH: Would they have old consoles?

LIBRARY LADY: Yes, they're very popular, Nintendo, Atari—

JOSH: And games? Like Super Mario brothers?

LIBRARY LADY: Probably.

JOSH: Sick!

BEN: What if you borrowed something and broke it? Stuff gets broken all the time in our house.

LIBRARY LADY: They'd be delighted.

BEN: Huh?

LIBRARY LADY: They want to avoid waste – so much is hardly used before it's thrown away. If you used it enough to wear it out, that's brilliant.

BEN: This sounds too good to be true!

NAOMI: Sounds grubby. It's hot.

Naomi passes Steve the knitting and takes a perfume spritzer out of her designer handbag and liberally sprays it on, triggering a coughing fit from Devanika.

LIBRARY LADY: If the idea takes off, there'll be different levels. For example, a more expensive gold option would let you borrow luxury items, like jewellery, art, even a boat.

STEVE: Where do I sign?

He starts to knit.

LIBRARY LADY: The most popular items—

Naomi watches Steve knit.

NAOMI: You're surprisingly good at that.

STEVE: I'm good with my hands.

LIBRARY LADY: Are tools—

STEVE: *(to Needles)* Bet that surprised you, didn't it Granny?

NEEDLES: I'm sure there's more to you than meets the eye, duck.

LIBRARY LADY: *(loudly)* The most popular items are things that are only used now and then – gardening tools are popular, carpet cleaners, kitchen items. Fun stuff too, like party gear, golf clubs, instruments, games.

Andrew walks around the table distributing fact sheets.

ANDREW: This study reports that drills are used on average only eighteen minutes a year and emissions from their use are just two percent of the total emissions, the rest coming from their manufacture, distribution and disposal.

Devanika looks up at him as he drops the fact sheet in front of her. Andrew looks away quickly when she meets his eye.

ANDREW: Library of Things borrowers collectively saved one hundred and fifty thousand pounds last year, and it saved ninety tonnes of emissions.

BEN: I could save how much?

ANDREW: Ninety tonnes.

STEVE: Da-da!

Steve shows a perfect line of knitting around the group and chucks the needles over to Sarah, who has to drop her notes to catch them.

Ben watches Andrew write figures on the whiteboard under the heading, Library of Things.

BEN: Hang on, that's really low.

ANDREW: It's realistic. The London Library of Things has grant funding, free space from the local authority, plenty of volunteers and is located in the perfect area – lots of densely packed people, high income, but little space. Yet less than one percent of the population in easy travelling distance use it.

His marker squeaks as he writes 'poor' by carbon savings.

BEN: You get us excited about the idea then you shut it down. Why do that? It's not fair!

SARAH: How many here would use a Library of Things if it were nearby?

Ben and Josh put their hands up straightaway. Steve shakes his head.

DEVANIKA: I buy my books new. Probably now I'll use the library, but the truth is, I never did before.

NEEDLES: I'd use it when my grandson visits. Before it would have been for the toys, now he'd be wanting to try out a guitar or computer game.

STEVE: Josh would have nabbed them.

BEN: I'd want the guitar for my son.

LIBRARY LADY: Eighty percent of household items get used less than once a month. With broad membership, there'd be plenty for everyone.

STEVE: On a sunny day, everyone would want the barbecue.

BEN: They said you could reserve.

NAOMI: But then you have to think ahead. This is why it won't work. You got your own stuff, you know it's there, you don't have to worry.

Andrew adds a column marked 'take-up' to the whiteboard and writes one percent. Ben looks increasingly agitated.

BEN: But we had three out of six. That's fifty percent.

JOSH: What about my games?

ANDREW: We could choose to pour funds into Libraries of Things or extending existing libraries to include toys and tools, etc. It would help, but it wouldn't be sufficient.

LIBRARY LADY: It's not just carbon though! The manufacture and transport of goods causes deforestation, loss of habitat, loss of biodiversity, pollution, toxic waste—

Everyone jumps as Ben interrupts, shouting.

BEN: It would be sufficient for me! What about me – do I not count? Why do I never count?

Andrew stands like a robot, not responding. The knitting needles click-clack at a fast speed until the din subsides, then return to a steady click-clack.

Richard stared into space, processing what he'd seen. The sound of the knitting needles in the background was like a metronome ticking off his thoughts.
Ben appears to resent Andrew or Josh more than Steve.
Click-clack.
Steve is stirring up Ben's resentment.
Click-clack.
She said her retirement hobby was gardening. So why has Marnie stopped mowing the lawn?
Click-clack.
Maybe it's passive aggression. Retire and do some gardening or I'll let it all grow over?
Click-clack.

Chapter 8

Our faculty meeting was online again. GG, Percy, Marcel and I attended for appearance's sake, but had our microphones on mute and cameras off.

Marcel: Here's an avatar for you, Chip!

Me: Chip?

I was delighted when I saw the image of a perky chipmunk with a mortarboard hat.

Marcel: Check this out for GG.

I laughed at a cartoon of Eeyore from Winnie the Pooh.

Percy: Perfect.

GG: You're not calling me Donkey!

I found an avatar of Sam the Eagle from the Muppets. The stern expression, black knitted eyebrows, and beak were uncannily reminiscent of Percy. I didn't quite dare. Then I became aware of what Jenna was saying.

'Those of you who are assigning marks through the NSS period, be aware that student satisfaction comes from getting good marks.'

I raised a virtual hand.

GG: What are you doing?

'It's our student satisfaction scores that determine the status of this wonderful university,' Jenna continued, ignoring my hand.

Me: Evil prevails because good people do nothing

Colin raised his hand.

'Colin, go ahead.'

'Just to clarify, are you asking us to give high marks in order to get good feedback?'

I was pleased. It's risky to be the only one making a stand.

'NSS affects student numbers, and therefore the budget for our faculty,' Jenna said.

'Makes sense,' Colin said, and lowered his hand.

I unmuted.

'Giving high marks to poor students will rightly upset hard-working students who earned their mark,' I said.

'One disappointed student can cause a lot of trouble, not just on the NSS but social media,' Jenna said.

Percy: Emily!

'You're essentially asking us to give them more than they deserve in order to get high marks from them.' I interrupted Jenna. 'That's…'

Marcel: Corruption!!

'Problematic.'

Colin unmuted. 'NSS scores determine the status of our university, which determines student numbers.'

'There are other ways to raise our reputation,' I said.

'Let's hear your suggestions, professor,' Jenna said.

'I could do a talk – a public one, an inaugural lecture.'

'That would be wonderful,' Jenna said. 'Liaise with our marketing team to get good reach. The more prestigious the audience, the better.'

I nodded and switched my camera and mic back off.

Me: Let's do our own NSS survey. If Jenna could choose between having every student graduating without having learned a thing but they all give 5-star NSS scores or students leave properly educated but with below average NSS scores, which would she choose?

Marcel: We need a four-part Likert scale

Me: 1 definitely choose NSS, 2 probably choose NSS, 3 probably choose education, 4 definitely choose education

'But my point still stands about NSS scores,' Jenna said. She stared pointedly to the left of the screen, and it occurred to me she was probably addressing me.

I started to compose a response in the chat for everyone, but deleted it. There was little point.

Percy: One.

GG: One

Marcel: Have you got ethical approval for this survey?

Me: So we agree. Our Dean would choose NSS scores over actual learning!

Marcel: Whoops!

GG: You sent that to everyone!

There was a horrified pause while we waited to see if she'd been following the chat.
Nothing.
Then eventually the message came via the chat to everyone.

The Dean: I would! ☺

My mouth went dry. But beyond concern for my position, I felt an unexpected twinge of pity. There was something sad about the smiley emoji.

*

Afterwards, I began to worry. It was all very well pulling that kind of stunt when you were a valued member of staff, or had a clear conscience, but I was on shaky ground. Using students without their knowledge was a disciplinary matter and if Colin's attitude was anything to go by, they were already regretting employing me. Giving up the consultancy was out of the question, but perhaps there was still a chance to get official approval without violating confidentiality. If it was the same system as in the Business School, applications would get assigned to an individual and they'd only pass it through the committee in exceptional circumstances. From what Percy had said, Obi was my best bet. If he was new, he'd be eager to please. I checked the staff pages, looking for a way in. I soon found it and it was better than I could have hoped.

I tracked Obi down in the shared room allocated to the postgrads.

He recognised me immediately. 'You're the one from the Business School.'

'Not any longer. I've come to find out more about your Join the Dots project.'

He stepped aside and waved me in. 'You can't miss it.'

'Oh my word!' I gasped. The image on the webpage had given no indication of the scale. A huge collage took up the wall. A series of large dots filled the space, each one with a picture in it. Above it was the title #JoinThe Dots.

I sensed Obi watching me as I took it in.

'Impressive, isn't it?'

'It's amazing.' I stepped closer to see the details. In one dot was a photo of a clear lake surrounded by swaying grass. A crayon drawing of children playing in another dot partially overlapped it. I traced a line to another dot, which had a photo of a desert. Someone had joined it to the first dot and scribbled "before and after." Then on another dot was a t-shirt and a pair of jeans that created a triangle with the first two dots.

'Did you do all this?' I asked.

'I got school kids to explore the environmental impacts of their clothes and find photos or draw pictures and I stuck the best of them up here.' He pointed to a picture of the periodic table with various chemical elements highlighted.

'These are the chemicals that leak into the soil and water supply from the dyeing process and this one here is from the tanning process and joins to the leather jacket.'

'What a great idea.'

'This is my favourite.' A colourful dead octopus lay on its back, all eight tentacles pointing vertically up in the air. 'It's not strictly accurate. Pesticides from cotton pollute the rivers more than the sea, but it's such a great drawing I couldn't resist.'

'What on earth is this?' I pointed to what looked like a brown turd with a credit card poking up out of it.

'Exactly what it looks like,' he replied with a grin. 'Someone estimated we have about a credit card's worth of plastic in our bodies from the microplastics that have seeped into the water supply.'

'That's brilliant.'

'Touch it,' he said, his face alight with pride.

I followed the trail from the dot with the credit card with my finger and found it connected to a picture of a washing machine and finally to a photo of a sequined top.

'It really does help us to join the dots.' I felt a rush of warmth for him. This was why I'd joined arts and humanities. We may be different ethnicities, ages, and genders, but here, at last, was someone truly simpatico.

'It ticks all the boxes,' I cried, delighted. 'Impact, knowledge exchange, sustainability, interdisciplinarity.' I paused. I'd wanted to be the one to write the book on edutainment, but credit where it was due. This was exceptional. 'It's edutainment,' I pronounced and beamed at him.

His smile disappeared. It was as if I'd uttered a dirty word.

'We're not accountants here. It's art. You wouldn't understand.' He sat back at his desk and turned towards his screen.

I hesitated, then left. I'd blown it.

Lecture 5 Human Rights and Ethics of Consumption

In our story, the library lady implicitly joins the dots between our buying behaviour and the impacts on the environment. Lawyers and human rights theorists would approach this using the language of rights – our right to consume versus the rights of affected communities, present and future.

Despite resting on shaky philosophical foundations, the concept of human rights has been influential across the world, from the French Revolution to the American Constitution.

The seventeenth-century philosopher, John Locke, developed the notion of natural rights which should be protected. He proposed three key rights: right to life, freedom, and property. He argued that these are God-given universal rights that apply to everyone, irrespective of gender, race, or class.

Does his proposal stand up to scrutiny?

Transcription note. Recording paused for debate. The students' critical thinking is progressing as revealed by the points they raised.

Music student: What about animal rights?

Another student: Should foetuses have rights?

Keen girl at the front: Why those three rights?

Mouthy lad at back (amid much whooping and backslapping): Right to party!

The keen girl at the front turned around and glared at them.

Mouthy lad at back: What about right to free speech?

You have raised some topical issues. Who or what are granted rights will have practical implications in the laws we pass and what we deem to be acceptable. For example, Ecuador's constitution was amended in 2008 to grant legal rights to nature and this has proved an effective way to protect its forests and coastal ecosystems. Similarly, the Whanguanui River in New Zealand was granted legal personhood. Also, what rights should be included? Is the right to property more 'natural' than the right to free speech? Like Hobbes, Locke agreed that a key purpose of law was to protect property rights. Locke thought that once you mixed your own labour with the land, you have the right to call it yours. He proclaimed, 'All the world is America', meaning that it was unowned and therefore those who worked it to turn a profit could claim it. [ref decolonisation] Locke failed to consider the Native American tribes that lived there before colonial powers seized the land.

[ref critical thinking] Thinking critically about any proposal involves asking key questions such as, do they have vested interests that will bias their thinking towards a particular conclusion?

Locke owed his living to the propertied Earl of Shaftesbury. Hobbes similarly wrote under the patronage of the landowner, the Duke of Devonshire. The wealth and political influence of such landowners derived from the Enclosures Acts that seized property from commoners who'd worked it for centuries. Their income typically also derived from the colonies and, often, the slave trade. Locke himself had drafted documents related to the slave trade in the US. To be fair, while complicit, there's no evidence that Locke supported slavery, and his leanings were relatively egalitarian. But he wrote within a period where politics was the preserve of wealthy landowners who took for granted their right to seize property from those less powerful and then write laws to protect it.

A key question is, how do we decide something is a "right", rather than a "nice to have"? This illustrates my point that human rights theory lacks a solid theoretical basis. Locke declares they come from God. But what if you're not a believer? Even if you are, how does Locke know that these are the three rights God would have chosen and not others? For example, Thomas Jefferson proposed three foundational rights in the United States Declaration of Independence: life, liberty, and the pursuit of happiness. He argued we can derive additional rights from these, such as the right of movement, speech, and religious expression. Rawls also claimed that there's a link between distributive justice and rights. For example, the right to property is meaningless if the economic system results in such inequality that there is little certain sectors of the population can afford to buy.

One way to determine if rights are legitimate is to ask, at whose expense will this right be enforced and who has the duty to respect the right? For example, if you have the right to breathe fresh air, this imposes a duty of manufacturers not to pollute the environment.

In our story, the library lady said, *The manufacture and transport of goods gives rise to issues such as deforestation, loss of habitat, loss of biodiversity, pollution, and toxic waste.*

In the past, the wealthy lost sight of the fact that their standard of living depended upon the oppression of others and devised laws, norms and institutions to protect the value of their ill-gotten gains. Similarly, today we gloss over the link between our consumer behaviour and the environmental and social impacts imposed on others. Consider fashion.

According to the UN Environment Programme, next to agriculture, the fashion industry is the highest consumer of water globally. Producing one cotton shirt and a pair of jeans requires about 2,700 gallons of water. It's the third most polluting industry, with water from textile-dyeing polluting rivers and streams. Synthetic fibres take centuries to biodegrade, and about a third of microplastics in our oceans come from laundering of such textiles – the equivalent of fifty billion plastic bottles.

Fashion is estimated to be responsible for ten percent of global carbon emissions. The production of synthetic textiles consumes large amounts of petroleum and releases volatile chemicals into the environment. The tanning process of leather is especially toxic due to the chemicals required, such as formaldehyde and coal-tar derivatives. Cotton is environmentally harmful as the pesticides used undermine the ecosystem and present health risks to farmers.

Global consumption has risen to around eighty billion new pieces of clothing every year, four hundred percent more than twenty years ago. The fashion industry produces obscene amounts of waste, with the majority of textiles going to dumps.

The industry is also notorious for its sweatshops and there is child labour and forced labour in many developing countries.

Despite the high social and environmental costs of fashion, some firms destroy unwanted items to protect brand value rather than risk them being sold cheaply. The luxury brand, Burberry, was criticised for burning unsold clothes and accessories worth over ninety million pounds over five years to prevent them from being sold at a discount.

But changes are happening. There's greater awareness among consumers, which has led to a growing market for second-hand clothes. For example, shoppers can send their unwanted clothes to specific platforms and others can buy these at a lower price than the original. Another trend is renting or swapping.

Transcription note. The keen girl in the front put her hand up to share that she always bought pre-loved clothes and vintage fashion. Another added that she engaged in clothes swaps regularly. They started trading details of fashion swap apps. Even though their motivation was to save money, I was delighted. It's nice when ethical conduct coincides with self-interest.

Using a Library of Things, buying second-hand, or using apps that enable you to borrow or lend thus becomes a moral act. Buying new therefore, especially from brands that show such disregard for the environment that they burn clothes rather than see them sold at a discount, is to be morally complicit.

Just as the arguments that raged in the 17th and 18th centuries justified slavery on the basis it was good for the economy, could we see parallels today in the way we justify our throwaway consumer society by talking about the need for economic growth?

Transcription note. Recording paused as the Dean interrupted the lecture to encourage the students to complete the National Student Survey. She was wearing a Burberry jacket.

*

This was what I'd hoped for when I'd joined the faculty, lunch and a laugh with like-minded colleagues. I entertained them with the story about Jenna entering the lecture, demanding the students complete the national student survey then and there.

'I'd just created the impression that anyone who bought new clothes was the moral equivalent of a slave owner. Then in she walks, perfectly kitted out as if she'd come from a fashion magazine. Burberry cashmere jacket with matching bag, scarf, and shoes. Burberry, who I'd just had a pop at for burning their stock to preserve brand value. The students were doing so well, too.' I turned to GG. 'One of your music students made a good point about whether animals have rights.'

She picked up her phone and showed me a video. 'Watch this.'

I put down my fork and tried to focus on the screen thrust in my face. A lonely baby orangutan wandered out of a decimated plantation, leaving behind tree stumps and scattered foliage. Sad music played in the background. It looked around, frightened.

'She's lost her home and family,' GG said, tears welling in her eyes.

Percy and Marcel avoided eye contact. They were clearly used to this. I was relieved when she pulled her phone back, but it was just to show me another.

In this video, fires raged through forests. A koala clung to the top of a burning tree. There's no way it can escape the flames.

'Take it away!' I shouted. It had come out louder than I'd meant.

'No one ever thinks about the animals,' she said.

'We can only handle so much pain.'

She looked at me disappointed and put her phone away.

'I hope you don't mind me interrupting your esteemed and wonderful professor to talk about something very important.'

Marcel imitated Jenna's voice.

'They just glared at her,' I laughed, grateful for the change of subject. 'She was so sycophantic it was embarrassing, listing the shopping vouchers they could get for completing the survey by a certain date.'

'Jenna's desperate,' Percy said. 'We need a fifty percent response rate for the NSS to count.'

'It disrupted my lecture. I'd led them to quite a dark place, and I wanted to pull them back a bit before the end. They've enough to worry about with the climate crisis, poor loves, they don't need every shopping trip to be a moral maze.'

Marcel and Percy laughed, but I no longer found it funny. Was my brother Lee a victim of the climate crisis? Apparently, the prevalence of heart attacks increases during extreme temperatures. I don't know. I do know that with my brother went the yardstick against which I measured myself. The joint repository of memories of Mum and Dad. The one person who could help me remember the name of my first hamster, reminisce about family holidays, or tell me whether I'd had chicken pox.

'Are you OK?'

I looked up to see GG gazing at me with concern.

I managed a smile and returned to my curry. I had no stomach to explain. No one likes a moaner. Fay had made that clear. I chewed on my rice and fell to brooding again about my interrupted lecture.

'Jenna's out of order,' I declared.

'She is,' Percy agreed.

'I'd timed my lecture to perfection. The last ten minutes were about trying to get some clarity to help them understand their feelings of dissonance.'

They nodded, but I wasn't done. I was a moral philosophy professor with an unfinished lecture.

'We see in the news that this or that company reports a loss of profits, and we feel vaguely responsible, like we've been bad consumers and haven't spent enough. At the same time, we feel terrible when we see news of floods and fires devastating communities or videos like GG's. This leads to an uncomfortable feeling that suffuses everything with a vague feeling of guilt. We don't join the dots because we're encouraged not to. The reason that the abolition of slavery took centuries was because of the argument it would be bad for the economy. What they really meant was bad for the wealthy. I wanted them to consider the connection between human rights to life and their right to consume. To debate both the extent and the limits of their culpability.'

Marcel banged the table. 'Hear, hear!'

'You should do that talk you promised,' Percy said. 'That will bring in the punters.'

'Show them the videos,' GG urged. 'I have a playlist set to music.'

'All the money goes to STEM subjects because no one thinks humanities are worth anything,' Marcel said.

'Why Moral Philosophy is the most important subject in the world,' I said.

They all spoke at once.

'Apart from Music.'

'History.'

'English.'

I remembered again Jenna's puzzled face as the students glared at her and laughed along with them. It's a sad fact of human nature, but there's nothing like a spot of schadenfreude to lift the spirits.

Chapter 9

I emailed Jenna to confirm I'd do a talk. I wanted to make the case for academia and for the relevance of philosophy.

It's funny, I'm still arguing with them even now.

Lee started it. Our first marriages had finished a few years ago, but unlike me, he'd not found anyone else. I'd hero-worshipped him growing up, but once the ten-year age gap had narrowed, we could talk as equals. He'd encouraged my growing relationship with Fay, and the three of us had taken to hanging out at mine. I was denying I felt empty nest syndrome when Adam had finally moved out.

'She was the same when our parents died,' he'd told Fay. 'If she doesn't like it, she won't acknowledge it.'

'I was as upset as you were,' I protested. 'But they had a good life. They're gone. It's sad, but who wants to dwell?'

They looked at me as if there was something wrong with me. One likes one's partner and brother to get on, but not when they gang up on you.

'There's always an upside, that's all I'm saying.'

'And the upside is?' Lee asked.

'Fay and I might not have got together while Mum and Dad were alive.'

'What?' She looked surprised.

'I don't know what they'd have thought about it.'

'I think they'd have been fine,' said Lee. 'It would be out of their comfort zone, but they'd have got over it.'

'Are you saying you turned lesbian because they died?' Fay asked.

'Worrying about telling them might have been a barrier to

taking that first step.' I smiled, remembering our first tentative kiss. What a big deal it had seemed, then how natural it had become.

Fay looked thoughtful.

'I'm saying it was an upside, that's all.' I tried not to sound defensive. 'I can look at everything I've lost, or I can look at what I've gained. I prefer to water the flowers rather than the weeds.'

'Then the weeds take over. You become complicit,' Fay said.

I was about to add that I also didn't accept that I'd "turned lesbian," then thought better of it. It would be a hard point to argue when we'd just got engaged.

'We fell in love, and we happen to both be women. It doesn't have to be a political issue,' I said instead.

'Our hetero-normative society makes it political.'

'You did just say you wouldn't have been with Fay while our parents were alive,' Lee pointed out.

'You can challenge prejudice without politicising everything.'

'This is the trouble with you philosophers,' Fay said. 'You put things in boxes – here's politics and here's homophobia and they're in separate boxes and one doesn't influence the other.'

'Then you understand nothing about philosophy,' I cried. 'This is exactly the point Wittgenstein – the *philosopher* – was making.' I took Fay's hand. 'I've lost my parents. I got divorced. I met you and my life took a direction I never would have imagined.' I clasped Lee with my other hand. 'And now we have the time and space to talk as adults. It's an upside.'

I smiled at them; argument won.

'You're so academic.' Fay was dismissive. 'You toss around ideas, and make arguments, but there's a real-world outside your ivory tower.'

Well, I'm showing her now. No one could say what I'm doing lacks real-world impact. She had her battle to fight, fair enough, but I have mine.

*

Dear class,

Your next essay is on the ethics of consumption. What do you believe are the extent and limits of our moral responsibility in terms of our consumer choices? You can come to any answer you wish as long as you justify it. Reference the moral theories we have covered where they help, but I also encourage you to reflect upon your own experience.

*

Dear Professor

As I got such a low mark for my first essay, please would you read what I plan to submit for the second?

Thanks

Emily ☺

Dear Emily,

I don't pre-read students' submissions. But as per my feedback on your first essay, I need to see that you have thought for yourself. GenAI could give automated replies to an essay question on moral responsibility or the ethics of consumerism without the least understanding. If you'd like more precise guidance, please come along to the class or chat with me before or after the lecture. I'd be delighted to assist.

*

To family chat: Just a reminder for games night this evening. Look forward to seeing you all. Mum xx

Tom: 👍

Adam: You don't have to sign off mum, we can see it's you

Adam: from your son Adam

Adam: ☺

I hoped Martha was coming. I was keen to engage her in the question I'd set my students. Tom needed to stop being so protective. Martha was a successful, independent young woman. If she couldn't handle a friendly debate about the ethics of marketing, then she'd never fit in.

Back home in my empty house, self-doubt set in. Debates with Lee and Fay had been robust, but this generation were different. Maybe it was me who no longer fitted in.

*

Adam and Tom arrived together.

'I picked him up on the way,' said Tom. 'That way he can't be late.'

I looked past them down the drive. 'No Martha?'

'She can't make it, she, er—'

'It's fine,' I interrupted. I couldn't bear to watch him think up an excuse. I'd obviously upset her, and my boys were still treating me with kid gloves.

Tom pulled a bunch of flowers from his bag. 'I brought these. They're just from the garage.'

I took them and peered at the label.

'Actually, they're from halfway across the world.'

He rolled his eyes and surveyed my drive critically.

'How about I sort your weeds out?' He nodded towards the dandelions growing through the path.

'Who are you?' Adam cried, disgusted. 'Bringing flowers. Weeding!'

'Just grown up. You could try it,' he responded, grinning.

My heart lurched with love. Tom looked like Lee used to when he talked down to me. I knew what he was trying to do, but nobody could take Lee's place.

'I like weeds,' I said. 'They're good for the ecosystem.'

'I can plant some if you like,' Adam suggested.

'They grow naturally, love.'

'Do I still get brownie points for offering?' he wheedled, following me inside.

I laughed. 'OK, but I'll still kick your arse at Risk.'

Once I'd dug out a vase and sorted everyone out with drinks, I opened the board game chest.

'Does it work with three?' Adam sounded doubtful.

Tom glanced towards the Monopoly, and hesitated.

'Let's see.' I pulled out the Risk and shut the lid.

We dealt out the mission cards and laid our troops.

Adam was lucky from the start.

'If he's got *Conquer Australia and North America*, he's almost won already,' Tom complained after Adam's lucky dice in his first battle.

'Attack him in Australia then.'

'I don't have enough troops. I'll attack you in South Africa.'

'That's where your flowers came from.'

'Ha ha.'

'Nothing funny about their carbon footprint.'

'That told you.' Adam punched Tom's arm, pleased that the flowers had backfired.

'Most mums would be happy their son brought flowers,' Tom grumbled. He was used to me though, and I could tell he was more upset at Adam's delight than my comments.

'Some local daffodils would be lovely in spring, love.' I threw a one, and shrugged as Tom moved his army in.

'I'll bring you some weeds.' Adam picked up the dice and threw a six. 'Right, bro, that's you gone from Australia.'

Forty minutes later and Adam had won. There was a brief silence. It was too early for them to leave.

'So Mum, how's your new job?' asked Tom.

'Suck up!' Adam burst out, incensed. 'You'd never have asked that before.'

It was true. Since he'd met Martha, he'd learned some manners. I didn't mind because I was pleased to be asked.

'Excellent, actually. I'm writing a whodunnit?'

'Huh?' Adam looked baffled.

'It's an innovative new teaching method. It's a fun challenge, and I always had aspirations to be a writer.'

'Did you?'

'Don't you teach philosophy?' Tom asked.

'I do. I'm using a real-life… I, er, I made up a murder and I'm setting up my characters, so they all have a different motive—'

'What's that got to do with philosophy?' Tom exchanged a bemused glance with Adam.

'Every character represents a different section of society and every motive ties into an ethical theory. I talk about distributive justice and human rights and the ethics of consumption. For example…'

I tailed off, noticing that they were checking their phones.

'Shall we play again?' I asked.

Adam looked up. 'It's no good with three.'

There was an awkward silence because he was right. After Dad died, Lee had kept the tradition going with the next generation. When the boys were in their difficult teenage years, games had provided a way to connect that they could still enjoy. Then later, Fay came along when Lee couldn't make it. I wasn't enough on my own.

Tom scooped up the soldiers. Adam glanced at the clock.

'Go on you two, get off,' I said brightly, standing up. 'I'll pack it away.'

They jumped to their feet and gave me a hug. They were out of the door in moments.

I waved them off. 'Love to Martha,' I called after Tom.

'Sort your weeds out,' he called back. He was grinning, but I suspected he worried my place didn't look tidy enough for his girlfriend.

I shut the door and went back into my empty house. I didn't mind because the next chapter was already writing itself.

I put the Risk away, switched on my laptop and started typing.

Murder in the Citizens' Jury #9: Just World

Richard watched the footage but couldn't concentrate. His mind kept returning to the weeds growing between the paving slabs on his drive. Marnie wouldn't let him touch them. It seemed like a metaphor for their marriage. They were in separate bedrooms now. This morning it had been a relief to get out of the house. What would it be like when he was there all day?

The word "murder" snapped him out of his ruminations. He rewound and leaned forward to listen.

POLICE OFFICER 1: What was your relationship with the victim?

NAOMI: We didn't have a relationship.

POLICE OFFICER 2: We heard that the two of you often stood in the way of policies being voted for.

NAOMI: That's not fair! That makes it sound like we were the villains!

POLICE OFFICER 1: How did Steve get stabbed with knitting needles?

NAOMI: I didn't see, but it might have been Devanika.

POLICE OFFICER 1: Why is that?

NAOMI: She hated him.

POLICE OFFICER 1: Did you actually see her stab him?

NAOMI: No, but I saw her in her car on the first day. I didn't know who she was then. And she was crying. Like full-on ugly crying.

POLICE OFFICER 1: Did you ask her about it?

NAOMI: No, because she scared me. She was so intense. One

time she looked like she wanted to murder me!

POLICE OFFICER 1: When was this?

NAOMI: It was after the debate about Libraries of Things.

Richard opened the file marked CCTV Day 3 and fast-forwarded to the point when it looked like things were wrapping up. Everyone was talking at once. Sarah was in a debate with Naomi while the Library Lady was seeking her attention to say goodbye. Once she'd left, the voices became distinguishable again. Richard pulled out some sandwiches and ate while he watched.

DEVANIKA: Don't you care that the products you market as natural are linked with cancer and fertility issues?

NAOMI: They're natural! Mostly.

NEEDLES: Arsenic is natural.

DEVANIKA: Look at you! Nothing natural about you at all. Is there even a face left underneath that makeup?

SARAH: Devanika, please!

NAOMI: I know what your problem is.

DEVANIKA: Really?

NAOMI: Karma.

BEN: Huh?

NAOMI: All suffering in life is because of past misdeeds.

BEN: You're saying that everything bad that happens to us is our own fault?

Josh nods to himself sadly.

NAOMI: Yes. We're responsible for our own suffering.

Devanika stands up and shouts.

DEVANIKA: So, if someone gets sick, or even, I don't know,

loses a baby, you're saying it's their fault?

NAOMI: I suppose so.

DEVANIKA: Are you fucking serious?

NAOMI: Or maybe it's the baby's fault – past life.

The click-clack of the knitting needles sounds loud and fast as Devanika and Naomi glare at each other.

STEVE: I get it. You're responsible for your own luck. *(To Naomi)* Me and you worked to get where we are. No one handed it to us on a plate, did they?

DEVANIKA: It's the same old story, blame the victim. But calling it karma! That's a new low.

SARAH: Just-world syndrome.

DEVANIKA: What?

SARAH: It's why people blame the victims. People like to think the world is fair, so the only way they can cope with injustice is to say that the victim deserved it.

NEEDLES: But they got it all wrong. If you want a just world...

She stabs her needles at the group to emphasise her point.

NEEDLES: You got to *make* it just.

Richard wondered about that final phrase. He was in no hurry to get home. He settled back in his chair to watch the police interview with their prime suspect.

POLICE OFFICER 1: We've done some background on you. You've been a member of several guerrilla groups.

NEEDLES: Just the Guerrilla Grannies, dear.

POLICE OFFICER 1: In the eighties you were a key member of the Deadly Knitshade Group protesting at Greenham Common Peace Camp.

NEEDLES: It were the weapons inside that were deadly. Not
    us, we were just knitting. Knitting for peace *(cackles)*.
    Some of the guys couldn't stand being left out. 'We want
    to protest too!' 'You do your thing, laddies, leave this
    to the girls,' we'd say. Some of 'em even dressed up as
    women to get in. We'd have a bit 'o fun with them. Give
    'em a wee poke with our needles.

POLICE OFFICER 1: Did you give the deceased a 'wee poke'?

NEEDLES: Bit more than a poke, weren't it? Still, that's why I
    were brought in, to diffuse any tension.

POLICE OFFICER 2: What tension was there?

NEEDLES: That Naomi caused a bit of trouble with her
    obsession with everything having to be new and shiny.
    Bless her heart, she didn't like the repair idea at all. And
    Devanika didn't like her, or Steve neither.

POLICE OFFICER 1: Devanika disliked Naomi and Steve. Go on.

NEEDLES: I did me best, but no amount of knitting could take
    the tension out of that one.

POLICE OFFICER 1: What were your views of the deceased?

NEEDLES: Well now, he thought a lot of himself. All charm to
    start with, but it didn't last. Not when he couldn't get his
    way.

POLICE OFFICER 1: Excuse me, I won't be a moment.

   He stands up and talks to someone off camera, then returns.

NEEDLES: Anything up dearie?

POLICE OFFICER 1: Do you wear lipstick?

NEEDLES: Not me duck. Found on the body, were it?

POLICE OFFICER 1: Which of the group wore lipstick?

NEEDLES: Andrew.

POLICE OFFICER 2: Andrew?

NEEDLES: He's a dark horse, that one.

*Police Officer 2 makes a note but stops when Needles
cackles with laughter.*

NEEDLES: Just having you on, love. No, it's Naomi who was full
of the makeup.

Police Officer 1 returns to the table and packs up his stuff.

POLICE OFFICER 1: We'll have to resume this later.

One thing was for sure, Needles was sharper than she
looked. She'd picked up on the lipstick straightaway, and
her failing memory seemed a touch too convenient. Richard
understood why they'd had her pegged for the murder. It
was her knitting needles, after all. Still, they had everyone's
fingerprints on them except for Andrew's. He remained to be
convinced.

Chapter 10

It's a shame I didn't record the last class as we had a productive discussion about the last chapter. Students were interested in the Just-world theory. The news was full of a devastating flood that had killed thousands in Europe. We discussed how difficult it is for us to take in, and how we find ourselves more upset about a dog that drowned locally than thousands of people dying elsewhere.

The keen girl at the front expressed guilt about this. I reassured her it's OK. We need to protect ourselves so we don't go mad. If losing one person has you in bits, what about when there are thousands? To have empathy for the world is a big ask. We know rationally that every single figure in that headline of 'thousands dead' is a real person who left behind loved ones. We can't even bear to think about what the victims themselves must have suffered. This is where ethical theories come in handy, I told them. You can apply them methodically and engage your brain to ensure that actions and decisions are fair and operate to minimise harm and maximise wellbeing, without having your heart broken at every instance of suffering you see in the media.

Many admitted that they didn't watch the news. This incensed the few students that did. But it's not that surprising. We didn't evolve to have the most horrific and distressing events from across the globe presented to our poor wee brains 24/7. No wonder we're anxious.

We took a poll and over half the class put their hand up when I asked who suffered from climate anxiety. Many were surprised at how many others shared their fears. The lads at the back who didn't put their hands up were accused of being climate deniers.

The keen girl in the front said that denial is stupid. It's like when you go out thinking it won't rain and it chucks it down and you are unprepared. I agreed with her – that was stupid. I suggested, though, that denial was rational when the worst has happened and there's nothing to be done.

I let them argue it out for a while between themselves while my mind wandered. I came back to myself when the girl at the front asked if I was OK. I found I had tears in my eyes.

*

Submission: Ethics of Consumption, by 2813456

When we talk about moral responsibility and the ethics of consumption, then we must distinguish between individual responsibility and society's responsibility. The best metaphor I could come up with was to think of my actions as a pebble thrown into a lake. The ripples caused by our actions in our lake are our moral responsibility. I don't feel I can do much about the big challenges we face or ripples in other lakes, but I can be responsible for my area of influence. So when I vote or buy something, that's my ripple. Also, I can try to create a bigger plop by engaging in activism by writing to businesses or MPs like Devanika did. Or I could make a difference at work. For example, I've a part-time job in a supermarket and there's lots of food waste. I could suggest they have a special discounted aisle to promote seasonal vegetables as that has a lower carbon footprint. I thought of that because I liked the first bit you wrote about Josh when he took free vegetables that were in season (did you write the whodunnit? If so, it's not bad!)

But then I thought, are we entirely responsible for our own plop? What we consume depends a lot on marketing and advertising. It must do or they wouldn't spend so much money on it. I didn't realise what a big difference it made until I went to Cuba. I liked your bit about Cuba by the way. I felt so at peace there. At first I thought it was because there wasn't much internet so I couldn't go on social media, but it wasn't until I came home that I realised how much we're sold to all the time. In Cuba there's no advertising. But when I got back, even in the airport, I was bombarded with adverts everywhere telling me what to buy. It was like when you're outside and the noise of a lawnmower stops and the silence suddenly seems peaceful, and then when it starts again, you notice the intrusion. It was like that.

Another thing that upset me was when my music lecturer played Bach's *Air on a G-string*. It lifted me up. I literally felt it in my heart and wanted to cry with joy. The way the music dipped and soared, my spirit soared with it, and for a moment I believed in God. Then I played it to my mum and she told me it was from the cigar advert and laughed. But it upset me and it's only now I understand why. I told mum how I felt but she just said the cigar advert was really funny. But now I reflect deeply on it, it's outrageous that a company who makes a product that's addictive and harms our health can use the most beautiful music in the world to sell itself. Then I started thinking about how literally all the best music in the world has been used to sell products. It's like the marketing people are hijacking our brain connections for their own purposes, so they determine what we think about when we see their product. Should we have a human right to our own associations?

In conclusion, I hope you don't mind that I haven't brought in many moral theories, but I'm not doing a philosophy degree. I'm a music student, so this is just an option.

*

It was the last of the essays. I was in no rush to go home, so I put on *Air on a G String* while I wrote my feedback.

> *Mark: 65%*
> *Feedback: I like your creative approach to this*
> *answer. There are areas you could improve. For example,*
> *the tone and language were rather informal for a piece*
> *of academic work. The conclusion too felt rushed and*

*incomplete. However, you clearly thought deeply about the
topic and presented insightful arguments. I'm giving you a
2:1 as a thank you for reminding me of a beautiful piece of
music that I haven't listened to for a long time, although I
suggest you check the spelling!*

I submitted my feedback and surrendered to Bach. The
student was right. It was exquisite. The sky outside was dark,
most office lights were out. I felt like I was alone in the universe
in a bubble of sound. The bittersweet high notes of the violin,
and underneath the low notes, holding it all together. The giant
double bass, the strings being plucked in the same sequence over
and over, ponderous, inexorable, funereal.

I snapped it off. The ping of an email notification broke the
deathly silence.

> *Dear Iris,*
> *How are the students coming on? Have they*
> *covered the relevant theories and been exposed to*
> *the key dilemma yet? I don't mean to question your*
> *professionalism but having to wait when there's great*
> *pressure on me to resolve the situation is stressful. I tried*
> *again to make the decision myself. However, my personal*
> *situation is making it impossible for me to think as clearly*
> *as I normally would. Apologies if I'm pressuring you. I*
> *have every faith you'll deliver.*
> *Kind regards*
> *Robert Ash*
> *Director of Public Prosecutions*

Grateful for the distraction, I composed my response.

> *Dear Robert*
> *I understand how frustrating it must be to do*
> *nothing and trust an outsider. It's also a prompt to*
> *increase the pace. Over the next six weeks, I'll cover the*
> *ethics of private justice, utilitarianism, virtue theory and*

discourse ethics. We also need some more climate stuff.
That, together with Kantian ethics to represent absolutist
approaches and justice theories covered earlier, should give
them sufficient grounding. I hope that puts your mind at
rest.

> *Kind regards*
> *Iris Tate*
> *Professor of Moral Philosophy*

My phone rang as I was standing in the deserted foyer, looking for my staff card to exit the building. It was the DPP.

'Six more weeks!' he barked, interrupting my polite greeting.

'Yes, it takes time to—'

'I don't have time. Have you even set the dilemma yet?'

'I can't until I've done the murder.'

'You haven't done the murder?'

I bristled.

'I'm sorry,' he said immediately. 'The pressure is driving me into early retirement.'

I sat down on the chair by the door, hugging the phone to my ear.

'I'd hate to retire,' I said, 'all that time to fill.'

'I'd planned on gardening, but my wife's taken up wildlife gardening, which apparently means you do very little.'

'Oh, really? Me too.' I was keen to distract him because what he was asking was impossible.

'Anyway, Iris, to get back to my point—'

'I'm sorry to hear you're under pressure. What's the problem?'

I listened carefully as he told me what was making it hard for him to think objectively. I murmured encouragement now and then to keep him talking while mentally adjusting my plot.

He stopped. 'I shouldn't be offloading on you like this.'

'It's fine. Helpful actually.'

He laughed a little nervously. 'Remember, confidentiality and all that.'

I made soothing noises. It would be a waste of breath trying to explain the necessity of building up to the murder.

He talked over me, his tone suddenly abrupt.

'Can you do the murder now, set the dilemma and get me an answer?'

'It's not that easy.'

'Why not?'

'I've got to do all the theories.'

'Can't you do that after you've set the dilemma?'

'No.' My answer was immediate. What would I do for the rest of the semester?

'I wouldn't have employed you if I'd known it would take so long,' he barked.

'It's not like you're paying.' I got to my feet and paced up and down. 'The department is losing precious consultancy money. I could lose my job if they found out.'

I heard footsteps coming down the stairs. I rummaged frantically in my bag for my staff card and flashed it at the sensor. The doors slid open, and I hastened outside. The path to the road was lit up. I scuttled instead to the dark shadows where the bins were. Over my beating heart, I heard Robert saying something about non-disclosure agreements. I put my hand over the phone.

Colin emerged from the building. He stood on the steps and looked around. I held my breath. For a moment, he seemed to be looking straight at me. He walked on towards the car park, and I exhaled with relief. Once he'd gone, I put the phone back to my ear. Robert was still talking.

'If it will speed things up, I'm still happy to pay.'

'I can't ask for ethical approval once we've started.'

I ended the call and stood in the shadows, wondering what Colin had heard.

The mournful sound of Bach seemed to linger in the air. I couldn't face going home. Anyway, I had some ideas for my story. I turned around and let myself back into the building.

Murder in the Citizens' Jury #10: On-Demand Buses

Richard got straight to work the minute he hit his office. The mystery of the unmown grass and weeds had been resolved at least. His wife had got into wildlife gardening. It was a worry. To be precise, the wildlife gardener was a worry. The sooner he got this wrapped up, the better. He pulled up the interview with Devanika, and watched old school, pencil and notepad in hand.

POLICE OFFICER 1: You were seen crying in your car the first day. Do you deny it?

DEVANIKA: None of your business.

POLICE OFFICER 1: It's a murder enquiry!

DEVANIKA: Unless he drowned in tears, it's not relevant.

POLICE OFFICER 2: We found traces of lipstick on the victim.

She looks at Devanika's mouth.

DEVANIKA: I don't wear lipstick. Not anymore.

POLICE OFFICER 1: Ah yes. We've done some background checks. You launched a petition against the company *Fabulous Cosmetics*, calling their marketing blurbs misleading and accusing them of 'falsely selling hormone disruptors, pretending that they're harmless, destroying our health and our fertility.' Surely they do safety testing before they can market products like that?

DEVANIKA: The studies only look at chemicals individually. We're taking them in cumulatively. It's in our cosmetics, and run-off from farms! Poisons on our faces and seeping into our rivers! People like them, they're the murderers.

POLICE OFFICER 1: A court of law will decide who the

murderer is.

Devanika scoffs.
Richard made a note: 'No respect for law?'

POLICE OFFICER 1: We checked the financial records of all
the persons of interest.

DEVANIKA: Ben's the one who's always crying about money.
And you should look at Naomi if you think that's the
motive. She's constantly buying stuff (*leans forward*) and
I know her job's in danger.

POLICE OFFICER 2: How do you know that?

DEVANIKA: You pick things up.

POLICE OFFICER 1: You and your husband have high-paying
jobs, so can you explain why, over the last two years,
your credit score has nose-dived from excellent to bad?

DEVANIKA: It was Naomi who was broke. That much was
obvious when we were discussing demand-led buses.

After that, there was nothing of interest. Richard made
himself a cup of tea and returned to watch the CCTV footage
from Day 4 of the citizens' jury when they'd discussed demand-
led public transport. Josh was now knitting easily. Was it
deliberate that everyone had a go with the knitting? To make
fingerprinting trickier perhaps?

Marnie had knitted when Laura was young. She was dying
for a reason to knit again. They were both looking forward to
grandchildren. It was after Laura had announced she was ready
to try for a baby that he'd finally taken the plunge and handed
in his notice.

The exasperation in Steve's voice brought him back to the
recording.

STEVE: On-demand buses come when you call them.

SARAH: Like Uber, but with buses.

NEEDLES: Ooba?

BUS MAN: Forget checking out the timetable and waiting at
a bus stop for a bus that always goes to the same place.
With demand-led transport, you say where you are and
where you want to go.

NEEDLES: But how?

*Steve raises his voice and taps the table with each word for
emphasis.*

STEVE: How many times? You. Download. The. App.

NEEDLES: App?

BUS MAN: There'll be lots of buses and they'll learn typical
patterns and the algorithm will—

Josh shows Needles his knitting.

NEEDLES: Oh, that's much better. You picked that up quick.

Josh beams.

STEVE: Let's move on so we can get out of here alive.

The offhand remark jolted Richard back to reality. He'd
been concentrating more on understanding the principle of
demand-led buses than following the dynamics. The thought of
transport that came when you called it was appealing. Laura's
teenage years had been a nightmare, with her needing lifts
here, there, and everywhere. Decent public transport would
have made all the difference. He picked up his pencil and pad
and continued listening.

BEN: I couldn't manage my kids on a bus. It's enough hassle
just getting them in the car.

NAOMI: Will people go for it? No offense, but buses are
grubby.

BEN: (mutters) Too good to travel with us plebs.

NAOMI: It's just having your own car is more convenient,

especially if you've got a lot of stuff, and like your own space. I'm getting an electric anyway, soon as I can afford it.

BUS MAN: That won't do. Cars have embedded carbon and use limited resources. The solution isn't to get an additional EV or even swap, it's giving up private transport and having an extensive, high-frequency, efficient, demand-led public transport system. *(He turns to Steve)*. In rural areas like yours, can you imagine what a difference it would make?

DEVANIKA: Men wouldn't give up their cars. It's a power trip for them.

STEVE: Do you have a car, Dev?

DEVANIKA: Yes.

STEVE: So much for our climate champion.

DEVANIKA: Actually, I have a car-share app, so when I'm not using it, others can borrow it.

NAOMI: Do you make a lot of money on that?

DEVANIKA: I made three hundred last month.

NAOMI: Who is that with?

DEVANIKA: Hiya car.

Naomi makes a note. She notices others watching her in surprise.

NAOMI: For the environment you know.

Devanika looks at Naomi, eyebrows raised in disbelief.

Richard also didn't buy the environment motivation, but he suspected money had little to do with this case.

It was nearly four. If he got the earlier train, he might get back in time to meet the gardener. There was another hour's worth of footage to watch for this session. He'd noticed hostility in Devanika's voice when she talked to Steve, and it was getting more pronounced. Sighing, he pressed *play*. When he finally had the time to put his family first, he hoped it wouldn't be too late.

STEVE: I actually like this idea. This would be good for my business. I can never get enough workers for harvest time. The youngsters up for that kind of summer work can't get to the farm, and cabs are too expensive.

DEVANIKA: Probably pay them below minimum wage.

STEVE: Also handy if you want a drink. Then you don't have to choose between having a few whiskies after work or carting your kids from place to place because there's no public transport.

DEVANIKA: I'm guessing you chose whisky.

STEVE: The kids don't bloody work all day like I do!

DEVANIKA: A yes then. *(To bus man)* Don't be fooled by Steve here. He may like the idea of more buses, but he won't give up his car, or is it cars? *(To Steve)* I bet you call your car 'she'.

Steve smiles and nods.

DEVANIKA: I bet you just love putting your foot down and feeling her go. The guttural vroom of the engine.

STEVE: Yup! She accelerates like a bitch, pushes you right back in your seat, and is absolutely silent. Cos she's a Tesla. Weren't expecting that, were you?

Devanika doesn't respond.

STEVE: Alright, I'll help you out. I've got an SUV too. Huge four-by-four gas guzzler.

The bus man follows the exchanges, waiting fruitlessly for an opportunity to intervene.

DEVANIKA: That's why you like to plough, isn't it? It can't be due to cost because the no-dig method is cheaper as you don't have to drag a plough across the field.

STEVE: You're an expert on farming now, are you?

DEVANIKA: Huge blades cutting into the earth, churning up
the ground. It gives you a thrill, doesn't it?

SARAH: I chaired a session on regenerative farming and
the expert said that the no-dig method is more
environmentally friendly and saves money. It's not just
organic farming—

STEVE: Organic farming is gay.

Richard looked up sharply at the snarl in Steve's voice. His
smooth air of indifference had disappeared, revealing an angry
man. Sarah was staring at Steve in horror. His outburst had
been inappropriate, but that look of shock was turning into one
of suspicion. Richard glanced at the timer. Just a few minutes
to go. Devanika was back on the attack. He leaned forward and
watched closely.

DEVANIKA: The solution is to put women in charge. Men like to
blow things up – no sense of nurture or care.

BEN: We're not all the same. What about Maggie Thatcher?

DEVANIKA: She had to make her way in a man's world, that's
why. It's still male values that rule – of domination and
control over nature – exploitation not regeneration.

STEVE: Don't take any notice of 'Dev', I like this idea.

DEVANIKA: Dev's a boy's name. It's Devanika... Stef!

STEVE: Don't call me Stef.

DEVANIKA: Why not Stef! Don't you like being called Stef?

STEVE: (shouting) Stop it!

JOSH: Stop it! Stop it.

DEVANIKA: Stop what? Stef!

STEVE: That's my wife's name!

NAOMI: Wife?

STEVE: She ran off with the organic farmer.

Devanika lets out a shout of laughter.

DEVANIKA: Was that before or after you changed the farm?

STEVE: None of your business.

DEVANIKA: No really, we're interested. Did you overturn the organic farm as revenge for him running off with your wife, or did she run off with the organic farmer because she was so disgusted by you?

Richard pressed *pause*, and the images froze on the screen. Everyone was looking at Steve. There was accusation in Devanika's eyes. Cold hatred in Steve's. Josh looked upset. Why? Naomi was also looking at Steve. She looked shocked – by the violent outburst or the mention of a wife? Andrew's face gave little away. Sarah looked worried. He pressed *play*.

Silence except for the click-clack of knitting. It sounded ominous, like a clock ticking down to death.

*

Lecture 6 Feminist Ethics and Eco-Feminism

Devanika's position in this chapter reflects eco-feminism, in that she equates respect for nature with a female perspective, and exploitation of nature with a patriarchal position. Gender is a sensitive topic right now, but the benefit of an academic environment is that we bring to such debates reasoned argument, reference to evidence and an objective stance. Although... a feminist methodologist might claim that statement in itself is a gendered position, valuing objectivity over subjectivity and intuition. As we can see already, there's plenty here to unpick.

Most research up till the late twentieth century was based on all-male samples, from seat belt design to psychological experiments. For example, Lawrence Kohlberg's Moral Development Scale was based on research which exposed boys to ethical dilemmas. The best-known example was of a man who needs medicine to save his wife but can't afford it. The question is whether he should steal it to save his wife's life. The answer itself wasn't as significant as the reasoning behind it – why they said yes or no.

Kohlberg classified answers into those that reflected various stages of moral development. Stage one is based on chasing rewards and avoiding punishment. Stage two is self-interest – what is good means what's good for me. In the example given, stealing is bad, as he may get caught and punished. After the age of seven comes stage three, where children want to please those around them and to be seen as good. For example, if social norms dictate husbands should protect wives, then he should steal the drug. Stage four reflects an awareness of law and order and obeying rules. Stealing is bad because it's against the law, for example. According to Kohlberg, many don't progress beyond this level. However, he claims about fifteen percent achieve higher levels, which require abstract reasoning. Stage five draws on notions of the social contract and gives rise to answers such as stealing would be good because human life is a more fundamental right than property. Stage six, the highest level of moral reasoning, is based on concepts of justice and universal ethical principles and may call into question the social structures that give rise to such dilemmas.

Kohlberg's scale was used in numerous studies to measure moral development, yet female respondents typically scored lower than males. This is surprising, as most studies on behaviour that include gender as a variable show the opposite. I have supervised hundreds of student dissertations on ethical consumption and sustainable business, and if there are gender differences at all, they lean towards female respondents showing higher scores on ethics or sustainability than male respondents. Would anyone like to offer a critical perspective on such results?

Transcription note. The keen girl in the front put her hand up to suggest that most studies measure intentions, not actual behaviour. One student said women are under greater pressure to present as ethical. Another said this didn't apply as questionnaires are anonymous. The girl in the front row claimed we internalise such expectations. We concluded we should measure behaviour, not just stated intentions. The level of critical thinking is improving measurably as the course progresses.

Carol Gilligan, Kohlberg's research assistant, challenged the scale's validity because the sample used was all male and therefore reflected a masculine view of morality. Gilligan claimed women prefer to resolve conflicts in ways that strengthen relationships. Whereas men are more likely to adopt a 'morality of justice', preferring to justify ethical decisions based on abstract moral rules, women typically adopt a 'morality of care', based on values of inclusion or feelings of compassion or love. Therefore, studies of moral development based only on abstract notions of justice have a male bias.

These are not mere academic arguments – let me share with you a personal anecdote. One time, I was playing a board game and one player wasn't enjoying the game and suggested a minor rule change. Two players were happy to change the rules because their goal was for everyone to enjoy the game, but the other two wouldn't accept changing them partway through. I can't report a clear gender split, but the point is, would it be correct to say that sticking to the rules is objectively more 'moral' than amending them to keep everyone happy? Carol Gilligan thought not. She said society benefited as much from the subjective care and compassion women exhibited within their relationships as by the "objective" rules and regulations predominantly devised by men.

You might assume feminists would applaud Gilligan for standing up for her gender, but they criticised her for gender stereotyping and perpetuating the exploitation of women. The argument goes that, most caring roles occur within families and are unpaid, and jobs in the care sector are paid poorly compared to jobs in other sectors. These are roles traditionally occupied by women. Thus, to assign care and compassion as feminine attributes is to perpetuate gender inequality. If Gilligan portrays women as more caring, and this hampers them financially, her view disempowers women as much as it seems to stand up for them.

Transcription note. The lecture was interrupted by laughter from the three lads at the back. I asked them what was funny. The ringleader said that honest people answering surveys would admit that they wouldn't always be ethical, but those who lie to appear better than they are would always tick the most ethical answer because they were actually very unethical. Then he said, 'Wouldn't it be hilarious if all research into ethical intentions was one hundred percent wrong!'

I thanked them for their insightful observations and told them I'd try to be pleased at this evidence of critical thinking, rather than concerned that our results were suspect.

Feminist researchers refer to patriarchal ways of knowing and are concerned with discrimination and oppression of all kinds, not just with gender. Particular emphasis is placed on who decides the rules of the game, and in whose interests? Which voices are privileged, and which voices are unheard? Language itself is criticised for being biased, with male versions of terms denoting power, and female versions denoting sexuality – 'master' and 'mistress' are examples.

Eco-feminism emerged in the seventies and developed into a movement that drew parallels between the exploitation of nature and the oppression of women by patriarchal society. Some branches also extend to include any oppressed groups, such as indigenous cultures or LGBTQ+. Another camp, cultural eco-feminists, asserts that women have a closer affinity with nature due to their maternal roles. Some branches have roots in spiritual notions of Mother Earth and nature-based religions. As before, though, this approach can lead to accusations of gender stereotyping. Perhaps as gender roles are more relaxed and men increasingly participate in childcare, the gender element may fall away so that we may talk about notions of care and control without assigning specific genders to such terms. As Ben said in the story, *What about Margaret Thatcher?* There are many high-ranking female politicians and leaders who appear more controlling than caring.

I began this lecture talking about feminist ethics, so perhaps we should instead de-gender the discussion and refer to the ethic of care.

*

As the students filed out, I scanned the attendance list for Emily. As usual, there was a blank space next to her name.

'Great lecture.'

I looked up to see the keen girl at the front had paused by the podium.

'The games example reminded me of my flatmate who gets upset and demands to change the rules when she's losing.'

'That's wrong, whatever the gender,' I said.

'What game were you playing?' she asked.

I swallowed, my throat suddenly constricted. She'd caught me off guard.

'Monopoly.'

'Where did you stand on changing the rules?'

I mumbled something and hurried away.

I paused at the door of the staff canteen. I turned around and headed back. I veered off down the meandering path and collapsed into the bench by the stream. I took deep breaths, staring at the reflection of the willow bouncing off the glassy water as the memories flooded in.

Friday night is games night. I'd made it clear to Fay right from the start. I was determined to keep it going because, since they'd left home, it was the only time I got both my boys in the same room. Fay seemed delighted to go along with it.

'Monopoly was invented by a woman,' she'd announced

140

the first time we tried to play. 'Lizzie Magie. She'd meant it as a cautionary tale against capitalism to show how it leads to wealth accumulating in a few hands.'

'Do tell,' I'd said.

'The original version was a game about cooperation, with the one we have now as the alternative.' She'd watched, satisfied, as we took this in. She held forth, eyes shining, about how Lizzie would be turning in her grave to see that some man had claimed credit for inventing it, and worse still, that the game no longer promoted the benefits of collective achievement, but now stood as a symbol of unbridled capitalism. We were transfixed, the game forgotten.

'This same Lizzie Magie,' she proclaimed, her face lit up with awe, 'was also a stand-up comedienne and inventor of a patented typewriting device.' She nodded significantly as if Lizzie's achievements were somehow her own, and they were, because without Fay, we'd none of us have known this fascinating fact. A sudden inversion of everything we'd assumed.

'What about relatives?' I cried. 'Could they not put this historic injustice right?'

Fay shook her head. 'She never had children.'

'What a shame.'

And then Adam and Tom had said they didn't want kids, as if it were no big deal.

Be that as it may, we never got to play a proper game again. In light of later events, I see it as passive aggressive.

I checked my phone. Nothing on the family chat. Clearly, if I didn't take the initiative, Adam and Tom were happy to leave it. I wasn't ready to out myself as 'needy mum', but maybe they'd appreciate my magnum opus. Either way, it would be a good excuse to contact them.

Hi boys. I've attached one of my chapters. See the bit about weeds!

Chapter 11

Faculty meetings were back in person. I joined GG in the queue of colleagues filing into the lecture theatre.

'Are you OK?' GG asked.

'Fine.'

She looked at me intently. 'Your eyes are red.'

'I'm just tired.'

In front of us, Sue was slagging off a colleague to another woman.

'After all the hoo-ha, she's contributed nothing.'

'Nothing,' her colleague agreed.

'We're threatened with redundancy, and they employ her.'

'They said she'd bring in consultancy money.'

'She's brought in nothing.'

GG looked uncomfortable. With a shock, I realised they were talking about me.

We siphoned off quickly to join Percy and Marcel on the back row.

The murmur of chat died down when Jenna took her place at the podium to speak. 'Many of you have complained that you don't have time to do research on top of teaching, so we are excited to report we're piloting an AI tool which is currently free for academics to use.'

'I don't have time to learn about software,' Marcel said.

'The AI plus the dictation function means it's easy as pie. You talk, the microphone picks it up and then you can feed it into the AI software to tidy up.'

Colin stepped up to the podium. 'So there's no excuse now. We want every member of staff to post their research plans by the end of the month.' He spoke louder over the noise of dissent. 'This isn't news to you. You should all have been working on your research already.'

Someone waved a hand. 'What do you need?'

'Either a draft outline of a paper, monograph or book – not fiction.' He glared at me. 'Or details of any consultancy, or a grant application or a completed research design with ethical approval.'

GG raised a hand.

'If it doesn't get ethical approval, then think of something else,' Colin said.

She put her hand down.

'Will we get fired if we can't?' GG muttered to me; her expression agonised.

Marcel took control and stood up. 'Are you saying that your new AI software justifies making us work like dogs?'

Colin went to speak, but Jenna put her hand on his arm. 'It's understandable to be nervous, but old dogs can learn new tricks.' Jenna looked aghast at what she'd said. 'Not that you're old or a dog... erm. Let's have a go together. I'm sure you're not the only one who is hesitant about new technology.' She smiled at him reassuringly.

'I accept your challenge.' The last word came out particularly French, sounding more like *Shallonnsha*.

He edged out of the back row and walked up to the podium where a laptop was connected to the screen. Jenna opened a document and pointed the cursor at a microphone icon. 'Just say out loud a title for a paper clearly. We will all see it typed out on screen, and you'll appreciate how easy it is to use.'

Marcel coughed dramatically and stepped closer to the microphone.

'We... er... must... er... hold the World Bank to account—'

We watched as the words formed themselves on the screen

Weir master old SeaWorld bonker to a cun...

The room exploded into applause as the software rapidly changed the final "t" into four asterisks. Marcel took a bow and returned to his seat, shrugging and gesticulating grandly.

'Did you do that on purpose?' I asked him when he sat down.

He shrugged again and grinned.

Colin looked annoyed. I raised my hand, keen to change the subject before he returned to the topic.

'What do we do about students who use AI to write their essays?'

'We have procedures in place to address issues of plagiarism resulting from AI,' Jenna responded.

Everyone spoke at once.

'It's just a link to another site.'

'Plagiarism software doesn't pick it up.'

'I typed my essay question into ChatGPT and got a perfect answer.'

Jenna interrupted. 'We make it clear there are harsh penalties, where proven.'

'We can't prove it.'

'Why can't we switch to exams?'

'We don't have the space,' Jenna responded.

Percy raised his hand. 'We had room for exams last year and we have fewer students now.'

She ignored him. 'Those courses which do have exams must switch to coursework.'

'That's ridiculous.'

'It's just about costs.'

'If you're worried, we can do online exams,' Colin said.

'That disadvantages students who don't have quiet spaces with a good connection,' I said.

'And they can still cheat,' Percy added.

'There's a Scandinavian country where schools do without marking and apparently everyone learns really well with no assessment,' someone said.

We all paused to savour the heady vision of education for its own sake.

Colin broke the spell. 'This is a serious matter. We're not doing exams, and lecturers must not accuse students of plagiarism or deduct marks without proof.'

GG nudged me. 'Why is he looking at you?'

'Emily?' Percy suggested.

'Probably.'

'Don't worry about AI,' Jenna said desperately. 'Students will use it in their workplace.'

'Then how will we know if they understood anything?' I asked.

Colin and Jenna looked at me as if I were on a different planet.

'I encourage staff to lean into this,' she continued. 'AI is a tool that we should embrace rather than resist.'

I stood up. 'We must not forget that our mission is to educate and to assess. I'm not wedded to the assessment actually. I like the idea of that Scandinavian country that doesn't mark, but if we assess, then we must do it with integrity. As professor of moral philosophy, maybe it's down to me to make a—'

'Are you claiming ethical superiority because you teach moral philosophy?' Colin stared at me; his lip curled in a knowing sneer.

I flushed and collapsed back into my seat.

The meeting moved on to redundancies. I paid no attention, because I'd just realised I hadn't yet broken the rules. Colin, if he knew, had nothing on me. The consultancy element didn't officially start until I set the final assignment. There was still time.

After the meeting, I headed to Obi's room. I paused to collect myself, then sauntered past, casually looking in. He saw me. I feigned surprise and gestured towards the door. He nodded, and I went in.

'Hello?' His inquiring tone offered no obvious way in. I couldn't get directly to the point until we'd established a rapport. Not too friendly. A professor wouldn't suck up to a newbie – he'd smell a rat. Now I'd hesitated too long, which left me with only one option.

'I left the Business School at great cost because of the tick-box mentality. So, when you accused me of being like an accountant, I was…' I forced myself to say it, 'triggered.'

'I'm so sorry, Professor.' He looked so apologetic, I felt bad. Still, needs must.

'Call me Iris.'

'I'm the same. Percy wanted me to be diversity manager just because I'm black.'

'It would be too much on top of the ethics committee.' That was smooth, if I say so myself.

'And he's so dismissive of my art.'

'Even your masterpiece?' I gestured towards the Join the Dots canvas.

'He wouldn't call it "art".' Obi made quotation marks in the air.

I nodded sympathetically. 'People like certainty. Art throws them because they can't define it.'

'You're right.'

'I know.' I pulled up a chair and sat beside him.

He picked up a mug and pointed to a smudge of lipstick on it. 'Percy said he supposed I'd claim that the smudge was as good art as the *Mona Lisa*.'

I grinned, picturing the scene. 'What did you say?'

'I said yes, just to wind him up, and then we got caught up in a ridiculous argument about whether there's such a thing as good or bad art.'

'I grappled with these subjective/objective dilemmas in my twenties,' I confided. 'It drove me mad. It's a side effect of being a philosopher. You can fall down these rabbit holes, but I'm more interested in real-world problems now.'

'If Percy and the rest truly cared, they'd include diverse thinkers on the curriculum,' Obi said, putting down the mug.

'I covered Ubuntu in the Business School as part of the sharing economy lecture.'

'Sharing economy?'

'Yes. Many don't know that there's an open-source alternative to Windows called Linux where an online community cooperates to design and share applications. Ubuntu is the most popular distribution. It doesn't track personal data, it's free and non-corporate. It's a lovely model of alternative…' I noticed Obi looked puzzled. 'What's the matter?'

'I am because you are,' he said. 'That's Ubuntu. It's an African philosophy.'

I thought quickly. 'Of course, yes, it's not just about online communities. Does it er… inform your approach to ethics?'

'I suppose I take a more collective perspective.'

'So, you'd consider the broader context when reviewing ethics applications?'

'Hello?'

I looked up. Standing hopefully at the door was a student. 'Am I interrupting?' she asked.

'Not at all.' Obi smiled at her.

She smiled back at him.

'Come on in. Take a seat.' Obi gestured to the chair where I was sitting.

'I'll come back, shall I?' I stood up to go.

He nodded without looking at me.

'I so love your canvas,' breathed the student, slipping into my chair.

I let myself out.

Back in my office, I checked out the dictate function. I pressed the microphone icon. It wobbled and then pulsed. I was good to go. I typed "moral philosophy of Ubuntu" into the search engine. I spoke aloud as I digested the contents.

'Ubuntu involves ideas of human dignity, reciprocity, tolerance, consensus, working together. All laudable qualities… but it's not obvious what they mean for the dilemma.'

I stopped to check. There was no punctuation, and it had reproduced "Ubuntu" as "open to". I corrected it and continued.

'I won't talk too much about that. The paper isn't about the dilemma; it's about the process. The title of my research paper is Storytelling for Pedagogy.' I paused, as it hadn't understood the last word. 'Storytelling for education,' I said instead. It was happy. I stood up and picked through the books on my shelf, talking more loudly.

'Setting the story in a citizens' assembly is topical due to the upcoming referendum. Few students were even aware of it, so this is an opportunity to remind them there's a world outside of the university bubble. What happens to our constitution will affect them all. The politicians will only talk about policies that create economic growth in the short term because they're in hock to business interests and dependent upon the media. So it's down to us artists. That will go in my talk. We must speak up. But we must be canny. We can think we're rebelling when we're playing into their hands. When I told Lee how the Business School had funded my trip to Cuba, he said I was their "Che Guevara t-shirt." He was right. You have the ultimate icon of rebellion stencilled on your t-shirt – the handsome revolutionary Che, and it's made from non-organic cotton, manufactured by sweat shop workers, using huge amounts of water and pesticides and sold to you so you think you're standing against the system. But the artists – we soldier on. Look at Obi! Look at me. We are the flag-wavers. Obi's Join the Dots points out the problems and my climate assembly lays out the solutions – here's how to avoid your doom. It is genuine entertainment education.'

'What are you doing?'

I stopped my pacing and turned around to see Percy and Marcel at my door. They regarded me with suspicion.

'Are you using the dictate function?' Percy asked.

'So what if I am?' I stood in front of the screen. I couldn't recall if I'd revealed confidential information.

Marcel approached to look at the screen. I tried to shield it, but he took no notice and peered over my shoulder.

'It's gobbledygook,' he said with satisfaction.

'Is it?' I scanned it quickly. The first paragraph stood out, but the rest was a mess.

'You look relieved,' Percy accused.

'I'm just going to ask her,' Marcel said.

'Ask me what?'

'Are you a plant?'

'What?'

'You didn't strike, you're from the Business School.'

'You work late,' Percy added.

'You're jumping through every hoop, no matter how ridiculous, and with a smile on your face.'

'How's that make me a plant, for God's sake?'

'You're too full of yourself. It's as if to show us how it should be done.' Marcel waved his arms. 'Look at me! I work late and I like it and I edutain and tick the boxes. If Iris can do it, why can't everyone?'

'I don't see them as tick boxes. They matter.'

'And you did that speech about it shouldn't be them and us. Classic thing for management to say.' Marcel paused and searched my face. 'There's something off about you. You're too cheerful.'

'What about when I called Jenna out on NSS scores?'

'GG doesn't think you're a plant,' Percy said. 'She thinks you're hiding some secret sorrow.'

'Even when we're mean to you, like now, you take it in your stride.' Marcel held out his hands as if to a jury. 'Proof.'

I had to give them something. 'OK, the reason I'm cheerful even when you're mean is that I liked it when my older brother was mean to me, because I liked the attention. But he was just making sure I didn't get too above myself.'

Percy tilted his head, considering.

'And while you're busy complaining about the requirement to post our research, I've done it.' I grabbed the mouse. 'There we go. Saved. Uploaded.'

'It's unreadable,' Marcel said.

'I narrated it using methods they suggested, so I've done my bit. Anyway, I bet no one reads what we post. It's just to ensure we're on the case.'

'She's not a plant,' proclaimed Percy. 'No one's that good an actor.'

'I played all three roles in *Dr. Strangelove* at university.'

'Of course you did.' Marcel still looked dubious.

'I'm not a bloody plant. Colin hates me for a start.'

'That could be evidence either way.'

'How do you figure that?'

'He'd hate it if you got called in to spy on us. He'd feel threatened.'

'He'd want to be the plant,' Percy said.

'Weed more like,' I said.

Marcel burst out laughing and clapped me on the back. 'OK, I believe you. Come to the pub with us on Friday.'

'Hmm.' I narrowed my eyes.

'I'll buy you a drink,' he promised.

I checked my phone. Still nothing on the family chat.

'All right.'

Chapter 12

Dear Professor,
Thank you for my mark. I was worried about the
term 'plop' but I couldn't think of a better one and I know
I didn't add many theories. I usually do rubbish in these
kinds of essays, so this will help. I'm so glad that you gave
me a 2:1 for the Air on a G-String. I got the spelling right
this time. My mates thought I meant it was about sexy
underwear! They're all taking the mick now! By the way,
when do we find out who the murderer is?

I chuckled and began an email to explain it was his capacity for reflection and independent thought that got him the mark but was distracted by an email from Emily. My heart sank. Her essay had been anodyne. The language had been sophisticated beyond the level of English revealed in her emails, yet it had lacked the slightest hint of personal reflection or critical thinking. I'd felt a strong temptation to mark it higher than I should to spare myself the inevitable complaint but reminded myself of my promise to Percy.

Dear Professor
I was disappointed by my mark. It makes me
anxious that I may not pass your course, and I need to or
I'll have to resit, which will cost my parents a lot of money
and they'll be upset with me. The thought makes me very
anxious. Please can you push my mark up so there isn't so
much pressure on the last essay.
Thanks
Emily

I toyed with a number of responses. Sorry to hear about your distress. You can have a 2:1 for anxiety, but for moral philosophy… Unfortunately, anxiety isn't listed as a learning outcome. Perhaps if you put more effort into turning up to lectures than complaining…

I gave up. There was no answer to give. I filed it away.

*

Murder in the Citizens' Jury #11: The Plant

Richard had been hijacked by reporters on the way to work. The Prime Minister had repeated his lies about personal carbon allowances. 'Why wouldn't he?' Marnie had asked. 'You let him get away with it before, so why should he stop?' Now Arthur was ill. The 82-year-old environmental protestor that Richard had put in jail had a name. And everyone knew it. They knew his name too, and it was him they held responsible. Even more than the Prime Minister who'd made the law so harsh. But the PM had his supporters. No one was rooting for Richard. Least of all his wife. The only thing that kept him going was the glimmer of hope in the case.

A fast-forward of footage from the CCTV camera in the lunch area had shown little of interest and been ignored. Richard had asked them to double check everything, and it turned out the interesting parts were on the audio. The tech guys had boosted the sound, and Richard would be the first apart from them to hear the selected highlights. The first file was labelled 'Day 4' – the day they'd discussed demand-led buses. He pressed *play* and sat back, notepad in hand.

He understood immediately why it had been missed. The footage showed a partial view of a small room with chairs around the side. Only one end of the lunch table is visible, showing an abandoned plate with half a sandwich on it. The camera is inconveniently angled to focus on a corner of the room by the door where little is happening. After a few moments, he hears a voice. It's Andrew. It sounded like he was talking into a phone.

ANDREW: No, they don't know who I... (pause) Too risky...
someone's coming.

*The camera catches the arm of someone walking past, who
turns and looks back, presumably at Andrew. There is the
flash of a Rolex. It must be Steve.*

*Sarah enters shot and puts down a plate with a few crusts
on it and walks out of shot towards Andrew and speaks in a
low voice.*

SARAH: I need to talk to you.

ANDREW: Oh?

SARAH: I know when I'm being lied to.

ANDREW: Oh... oh?

SARAH: When someone's not who they're pretending to be. You
know what I'm talking about.

ANDREW: Er...

SARAH: I've chaired numerous citizens' assemblies, and
without exception they've been calm, considered,
respectful. This was chaos from day one. It can't be a
coincidence that this is the first one to be granted legal
authority.

ANDREW: What are you saying?

SARAH: There are plenty who'd like to see them shut down.
The ministers with vested interests won't just sit by and
watch their power seep away. They've put in a plant to
stir things up.

ANDREW: You mean...

SARAH: Steve.

ANDREW: Steve?

SARAH: Right from the start, he's been provoking Devanika
    and look at how he's stoking Ben's resentment against
    Josh. And how did he know I was gay?

ANDREW: What if you're wrong?

SARAH: I'm not going to let one man sabotage our best chance
    of averting the climate crisis. I won't let him get away
    with it.

That was the only audible snippet from that day, but it was
thought-provoking. There'd been determined steel in Sarah's
voice. How far would she go to protect her beloved citizens'
jury?
Richard watched the rest of the footage from the police
interview with Sarah.

POLICE OFFICER 1: You don't deny it was your idea to have a
    knitter? That the murder weapon was available because
    of you?

SARAH: I can show you research that having a knitter present
    can instil a sense of calm.

Richard paused to check the research Sarah had
mentioned. It backed up her argument that crafts can reduce
stress. Slightly disappointed, he pressed resume.

POLICE OFFICER 1: Have you heard the phrase 'accessory to
    murder' before?

SARAH: Naomi probably thinks that's an earring brand.

Sarah laughs, but the police officer continues staring at her.

SARAH: For God's sake, you can't seriously think I'd want this!
    I've given up everything for this citizens' jury.

POLICE OFFICER 2: Why?

SARAH: Why? Because we've tried everything else, and it's
    not worked, but this does. Citizens' juries have been my

life's work.

POLICE OFFICER 2: This murder throws their future into
    doubt.

SARAH: Exactly. I can already see the headlines. 'Judge,
    Jury, Executioner,' and the speeches. 'People don't go to
    citizens' juries to be murdered.'

Richard noticed the two police officers exchange a look.
There was a palpable drop in tension. Sarah's response had
convinced them. It convinced him too.

*

The ding of email notifications had become too regular to
ignore. With reluctance I saved my story and checked my inbox.
I immediately wished I hadn't. Endless requests to complete
tedious jobs that seemed pointless when set against my current
mission, another request from Robert for updates and finally one
from Colin.

> *Dear Iris,*
> *As Jenna is away, she asked me to talk to you about*
> *another complaint from a student. Please see me in person*
> *at your earliest convenience.*
> *Kind regards*
> *Colin*
> *Assistant Dean*
> *Faculty of Arts and Humanities*

I panicked, then read the email again and calmed down.
If it was a student complaint, then at least it wasn't about not
declaring the consultancy. Probably.

*

In the pub, I waited until my colleagues had stopped complaining
about their workload – we were on the second bottle by then –
and showed them Colin's email. 'He sent it at 5 p.m. on a Friday.'
    'Classic dick move,' Marcel said.

155

Percy put his glasses on and peered at it. 'Colin has no authority over you. You outrank him academically.'

'I don't know what I've done.'

'It will be Emily,' said Percy. 'She emailed me saying she was disgusted I hadn't added my pronouns to my email signature. Now Colin's demanding we all add our pronouns.'

'Did you add yours?' GG asked me.

'No. Surely the whole point is not to be pigeonholed by gender.'

'He hasn't contacted me, but if he insisted, I'd put per,' said Percy.

'Bit self-referential,' Marcel commented.

'Not for Percy. Person.'

'Ah—'

'Surely that's not what Colin wants to talk to me about?' I interjected, but Percy was warming to his theme.

'Someone has to protest against the use of they/them as a singular pronoun.'

'Don't let Emily hear you say that.' GG looked round.

'Does she identify as something?' I asked.

'None of us have met her,' GG said.

'It doesn't matter if she's black, white or purple, or identifies as LGBXYZ, she's still a troublemaker,' Percy declared.

I raised my eyebrows.

He saw our expressions and pulled a paper from his bag. 'You dish it out, but you can't take it.' He brandished it in our faces. 'Why Men Are Predatory,' he read. 'It doesn't say, why are some men predatory. No, the headline assumes we're all the same. We wouldn't be allowed to make such generalisations about you women.'

'You're not allowed to say, "you women."' Marcel wagged a finger.

'Have you noticed in films these days, the man never gets the woman?' Percy continued. 'She wanders off to do something interesting, and he's left looking like a twerp.'

'Do you watch romcoms?' I asked, surprised.

'Kate enjoys them. My point is, every man on TV these days

is either an idiot or controlling. Let me tell you, women can be controlling.' He shot us a meaningful look.

'Kate?' GG looked incredulous.

'What goes on behind your net curtains, Percy?' Marcel topped up his glass.

'I have to watch romcoms for a start.'

Marcel snorted with laughter, spilling the rest of the wine.

'My round,' I jumped up and headed to the bar, staggering a little. The pub was filling up. It was around the corner from the campus, and I waved at some ex-colleagues from the Business School. They nodded back but didn't come over. I'd upset a few people when I'd left, although I didn't flatter myself it was because of my charming personality. I was just the goose who'd laid the golden egg for a while. Now, though, I was among my own kind. I looked over at my little group fondly – Marcel gesticulating, GG looking solemn, Percy shaking his head.

I returned to the table with another bottle of red. 'What are we talking about?'

'How they thought you were a plant,' GG said.

'Well, she's such a keeno,' Marcel said. 'How do you have time to write a story?'

'You spend your time raging. I pour that energy into productivity rather than complaining.'

Percy frowned. 'Bit rude.'

'The drink's loosened her tongue.' Marcel poured the wine. 'Have some more.'

'Honesty is a virtue.' I took a swig. 'I pay you the compliment of assuming you can take it. Obviously, I wouldn't dare be honest with students.'

Percy and Marcel nodded. There was a tacit understanding that the younger generation was different. It was unclear where GG fell.

'I thought moral philosophers were supposed to be nice,' GG said.

'Jesus wasn't nice,' I responded. 'He called stuff out when he came across it.'

'Are you claiming to be Jesus now?' Percy raised an eyebrow.

I drained my glass and banged it down, harder than I'd meant.

'Percy's hit a nerve!' Marcel grinned and cocked his head at me.

I stood up, reeling slightly.

'Not at all. Just off to the ladies.'

I hovered by the sink for a bit, then checked the mirror. A fuzzy image stared back. I washed my hands and returned to the table.

Percy was waving his glass and holding forth. 'I checked all the regs—'

'What's this?' I asked.

'How Emily fucked over my wife. I told Kate, it's her own fault.'

'That's nice.'

'Psychology's fault then, their obsession with self-esteem.' Percy topped up my glass. 'I said, if you psychologists would focus on self-respect rather than self-esteem in your research, we may not have bred ourselves a generation of narcissists.'

'Pah!' said Marcel in agreement, or possibly dissent.

'It's all about identity politics. It's a distraction, isn't it?' Percy glowered around the table; his brows knitted majestically. 'I can't tell you how bored I am with the endless navel-gazing of what does it mean to be a man, or what it means to be British.'

'What does it mean to be a citizen of this planet and utterly beholden to it? That's what I want to talk about,' I cried.

'Is that going in your talk?' GG asked.

'It certainly is!' I glugged my wine. 'Every time there's a legitimate complaint against the powers that be – they've rigged the rules in their favour, undeclared business interests, trashed the environment, they just press the patriotism card and suddenly it's all about nationhood.'

'You English, you think you're some big-shot country, but you're nothing since you left Europe.' Marcel downed his wine and poured another. 'In France, law has changed, so business must address society and the environment.'

'Has it?' My arm slid on the table as I leaned forward.

'Only in France have they banned planned obsolescence—'

'It's capitalism.' Percy cut him off mid-rant. 'You can't ban it.'

'What's that?' GG asked.

'They design products to fail because it makes them more money.' Marcel waved his glass around. 'France has right to repair. They must show how and make parts available even if it isn't profitable. I bet you don't teach that in the Business School?'

'I'll tell you what's going in my lectures now,' I slurred. 'Ubuntu.'

'Don't tell me you're ticking the decoloniality box now,' Percy said.

'How dare you imply it's a box!' I put my glass down and jabbed a finger at him. 'I tell you, Percy, I looked up to you and not just because you're tall, but that you can think it's about ticking a box?'

Marcel leaned back and gave me the floor with a wave.

'For years, I've reeled off Greek male shite and told myself it was moral philosophy. Plato spread the idea that we're better than nature - that the real perfection lies in some heavenly beyond. We're lost in dreams of some afterworld and dismiss nature as nothing.' I sniffed. 'It's like these space tech bros who want to sod off to other planets without a thought for this wonderful Earth. And next thing you know we're blind to the complex web we're a tiny part of.' I glared around at them.

'Blind!' I thundered, and they jumped.

Marcel laid a protective hand on GG and Percy's arms. 'Give her space.'

'And I know people who are climate anxious...'

Percy opened his mouth to speak. I stared at him, and he took a sip of wine instead.

'My friend wants to get a smallholding and guard it with guns,' GG said.

'Yes, because we've been literally taught to think that way. Our individualistic, self-interested consumer society is all about me first. And I tell you, we're all fucked. But Ubuntu...'

I steepled my hands under my chin and looked at them in turn.

'Tell us about Ubuntu, Chip,' Marcel encouraged.

'Ubuntu is about survival. Ubuntu is the truth that our survival depends upon our community's survival. We'll need farmers and dentists and engineers—'

'Musicians?' asked GG.

I hesitated for a moment, then allowed it.

'Yes.'

She looked pleased.

'Ubuntu says, "I am because you are." "One finger cannot pluck a seed."'

'Hazard at one o'clock,' said Marcel, cocking his head towards the door.

We turned to look. Colin had entered the pub.

We spun back around. 'I'm going to use my English superpower of extreme politeness and confound him with kindness,' I declared.

'It won't work,' Percy said.

Marcel topped up his and GG's glass and waved the bottle in the air.

'No more for me.' Percy stood up to leave. 'Kate will wonder where I've got to.'

GG turned to me. 'Are you married?'

Her question caught me off guard. I hesitated. They looked at me with interest.

'Don't you know?' Marcel asked.

'I think yes.' Percy shrugged on his jacket. 'Consider the bowed down, oppressed look.'

'Let's put it this way, there's no one at home waiting anxiously for my return.' I hailed Colin as he walked past.

'Hi Colin.' My greeting was overly hearty.

Marcel put the bottle back on the table and raised his eyebrows at me.

'Oh. Hello.'

'Would you like to join us?' I patted the empty seat.

He looked surprised. 'Oh. OK.' He sat down between me and GG. 'Hello Georgina. No more musicals, I hope?'

The atmosphere froze. GG glared at the table.

I grabbed the wine to top up our glasses, but it was empty.

'Would you like a drink?' Colin asked.

I regretted my impulse already. Machiavelli says that the worst thing you can do is accept a gift from your enemy. Refusing it can be seen as a hostile act. If you accept, you're in their debt. I didn't want to be indebted to Colin. Anyway, the sadness had come upon me. I could no longer sit and be jolly.

'I'd better get off too,' I said.

GG and Marcel looked at me, aghast. I felt bad for them, but they'd forgive me. I wasn't so sure about Colin.

*

Murder in the Citizens' Jury #12: Repair Bill

'Back in the seventies, appliances were expensive, and most people rented them. We repaired televisions rather than threw them away. A fridge from the sixties was built to last sixty plus years, whereas today, not more than twenty. We're not shown how to maintain or clean appliances to extend their life.'

Josh listened intently to the repair man. His mouth was dry. He'd been told not to mix his meds with anything else, but cannabis didn't count. He needed it anyway to calm his anxiety. He poured a glass of water and looked around the room. Needles was knitting and nodding. Devanika was staring at Andrew, looking puzzled. Steve was eyeing up Naomi. Ben looked sleepy in the heat. Sarah was trying to close the blinds. Naomi looked bored.

'Extending the lifetime of smartphones from three to ten years would save six million tonnes annually – a forty percent reduction.' As the repair man spoke, Andrew jotted down the numbers.

Josh wondered how old Andrew was. His calm air reminded him of his dad. A wave of emotion rose in him, stopping his breath for a moment. Stay calm. Ride it out. It's just the hash cookie kicking in.

'Producing a smartphone requires twelve thousand litres of water. It contains eighty grams of metal, which means drilling through six kilograms of ore, and it emits seven kilograms of emissions while it's being produced.'

As Sarah adjusted the blinds, a ray of light shone a spotlight on the brand-new iPhone peeking out of Naomi's bag.

'I always recycle my old phones,' she said, looking around.

'Recycling isn't the issue,' the man explained. 'You can't get back all the materials in a product. Repairing means we don't have to keep making products and causing these environmental impacts in the first place.'

'This is sounding like the library of things proposal,' said Devanika.

'Very perceptive,' agreed the repair man. 'Most libraries of things have an associated repair café, as the principles are the same. Avoiding waste, extending the life of a product.'

'You modern folk, you chuck stuff away without a second thought,' said Needles.

'The thing is Granny, that stuff is cheap, and time is precious,' said Steve. 'I'd rather be playing a round of golf than huddled over some workbench with a screwdriver.'

'I took the kids to a repair café once, as we had so much broken stuff, but they got bored waiting. To be honest, I don't have time,' Ben said.

Needles gazed at him sternly. 'You say you love your kids, young man. You keep going on about them and how scared you are for their future.'

'I'm bloody terrified. I saw the film too.'

'We've got to help our young people prepare. My grandson don't even know food comes from the ground. He couldn't tell a screwdriver from a piece of string.' Needles knitted furiously, shaking her head. 'I told him, forget about your exams sweety, they won't help yer. His mum won't let me see him now cos she don't like what I have to say. But he's so vulnerable, he wouldn't have a clue, the sweet babe. He needs to be taught, don't he?'

Ben jumped as a needle was pointed at his face.

'As their father, you should know how to repair things and show your children.'

'My dad used to show me how to repair stuff,' said Josh.

'I also need to fix the fence, sort the tap, help Millie with her homework, and sell everything we don't need on eBay so I can pay the energy bill,' Ben snapped at Josh.

'It's easier to buy new, isn't it?' Naomi appealed to the group. 'You get the latest thing with instructions and guarantee. All nicely wrapped and shiny.'

'Colonialism rules supreme,' said Devanika. 'We enjoy our latest smartphone and let the developing countries deal with the toxic waste.'

'When was the last time you repaired your phone, Dev?' Steve asked. Naomi shot him a grateful look.

'It's Devanika!'

'You didn't answer the question.'

The repair man jumped in. 'You made a good point, Devanika. E-waste is increasing rapidly all over the globe and poses significant hazards. The toxic materials, heavy metals and acids leak into the soil and contaminate water supplies. You see increased prevalence of cancer and birth defects in surrounding communities. Children are especially vulnerable, affecting brain function and development.'

'It's capitalism. The manufacturers design products not to last because that's the most profitable business model,' said Devanika.

'What can you do? You can't exactly pass a law about it?' scoffed Steve.

'You can,' the repair man countered. 'France implemented a right to repair policy.'

'I took my radio alarm back and they wouldn't repair it,' said Needles. 'Said it would be easier to buy new. "Young man," I said to him, "this isn't even thirty years old, and you want me to chuck it away?"'

Ben snorted involuntarily. Steve laughed, Devanika shared a sideways smile with Josh, and Naomi collapsed into giggles.

'Yes, just like you. He laughed in my face,' said Needles.

'It isn't funny,' the repair man insisted. 'Sorry to get heavy, but we all saw the same video. These figures matter. Over two hundred million smartphones are sold every year in Europe.

Each time one of these phones is made, it releases more carbon emissions.'

The anxiety of his tone and the increasing speed of the knitting needles created a panicked hush as everyone remembered day one and the video.

'It's urgent, people. Repair and reuse are the key. The future of our planet depends upon it.'

Josh felt his anxiety mount. 'This is getting heavy. I gotta watch my mental health.'

'The thing is, even if there are repair cafés, doesn't mean we'd use them,' said Naomi.

'But I like this one,' Josh cried.

'Most of us don't know how to repair,' said Devanika.

'That's why crafts are important,' said Needles, waving her knitting in the air.

'YouTube videos show you how to repair things,' said Josh.

'And what if the internet goes down and you don't have Goggle?' Needles warned. 'You'll rue the day.'

'She's right,' said the repair guy. 'Back in the day, the three R's meant reading, reckoning and repair. We propose they teach it in schools.'

'I loved design and technology,' said Josh wistfully. 'It was the only thing I was good at, but then they stopped running it.'

'People report immense satisfaction and empowerment when they learn how to do something for themselves,' said repair man.

'We were without Google last year,' said Naomi, suddenly coming to life. 'For five days. I was up in Scotland with my sister during the blackout. We couldn't get television, and everything had run out of charge, so we worked out how to repair the torch and then managed to fix the old transistor radio. It was actually amazing.'

Repair man lit up. 'Exactly! Now imagine if our culture changed. What if, instead of having the marketing people calling the shots, getting us to buy, buy, buy, how about we value what we have? If we consider everything as precious as gold and throw nothing away, but repair and re-use? Preserve our precious world instead of trashing it? The repairers would be the new elite, valued as they should be.'

Josh beamed, the dream of a world where he felt useful hovering like a mirage on the horizon.

Steve tutted. 'You just lost Naomi, mate. She's in marketing.'

Josh looked at Naomi, gutted. She was shaking her head.

'Are we ready to get some figures on the board?' asked Andrew. 'Although I suspect we may have the same issue as with the library of things.'

Josh crumpled in his chair, folding up his disappointment into himself. He watched through knitted brows as Andrew consulted his notes and wrote 'one percent uptake'. Andrew looked up and caught Josh's eye for a moment. A flicker of alarm registered behind his opaque expression.

Chapter 13

Dear Iris

With reference to my last email. May I request again that you update me on your progress? Have you covered the murder and set the dilemma yet? I'm also still waiting for you to send me the materials you are using.

Kind regards
Robert Ash
Director of Public Prosecutions

Dear Robert

Sorry for my belated response. There's no point setting the dilemma until the students are equipped to answer it. Surely an unconsidered answer is worse than a late answer? It takes time to acquire the necessary knowledge and reasoning skills. I need to cover indigenous moral philosophies and non-western approaches, which is essential if we're to decolonise the curriculum. I planned to set the final assignment at the end of the term as that's what they expect, and I'm under pressure to ensure they're happy. I attach an outline of the remaining lectures.

Kind regards
Iris Tate
Professor of Moral Philosophy

PROPOSED OUTLINE FOR UPCOMING 5 LECTURES

- Discourse ethics: This approach claims that the moral action is the one that would be decided upon by a group of rational individuals in open and power-free debate. You can see how that's relevant here.

- Utilitarianism: This is essential because it goes to the heart of the dilemma. Can we make moral choices by adding up the numbers of those harmed and benefitted? If an act that seems wrong in itself is likely to save many lives, can it be called 'wrong'?

- Cross-cultural ethics. Confucius, for example, gives due heed to the practical problems posed in specific contexts. I particularly want to include a section on Ubuntu. Many associate it with African tribal societies and values, but variations of it are seen across the world. A core value is simply survival, and Ubuntu pays attention to how survival depends upon strong communities. 'I am because you are,' is a well-known Ubuntu saying. For example, a key idea is the Collective Fingers Theory: 'a thumb although it is strong cannot kill aphids on its own.' This African proverb highlights how we must cooperate to survive. Of course, community and cooperation are essential everywhere, but individualistic libertarian values obscure the extent to which our wellbeing depends upon the efforts of others. They also ignore our dependence on the planet itself.

- Moral Relativism: I know from experience that when faced with seemingly impossible dilemmas, students often fall back on the idea that there's no 'right' answer and give up. We don't want that.

- Virtue Ethics: This is essential for two reasons. By comparing the proposed key virtues of different societies from China to ancient Greece, we can see how similar they are. This reinforces the notion that one can speak of 'right' and 'wrong' without being culturally imperialist. It also allows us to consider where cultural differences reflect similar values but different priorities. Greek and Chinese philosophers may appear to agree on the virtues superficially, but for Plato and Aristotle, the goal is happiness, and the focus is on the individual. Confucius is more concerned with family and community.

*

I pressed *send*. Robert had also requested the readings, but that was too risky.

My heart sank when I saw a reminder appear on my calendar. I had ten minutes to grab lunch before my appointment with Colin.

On the way to get some sandwiches, I was beset by doubt. I turned back, ignoring my rumbling stomach.

> *Dear Robert*
> *As a compromise I could skip the lecture on*
> *discourse ethics so I can deliver an answer a week earlier.*
> *Trust me, I'll get you an answer soon.*
> *Kind regards*
> *Iris Tate*
> *Professor of Moral Philosophy*

The DPP rang while I was on my way back from the food kiosk.

'Hi,' I mumbled through a mouthful of hummus wrap. 'Are you OK with my plan?'

'I need it earlier. Can you set the assignment before the cross-cultural lecture?'

I struggled to swallow my food in time to protest, but he was already continuing.

'I know it's important to decolonise the curriculum, but that one seems to me least relevant to the dilemma.'

'It's not about ticking a decolonisation box,' I said, struggling to keep hold of my water and wrap while holding the phone. 'The problem is that western approaches have crowded out perspectives that are essential to our flourishing. Oh!'

I dropped my flask and had to run after it as it rolled down the hill. I managed to grab it before it went into the stream.

'The future of humanity may rest upon the choices they make,' the DPP was saying.

'If we're talking about saving humanity, it's already too late to avert many of the impacts of the climate crisis.' I made my way to the bench by the stream while talking. 'We must develop resilience. The fact is that the individualistic cultures are going to start prepping and buying up toilet rolls, food and, in the US, probably guns, too. That will make everything worse.' I sat back on the bench, warming to my theme. 'Come the likely infrastructure breakdowns, we'll need local food-growing cooperatives, community-energy projects, local currencies even. The only thing that will get us through are the cooperative values embodied in Ubuntu.'

'It's not relevant to the dilemma,' he responded. 'Do I prosecute or don't I?'

'Few students bother turning up to the last lecture if you've already set the assignment,' I explained. 'They assume it's an optional extra.'

'I'm not asking you to omit cross-cultural approaches – just move them to after my assignment, that's all.'

'I'm fed up with this kind of thing always being seen as an add-on rather than fundamental,' I barked down the phone. 'It was the same thing in the Business School. Every staff briefing day, they'd put my talk on integrating ethics and sustainability into the curriculum right at the end when most had gone home.'

'I'm sorry, it's a fair point,' he hesitated. 'But will you do it anyway?'

I sighed and trudged over to Colin's office to be told off.

*

I didn't like the way Percy demonised Emily, but it turned out he was right.

169

'We received a student complaint that you've been awarding high marks based on someone referring to a piece of music you liked, even though it had nothing to do with the assignment.'

'That's not quite true.'

'Marking has to be fair.' Colin gazed disapprovingly at my mouth.

'Of course.' I wiped off a smear of hummus with my thumb. 'Students take marking very seriously.'

'The trouble is when others have failed the assignment—'

'Emily.'

'How do you know it's her?' Colin pounced immediately. 'Marking is supposed to be anonymous.'

'Because she wrote to me complaining, as I assume she did to you.'

'Jenna was specific about the need to give high scores.'

My God, he was blatant.

'Just to make it clear, it's fine for you to give high marks to the student. I'm sure you had a good reason beyond music.'

'Thanks for that, at least.' My polite smile remained rigid on my face.

'But when you fail another student, especially within the NSS period, then questions will be asked.'

'Let's make it clear, I didn't give her a poor mark, her work merited it.'

'Even so.'

I ungritted my teeth and reminded myself of my plan to devastate him with politeness. I looked around for something to compliment him on. I couldn't bring myself to comment on his new suit. His thinning hair was shiny and reeked of fruit – enough to put one off strawberries altogether.

'You have a very tidy office,' I managed.

His brow furrowed, and he tapped the desk with a perfectly manicured finger.

'And lovely hands,' I added desperately.

He looked at me, confused.

I stood up to leave. I needed to make it up with Marcel and GG.

I'd hoped to catch Marcel on his own, but Percy was in there, sprawled in the chair.

'Go away.' Marcel waved his arms at me when I popped my head around the door.

'I heard what you did,' Percy said.

I took an involuntary step backward. 'Sorry.'

'You leave us with Colin and you're sorry?' Marcel said.

'I found out what he wanted to talk to me about.'

'I don't care.'

'Did he stay long?' I asked.

'Apparently, he stayed long enough to have GG close to tears!' Percy said.

'Colin made GG cry?' I came in and sat down.

'No,' said Marcel. 'But he suggested it was "inappropriate" for a young postdoc to hang out with us oldies.'

'Inappropriate?'

'I told him she has a teenage son.'

'She must be older than she looks.'

'She started young,' Percy said.

'Then GG said it's because they've stopped recruiting anyone new, so only the oldies are left,' said Marcel.

'They recruited me,' I reminded him.

'Yes, I told him that to wind him up, and then he insinuated there was something between me and GG.'

'What?'

'That's what she said, "what him?" she said.'

I tried not to laugh at Marcel's outrage.

'We told him it was ridiculous, but he said it was how things looked that counted.'

'He would.' I told them about Colin's response to Emily's complaint. 'I was speechless.'

'One expects such breaches of academic integrity to at least be decently covered up,' Percy said.

'I wanted to ask him if his lack of shame indicated stupidity or had standards dropped to such a degree that upholding them now was considered a luxury we could no longer afford?' I stood up, feeling the need to pace. 'The future of humanity is at stake, and he's worried about one student's mark.'

'The future of humanity?' Percy raised an eyebrow.

'Bit grandiose,' Marcel commented.

I stiffened, flashing back to Fay's parting shot. 'It's not up to you to save the world.' I'd yelled something after her, something about nothing being so lonely as being misunderstood.

'Ah! Is this for your talk?' Marcel asked.

'Yes,' I said quickly.

'If anything will save us, it's learning from history.'

'Yes indeed,' I said.

'You should talk about how the metric has replaced what it stands for,' Percy said. 'Jenna would prefer top student satisfaction scores than to actually educate them.'

'As Chip told the whole department.' Marcel grinned.

'It's like profit in business,' I said. 'The moral justification for laws that allow businesses to pursue profit as their prime purpose was the belief that it would benefit society through efficiency, competition, etc. Historically...' I emphasised the word for Marcel's benefit, 'the goal of profit maximisation is subordinate to the goal of societal welfare. But...' I resumed pacing, 'the means and the end have become inverted. So now it's the market in charge, and society must do its bidding for better or worse. This is why, Marcel, you were right.'

'Naturally. How?'

'France is ahead of the game.'

'Always.' Marcel nodded.

'The rest of the world must follow suit and rewrite the rules of business to put society first.'

'You're correct, my friend.'

I stood up to go.

Marcel and Percy were appeased. Now for GG. I went past her room, but she wasn't in. I returned to my office to restructure my course.

*

I uploaded an amended lecture timetable to the module content

172

page. A reminder came up on my calendar that today was the deadline for posting our research plans. My act of bravado uploading gobbledygook might be a step too far. I pressed the mic icon and talked slowly.

'Storytelling for education. The first step in ethical decision-making is to consider who is benefited and who is harmed by a decision or policy. In business or government, this involves conducting a stakeholder analysis. This can make for dry reading, as the groups affected can seem distant. My story set in a citizens' jury allows stakeholders to become characters and as such, we identify with them and their needs more easily. We can then view any policy from the perspective of a variety of people, all of whom have a unique relationship to the proposal.'

I read it through and saved it. Another thought occurred. It's not so relevant, and I'd made a vow not to go on about Wittgenstein, but one has to allow oneself the odd treat.

'I wonder what Wittgenstein would make of my equating characters with stakeholders. Take the word "repair." It's one word with many connotations. Repair to Naomi threatened her livelihood. Why buy new if you can repair? To Steve, it was a waste of time. To Needles, it was resilience, to Josh, a father's love and sense of competence and to Ben, one more thing to feel guilty about. Like Obi's join the dots – the issues presenting out at refracting angles to interact with the needs, wants, and expectations of a diverse, yet representative group of people, each one seeing it differently.'

I saved it again. It wasn't much, but they'd only asked us to make a start. I had a chapter to write. Just one more sentence.

'It's a bit like the question of what is "good" art? Wittgenstein would see the object – whether it be a painting or a climate policy – as existing in a universe of constructed meanings. For example, there's an overlap between "stakeholders" and "characters" when seen from my perspective as a lecturer previously from the

Business School turned storyteller. But few others would see it the same way.

'I must read Wittgenstein properly, but it would be more fun to resurrect him. What's that radio show where you have to decide which historical characters you'd invite to your dinner party? Maybe there isn't a show. If not, there should be. I'd be on it, famous for breaking ground in this new field of edutainment. I'd have Wittgenstein and Socrates at a table for a chat. And Lee, because who says they all have to be famous? They're all men, but I'd have Fay.

'The pressure from Robert is relentless. It's hard enough anyway to align the story with the theories. It's next to impossible with Robert rushing me. This is what he doesn't understand. What I'm doing here is art. I'd love to talk to him about it, but if I sent him the readings, he'd just see them as a waste of time.

'I'd like to write more about the Prime Minister spreading misinformation. It's the lack of laws to protect the public from such antics that make citizens' assemblies so important. Too many of those at the top are toxic male types. Still, I have Steve, who typifies the individual bent on devouring the planet for his own gratification. He uses everything that comes his way – nature, money, Naomi?

'I'm not happy about delaying cross-cultural approaches, but maybe I can represent these through a character. Beyond Devanika, I haven't considered ethnicities. I see each character more as a type. Naomi typifies the materialistic millennial, locked into a corporate job that promotes excessive consumption. Naomi is also a Japanese name. If I make her Japanese, then Martha won't think it's about her. It's not, but they could think that. No. It's too late to change things now and it might look like tokenism. Also, once readers get an image in their head, if you then present someone differently, the magic bubble lifts, and the mechanics are revealed.

'I must remember to check this before saving.

'I've been jumping through hoops set by others – publish, make money, solve a dilemma. Confidentiality is a tricky dilemma. It's a shame it's one I can't share with my students. I must also check if the autosave is on. But I shouldn't have to be skulking around. It's alright for Robert. He's retiring, so what has he got to lose? I'm the one putting my job on the line. I haven't seen my sons for weeks. Now Fay's not around, things aren't the same. Robert's not the only one with family issues and I'm not crying over it. He wants confidentiality but he has no appreciation of what he's asking of me. I've put all that effort in, and I've had no acknowledgment from Colin or Jenna either. I gave them what they asked for in trumps, and not a peep. You'd think Obi would be interested. I enthused over his join the dots, which was magnificent, but he didn't even inquire about my work. Lee would have appreciated it. And Fay.

'If I could confide in my colleagues, they wouldn't think I was "sucking up". The students are mark-grubbing and distracted, although there are a few standouts. The keen girl at the front. A bit earnest, but thoughtful. Then the mouthy lads at the back. Some lecturers might see them as a threat, but the cocky one gets right to the heart every time. He often goes wrong too, but if he didn't, he wouldn't need me. He overturned my faith in behavioural sciences with a casual joke. And the sweet lad from music, who'd swooned at Bach. What he said was surprisingly deep and dark, and beautiful too. It's like in that one piece of music, *Air on a G String*, is the choice facing humanity.

'On one hand, represented by arts and humanities, is Bach, speaking to the soul. Music so exquisite and perfect and sublime it makes you believe in God. On the other, represented by business, is the cigar advert. Take a product that for decades was the most legally harmful of all – not just a cigarette with its cancer and tar, but the unfiltered fat brown cigar that tears at your lungs, the very organ you use to breathe, and rips them raw. And it uses Bach's music to do that. And that young lad's mum thought it was OK because it was funny. It's all there. These few students make it all worthwhile. But even them, actually, let's not romanticise them, none of them thought to comment on the story writing. The interweaving of moral philosophy and climate policy and democracy and the murder, which I haven't written yet, but I will. And the murder will be a metaphor for climate change, because they all did it. No, someone must be responsible, or there's no dilemma for the DPP. Robert doesn't realise the artistic sacrifices I'm making here.

'Fuck Robert, and fuck Fay too.'

*

Murder in the Citizens' Jury #13: Saviour complex

Richard was still seething at the way his retirement party had been hijacked. He'd tried to delay it on the grounds that he couldn't retire till the case was done, but apparently a special guest would make an appearance. Was he supposed to be honoured that the Prime Minister had turned up? The PM had shaken his hand in front of photographers before he could protest and audibly thanked him for getting him off. As if he, Richard Beech, Director of Public Prosecutions, approved of lying to the British public.

He loaded up the lunchtime footage and listened while glaring out of the window at the Houses of Parliament in the distance. He vaguely took in the click-clack of knitting needles and murmur of conversation in the background, too faint to make out, all the while thinking of everything he could have – should have said. He didn't want to be seen as one of the PM's cronies, but his biggest fear was what Marnie would think.

Richard heard footsteps, an exasperated *tut*, and the sound of a chair moving. He returned to his desk to watch.

Naomi wanders briefly into shot, talking inaudibly on the phone, oblivious to her surroundings. He turned the volume up and listened. It's Sarah speaking. She and Needles must be sitting right underneath the camera.

NEEDLES: I had hopes for that lass when she was talking
    about repairing that radio.

SARAH: Me too. I shouldn't say this, as I'm supposed to be

impartial, but for a moment I was irritated with her.

NEEDLES: Were you, love?

SARAH: Chairing a citizens' assembly is a bit like being a therapist. You can't bring your own baggage to the situation.

NEEDLES: Bags?

SARAH: My partner and I split up over this.

NEEDLES: I'm sorry to hear that, duck.

SARAH: She complained that I never had time for her. She didn't mind my being a chair for the Citizens' Assembly on same-sex marriage as it was for the cause. But when I accepted this one, she said I cared more about the planet than spending time with her. Said I was – what was it – yes 'grandiose' for wanting to save the world.

NEEDLES: Ooh, that's harsh.

SARAH: Accused me of having a saviour complex. I was furious. Talk about gaslighting!

NEEDLES: Gaslighting?

SARAH: She was basically medicalising my concerns. I knew then that I had to jettison her, but it still hurts.

Sarah's voice went quiet. Richard turned up the volume to hear.

SARAH: They'd say that splitting up with a long-term partner the week before counts. I didn't disclose it, because I wanted to make sure nothing would go wrong. So don't say anything, will you?

NEEDLES: Course not. Don't you worry, duck.

Richard typed the word "jettison," into the online thesaurus: 'get rid of', 'dump overboard' 'dispose of.' Quickly he searched for the photograph of the list of names that had been found on the scene. Someone had circled Steve's name several times, but Naomi's name had also been circled. Steve's behaviour hadn't endeared him to Sarah, and here was evidence that she had issues with Naomi, too.

He checked through his notes for mentions of Sarah – day one – something about a baby. He fast-forwarded to the time code he'd listed and watched again.

SARAH: This citizens' jury is my baby, and it's a climate
      solution in itself. If anything is going to change our
      world, it will be who makes the decisions and on what
      basis. So I'll be making sure it grows up smoothly.

He watched Sarah's face, noticing her smile harden when she looked at Steve. Richard paused the recording to consider her expression. You could even call it a glare.

He jumped to his feet, energised, and paced, thinking through everything he'd watched. Sarah had baggage. She'd obviously been deeply hurt by her partner's comments. Perhaps Naomi's likeness had triggered a repressed fury. Maybe it was her, after all.

He paused to consider why he was so excited. It wasn't like he wanted Sarah to be the murderer. He'd trained himself not to want anything. If he did want anything, he'd want the murder never to have happened and put him in this position. He had to admit, though, he definitely wasn't keen for it to be Needles. With the murder weapon being knitting needles, she was the obvious suspect, but he couldn't face being hated for putting away another pensioner.

If it made a difference what he wanted, then he'd have prosecuted the Prime Minister for the misinformation he spread, the impacts of which would be felt for decades at least. If what he wanted mattered, he wouldn't have prosecuted the 82-year-old environmental protestor. He'd fallen ill while in prison and they were making out it was his fault. Marnie had played the news item to him accusingly the moment he got home. It was a rerun of Arthur's interview the day he was arrested. Eyes watering with emotion, the old man had told the camera how he was a retired probation officer who respected the law. But when the law was allowing the earth to be destroyed, and his granddaughter was too scared to have children, he considered it his duty to protest. Then it cut to the sombre face of the journalist who said the old man was ill and may not recover. He'd become a national treasure, which made him, Richard Beech, the villain. He hadn't made the laws that meant automatic jail time for any destruction of property. It was unfair, but the media were just doing their thing. It was his wife that he was finding it hard to forgive. He'd begun by trying to appease her, but now he was angry at the way she too was ganging up on him when he needed her support. Why couldn't she understand? He was just doing his job.

*

My vision was blurring and my body ached from sitting in one position. With a final muttered 'fuck you', I uploaded what I'd written. Next—

There was a knock at the door. Jenna entered, and I quickly shut down my laptop.

'I hope you don't mind. You haven't responded to my emails.'

I bit back a 'fuck you' and said something apologetic.

She went on for a bit about my talk and I responded with positive words until she went away.

I stood up, gazing out of my window. It wasn't yet dark. There was something on my mind. I saw a few students heading home after the last lectures. That was it. I needed to apologise to GG. If I was quick, I'd get her before she went home.

I caught GG as she was leaving the lecture theatre.

Her sad brown eyes reproached me as I rushed up.

'I'm sorry GG for…' I stopped, suddenly lost. I wanted to say for not inviting her to my dinner party, but that was imaginary.

'Why did you do it?' she asked.

I shrugged helplessly.

'Why did you invite him to join us and then leave?'

'Colin. Yes, that was bad.'

'I don't understand?'

'I wanted to prove I could win him over with niceness.'

'But you don't like him?' She looked at me, puzzled.

'Sorry, it was stupid. Marcel told me what he said to you.'

'He's always mean about my music.'

The early evening air was soft and heavy.

GG waved at a couple of students who were wiping their eyes.

'Are they yours?' I asked.

'Yes.' She looked satisfied. 'My music makes them cry.'

'Right.'

The rays of the setting sun cast a poignant beauty to the campus, shooting me through with loneliness.

'Are you off home now?'

I saw a question in her eye. After my evasiveness when she asked if I was married, I'd probably been the topic of speculation.

'Not yet. I've got to work out the best climate policies to include in my story.'

'I know a sustainability expert who can help.'

'Thanks. Also, I've got to reorder my lectures. I had to lose the one on discourse ethics.' As we walked back, I made do with an audience of one. 'Habermas said only in debate can we test the moral validity of a proposition.'

'Like in citizens' assemblies?' she asked.

'Yes, it's based on the assumption that we can think rationally about what's best for us.'

'I hate it when people try to tell you what to teach,' GG said.

'It has some problems with it anyway. History offers numerous examples of disadvantaged groups being complicit in their own oppression. Many women were critical of suffragettes and feminists, for example. We internalise society's assumptions about us.'

'Do you think we know we're doing it?' she asked.

The pink-yellow light created a dreamlike feel. I couldn't face returning to my dark office.

'Shall we sit by the stream for a while?' I pointed to the path down to my bench. 'It reminds me of something Fay said to me.'

'Fay?' GG looked interested and followed me down to the bench.

We sat and watched the reflection of the trees in the rippling water.

'Isn't it strange?' I said. 'We can lecture on a subject, year in and year out, and never notice how it applies to ourselves.'

'Uh-huh.'

'Did you ever watch *Downton Abbey*?'

GG nodded.

'I was watching it with Lee, that's my brother, and Fay. I was commenting on how the butler had so internalised the class structure, he was more critical of staff who got above themselves than the master. Then Fay claimed I wasn't so different and pointed out I hadn't ticked the LGTBQ+ box when we did a survey.'

I checked GG's reaction and continued.

'I hadn't thought she'd noticed. But she wasn't blaming me or anything. She just said, "it was interesting." I told her I'm not keen on categories. Lee had a pop at me for going on about Wittgenstein, but in a nice way, because we get on well. Got on well. And he knows me because it was a Wittgenstein thing.

'And then Fay asked, "Are you saying there's something wrong with being LGBTQ+?" I said, "Of course not, because an ethical analysis begins with the notion of harm, then if no one is harmed, there's no issue of right or wrong to address." Then she made some point, and she was referencing my parents here because they're, they were very traditional. "Could one say there's indirect harm to societal values?" she suggested. I went along with it because I was impressed to see she was using the Socratic method to interrogate my statement.'

GG looked confused.

'It's where you ask questions as a way to challenge assumptions,' I explained.

She nodded, and I continued.

'I told her I'd brought two children into the world – not that it

should be a requirement. Then she asked if that was my parents'
voices in my head and if they'd have disapproved?'

'Would they?' GG asked.

'Probably. And I admitted as much to Fay. "Because there's
something wrong with it?" she asked. And I said, "They just
internalised society's norms like we all do." Lee was grinning
because he saw I'd been caught in my own trap. I didn't mind
because one can't win every argument. Then she asked me if I
felt shame. I denied it. And she said, "There's no shame in feeling
shame. I'm not shame-shaming you." And I said, "I'm a rational
woman in a progressive environment. I'm almost trendy." Then
she said, "But…?"'

I paused and GG smiled at me encouragingly.

'I had to admit that I was aware of actively choosing not to
feel shame. That shame was present as something I needed to
argue myself out of. Part of the mental architecture that one is
constantly dismantling.'

GG looked solemn. 'Is that why you didn't say anything at
the pub?' she asked. 'Were you worried they'd make you Diversity
Manager?'

I laughed, but then I saw another question in her eye. She
was going to ask me more about Fay. I felt a 'fuck you' returning.
I looked at a nonexistent watch.

'I'd better get back to my whodunnit.' I stood up to go.

'How's it going?' she asked as we headed back.

'I'm building up to the murder.'

'I can set it to music, if you like?'

We got to the main path and saw Percy and Marcel on their
way home.

'Bit early for you, isn't it, Chip,' Marcel said. 'It's not midnight
yet.'

'GG's trying to talk me into Murder in the Citizens' Jury –
the musical.'

'Coming to the pub?' Percy asked.

GG shook her head curtly.

'Oh dear.' I looked after her as she walked off.

'She's got no sense of humour when it comes to her music,'

Marcel warned.

'One drink while I tell you why we're broke,' Percy said, walking briskly, 'and then I have to get back to Kate.'

'What's this?' I asked, following them.

'Percy's found out why we've got no money.'

'You know Jenna said our student numbers were low?'

'Yes?'

'It's not because we're boring lecturers like she implied.'

'Why then?'

'Apparently last year they cut admin numbers by half, so they didn't have enough staff to process student applications.'

'And they have the nerve to blame us.' Marcel stopped and spread out his arms in indignation.

'It gets worse.' Percy stalked on.

We scampered to keep up with his long-legged stride.

'To remedy this, Jenna employs an expensive consultancy firm—'

'Your mate,' Marcel added.

'—to do focus groups on why students didn't choose us.'

'You couldn't make it up.' Marcel looked delighted. Discovering a new cockup by management had put him in a buoyant mood.

'That's why they're making academic staff redundant.' Percy glared at me. 'And it will be GG next.'

'It's the system,' I said as we entered the pub.

Once we were seated with drinks, I expounded on my point. 'The least useful people are the ones who get to keep their jobs, as they're the ones conveying information to those holding the purse strings. Middle management.'

'Can you believe Jenna's away again?' Marcel said.

'It's her mental health.' Percy sniffed.

'How do you know?' I asked.

'I have to do the programme review report because she finds it so stressful.'

'That's my point,' I said. 'It's the job of middle management to be hated. That's probably why Jenna takes so much time off.'

'First Kate, now you.'

'Now me what?'

'Is it the sisterhood or something?'

'Is what the sisterhood?'

'Now Kate's moved onto researching the menopause, everything's down to bloody hormones. I don't want to sound insensitive…'

'Don't worry.' Marcel was bright-eyed in anticipation of an outburst. 'You're in a safe space with us.' He patted Percy's arm.

'I've got a student who doesn't want to do a group presentation during her "time of the month" but if I let that go, then unless they all sync up—'

'They do that apparently,' Marcel said.

'One lad last week begged me to let him off his presentation due to fear of panic attacks. I said, "Just do it" and afterwards he thanked me and said how much doing it had improved his confidence.' Percy looked around at us. 'I said, "Write and tell that to the bloody management, because people damn sure complain if they don't like it."'

'Did you really say that?' I asked.

Marcel shook his head at me.

'But the point stands, doesn't it?' Percy demanded.

'Which point?' I asked. 'The fact no one tells you when you got it right, or that people should tough out their fears.'

'Both.'

'It's a dilemma.' I sipped my wine and mused. I'd use Rawls' theory of justice for this. 'If you were about to magically switch places with a girl—'

'Like in *The Hot Chick*?' Percy suggested.

'Is that one of your romcoms?' Marcel asked him.

'And you knew you could be one of the eighty percent of girls who experience painful periods for one or more days a month. What would you say was a fair system?'

'But what about Jenna?' Percy's brow furrowed.

'She took the job of Dean at twice what we earn, and she's been off half the semester,' Marcel said.

'I'm just saying—' I began.

'If she can't hack it, then she shouldn't take the money,' Percy interrupted.

'While people like GG worry about being made redundant,' Marcel added.

'After losing all our money on consultants,' Percy reminded me.

'If she's being paid to be hated, it's the only part of her job she's successful at.' Marcel waved his glass around.

Percy clinked his glass against Marcel's in agreement.

'I'm just saying, being employed as a human shield for the higher ups to protect them from the fall-out from their decisions can't be much fun.'

They paused drinking and looked at me. I realised with a shock they assumed I was showing sympathy.

'That's why we should sack the Deans.' I took a nonchalant swig of my wine.

'Yes!' Marcel was ecstatic. 'Sack the Deans.'

'We can sympathise with Jenna,' I conceded with a kind smile. 'It must have sounded good – promotion, more money. She probably didn't realise until it was too late that her job is to be hated. But our natural sympathy doesn't mean we should allow her power at a cost to the rest of us who actually do useful work. We should still…'

'Sack the deans,' we said in unison.

'And their assistants,' Marcel added, looking over my shoulder. I turned around to see Colin on his way to the bar.

I fought a craven urge to run after him and find out what he'd heard. Colin turned around and saw me looking. I flashed him a bright smile and looked away quickly before anyone noticed.

'Iris, you're right,' Percy boomed, oblivious. 'We should sack the deans.'

Marcel gestured towards my empty glass. I shook my head and stood up. Suddenly, I was desperate to get back to the safety of my fictional world.

Murder in the Citizens' Jury #14: Cabbage

Richard's colleagues had invited him to lunch as today was the day he'd expected to retire. Normally, he'd welcome a break from his desk, but he was too eager to see what the rest of the footage held. At his level, it was a long time since he'd been the first to see potential evidence. He'd forgotten how exciting it could be. There'd been no packed lunch from Marnie for weeks now, so he nipped out to buy some sandwiches and rushed back to see what happened during lunch hour on Day 5.

The camera is still focused on the corner of the room. At first, he misses it because he's struggling to make out the murmurs of conversation. Mostly people grumbling about the heat and complaints about there being no window. Someone opened the door and left it open. That seemed to be it. Richard rewound and then he saw it. Devanika is just visible in the shadowy area behind the door. She looks around and then puts her hand down her t-shirt to adjust something concealed in her bra. She moves quickly out of shot. On the floor, there's something green that wasn't there before. Cabbage.

Richard paused the footage and typed, "Why would you put cabbage in your bra?" into the browser. When he saw the answer, another piece of the puzzle fell into place.

He resumed watching. The sound on the next section was barely audible, but the sound engineers had added captions to assist him.

Devanika emerges from behind the door just as Josh appears. His eyes are bloodshot. She retreats into the shadows.

Josh turns towards someone who is out of shot.

BEN: How come you were allowed out?

JOSH: Just in the courtyard for a smoke.

BEN: That's not tobacco. We have to decide soon. Some of us
     take this seriously.

*Josh leans out of shot. His right arm is seen stuffing
biscuits in his pocket. He returns to stand by the door and
munches, looking stoned.*

*Devanika emerges from behind the door, making him jump.
She stands next to him.*

DEVANIKA: You look familiar as well.

JOSH: As well as who?

Devanika nods over at someone who is out of shot.

JOSH: I haven't seen you before. But when you were shouting
     at Naomi, I thought...

DEVANIKA: Do you go to that Buddhist refill shop?

JOSH: Yes. Jesus! It was you shouting at the guy at the till
     because they'd run out of organic wheat germ.

He looks at Devanika, alarmed.

DEVANIKA: He said they'd lost their supplier. I bet it was
     Steve.

JOSH: But you were raging at him. Proper raging. You scared
     me.

DEVANIKA: I was in a bad way that day. Sorry I scared you.

Josh relaxes slightly but still looks nervous.

Richard paused the recording to scribble some notes.
Jurors knowing each other from outside the citizens' jury
complicated things. At the very least, it could muddle theories
about motivation. He pressed *play*, and the recording resumed.

JOSH: Sometimes I wish I could scream and scream like you

did.

DEVANIKA: You should let it out.

Josh shakes his head.

JOSH: You know what does make me feel better?

DEVANIKA: What?

JOSH: I always go home via that house where they leave out vegetables on their doorstep. There's a whole street that does it. They all grow different things and when there's a glut they have boxes saying 'please take these so they don't go to waste'. You get all sorts.

DEVANIKA: That's a great idea.

JOSH: I know it sounds stupid, but I dunno, the way they put it – asking you to 'please take them', it makes you feel you're doing your bit to prevent food waste.

DEVANIKA: You know you're all right, Josh.

JOSH: Thanks.

DEVANIKA: I hate the way they're picking on you.

JOSH: Ben has it in for me. Don't know what I ever did to him.

DEVANIKA: It's Steve egging him on.

JOSH: Steve looks a bit like my dad.

DEVANIKA: You mention your dad a lot.

Josh suddenly shouts, making Devanika jump.

JOSH: It wasn't my fault. I didn't even want to go on holiday, but he insisted. To cheer me up, he said. It wasn't my fault. I didn't even want to go.

Josh stares at Devanika. She recoils, disturbed by his intensity.

Richard exhaled slowly and sat back in his chair. There were now two more suspects. First Devanika, and now Josh, seemed to have mental health issues. It wasn't going to help him wrap this up any quicker. He no longer minded. The way things were at home, frankly, it would be awkward if he was there the whole time. He stood up and walked to the window and gazed out at the London skyline. Big Ben was lit up, its reflection glimmering gold on the inky blackness of the Thames. Opposite the London Eye was illuminated by an ethereal pink glow. When he'd first started here, he'd been blown away by the view. It was even more impressive now. Back in the nineties, the London air had been thick with exhaust, and he'd come home filthy every night. The city had cleaned up once they'd banned leaded petrol, and now it sparkled. Soon the city would become quieter as electric cars replaced the old engines. Or maybe demand-led buses would take over entirely. Would he even notice, retired in the country? He supposed they'd come into town now and then for the theatre. But the days of putting on their glad rags for an evening out seemed far away.

Why was he in such a rush to give it all up, anyway? It wasn't the hate coming at him from all sides for prosecuting the old protestor, or not prosecuting the prime minister for lying. These things blow over. It was Laura's statement she was ready to have children that had decided him. He'd been too busy to be the father he should have been to Laura – something he'd increasingly regretted. He couldn't wait to be a grandad. Hopefully, it would also bring him closer to Marnie.

He stared at the screen, which was paused on Josh's agonised expression and Devanika's look of fearful concern. The defence could plead insanity. Not a great way to end one's career, but he'd take that over having to prosecute the old lady.

Chapter 14

In the last class, the students debated what moral responsibility we should assign to Josh. His medications may have combined with his cannabis smoking and prior issues to tip him over the edge. I asked whether we should hold him morally responsible for his actions, even if they include murder. It wasn't my best class, but this is more of a legal question anyway and doesn't tie directly into the DPP's dilemma.

The students could tell I wasn't on form. Every time I put forward an argument about responsibility, I flashed back to our discussions over Monopoly. The first time we played, the game got no further than a debate over whether to claim rent while in jail. The boys thought not because prison was supposed to be a punishment. Fay said that most people were in jail because of lack of options and poor role models growing up. Adam said she had a point. If you have no control over your genes or your environment, can you be held responsible for your actions? Fay got excited and said that was an interesting question. Then Tom said that implies there's no such thing as free will. Then we discussed what that meant for our penal system. I remember sitting back, silent for a moment, watching them debate issues of moral responsibility and free will versus determinism, enjoying their excitement in the ideas. Observing them as they began to appreciate the real-world implications of such beliefs. I'd tried fruitlessly to engage my sons in philosophical debates for years, and Fay had managed it effortlessly after knowing them just a few weeks. That phase, the one I later referred to as the 'lovey dovey' phase, began at that moment, with my heart so full, I thought I'd cry. Then, every time we meet, there's that point of connection, and then another. Love songs have meaning. I want to write one myself, but knowing my limits, settle for bad poetry. I feel vulnerable and, seeing the vulnerability reflected in her, feel reassured.

Until it all changes and I realise it was a mirage.

The girl in the front row came up to me after the class, all bright-eyed, and told me she had a good dilemma I could use. I felt irritated, as if it were an attack on the dilemmas I'd posed. I pretended to be busy and rushed off.

I sat on my bench by the stream feeling bad. The keen girl at the front had looked gutted when I'd left so abruptly. Colin and Jenna would wag their fingers and remind me of the NSS scores. But my concern was the fragility of the students. I don't remember being so easily upset when I was that age. Was it volatile chemicals in the air affecting our nervous system? Social media? Fear of the future? Or was it just that the stiff upper lip approach was out of date? I'd been told off for being a baby when I'd cried as a kid, so learned not to. If crying had been rewarded, would that be better or worse? Then how do we deal with the Emilys of the world? I'd love to debate it with the students, but it was too charged. Or my parents, but they'd gone.

I turned my phone back on and checked the family chat. The last message on it was from me, attaching a chapter. I looked at the photo, Fay smiling into the camera, me with my arms around my boys. Adam was pulling a face. Lee was gazing slightly to the left, looking wise. Lee would say… I stared at his face, reaching for him with my mind.

I jumped when the phone buzzed in my hand.

Tom: Sorry not been in touch.

Adam: We were worried you'd make us read your mystery thing.

Tom: Adam's not read anything longer than an email since school.

Adam: True that.

Tom: but Martha said you'd be more upset at us avoiding you than not reading your book.

I came to life.

Me: Bless her. This Friday then?

Tom: We're in.

Me: Martha too?

Tom: 👍

Me: ☺

Me: Did you read any of it?

I waited. Nothing.
Then a buzz. It was the DPP.

How's progress? Have you set the dilemma yet?

Nearly there.

I stared at the stream and tried to focus on the murder.
I was distracted by someone waving at me. It was the girl from the front row. I beckoned her over. She came to join me on the bench.
'Hi Professor.'
'Hello. Tell me about this dilemma of yours.'
She shook her head. 'It's silly actually, and illegal.'
'Sounds great, tell me,' I encouraged.
'You know that bit at the start of your story when Needles tells her grandson that insects hold everything together?'
I nodded.
'I liked that bit because it's so true and I think if our political leaders appreciated how we depend on nature, then they'd make different decisions.'
'OK,' I said, 'but how is that a dilemma?'
'We should secretly feed them magic mushrooms.'
'Right. Erm. Talk me through your thinking.'
'Research shows magic mushrooms make people feel

connected to nature and then they're more environmentally friendly.' She shot me a sideways look to check my reaction.

I kept a straight face. 'Go on.'

'I think a good essay question is would it be ethically right to give leaders at the next climate decision thingy magic mushrooms because it's been shown that it makes people value nature and see themselves as part of the whole ecology.'

'Without them knowing?' I asked.

'You could add them to a quiche or something. That would be the ethical dilemma, you see?'

'I get it, but there's a more practical issue. If they didn't know they'd taken magic mushrooms, wouldn't they be worried about what was happening to them?'

She looked disappointed. I sought for something positive to say.

'Much better to find a way for them to take it of their own free will,' I said. 'Then you don't violate the human rights issue and practically it would be more effective.'

'Good idea,' she nodded with enthusiasm. 'We'd also want to target those least interested in climate for maximum effect.'

'You've obviously given this a lot of thought.'

'How could we get them to take it voluntarily?'

'Your target group might be the toxic male types. You'd need to think what would appeal to them.'

'How?'

I mused. 'Maybe spread a rumour in their echo chambers that magic mushrooms can increase virility?'

'Do they?' she asked.

'Not as far as I know,' I confessed. 'But the climate deniers are the types who believe what they want to believe rather than evidence, so it doesn't matter. They'd be gasping to get it.'

'We could link to a secret website where they can get hold of it,' she suggested.

'Yes, then prime them with images of bountiful nature. They'll be going in with sex on their minds, so we need to shift that to ecology.'

'Brilliant!'

'It could just work.'

'So, will you set it as a dilemma?' she asked.

'No.'

Her face fell.

'What made you think of this idea?' I asked. 'Have you tried them?'

'Not yet, but everybody says—'

'People you know?' I interjected.

'No, well, YouTube and such, but they all say it's amazing, and they had this incredible experience. And it helps with anxiety, and…'

'It's not my area of expertise so I won't comment, but what I can tell you with absolute fact is that you don't need magic mushrooms to appreciate nature.'

'But they say—'

I put my finger to my lips, and we listened to the evening chorus of birdsong. I nodded towards the stream where trees were reflected on the dancing water. A dragonfly in iridescent blue flitted across the surface. A series of quacks heralded a raft of ducks engaged in noisy conversation.

She watched, smiling, as the ducks headed downstream.

'Beware of the ravers,' I said after a moment.

'Ravers?' she asked. 'Like dancing on E kind of thing?'

'No. The ones who go on about how amazing everything is. If there's a diet or new fad, it will change your life forever. You'll be transformed by cold water, eating berries or whatever. If it's a holiday resort, it will be absolutely stunning, the best book/movie/restaurant ever. You try, and it's all right, but not that great.'

She nodded in recognition.

'I used to assume that they really experienced everything at this wonderful level, and there was something wrong with me,' I told her. 'My brother first alerted me to the existence of these ravers, and once I saw them in that light, they never affected me again. He was wise.'

'My friend is like that,' she said. 'I don't know if she raves deliberately to get an audience and make out she has a more fabulous life.'

'They're a hazard no one tells you about. No one raves about the normal stuff, like sitting here, chatting about life, watching the sun sparkling off the stream.'

'I'll call my friend out about her raving,' she said, standing up to go.

I laughed. 'You do that. What's your name, by the way? I know you as Smart Girl in the Front Row, but I haven't yet matched up names with faces.'

'Zoe. Zoe Jones.'

Her name rang a bell.

'Nice to chat, Zoe.'

'I'll tell Emily all about our conversation.'

I remembered now. Emily had wanted the 3 p.m. class to be with her friend Zoe.

'In fact, I'll rave about it!' Zoe shot me a shy smile and walked on.

I tried to return to my plotting, but I could no longer concentrate. If Emily had bought down Percy's wife for talking about gender differences, what could she twist this into if I failed her?

'We were only joking about?' I imagined my defence.

'Distributing Class A drugs to government officials is no joke,' would be the stern response from Jenna, Colin nodding solemnly next to her.

*

Dear Emily,

I'm aware you are worried about your progress. I've been hoping to see you in my lectures, but I'm also available if you'd like to come to my office to discuss any issues you may be having. We have two more assignments to go. I don't pre-read submissions, but I am always happy to talk through your ideas.

Kind regards

Iris Tate

Professor of Moral Philosophy

Chapter 15

The encounter with Zoe had reinvigorated my interest in the students as individuals. They wouldn't just be the victims of past inaction, but also the changemakers. To teach them effectively, I had to understand their world and what was shaping them.

I'd had little success shaping my sons. The harder I'd tried to influence them, the more they'd pulled back. It had been Lee who'd been the bridge. His male solidarity, combined with the wisdom that had guided my own values, had kept the family bond strong. My greatest fear when Lee died was that I'd lose my boys. I was just too sad and too female for them to bear at that age when they both hate and love you. Tom, bless him, was atoning now for how he'd been. His guilt making him unable to hear my reassurances that I understood. It was him who'd had a right to a functioning mother. He didn't need to bring me flowers. I'd handled that badly, but maybe it didn't matter. It was Martha who was shaping him now.

I beamed in relief when I saw her step out of the car with Adam and Tom. Her thoughtfulness when she'd prompted Tom to contact me had been touching.

I beckoned them in.

'I'm so glad you came, Martha. Risk is better with four.'

Thirty minutes later, and the game was in full swing. I smiled around at everyone strategising and making alliances and threats.

'If your red army are still in Iceland next turn,' Tom warned Adam, 'then I'm coming for them.'

'But if you weaken me and Mum's mission is *Kill all red troops*, she'll win.'

'I'll leave you alone.'

'Attack Martha. She won't respect you if you do her favours just because she's your girlfriend.'

'Yes, I will.'

'I'm getting a set next go, and then I'll have my revenge.'

'Bring it on.'

'Mum, will you do a peace treaty?'

'Just for one round.'

'Your turn.'

The game ground to a halt when Adam got a set and had eighteen troops to play with. 'Hurry up.' Tom tapped the table impatiently.

'How's work?' I asked Martha while we waited.

'We're launching a probiotic bodywash.'

'A what?'

She came to life. 'You know everyone's taking probiotics for their gut health?'

I nodded.

'A focus group found people are worried about standing under hot showers in case it washes off the good bacteria on their skin, which is very ageing.'

A probiotic cream sounded just about plausible, but bodywash? 'Surely it can't work?'

'It's doing well in the trials.'

'But does it actually work?'

'Yes, because we get the green market too, so that's an extra price premium.'

'Your turn, Martha.' Adam was finally done.

She threw the dice and took out two of Adam's troops in Europe. Southern Europe, where fires had raged out of control last summer.

I lasted for another round before I posed the question on my mind. 'You charge extra if something is environmentally friendly? You don't see a problem with that?'

Tom's attention switched abruptly from the board to me. He put his hand protectively on Martha's arm. 'She's just doing her job, Mum.'

'So am I.'

'Your turn, Tom,' Adam reminded.

'I'm attacking you in Iceland.'

'If you wanted to be green, you could advise turning down the temperature of the water,' I suggested.

Tom glanced over while he continued his battle with Adam. He looked reassured by Martha's air of confidence and threw his dice.

'We thought carefully about what claims to make, and whether to play the green card.' She had the air of someone who'd got the answers right in a marketing exam.

'Are you saying that the environmental impacts of products are optional?'

'It can backfire when you make claims that aren't true,' she explained. 'That's why we made no claims about the probiotic bacteria, because it would probably get washed off by the shower before it made any difference.'

'It's literally greenwash, Martha, because if you wanted people to have healthy skin and low environmental impact, you'd advise tepid water and shorter showers.'

'We didn't explicitly say it was green. It's done through the packaging.'

'I mean impact in the actual world – not the world of marketing.'

'For God's sake.' Tom threw the dice so hard it scattered all the troops. He didn't bother putting them back, and sat, arms crossed, glaring at me.

Our games were always an opportunity for debate, but Martha was still new. I'd gone too far.

They left early. Martha said they had a friend's party they wanted to get to. She was trying to be polite, but it made me feel worse, like this was a pity visit squeezed into their busy schedule. Adam just shrugged and sloped out after them.

It was for the best, really. I had my story to be getting on with.

Murder in the Citizens' Jury #15: Tipping Points

FOOTAGE FROM LUNCHTIME CCTV. DAY 5 [eco-anxiety trigger alert]

Naomi approaches Sarah.

NAOMI: I've been wanting to say something. You know that film we watched about the tipping points?

SARAH: *Breaking Boundaries?*

NAOMI: I thought it was too much.

SARAH: What do you mean?

NAOMI: They said the Greenland icecap has passed the tipping point, but there's still the Arctic icecap, isn't there?

SARAH: Yes. The climate has been kept stable by the two polar icecaps. We're losing one and if we carry on as we are, we'll lose the other.

NAOMI: Look, no offence, but you need to be more positive.

SARAH: I'm sorry?

NAOMI: Don't worry, it's fine. It's just, I'm a marketing person. I'm trying to share my expertise with you. I'd spin it so people have more hope. It's like with beauty products, they buy because they hope it will stop them ageing and all that. That's what people spend the money for – they're buying the dream. You discourage people if you make it too bleak.

SARAH: That wasn't a marketing video. They didn't make up the figures to get a certain psychological effect. These are scientists' estimates.

NAOMI: Uh-huh.

SARAH: If anything, they underestimate. We're giving it to you
    straight, Naomi, no spin.

NAOMI: Oh.

*

I pressed save and stood up. I had a pain in my elbow where I'd
leaned on the table. I rubbed it and a tiny soldier fell off, leaving
an indent in my flesh where a miniature bayonet had pressed
into the skin. It was past midnight. I left the Risk and stumbled
upstairs to bed.

I lay there, my mind whirring. Did Martha know the difference
between actual impacts and marketing blurb? I suspect it was
more that she believed it didn't benefit her to. I'd like to argue
to her that it did. Lee may say *softly softly catchee monkey* all he
liked, but my job is to tell it like it is. That's why everyone hates
philosophers. They killed Socrates after all.

I put aside thoughts of the evening and tried to focus on my
story. Should I write the murder first, as Robert suggested, and
then the ethical theories? That doesn't make sense. We need a
well-informed answer. The right answer.

I tossed and turned over what that might be, then ended up,
as I did most nights, reminding myself this was why we were
consulting the students. They must decide. It matters that they
get it right, I tell Robert in my head. A compromise then. One
more ethical theory, then the murder, then the virtues. But first
to finish the story. The Risk board hadn't been put away yet, but
I mustn't allow myself to be distracted. The important thing is
to be getting on with saving the world through climate fiction. I
had to find a climate policy worth killing for.

But what if I spawn a class full of vigilantes?

It was my prof, your Honour. I imagined the mouthy guy at the
back in court. *It was 'er who said it was the right thing to do.* He'd
developed a Cockney accent for some reason.

'Same here,' Zoe says. 'I wanted to get a first, so I poisoned
the lot.'

Colin is on the jury, looking stern. I'm in trouble.

200

Now I'm in the dock.

'How do you plead?'

I turn to look at the jury. Martha's there, and Tom and Adam and Lee. Colin's gone, thank goodness, but I still have the question to answer.

'Guilty or not guilty?'

'It depends on what you mean by guilty?' Wittgenstein has popped up to defend me.

'None of your nonsense,' says the prosecuting counsel. It's Kant, his white wig rivalling the judge's.

'Just answer the question.' I recognise the voice. It's Fay.

Everyone looks at me.

'Guilty, your honour,' I say eventually. It's a relief to admit it.

Fay looks disappointed.

A battalion of blue troops march up the court, bayonets pointing forwards. Red troops appear banging on drums. Someone throws dice, and they scatter everywhere.

Chapter 16

> *Dear Mel*
>
> *GG gave me your email. I need your advice as a matter of urgency. If you could pick a climate policy worth killing for, what would it be?*
>
> *Kind regards*
>
> *Iris Tate*
>
> *Professor of Moral Philosophy*

The answer came straight back.

> *I have 25 minutes before my next lecture. I'm Building A5, room 312.*
>
> *M*

I arrived out of breath ten minutes later. Mel's office stood out for the colourful poster of global warming stripes going from blue to bright red, tracking temperature rise since the industrial revolution.

Inside, I saw an angular woman with cropped dark hair tapping at her keyboard. I knocked on her open door.

'Come in,' she said, swivelling around in her chair.

'Thanks for getting back to me so fast.' I shut the door behind me.

'Tipping points, and all that.' She glanced at the clock. 'About a climate policy worth killing for…'

'Yes, I'm only asking because…'

She waved away my explanation. 'I don't need to know why.'

I'd have liked to tell her about my book, but she was right, time was short.

'Everyone thinks it's just about tech.' Mel scanned files and shut them down while talking fast. 'They get all excited about what their new invention can do and then you do the sums and find out, yes you managed to capture one whole tonne of carbon dioxide, or power something with hydrogen, and the tech boys are all "da da!"' She made jazz hands. 'But they emitted huge amounts of emissions to get there. And each individual consumes about ten tonnes a year, so you have to do ten times that for eight billion people every year. It requires more resources than we fucking have to scale it up, but no one wants to hear that, do they?' Mel fixed me with an irritated glare. 'No, because business whispers in government's ears and all they say is economic growth. Economic growth – the fuel to keep everything going and we're fucked, because growth is the hot tap.'

'The hot tap?'

'Think of a bath.' She stood up and drew a crude picture of a bath on a whiteboard. 'Think of the water as the carbon dioxide in the atmosphere.' She drew a plug and water streaming out. 'Carbon capture, and planting forests etcetera that draws down the carbon, decreasing the heat. But we only have so much land and trees can burn, and carbon capture requires resources. And all the time we continue to have the hot tap full on. As a matter of policy.'

'People chase economic growth for a reason,' I said. 'It creates jobs, provides taxes to pay for services and all that.'

'Oh yes, GG said you were from the Business School.'

I bristled at her tone, but before I could speak, she'd moved on.

'Economic growth is measured by the Gross Domestic Product, which is basically production and consumption, but it's not the same thing as wellbeing. Never has been, and even more so now we have climate change in the mix.'

'Are you saying the best climate policy is to switch from the GDP to something like a wellbeing or planetary health index?' I asked.

'Most countries already have some kind of wellbeing index. The Office of National Statistics has also developed a new inclusive income metric which includes environmental data. So the real solution here is to give these media attention and get politicians and journalists out of the habit of reporting the GDP as if it's a measure of success. It's ridiculous as most things that we value aren't included in it. For example, sea level rises will flood huge tracts of land – most of London - coastal regions everywhere and GDP will rise as we rebuild on higher ground. This will emit even more greenhouse gas emissions, worsening the problem, but GDP is up – hurrah!'

'So the solution isn't so much developing a wellbeing index, it's getting journalists to report on it?' I asked.

'Basically, yes.'

It lacked drama. 'Anything else?'

Mel tapped her desk thoughtfully. 'It's high-carbon consumption that matters. Another contender for the top spot would be personal carbon allowances.'

'I've mentioned these in passing and I've covered carbon offsets.'

She snorted. 'The voluntary carbon market is a Wild West. I'm talking a government controlled mandated carbon ration.' Mel looked around for her phone, still talking. 'PCAs were proposed in 2007, and people were taking them seriously, but the global financial crisis knocked it off the agenda. We didn't have the carbon footprint software. We weren't scared enough. But we're fucking scared now, aren't we?' She fixed me with a stare.

I nodded.

'They were back on the agenda until the Prime Minister started going on about how most people would be worse off. It's a lie. He and his jet-setting cronies would be worse off. Personal carbon allowances threaten the privilege of those who fund him too. It's a bloody disgrace he wasn't prosecuted for misinformation. His lies may have cost humanity its future.'

Her next words passed me by because I was suddenly sure. That must be the climate policy Robert was talking about. It was Robert who'd decided against prosecuting, saying there wasn't enough evidence. Apparently, politicians lying to the public isn't illegal unless they actively mislead parliament too. It was probably exactly as I'd written in my story. He would surely feel bad about that. He must want to atone and that could affect his thinking. He was a hate figure now, especially when he prosecuted the old environmental protestor after letting the PM off. People didn't accept that just doing his job was enough excuse.

'Are you getting this?' Mel inquired with a sharp tone.

'Sorry, yes.' I came to and paid attention, nodding as she pointed to the bath.

'Imagine with every tonne of carbon dioxide we emit, more hot water is going into that bath and we're boiling ourselves slowly alive.' She found her phone and shoved it in her pocket. 'We used to tie our currency to gold as it was scarce, now carbon is scarce. We should ration carbon dioxide emissions, tie our currency to that.' She stopped abruptly, rubbing her chin. 'No, let's not get carried away. Keep it simple. Stick with personal carbon allowances. We need to switch that hot tap off, and that hot tap is consumption. High-carbon consumption. PCAs will fix that and fast. And we'll hardly notice. Is our wellbeing affected if we take two photos instead of two hundred, or launder at thirty degrees, not sixty? We're lavish and wasteful because we're encouraged to be.'

She snapped down the lid of her laptop.

'There we are, Iris. My top two policies worth killing for. Take your pick.'

Mel stood aside to let me go and locked the door. She set off, then paused and looked back at me.

'Do you know GG well?'

'Just as a colleague.'

'Don't let her play you her music.'

*

Lecture 7 Utilitarianism

Today, we'll consider the moral philosophy of utilitarianism. Unlike Kant's moral theory, it judges the morality of an action by its consequences. Utilitarianism is associated with the eighteenth-century thinker Jeremy Bentham, and nineteenth-century philosopher John Stuart Mill.

Bentham said: 'The greatest good of the greatest number is the foundation of morals and legislation.' In his book, he proposed a 'greatest happiness principle' whereby we should pursue policies and make decisions that will maximise happiness. His ideas were progressive in that they considered everyone's happiness to be of equal worth – a radical concept at the time. It justified the reform of laws that had previously just protected the privileged classes. This approach requires you to consider the harms and benefits to all parties of a variety of options, then choose the one with the highest ratio of happiness to pain for all concerned.

Utilitarianism sounds like a rational and quantifiable means to determine the 'right' thing to do in any situation, but can anyone think of any drawbacks?

Transcription note. I include a point made by the music student in full as it shows how the student's critical thinking ability has matured throughout the course.

Student: What about happiness and pain that has been caused by adverts?

Me: Do you have an example?

Student: Well, my mum was fine until she saw an advert selling security stuff with images of masked men approaching a house at night while the woman sleeps without a clue. Now she's on at my dad to get an alarm system.

Me: OK, go on.

Student: She says she'll be scared until she gets it. But it's expensive. So is the advert ethical, as buying the alarm system will make her happy by relieving her fear? But she wasn't scared until she saw the advert.

The student suddenly lost confidence.

Student: I dunno. Maybe there'd be more pain if she got burgled.

Me: No, you made a relevant point. This is known as preference manipulation. Well done.

I was encouraged by several other thoughtful responses. One asked if animals' happiness counted? Another asked if they

I'm delighted by your insightful comments. These points are all valid criticisms. Yes, it tends towards the end justifies the means approach – but whether that makes it immoral is open to question. Philosophers are perpetually haunted by the ghost of Wittgenstein, who rears his head regularly to claim that most philosophical debates come down to how you define your terms. If you define morality by the greatest happiness of the greatest number, then if the result of someone's misery is more happiness than pain overall, then by definition that is moral.

Transcription note. Zoe raised her hand again to ask whether that means it's right to allow torture if it saves people's lives.

Good point. One issue with this philosophy is that notions such as human rights and justice and moral duty are ignored in favour of maximising net happiness. However, J S Mill adopted a rule-based version which avoids many of these issues. Rule utilitarianism considers the consequences of following a rule of conduct. So, for example, an act of stealing, murder, dishonesty, or tax evasion may lead in particular instances to greater happiness than pain, but if we adopted stealing etc. as a rule of conduct, happiness certainly wouldn't be maximised. In this sense, rule utilitarianism begins to look more like Kant's categorical imperative, even though it's coming from a different place.

Consequentialism was popular with empirical thinkers who didn't like the vagueness of abstract duties or concepts such as human rights, which lack a clear foundation. They liked the utilitarian approach as it enabled a means to ethically assess an action based on its observable consequences. It also appealed to those who prefer to deal with numbers rather than words, as it involves quantifying benefits and harms.

However, you have pointed out some shortcomings of this

approach. The most obvious of which is that utilitarianism may ignore actions that appear to be wrong in themselves. Also, it isn't always possible to know the consequences of any action. Related to this are the questions you have already highlighted. Bentham and Mill may have counted everyone's happiness as equal, but just as we debated in the lecture on human rights, do we count future generations? In a time of climate change, we're more aware than ever before that decisions made now will have far-reaching consequences that cannot be undone once tipping points have passed. As someone once told me, you can philosophise at an iceberg as much as you like, but it will melt at zero degrees Celsius nonetheless.

Another difficulty is that when doing a utilitarian analysis, it's common to only include criteria that are easily quantifiable over less tangible factors. This isn't a shortcoming of the theory itself, but the way it's applied. Bearing all this in mind, consider this ethical dilemma which I took from a TV drama.

An MI5 agent is in the centre of London and gets a call telling him that the man coming out of Piccadilly Circus underground station may have a bomb in his rucksack. He's instructed to take him out. The agent asks how certain is this intelligence and is told that there's a twenty-five percent likelihood that the man is about to detonate a bomb that could kill two thousand people. He must decide quickly. Using a utilitarian analysis, what should the MI5 agent do? Should he kill the man?

Transcription note. One lad shot his hand up to say he should shoot the guy with the rucksack because twenty-five percent of two thousand was five hundred, so using probability theory, he would save more lives than would be lost. Another student said she thought he shouldn't shoot but couldn't say why. I asked if anyone could help her to justify this, considering less tangible consequences of shooting the man. The mouthy lad at the back asked, what if he was an inventor who was about to invent a device that would save thousands of lives? I responded that the point that the agent may be killing someone who could go on to save lots of lives isn't relevant because the same argument applies to all those the bomb (if it exists) may kill. The lad at the back muttered something dismissive.

Consider the less quantifiable consequences of shooting someone in cold blood in the middle of a crowded city. It will be news for a start. Will it be more likely to create fear of our security services or create trust? Currently, the UK is one of the most law-abiding countries. If I see someone building a bomb in the shed next door, or was a witness to a crime, I'd mention it to the police. However, if we see our security services more as threats than protectors, the level of trust breaks down and then who knows where that can lead? Trust is the most intangible of things but one of the most valuable. It can take years to build but moments to destroy. Qualitative consequences of actions may be harder to add up in the conventional way. Those who like everything cut and dried may dismiss them or give up, frustrated by the lack of certainty in assigning them a value. But assign them a value we must.

An example is the way we judge the health of our society using quantifiable criteria such as production and consumption figures. This isn't because these figures measure what's most important, but because they're easy to measure. Many have been calling for the Gross Domestic Product to be abandoned in favour of a wellbeing index..

Let's finish with a quote from presidential candidate Robert F. Kennedy back in 1968, which makes the point:

Too much and for too long, we seemed to have surrendered personal excellence and community values in the mere accumulation of material things. Our Gross National Product is over eight hundred billion dollars a year, but that Gross National Product counts air pollution and cigarette advertising, and ambulances to clear our highways of carnage.

It counts special locks for our doors and the jails for the people who break them. It counts the destruction of the redwood and the loss of our natural wonder in chaotic sprawl.

It counts napalm and counts nuclear warheads and armored cars for the police to fight the riots in our cities. It counts

*

GG arrived late. She joined us with an air of excitement, clutching a sandwich.

Percy looked at her, concerned. 'You look happy GG. What's the matter?'

'I have an idea for research.'

'Go on?' I encouraged.

Her eyes shone. 'It's about music and pain.'

'How music causes pain?' Marcel asked.

'No, how music can redeem pain.'

'Right. Of course.'

'I have a playlist for different kinds of pain,' GG explained eagerly. 'A playlist for disappointment, one for heartbreak, one for—'

'Having too much work,' Marcel suggested.

She shook her head. 'Not that. Do you think I should do one?'

'Definitely.' Marcel twirled his pasta.

GG's head bobbed and her eyebrows jumped up and down as she described her plan, interspersed at intervals with attempts to convey the kind of music she meant – one wouldn't call it singing, more various kinds of wail.

'So essentially you upset people with videos of abattoirs—' Marcel began.

'Thus also promoting veganism—'

'Then you ask them if they feel sad, angry, or guilty, and test out various… can we call it music?'

'Exactly,' GG nodded in agreement.

'You'll need ethical approval for this.' Percy brought her down to earth.

'Could be tricky,' Marcel said.

She looked downcast. I changed the subject.

'Your friend Mel was helpful.'

'Who's that?' asked Marcel.

'A sustainability expert. She suggested some climate policies.'

'For your talk?' Percy inquired.

'My story.'

'You should be working on your inaugural lecture.'

'I'm working on my whodunnit, but the talk will cover that too, so I am indirectly.'

'I thought it was about moral philosophy,' Percy said.

'I'm worried someone will bring up Wittgenstein.'

'So?' Marcel shrugged.

'He said that philosophy is a battle against the bewitchment of our intelligence by means of language.'

Marcel turned his hands up in incomprehension.

'Basically, that all philosophy is just confusion about the meaning of words.'

'Surely someone has refuted his argument?' Percy said.

'Wittgenstein would say it depends on what you mean by "refute." I don't want to take the chance.'

'The audience won't mind about such things,' GG said.

'That's the whole point.' I put down my fork. 'I must show them why moral philosophy matters. That's why couching it in a real murder—'

'A real murder?' Percy raised an eyebrow.

'Um. In the whodunnit,' I said hastily. 'I might talk about justice, too. What does justice mean when the victim isn't a grieving parent, or elderly couple scared to go back to their burgled house but a ninety percent chance that action or inaction in regard to the climate crisis means this many percent of people will die?'

'Good question.' He nodded approvingly.

'I might add that line to my whodunnit.'

'Enough of your whodunnit. We want to know about your talk,' Percy said.

'I could say a bit about the difference between basic human values and those embodied in our societal institutions and what happens when the two conflict.'

He looked interested.

'What gives your life value, Percy?' I asked.

'Upholding academic standards.'

'Don't tell Jenna, she'll make you academic integrity officer,' Marcel warned.

'She wouldn't let me do the job properly.'

'So your values and the values of the institution don't match. How does that make you feel?' I asked.

Percy glowered.

'Dangerous stuff, Chip,' said Marcel. 'I like it.'

'Jenna won't though,' GG said.

'Good,' Marcel said. 'I'm looking forward to it already.'

'Joking aside,' said Percy. 'You need to take the talk seriously.'

'Why is it so important?' I asked.

They all spoke at once.

'So you bring money in and I don't get made redundant.'

'To make the case for the humanities.'

'To annoy Colin.'

'What's it got to do with him?' I asked.

'He got his hopes up when Jenna made him Assistant Dean, but she only did that so she could slope off in term time,' Percy said.

'She's off to the Maldives.' Marcel threw his hands up in disgust.

'But no one's asking him to do a talk,' Percy said.

'Because we all know he'd be useless.' Marcel said. 'The better yours is, the more he'll hate it.'

'These external-facing events are a big deal.'

'Especially if they don't go well.' Marcel carefully avoided looking at GG.

'So take a break from your whodunnit, and work on your

talk,' Percy said.

I saluted. 'Sir, yes sir.'

He didn't look amused.

*

Murder in the Citizens' Jury #16: The Morning of the Murder

There was one file of unseen footage left – lunchtime on the day of the murder. Richard had so far stuck to his decision to watch events unfold in order. He was sorely tempted to watch, but motivation was about cause and effect. He wasn't going to cut corners on his last case. With reluctance, he shut down the lunchtime footage and opened the CCTV recording from the morning of the murder.

Chairs scraped and everyone talked over each other as they all sat around the table. Eventually, the hubbub died down and Sarah took charge.

SARAH: We must cover personal carbon allowances.

STEVE: PCAs are out.

Naomi loosens her blouse to get some air in.

SARAH: Naomi, you look worried. Any thoughts?

BEN: You liked the library of things idea, didn't you?

Naomi looks doubtful.

STEVE: You fancied the gold card option, didn't you, love, where you could borrow yachts and such?

Richard sat up at the endearment and rewound to check Naomi's reaction. Her face was obscured by Ben leaning forward to pour some water, but he noted that she'd let it pass without comment.

STEVE: We see alike on these matters.

NAOMI: *(sighs)* But realistically, it wouldn't get to that level.

JOSH: I like the repair bill.

NEEDLES: Me too.

STEVE: Aren't you supposed to just knit?

JOSH: Didn't you like the repair one, Naomi? You talked about repairing the radio during the blackout. It's satisfying fixing stuff, isn't it?

NAOMI: It was, but I know I wouldn't have done it if I didn't have to. I'd just buy something new.

STEVE: If demand-led buses get proper support and take off, the private sector will get involved and do smart buses, they won't be grubby.

NAOMI: They'll only get high demand if people give up their cars and no one's going to do that.

NEEDLES: Naomi doesn't like anything.

NAOMI: Why does everyone make me the bad guy? I only say what you all think.

SARAH: First, we need to go back to personal carbon allowances, then we'll make our final decision.

STEVE: We already have voluntary carbon offsets and they're just an extra business cost. On-demand buses will be good for business. Workers can get to my farm for a start.

DEVANIKA: For God's sake! Let Sarah tell us about personal carbon allowances so we can get on.

Steve sits back and waves at Sarah to continue.
Naomi dabs her face with a tissue.

SARAH: The idea—

NAOMI: There should be air con!

SARAH: The idea is that Government sets a personal and
      equal cap on emissions so everyone would receive the
      same carbon allowance. Once your allowance runs out,
      consumption would become more expensive. Those who
      don't use up their allowance can sell their remainder
      on the personal carbon market. This proposal is also
      referred to as personal carbon trading.

The click-clack of knitting echoes each statement.

SARAH: This encourages people to reduce their carbon
      footprint. For example, by flying less or using energy-
      efficient transport. It also benefits less well off or
      greener people.

BEN: How?

ANDREW: It's been calculated that seventy-one percent
      of low-income households would be better off under
      personal carbon allowances.

JOSH: Yay!

*Josh goes to high five Ben, but his hand falls back in his lap
when Ben ignores him.*

BEN: What about kids?

SARAH: Just like money, you get extra, like you do with child
      benefit and the disability allowance. If you vote for
      PCAs, a follow-up citizens' jury will decide the details.

STEVE: How will it affect high-income households?

SARAH: It's likely that you'd need to pay more than you
      usually would, depending on how much you went over your
      allowance. It acts as a progressive form of taxation on
      high-carbon consumption.

Steve shakes his head.

JOSH: I didn't get personal carbon trading.

SARAH: It's another term, that's all. Let's recap. There are
      a few different versions of the idea, but basically, the

Government gives everyone a...

NEEDLES: A ration, like during the war.

SARAH: Yes, just as in wartime, we ration what's scarce. In this climate emergency, we ration carbon emissions. Everyone gets an equal allowance of how much carbon they're allowed to produce. If you go under, you can sell your remaining carbon credits on the open market. That's the trading part.

Josh puts his hand up.

JOSH: What do you mean by producing carbon?

SARAH: Your purchases will come with a carbon footprint. So if you consume seasonal vegetables you'll produce fewer carbon emissions than if you eat beef, for example.

Josh nods.

BEN: My kids won't eat vegetables. Millie just likes beefburgers. The kids are too stressy to get on a bus.

DEVANIKA: Stop moaning about your children! You're lucky to have them!

BEN: I don't ever stop, and it's still not enough! This is the first break I've had since they were born. You lot swan around saying, 'I'll pay my carbon offset' or 'I might jump on a bus,' as if it's not a ton of hassle. And there's Josh (*Ben mimics Josh's slow drawl*), 'I'll just take time out from strumming my guitar to have a little tinker and repair something.' (*back in his own voice, shouting*) Why the hell should I? Why?

DEVANIKA: Leave him alone. Doing nothing is better for the planet than actively destroying it!

Devanika looks at Steve pointedly.

STEVE: Don't bloody start on me again!

Andrew moves to a whiteboard, which has columns and figures on it.

ANDREW: The key thing is that none of the other policies we've discussed work on their own. None got anywhere near one percent take-up. All together, they struggle to save a million tonnes. But, with personal carbon allowances and the financial incentive on us all to stay below our allowances, take-up on all of these things would shoot up. For example, fewer people would run their own car.

Andrew writes on the board. The pen squeaks as the numbers by demand-led buses go up from five million to forty million tonnes.

STEVE: Wake up, people! They'll start the PCA low and then tighten it like a screw.

ANDREW: In the second stage, embedded carbon would be included, increasing the advantages of borrowing and repair over buying new.

NAOMI: Surely not that many people would go to libraries?

SARAH: It's not just libraries. As buying new goods uses up carbon allowances, department stores would swap their toy, fashion and games departments for subscription services. You'd be more likely to buy your dad a year's membership to the sports department than a new set of golf clubs.

Andrew writes on the board. The numbers for repair cafes and libraries of things increase from five million tonnes each to sixty million each.

SARAH: There would be apps developing and expanding, like there are already, to swap fashion and games. You'd borrow and return.

JOSH: An Amazon of borrowing?

SARAH: Maybe.

Steve taps the table impatiently.

ANDREW: We estimate an additional sixty million tonnes for

the spillover effects as there'd be increased incentives towards home insulation, businesses would invest in low-carbon technology and so on. Altogether we can save as much as...

Andrew writes the figure.
The jurors look startled. Sarah smiles.

ANDREW: 220 million tonnes.

Josh whistles through his teeth.

BEN: Oh my God! It's the only thing that will get us there.

Richard observed their expressions – inquiring, concerned, hopeful, calculating. Steve's face was grim.

STEVE: It's bureaucratic and costly.

NEEDLES: So what if it's necessary? That's what Churchill said, weren't it? We gotta do what's necessary.

STEVE: Forget it.

DEVANIKA: You're not going to let him get away with this, are you?

SARAH: No.

Chapter 17

Dear Iris

Please can you provide some content we can send out to our comms team to promote your talk. This is what they've suggested so far:

'Professor Iris Tate, known for her groundbreaking and impactful work on ethical dilemmas in self-driving cars, will give an inaugural lecture on moral philosophy. She will present her innovative storytelling approach to teaching and learning.'

Feel free to add more details. The comms team are keen to get it in this month's alumni magazine, so please let us know by the end of the day.

Kind regards
Jenna

Dear Jenna,
Thanks. The blurb suggested is fine by me.
Kind regards
Iris

My response was rushed, as I'd just seen an email by Robert, marked urgent. I took a deep breath and opened it.

Dear Iris,
Despite having asked several times, I still have not received any of the readings or dilemmas you gave to your students. I must insist that you send me something straightaway.
Kind regards

Robert Ash
Director of Public Prosecutions

It was just as I'd feared. This was tricky.

> *Dear Robert,*
>
> *I confess that I haven't sent you the readings for a reason. Possibly I've done you a disservice in not trusting you with a full explanation. Further discussion would be better served in a phone conversation. Please call me when you are able.*
>
> *Kind regards*
> *Iris Tate*
> *Professor of Moral Philosophy*

I looked back over the readings while I waited for his call. I was still rehearsing my arguments when he rang.

His first words were promising, even if the curt tone wasn't. 'I'm listening.'

'As you yourself said in an earlier email, we both want a considered answer from the students, and we all want to do the right thing.'

'Go on.' His voice was tinged with suspicion.

'My worry was that you would be concerned that the readings were too close to reality. That you'd, er, flare up at any references to your private life.'

'Private life!' he barked.

'You're proving my point, I'm afraid.'

I heard a sharp intake of breath. Best not push my luck. I hurried on. 'Look, I know little about your backstory, but I had to make Richard a man the students could relate to. He has to be more than his job.'

'Richard?'

I squirmed. No point holding back now. 'Richard Beech.'

'For God's sake—'

'I know, but if you hear me out, you'll understand the necessity. I know from experience that students respond differently to dilemmas they believe are real. If they think of it as purely hypothetical, all they'd care about is getting good marks.'

He interrupted, 'I insisted on confidentiality.'

'I know, and if I can't tell them it's real, then the best I can do is to induce a sense of narrative transportation.'

'What?'

'That's when readers identify with the characters and feel their emotions and thoughts as their own. Here they need to identify with you, so the compromise I made was to make Richard's situation analogous to your own to create a sense of reality.'

'How analogous?'

I hesitated.

'Look, if I hit upon the actual climate policy, it was completely by accident, and the rest is in the public domain.'

'What climate policy?'

'Personal carbon allowances.' I held my breath waiting for the response.

'And the rest – the bits in the public domain.'

I winced as I told him. 'Well, er, prosecuting the old protestor and not prosecuting the PM, that kind of thing.'

'Oh.' His voice was flat. 'Iris, I understand what you're saying to me. Rather than explaining any further, I'd like to see the readings.'

'Which ones – there's a lot.'

'The remaining ones.'

'They won't make sense out of context, and I haven't written them all yet.'

'Just the next one then and the associated dilemma.'

'It's not the best one—'

'Can you just send it please.'

'Yes of course. Just give me a day to polish it up.'

'I'd like it now as is.'

'Right.'

He rang off. The call had gone as well as I could have expected, although he was a hard man to read. There had been little reaction to the mention of personal carbon allowances. It wasn't what I was using for the ultimate dilemma anyway. Perhaps I should have said that. Either way, I was confident I'd done the policy justice.

Murder in the Citizens' Jury #17: The Day of the Murder

The footage begins with a babble of talk and noise of scraping chairs as everyone takes their places at the oval table. The jurors look hot. Sarah in particular looks flustered. Naomi looks troubled. Josh is breathing hard and wiping his brow. Even the ever-calm Andrew looks on edge. It took a while before Richard could distinguish specific voices.

SARAH: We're running out of time. We must decide!

STEVE: I made my decision.

DEVANIKA: You're not in charge.

BEN: I thought we decided on personal carbon allowances.

> *Needles, Devanika and Josh nod. Naomi is looking down at her feet. She seems subdued.*

STEVE: The trouble with personal carbon allowances is that the drop in consumption will cause a recession, people will protest and we'll be rushing back to normal as fast as we can.

ANDREW: That's because a recession is defined as a drop in the gross domestic product – that is, retail sales and manufacturing go down. Let's do a thought experiment. Imagine everyone could get access to what they want without having to buy anything new, so they didn't need to work so hard. Wellbeing has gone up, but GDP – gross domestic product has gone down. Recession is just a word. Does it matter if consumption has gone down if wellbeing has gone up?

BEN: Then why is everyone chasing economic growth?

ANDREW: Short-term thinking and habit.

SARAH: Our last citizens' jury decided that switching from
        the GDP as our key metric of success to a wellbeing index
        was a crucial climate solution. Then we could change the
        conversation from what's good for the economy to what's
        good for us. The assumption that they're the same thing
        no longer holds up. Unfortunately, back then, citizens'
        juries had no actual power.

STEVE: What about jobs?

Richard paused the recording. There was something
different in the dynamic that he couldn't put his finger on.
The image frozen on the screen showed Steve sitting back in
his chair, arrogant, smug, legs wide apart. Strange when he
seemed to be losing the argument. Naomi's hair was out of
place – unusual for her. Her lipstick was smeared. He'd missed
something.
    The lunchtime footage! How could he have forgotten?
He knew why. He'd been distracted. His thoughts kept
returning to the family dinner last night. The old protestor
had recovered, and his daughter had forgiven him enough to
join him and Marnie for dinner. Laura had been excited about
the citizens' juries. Once the trial period was up, there'd be a
referendum, and everyone expected that they'd form part of a
new constitution – a House of Citizens to replace the House of
Lords. 'Then,' Laura had said, 'we'll try for a baby.'
    'You having children depends on citizens' juries?' he'd asked
her.
    'There's no way those in charge will ever prioritise the
climate,' she'd said. 'I can't bring kids into that world. But
there's only two months to go. Nothing can go wrong now.'
    No one yet knew about the murder. He'd thought his heart
would break.
    'Why are you looking sad?' she'd asked. 'I thought you were
looking forward to being a grandad?'
    'More than anything,' he'd said.

    Richard switched to the final lunchtime recording. The

excitement was now gone, but he still had his job to do. He loaded it up and listened. Naomi appeared to be on the phone.

NAOMI: It's just some appliances. Thanks for signing for them.

Naomi fans herself with an empty plate.

NAOMI: I miss the ice dispenser at home (beat). Did you see my new fridge? Great, isn't it? I had to get a new toaster and kettle to match the platinum finish.

Sarah is visible entering the door. She looks towards Naomi and frowns, then walks out of shot.

NAOMI: Whoops. Better go, we're not supposed to use our phone. Bye.

Ben passes briefly in front of the camera, heading towards Naomi.

BEN: That's how I recognise you!

NAOMI: What?

BEN: I deliver to you all the time. And you never say hello.

NAOMI: Sorry...if I stopped to chat to every delivery driver (pause) Anyway...

BEN: You know we must decide soon, don't you? The amount of stuff you've got, you've got to like the Library of Things.

NAOMI: My stuff is new.

BEN: Imagine if you could clear out everything you only use now and then, but get access to it anytime you want? You take your life in your hands opening our cupboard at home. It's crammed full. Bike rack, kids' toys, an easel from Millie's painting phase, breadmaker we don't like to throw away, tools right at the back somewhere we can't get to.

Steve saunters in, looks towards Naomi and winks. He heads towards them. There's a muddle of conversation hard to decipher. Ben passes in front of the camera as he walks away looking snubbed.

NAOMI: Thanks for rescuing me. He was on about his kids again.

STEVE: What's your situation? I bet you have a boyfriend.

NAOMI: We split up. I caught him... well, anyway, I was glad in the end. He took up too much space. Always complaining about my shopping, but it wasn't his money.

STEVE: You earn a fortune in marketing, I bet. So what if you can afford it!

NAOMI: Er yes.

STEVE: Why shouldn't you treat yourself?

NAOMI: Exactly. Now he's gone, my sister can finally come visit, although the spare room is still full of stuff. I had three books on minimalism delivered last week.

Steve guffaws.

STEVE: Three books on minimalism – that's funny. You're witty.

Naomi laughs politely, sounding uncertain.

NAOMI: How about you?

STEVE: I'm up for grabs.

NAOMI: Oh yes?

STEVE: Come with me.

NAOMI: What? Where?

STEVE: You'll see.

They pass briefly in front of the camera, Steve walking behind Naomi. His hand is on her lower back, pushing her through the door. The clock shows this was one fifteen – fifteen minutes before the next session started. Naomi looks excited. Happy.

Richard returned to the footage on the afternoon of the murder. Twenty minutes later, they're sitting around the oval table again. Steve, for once, is paying her no attention, but he looks pleased with himself. Naomi is sitting as far away from him as she can. She looks like a deflated balloon.

*

I read it through then lost my nerve. The first bit was too close to home. I couldn't remember exactly what Robert had told me during our last conversation, but I knew it had inspired some ideas for Richard's backstory. I cut the first section and sent the final part which mentioned nothing about his family.

> *Dear Robert,*
>
> *Please find attached the next reading and associated class. Hopefully you'll get a sense of how I link the plot line to various elements of the dilemma. Here we focus on the question of private justice. I know that's not the actual issue, but it allows students to practice dealing with dilemmas they can relate to. I'm also setting up motives for the characters. I didn't say, but I've framed it as a murder mystery to keep the students interested. I know for you, the 'whodunnit' element isn't of interest as you already know, but I'm sure you'll agree that keeping the students engaged is essential in our endeavour.*
>
> *Kind regards*
> *Iris Tate*
> *Professor of Moral Philosophy*

ATTACHMENT Class exercise. Ethics of Private Justice

If you'd have asked Naomi if she'd be up for having sex with Steve, she'd have hedged a bit. A shrug, maybe a slight smile giving away the answer might just be yes in the right circumstances. If you asked her if she wanted to be taken roughly in the accessible toilets, it would have been a resounding no. She'd want to be wined and dined and embraced in those strong arms, enveloped in the smell of his expensive aftershave, cherished and then perhaps, if the vibes remained positive, yes. Despite this, Naomi would never class what happened as rape. An ugly word describing something that wouldn't happen to someone like her. Naomi had style. Her makeup, her clothes with the flattering cut, the shiny hair and elegant jewellery was her armour, her attractiveness was her power. For someone to ride roughshod over all that and just take what he wanted cast her in a role of victim. This isn't how she liked to see herself. Instead, she berated herself for being weak for not shouting out. But who'd want to be caught like that? It was embarrassing mostly. So she put it out of her mind. The memory showed only in the sag of her mouth, the stray hair she didn't bother to smooth back, the slump in her posture.

So there we have it. Steve forced himself on Naomi in the toilets. No witnesses – his word against hers. I think most of us would like to see justice – maybe out of sympathy for Naomi, or to teach Steve a lesson. But she wouldn't take it to court. To report it to the police would cause further humiliation without achieving a conviction. This is no criticism of our legal system. It's proper that one shouldn't be convicted based on a single person's testimony. People lie, after all. There's no obvious motive for Naomi to lie, but a good defence attorney could surely find one if they looked hard enough. Had she been disappointed in love? Had she a gripe against married men who had sex with her even consensually? Yes. But does that mean Steve should get away with it?

If it was Naomi, can we truly blame her? Of course we can, and we should. Perhaps we could forgive a less final retribution – let down tyres or smashed windows or trash his reputation online perhaps? Murder takes it too far. But there's only so much that the legal system can do. She can't expect anyone else to know for sure in the way she can, so is there a case for private justice?

Debate.

Chapter 18

Dear Iris
I read in the alumni magazine that you're giving a talk on moral philosophy and will discuss "the innovative technique of storytelling". I wonder that you have not first consulted me on this. Please send me an outline of your talk so I can check you haven't revealed anything you shouldn't.
Kind regards
Robert Ash
Director of Public Prosecutions

Probably I should be pleased he hadn't mentioned the story extract and activity. I'd been worried he'd think they were too tangential to his dilemma. Still, rather than relief, I felt aggrieved. Surely some appreciation of the work I'd put in was due. A mention at least of the creativity of the approach. I reminded myself that he was a stressed Director of Public Prosecutions who probably hated fiction —especially murder mysteries. I'd planned to read an extract at my talk, but perhaps best not.

Dear Robert
I'm sorry you heard about my talk this way. I recall being asked to send off some blurb, but writing the whodunnit has taken all my spare time and I've had little left for anything else other than teaching and marking. I admit to having some unread emails, so it's possible I missed correspondence concerning my talk, as currently it's not top priority. I don't yet have an outline, but I'll be talking in general terms, and you need not worry that I'll

I heard a knock on the door and looked up. It was Colin.

'Can I help you?' I asked.

'You didn't respond to my email.' He looked around at the room, his lip curling. 'And I wanted to see for myself.'

'See what?'

'A student complained she felt uncomfortable visiting your office because of the state it was in.'

I surreptitiously swept crumbs under some papers. 'I admit it needs a tidy up, but I'm so busy—'

'With what? We gave you a light teaching load. There's been no consultancy…'

'Didn't you see my research notes? I also uploaded transcription notes that link to lecture recordings so you can see how I'm innovating in education entertainment. It will be a groundbreaking paper.'

'You must also answer emails and maintain a tidy space.'

'I'll donate some of my books to the library,' I said to show willing.

'We're reallocating the space. It will all be virtual soon.'

I gasped. 'But what if the internet goes down, or there's a power cut? What if you like real books?'

'It's not the most efficient use of space.'

'As a society, we continuously prioritise efficiency over resilience. Another example of short-term—'

'Save it for your talk.' Colin turned on his heel and left the room, leaving a faint smell of watermelon shampoo.

I pulled out an untouched crate that I'd shoved under my desk and took out a batch of files from my research on self-driving cars. I'd really cared about it back then. I threw them in the bin. We worry about these marginal trade-offs, when the real fear is that we'll be playing on our phones in the back seat while forces out of our control steer us to our doom.

Next in the crate was Hannah Arendt's book, *The Banality of*

Evil. She'd been pilloried for saying people who do bad things are often very ordinary. They just get caught up in a particular belief system. The less they question it, the more highly rewarded they are. The 'evil' consequences arise more from failing to reflect on what it means for others rather than any specific malice. This is why moral philosophy is so important, I tell my boys in my head. It makes us reflect.

I removed Edmund Burke from the shelf. Another eighteenth-century man in a white wig. He's famous for the quote, "The only thing necessary for evil to triumph is for good men to do nothing." He never actually said that. Anyway, terms such as "evil" get in the way, making us think it's a few rotten apples when it's the system at fault. I put him in a discard pile and place Hannah Arendt in his place. Next up is *After Virtue* by MacIntyre, reminding us we must also take personal responsibility. It can backfire if you expect people to be nicer than they are, but virtues such as courage, honesty, and justice will grow if nurtured. Without them, no society can thrive for long. We must build moral muscle in ourselves, our children and in society.

I looked at the family chat. Nothing. Of course there wouldn't be. It was down to me to make the first move. I availed myself of the invitation by the new AI assistant that had magically appeared on my phone and dictated my message.

> *Hi boys. I'm sorry if I upset you or Martha. Please let her know that I'm not judging. We're all complicit in destroying our environment. It's not just evil oil executives. They're not off the hook, but they're responding to the market. It's those who encourage us to consume more than we need. Martha is on the front line of that. And if you don't understand that after what happened, well, erm. I'd like to see you all again. It doesn't have to be games. I know it's not the same now. Love you. Mum xx*

I read what I'd written. The AI assistant had done well, but last time I'd sent a text longer than two lines, it came back as TLDR. I'd looked it up and found it meant 'too long, didn't read.' A reminder came up my lecture was due to start. I deleted everything after the first line, sent it and rushed off.

*

Lecture 8 Relativism

I'll begin this lecture by asking you to consider whether we can definitively talk about right or wrong, or is it all relative? Moral absolutism claims there are universally applicable moral laws, and right and wrong are objective qualities that can be rationally determined. Kant's categorical imperative would fall into this school of thought. Absolutists point to evidence that beliefs about fairness and justice are hard-wired into us as a species.

Ethical relativism, on the other hand, claims that morality is context-dependent and subjective. Relativists argue it's arrogant to judge the conduct of people from other cultures that are different to our own. The observation that practices that harm no one, such as same-sex marriage, are considered wrong by certain groups, provides evidence for the relativist position. The absolutist might counter-argue that such judgements are due to prejudice, ignorance or fear, and are personal preferences rather than moral positions. Moral nihilists claim that nothing can be said to be right or wrong in any sense.

Debate amongst yourselves – is morality whatever anyone thinks it is or are there universal values that transcend culture? Think of examples to support your view.

Transcription note. A debate about the ancient Indian practice of sati, where wives were thrown onto the funeral pyre when their husbands died, got out of hand. Terms such as misogyny and colonialism and cultural imperialism were thrown around like weapons. Zoe looked ready to cry, so I stepped in.

When we look at practices in other cultures that seem to us to be wrong, we can claim that our practices are morally superior, which smacks of cultural imperialism. Alternatively, one can say that morality is relative, which can lead to moral nihilism or amorality. However, you usually find that the core values are similar. What differs is the practical context and belief system. For example, we consider ritualistic killings as barbaric, but they may have been driven by values such as love and fidelity due to different beliefs pertaining to the afterlife.

Transcription note. I was pleased with how I'd handled that, but it turned out I'd missed the point. Zoe had come under attack for using the old British term Suttee, rather than the Indian term Sati. I wondered whether to bring in Wittgenstein, but felt we'd be out of our depth and moved on quickly.

In the previous lecture, we discussed utilitarianism – the philosophy that judges the morality of actions by their consequences. It seems on the surface to be relativist in the sense that actions may give rise to different consequences in different circumstances, yet it offers a single guiding principle that can be applied to any context. It advocates that the right action is the one that leads to the greatest ratio of good to harm for all those affected. We practiced adopting this rule of thumb in a few dilemmas, so your next assignment is to apply it to the scenario unfolding in *Murder in the Citizens' Jury*.

We know Steve is soon to be murdered. He's the only person standing in the way of a policy that could avert a climate crisis. Is it morally justifiable to kill Steve to ensure the policy gets through based on the principle of the greatest happiness of the greatest number?

Discuss among yourselves for five minutes. You don't have to have decided in that time but share your thought processes so we can get a sense of the pros and cons of such an approach.

Transcription note. I wandered the aisles, collecting questions. I was reassured that most of them were relevant. However, many students were uncomfortable with an assignment that had no clear right answer. They wanted me to give them so much guidance that they didn't have to risk thinking for themselves. I represent the gist of the conversation with the lads at the back to illustrate:

Me: How are you getting on?

Mouthy lad: We've given up.

Me: That's a shame. Why?

Mouthy lad: It's stupid because how could you ever know all the consequences?

Me: Are you saying that lack of perfect knowledge renders the approach worthless?

Mouthy lad: You said philosophy is like maths – like precise.

Me: Even maths allows for margins of error.

Other lad: But we don't know everything. Like, will the murder be discovered?

Me: I don't know.

Mouthy lad: But how can we get the answer right?

Other lad: Yeah. With this utility rule, you get a different answer than if you follow Kant's law.

Me: There's no law that applies in every single situation. If you find one, then you've proved me right as the law that there's no law is in itself a law!

I waited in vain for a smile. Wittgenstein would have found it hilarious.

Mouthy lad: But like with the MI5 agent last week, you said consequences would be different if they were publicised than if they weren't, loss of trust and all that.

Me: What do you think happens if you cover it up?

Mouthy lad: No one knows so you get away with it.

Me: Transparent processes protect organisations and institutions against temptations to illegal actions. The moment you cover something up, you risk creating a culture of secrecy. Under such a culture, other illegal acts can more easily occur.

Mouthy lad: Everything I say, you like say it's rubbish.

Me: Sorry. It's the dialectic – the Socratic form of argument. You subject an argument to interrogation.

Mouthy lad: It's annoying.

Me: Yes, it's probably why Socrates was killed.

Mouthy lad: Was he?

Me: Poisoned. But don't get ideas.

Laughter.

[To the class] Some of you made the valid point that one cannot know all the consequences. Generally, even rough approximations and estimates can give you answers that are in the right order of magnitude. Look up 'back of the envelope' or Fermi calculations for examples.

Some are getting frustrated with answers that may seem 'woolly'. Many of us are drawn to theories, thinkers, and leaders who offer us a sense of certainty. But don't mistake certainty for wisdom – indeed, there's a negative correlation. Those who talk as if there's a clear answer to everything are most likely to be talking rubbish. Attractive rubbish – but nothing that can stand up to critical scrutiny.

If you want a perfect world, you'll be perpetually disappointed. I like to think that if there were a God, then he/she/they must like to mess with our heads – keep things off kilter. Or perhaps it's only when things aren't quite aligned that you get dynamism in the system – the stuff of life. I advise you to embrace a little fuzziness.

[ref. interdisciplinarity] Look at the duckbilled platypus, for example, a mammal with a beak that laid eggs confused the biologists' neat categories.

But don't go to the other extreme and say that because there's no perfect certainty everything is equally good or equally bad. Like the Buddha said, seek the middle way.

It's not always a case of right or wrong, but trade-offs in values. For example, a business can please its customers with low prices, but this may mean exploitative wages for employees and less profit for suppliers. Sometimes, two values are in conflict. In lecture three, we debated the trade-off between freedom and liberty. What's 'right' is a moving goalpost – it changes with the context. But the principles used to help you make the moral decision remain firm. I've shown you the ones that have stood the test of time. These moral theories are tools to help guide your thinking, but they're simply that – tools. You still have to do the thinking.

*

Essay question: With reference to utilitarian theory, is it morally justifiable to kill Steve to ensure the policy of personal carbon allowances gets through based on the principle of the greatest happiness of the greatest number? Do you get a different conclusion using other moral theories we have covered?

Guidance notes: Feel free to look up extra sources on personal carbon allowances, often referred to as personal carbon trading. Please finish with a reflection on the decision you came to and your thoughts about it.

*

My colleagues were already eating when I arrived. I gave up on the queue for hot food and grabbed a sandwich.

'Sorry I'm late. The students had questions about the assignment.'

'GG's got a new boyfriend,' Marcel said.

'Boyfriend?'

'This is what happens when you lock yourself away. You miss the gossip.'

'How did you meet?' I asked.

'In the supermarket,' GG replied.

'He caught her messing with his stuff in his trolley.' Percy dipped his bread into his gravy.

'I swapped his tuna for dolphin-friendly tuna.'

'You're lucky he didn't report you,' Percy said.

'He took me to a SeaWorld protest on our first date.'

'Sounds like a match made in heaven,' Marcel said.

'What's he like?' I asked.

'Handsome, charming.' She frowned at her bean chilli as if suspecting it of containing meat.

'Sorry to hear that,' Marcel said, scooping up his risotto.

'We'll see how it goes.'

'How's your music and pain research going?' I asked.

'The ethics committee want me to review the design of the study.' She looked downcast.

'Bit unreasonable isn't it?' Marcel said. 'Not wanting you to inflict pain, then cure it – or not – with your playlist.'

'It sounds bad when you put it like that.'

'You could play them happy music instead,' I suggested. 'A bit of salsa always cheers me up.'

'Take this seriously,' Marcel admonished.

But unlike Percy and Marcel, I wasn't taking the mick. I saw how much she cared.

'What's kept you so busy?' Percy asked me, pushing his plate away and leaning back.

'The final assignment. I'm concerned that they'll focus on what they think will get them good marks rather than the dilemma.'

'Of course they will,' Marcel said.

'Don't you worry about it?'

'I teach genocide. As long as they don't think it's a how-to manual,' he laughed.

'It's not funny. With the climate crisis, you should teach students about community responses to disasters rather than genocide.'

'I agree,' said GG. 'Giving baddies all the fame is like rewarding bad behaviour.'

'Exactly! How many films and books are there about Henry VIII and Hitler who were complete bastards compared to people like Florence Nightingale or Nelson Mandela?'

'It's all about war and nothing about peace.'

'I can't think of one film about overthrowing apartheid or how we set up the NHS.'

Marcel clutched Percy's arm. 'The women are ganging up on us.'

'Kate's the same,' he replied.

'It matters what the students learn,' I cried, annoyed by their amused expressions. 'When someone is a surgeon or a heating engineer and some valve has burst – I don't know – a heart valve, I'd want that person to know their stuff.'

'I teach English,' Percy said. 'It's troubling when they mix up "their' and "there", but it's not the end of the world.'

'But it is!' I cried before I could help myself.

Marcel and Percy exchanged looks. They thought I was

being grandiose. I longed to confide in them. At least then they'd understand. Or would they? Perhaps they'd be like Fay.

Everyone had finished eating except for me. I pushed my sandwich away and stood up.

'We can wait if you're not done?' GG offered.

'I've got to tidy my office,' I said, forcing a smile.

I sensed her eyes on my back as I led the way out.

*

I rushed back to my room, feeling like I'd explode with the effort of keeping it all in. I wondered if I could now confide in Robert. Probably not, but the last lecture was innocuous enough. I sent him the transcript and essay assignment so he could see how I was building up to the ultimate dilemma. Hopefully that will keep him happy, and he won't ask for any more readings. Possibly I'd been foolish there, but I wasn't going to risk messing up the rest of my story because of tedious liability issues.

I checked the family chat. Still nothing. They wouldn't engage with the dilemma anyway. I needed Fay for that. Without her, my philosophical observations were jarring. They'd get defensive. *Mum's lecturing us again. We're not your students.*

I returned to unpacking. The next book in the crate was another Kant – *Critique of Pure Reason*. If I hadn't read it by now, I never would. It went on the discard pile. He's the one giving me grief for not going through the ethics committee. He must understand about the greater good, but it doesn't fit his neat little box called 'duty', so he judges it 'wrong.' But I can't get the answer because I know it has real life consequences. If I tell the students, it will mess them up too. I have a duty to them as well. I know it sounds like I'm rationalising, but we only have to watch that when we have vested interests that can lead to self-deception. I can't see any here. Well, I suppose I'm keener than the average person to make a difference in terms of climate action. That's to be expected. It's not like I have a saviour complex as everyone seems to think. It's not about ego, for God's sake.

At the bottom of the crate was a framed photo. My throat constricted. I didn't need to turn it over to know what I'd see.

Lee on his bike about to set off on one of his epic challenges. It had been Fay who'd taken the call. Lee had gone cycling on the hottest day of the year – tried to take on the South Downs way. It was a heart attack. Very sudden. That's when the photo had gone in the drawer.

I steeled myself and turned it over, and his face was so familiar. The warm tug of knowing here was someone I loved. Who loved me. Who'd teased me, taught me, supported me. He's looking me straight in the eye. He wants to know about Fay. I know you liked her, I say. But she hurt your little sis. She accused me of killing the messenger. You don't have to stay with me out of pity, I said. She said I should do what I like, change job, whatever, if that's what it took to cheer up. My brother is six months in his grave, and I'm being told to cheer up. I accused her of wanting me to be happy. If she died, people would be sympathetic. I'd be allowed to be miserable for years.

I tried placing the photo on my desk, but I couldn't bear it. I placed it in my drawer and picked up my phone.

Me: Hi boys. To make amends for last time, would you like to come over for Sunday lunch? Martha too.

I put on Fay's favourite song and wept for the three minutes it took to play.

Murder in the Citizens' Jury #18: The Afternoon of the Murder

Richard fast-forwarded to the point he'd left off before. With his new suspicions about Steve, he felt even less desire to solve the crime. Not that he was any closer – the number of suspects was growing with each bit of footage.

STEVE: What about jobs?

ANDREW: You said yourself, personal carbon allowances generate bureaucracy – there'll be no shortage of work, and repairing stuff takes time.

JOSH: I'd volunteer at a repair cafe.

Andrew smiles at him.

ANDREW: They'd be doing well under PCAs. They could afford to pay you.

JOSH: Nah, too much pressure if I'm employed. Anyway, I'd get lots of dosh from selling my spare carbon credits.

They all stop and smile at each other – except for Steve. Needles hums the tune from John Lennon's Imagine as she knits.

DEVANIKA: Is that John Lennon?

NEEDLES: I met 'im once at a peace rally. I was part of the Knittas for Justice group.

BEN: Never!

SARAH: What was he like?

NEEDLES: Lovely. Broke my heart when he got shot.

DEVANIKA: My grandmother was in the crowd when Gandhi got shot.

BEN: It's always the nice guys that get assassinated.

NEEDLES: Lincoln.

DEVANIKA: Malcolm X.

NAOMI: What was he in, the X Factor?

Sarah interrupts Devanika's mocking laugh.

SARAH: Naomi, you were right!

Naomi looks up, surprised.

NAOMI: I was?

SARAH: We need to be more positive. Yes, Lincoln got shot, but they overturned slavery in the end. When you look at history, there are positive tipping points too.

NEEDLES: I remember when the NHS and the welfare state came in. Changed things overnight.

SARAH: Exactly. For years I've been tearing my hair out waiting for change that never came and suddenly, it's happening. This citizens' jury is a tipping point in the right direction for once. Personal carbon allowances – finally a policy that will be truly transformative.

Needles starts humming again.

NEEDLES: Da, da, da...

Devanika joins in, then Josh, then Ben and Naomi and Sarah. They add words as Needles hums.

ALL EXCEPT STEVE: Imagine there's no...

They all sing their own variations simultaneously:

DEVANIKA: Countries

SARAH: Politicians

JOSH AND NAOMI: Da da...

BEN AND ANDREW: Hmm hmm...

Needles keeps the hum going.

Steve's face is stony.
Josh stands up and pretends to be the conductor and orchestrates them. Then, as it reaches the chorus, they sing the same words in unison.

ALL: Imagine all the people, sharing all the world!

Everyone bursts out laughing and clapping. Steve slams his hand down on the table, shocking everyone into silence.

STEVE: You're a bunch of hypocrites. Dev's on the moral high ground the whole bloody time, but she's not giving up her car.

DEVANIKA: I use the ride-share app.

STEVE: Josh's a parasite who needs people like me to work and keep the economy going so he can scrounge! Ben is just a seething mass of resentment. Naomi, we both know you're not such a good girl, don't we?

Naomi looks down, distraught.

STEVE: And Andrew – you're clearly hiding something.

The sound of the knitting needles plays loud and frantic. Everyone looks at Andrew.

ANDREW: You're right!

SARAH: What?

ANDREW: My name's not Andrew!

Sarah looks horrified.

SARAH: Then who are you?

ANDREW: I'm a Buddhist! I'm a Buddhist and my given name is Samudrapati. I'm sworn to a life of compassion for all living things.

DEVANIKA: That's where I've seen you before. In the refill shop. In your orange robes.

Andrew nods.

STEVE: For crying out loud.

ANDREW: I'm an auditor and a mindfulness and meditation
    specialist. They booked me in to do both and forgot to
    tell me you were going with a knitter instead. I kept quiet
    for fear you'd make assumptions about my independence.

SARAH: Well, thanks for that, er…

Steve leans forward and points to Andrew.

STEVE: Wake up everybody! This is a brainwashing exercise.
    Do we want a religious nut guiding our thoughts?

Sarah groans and puts her head in her hands.
Steve jumps to his feet and paces angrily.

STEVE: They've kept us in this room, away from outside
    influences, parted from our phones, like some kind of
    cult.

*The click-clack of knitting has an edgy note. Josh is
breathing heavily as light shines in his eyes.*

SARAH: (clipped tone) Will you close the blinds, please
    Andrew?

ANDREW: It's Samudrapati. Can we use the courtyard garden
    out the back?

*She looks at him in surprise. His face has lost that deadpan
look and come alive with authority. The sun's rays blazing in
through the window light up his head like a halo. She pauses,
then nods.*

SARAH: Good idea!

ANDREW: We'll head outside now for a mindfulness exercise.

STEVE: Here we go.

ANDREW: This is a process used by EU officials working
    on climate change policy. They've found it improves
    consensus building.

Steve remains sitting, his arms folded. Sarah nods towards

Josh, who is now hyperventilating.

SARAH: Come on. Leave everything here.

NEEDLES: I'll pack up my knitting.

SARAH: Everything!

Richard leaned forward to watch carefully. Needles put her knitting on the table. It was obscured by the bodies of everyone filing out. When the room was empty, the knitting was gone.

*

Imagine was playing the night we crossed the line. Fay would see herself in this, but she'd never read it. She'd got me into the ride-share app and meditation – although it's been a long time since I've had the desire to close my eyes and observe my thoughts. We got too close too fast, that was the trouble. Looking back, I was vulnerable after my divorce and even more so after my parents died. Lee had filled the space where family had been with extreme sports and look where that had got him. I'd filled the gap with Fay. We met at salsa class, something I tried when newly single. As always, there were more women than men, but after a while we didn't even pretend to look for a male partner. She'd hold out a hand, I'd take it and we'd be off.

We'd worked best, the three of us. Me, Fay and Lee. Our debates were coloured with love. They were safe. When I set forth in her circle, I felt a fraud. I was far from my ivory tower and not even a proper lesbian.

I often wondered, along with Wittgenstein, at what point one crossed the line from one box to another, and whether it mattered. With my first boyfriend, we took months progressing through the bases until we had sex. Then you knew you'd 'gone all the way'. But what counted with a woman? At what point would I have to tick the box LGBTQ+?

Fay objected to the term 'crossing the line' because, she said, it made it seem like we were doing something wrong. But I couldn't get the images out of my head of the lesbian porn I'd seen when checking my boys' browsing history years ago. "Pretty nakid lesbins" they'd typed. After correcting their spelling, I sat them down and told them actual sex was different to porn. I'd certainly hoped so. The women had long, sharp, painted nails, which surely no one would want near their tender regions. Fay told me later that the target audience was men, and porn produced by lesbians was different, but it would be the image my boys had in their heads when they pictured "lesbins". I cringed at the thought of my sons thinking of me that way. Maybe they still looked at that stuff now I'm not around to police them. I dealt with it by not thinking about it. Probably the same approach they took. People are too quick to dismiss avoidance and denial. It has its place.

I'd wondered about sex with a woman before Fay. I'd even had a chaste dabble with a girl at university. My assumption was that the principal difference with sex with a woman would be that what one thought of as the preliminaries would become the main course. I'd counted without the passion.

It began slowly. Hours chatting on the sofa, leaning into each other, cuddling, holding hands. This is just a physically demonstrative friendship, I tell myself. Then our eyes hold and a fire leaps into being. I look away. But I don't move. We get caught up in a new conversation. Our eyes connect again, and I can't look away. Fay stops talking and waits. Her mouth is right there, and I know she wants me to kiss her. The moment I do, Wittgenstein cautions, I'm in another box. Or is it me, or my mum, or the way my boys look at me? I pause. Our lips poised a millimetre apart. I feel her breath, soft and moist and warm. I breathe it in. She waits. I plunge and I'm lost. Like stepping into a warm bath and being immersed, held, surrounded and surrendered.

She nibbles my neck, and it's alive, electric shivers through my body. Sweet nothings, clothes removed. I hesitate. 'Is it Wittgenstein?' she asks, a smile twitching in the corner of her mouth. Her soft, full lips. I return to base one and we kiss.

'Tell me about old Ludwig Wittgenstein,' she says when I pull back. She caresses my flushed cheeks. 'I demand to see the original texts.'

I hesitate, and she smiles knowingly. 'I suspect, professor that you have appropriated him for your own ends.'

I laugh because she's right.

'Have you even read him?' she sits up, grinning.

'He's hard to understand,' I plea with outstretched arms. 'I never actually used him in a lecture. Well, hardly.'

'And you quote him all the time.' She wags a finger at me. 'Wittgenstein this and Wittgenstein that.'

'Stop giving me imposter syndrome,' I cry.

'I'm not *giving* it to you. Own it, baby'. We laugh helplessly. We remember we're naked, and my boys have left home. An exploratory touch, and another and it's red hot and there's nothing on my mind except love and sensation, not even next week's lecture.

Then suddenly I'm scared. Stranded without my guide in a strange new world with no brother and no mum and dad.

What I'm seeing now, in retrospect, is that it wasn't that Fay was so great. It's just more relaxed having a relationship when kids have left home and you're established in your career. You've developed a bit of confidence. Got to know who you are, kind of.

Chapter 19

I looked around my grubby kitchen in panic. The offer of food had done the trick, but I hadn't realised I'd let things go so much. The fridge yielded nothing they'd want to eat. I'd have to shop and cook and clean. I thought of Tom's finger running along my shelves, undusted for months now. The marking was piling up from the last assignment, and I still had lots more to write. It was supposed to be one reading a week, but the story was driving itself. I had a brainwave.

Me: Looking forward to seeing you. It will be tofu stir fry. X

They'd turn down the food for sure, but I'd made the gesture.

Adam: Sorry I just realised I have football on Sunday.

Tom: Cool. Martha's got me into healthy food these days.

Me: Change of plan. I'll treat you to a pub lunch.

Tom: 👍

Adam: Wish I hadn't made up the football excuse now.

Me: Too bad. Next time ☺

I imagined Adam's disappointment. But it wasn't just a lesson about lying. It would be best to have Tom and Martha to myself for this one.

I sent them details of a pub near the university that GG had recommended and made a start on my marking.

I began by estimating how global temperature will change if personal carbon allowances (PCAs) were adopted, then looked at how many deaths are likely to be averted by a reduction in temperature. I then looked at the less tangible effects of vigilantism and how that may impact societal wellbeing. To do this I had to make many assumptions.

I used the en-roads climate simulator to estimate how much greenhouse gas emissions and global temperature would go down if PCAs were implemented. I adjusted dials to show reduced use of coal and oil and more renewables. Based on the story, I also assumed people would purchase more seasonal vegetables and less red meat. I managed to reduce the expected temperature by one degree. It was scary that even doing this, it was still too hot.

It was hard to find data related to how many lives would be saved by a decreased temperature of one degree, but it seemed to be about twelve million over fifty years – more if we include the 'Quality-Adjusted Life Year' which is used in health policy. It would be easy to get a higher figure if you include things like increased probability of pandemics, but harder to get a lower figure.

If no one knew about the murder, there wouldn't be many other impacts. If it got out, then it could go either way. The threat of being assassinated might make leaders think twice about doing things or making policies (or not making them) that would harm the environment. But they'd probably just load up with extra security. Also, potentially good leaders might get put off going for positions of power in business or government if vigilantism became a thing. Then you could end up with your macho don't-give-a-damn types. But we seem to have lots of them anyway.

We could argue that PCAs will reduce happiness as people

can't consume as many high-carbon products and services as before without extra cost. However, studies show that happiness doesn't increase once a certain level of income is reached. After that, more money doesn't equate to more happiness. The figures also show that 71% of low-income households do better under PCAs, and if you consider everybody, not just the mega rich, then the ratio of happiness to pain is greater with PCAs than without. Also, climate change will affect even the wealthy due to food shortages, climate-anxiety etc.

If we don't use PCAs, we may use carbon taxes or green subsidies to reduce greenhouse gas emissions and encourage low-carbon practices and technologies. The main benefit of PCAs over carbon taxes is that they're more equal and inequality correlates with infant mortality and crime – including the murder rate. Therefore, a policy that's more equal should result in greater wellbeing. I checked online to see why we don't use PCAs already but apparently, they're expensive to set up. But when I looked at the cost, it was less than that railway that we stopped building halfway through.

In conclusion, it seems that it would be moral to kill Steve using the principle of the greatest happiness of the greatest number. The answer changes if we use Rule Utilitarianism or Kant's philosophy because we wouldn't say that murder be used every time someone stood in the way of a climate policy. It would violate human right to life, although again – what about the lives lost through inaction? I'm trying to embrace uncertainty as suggested but wish I could come to a clearer answer!

Reflection. Professor, you should have given trigger warnings! I've heard people say it was urgent, but I didn't realise that was actually true. I watched the documentary you mentioned in the story and was freaked out that they sounded scared. On the simulator I had to set deforestation to zero, set reforestation at 100%, switch to 100% renewables, stop fossil fuels and even then, we're still not far off two degrees. All these things we already know how to do, which reassures me a bit, but we've known how to do these for a while but still haven't.

I think a better dilemma is should you kill for citizens' juries because it looks like under these, we'd have more chance. I did some research and found that what Sarah said about citizens' assemblies was true and that in some countries they really do have power and are making good long-term decisions, and that there are campaigns to give them power in the UK too.

*

> *Mark 80%*
> *This is a well-researched and thoughtful response.*
> *You have partly anticipated the final dilemma!*

I'd have liked to have given more feedback, but my alarm sounded, reminding me that I was due at the pub.

I arrived at the same time as Martha and Tom. I spotted GG in a corner with her back to me. Panicked for no obvious reason, I steered us to the furthest table.

'Sorry if I upset you last time,' I said to Martha once we were in the queue for the carvery.

'Honestly, Iris, you did me a favour. I went on a course about greenwash last week and it turns out you're right.'

'It's always best to be honest.'

Tom took a photo of the huge hunks of meat.

'What are you doing?' I asked.

'I'm sending to Adam. *Ha ha. Mum says that will teach you.*'

'Don't send that!'

'Too late.'

'Chicken please,' Martha said when we reached the carvery.

'Beef for me, and some belly pork,' Tom said.

'What was that about healthy eating?' I asked him.

'I'm a work in progress.' He grinned and ladled on apple sauce and gravy.

'Nut roast,' I said.

'Lots of brands are being called out for greenwash,' Martha said once we were back at the table. I told my boss it might be an issue with the bodywash, so they sent me on this course.'

'Normally, only senior execs go on those,' Tom said between mouthfuls of food.

I chewed my nut roast and said nothing. The atmosphere, after all, doesn't care if the motivation is profit or ethics, it just responds to the level of emissions pumped into it.

Martha swallowed and leaned forward. 'Have you heard of greenhush, Iris?'

I shook my head.

'Companies now don't want to talk about any green credentials in case they get pulled up on it for greenwash. So we've changed the packaging from green to purple. People are getting very picky about this stuff.'

I thought about the implications. 'Does that mean they stop making untrue claims, or they're stopping trying to be green?'

'I'll show you the sample.' Martha rummaged in her handbag and pulled out a bottle of bodywash. 'Read the label.'

I paused eating and put on my glasses. 'Probiotic bodywash,' I read out. 'Now you don't need long hot showers to get clean.'

'What do you think?' Martha looked at me expectantly.

'She was inspired by what you said,' Tom prompted.

I sighed. 'But saying now you don't always need hot water implies that you do normally.'

Martha remained confident. 'I don't think it does.'

I spotted GG on her way back from the ladies and waved her over. Before we could get bogged down in introductions, I thrust the bodywash in her face. 'You're our focus group. What do you think?'

'Huh?' She peered at the label and shook her head, bemused.

'Do you need long, hot showers to get clean?' I asked her.

She shrugged.

'No clues. Just tell me what you think.'

'I know!' she proclaimed. 'Normally you *would* need long hot showers to get clean, but because that would wash off the probiotic stuff, if you use this, you don't.'

'Thank you, GG, you may be on your way.'

She glanced sorrowfully at the plates of meat in front of Tom and Martha and walked on.

I turned back to meet Martha's gaze. Point made.

'She's doing her best,' Tom said.

'It's not enough to do our best, we must do what's necessary.'

'Please Mum, don't go on one of your doom rants.'

Martha looked disappointed. Because she had failed to impress her boyfriend's mum, or because she realised I was right? I couldn't tell, but she wasn't the only one. I lowered my eyes and tried to finish my nut roast. Frustration and fear made it impossible to swallow. I found myself thinking of Naomi and how I could bring her around. How I could do something, anything, to turn the tide before it was too late. *Softly softly catchee monkey*, Lee whispered in my head. I wiped my eyes.

'OK, go on a doom rant,' Tom sounded desperate. 'Just say something.'

'I'm not saying you're not good at your job, Martha.' I gave up trying to eat. 'The problem is that you are.'

'Thanks, erm…'

'But it's like you wouldn't want a serial killer to be good at their job, would you?'

'What?'

'Mum!'

'No, you'd want them to get caught.' Lee's shaking his head, but the words can't be contained. 'Running hot water is the most energy intensive thing we do in our homes. Household energy makes up a quarter of greenhouse gas emissions. These lead to climate change and it's killing us. If you can't see that after everything that's happened. Honestly Martha, the world would be better off if you did nothing and planted weeds.'

Tom slammed down his fork. 'You're making her the scapegoat for the entire economic system.'

Martha pushed away her plate. 'I've had enough.'

'Me too,' he said.

'Are you done?'

I looked up to see the waitress.

'Yes,' said Tom.

His plate had most of the beef left on it.

'Don't you want a doggy bag?' I asked.

'We can wrap it up if you'd like,' said the waitress.

'No thanks,' he said.

'Yes, please for me,' I said.

'The carbon footprint of food waste is ten percent of all emissions,' I said after the waitress had taken our plates. 'GG would say that cow died for you. Methane is emitted from their burps – a greenhouse gas many times more potent than carbon dioxide…

They need to join the dots, so I pay no heed to Martha and Tom's stricken faces or Lee's voice faint in my head …*softly, softly catchee monkey*…

… and you can't be bothered to put it in a doggy bag? I don't mind you eating meat, but wasting it is an insult to the cow that gave its life and the environment.'

Tom jumped to his feet and his chair crashed to the floor. 'Is this what you did to Fay?' He looked horrified at what he'd said. He picked the chair up and sat back down.

'Sorry,' he whispered.

I paid the bill, collected my doggy bag, and we left in silence.

Home was deathly quiet. I set up my laptop on the kitchen table and laboured through more tortured assignments. Students had floundered back and forth, riddled with anxiety and uncertainty and all had ended up with some version of 'I don't know'.

Murder in the Citizens' Jury #19: Interviews with Suspects

Richard was frustrated. He'd watched all the footage, but the most important bit was beyond CCTV. Still, one comment had stood out for him. He dug out the police interview with Ben. He sat forward when he got to the interesting bit.

POLICE OFFICER 1: 'It's always the nice guys that get assassinated.' Did you say that?

BEN: I can't remember.

POLICE OFFICER 1: What happened on the last day?

BEN: We were all about to vote for personal carbon trading. You know what personal carbon allowances could mean for me? We might get to be a family. Might not have to feel the blood pressure go up every time you get a bill. Might mean some actual time with my wife! Steve was the only one getting in the way. And—

Ben stops abruptly, takes a deep breath, and speaks slowly and deliberately.

BEN: But this process is about... a group of concerned citizens coming together to calmly deliberate the way forward and come to a consensus. We were here to ask questions of one another and of the evidence in front of us, er... respecting each other's opinion and not talking over each other.

POLICE OFFICER 1: The deceased may have preferred to be talked over than stabbed.

BEN: That's the thing, right? We were trying to convince him. To calm him down. So we stepped in to... uh, give him a hug.

POLICE OFFICER 2: A hug?

BEN: Er, yes. As part of the process. So I couldn't see what happened.

POLICE OFFICER 1: Hmm. How did you feel about the deceased?

BEN: Seemed OK to begin with, but by the end...

He leans forward.

BEN: You spoken to Josh yet? You should talk to him.

POLICE OFFICER 1: Why do you say that?

BEN: You'll work that out when you meet him.

Josh

Richard loaded up the police interview with Josh.

POLICE OFFICER 1: How did you get on with the deceased?

JOSH: He was always having a go! But if he hadn't shut down the repair cafes, I could have helped. My dad would be proud of me.

POLICE OFFICER 1: You didn't like him then?

JOSH: I loved him.

POLICE OFFICER 1: You did?

JOSH: I never told him.

POLICE OFFICER 1: Did he love you back?

JOSH: Of course.

Police Officer 1 looks at Police Officer 2, confused.

POLICE OFFICER 1: Erm. Right.

The second police officer speaks up suddenly.

POLICE OFFICER 2: Did you kill Steve?

JOSH: Steve? I couldn't do it, even if I wanted to. I'd just had a panic attack, and I was shaking so bad I couldn't stand up.

Both police officers speak at the same time.

POLICE OFFICER 2: Did you want to?

POLICE OFFICER 1: What precipitated the panic attack?

JOSH: Huh?

POLICE OFFICER 1: Why were you so upset?

POLICE OFFICER 2: On the day of the murder?

JOSH: It was hot. And there's this old woman, and she's knitting, knitting, knitting, all the time, and it feels like she's controlling everything!

POLICE OFFICER 1: You felt controlled?

JOSH: By the knitting, man!

POLICE OFFICER 2: And then what happened?

JOSH: She gave me some knitting to calm me down. She said I remind her of her grandson. This is for him, she said. She'd do anything for him.

Police Officer 1 sits up, excited.

POLICE OFFICER 1: Did she say that in the garden, when you went outside?

Josh shrugs.

POLICE OFFICER 1: Before the murder?

JOSH: It's all a blur. You know I can knit really well now.

He holds up some knitting.

Richard read through the police notes on Josh's interview. They'd taken his comments as extra evidence against Needles. He made himself a cup of tea and returned to his desk to watch her second interview with the police. The first ten minutes were nothing special, but then it got interesting.

Needles

POLICE OFFICER 1: Before the murder, you were overheard shouting, 'This is for my grandson.'

NEEDLES: *(croaks)* I don't think I did any shouting love.

POLICE OFFICER 1: The murder occurred in the only place that doesn't have CCTV. How did you all come to be there?

NEEDLES: It were Andrew who took us outside.

POLICE OFFICER 1: Andrew?

NEEDLES: Although it turned out that wasn't his real name. Like I said, a dark horse.

POLICE OFFICER 1: And what happened?

NEEDLES: My eyesight's not so good, dearie. I couldn't tell you.

POLICE OFFICER 1: Try!

NEEDLES: We were sitting in a circle. Chatting, and such. Then suddenly he were screaming. Aiyee! He went. Poor love.

He rewound the last few moments. He detected a note of satisfaction in the way she said, 'poor love.' She'd also, very slightly, pointed the finger at Andrew.

Andrew

POLICE OFFICER 1: It was you who led everyone out to the garden where there was no CCTV.

ANDREW: I didn't know this would happen.

POLICE OFFICER 1: Why did you go outside?

ANDREW: It was hot. Josh was having a panic attack. We all needed some air.

POLICE OFFICER 1: Did you see the murder?

ANDREW: No.

POLICE OFFICER 1: I find that hard to believe.

ANDREW: Everyone was clustered around Steve, but I sat further back. I like to keep somewhat apart during the discussions.

POLICE OFFICER 1: So they were discussing stuff?

ANDREW: Um, yes.

POLICE OFFICER 1: Or arguing maybe?

POLICE OFFICER 2: Hugging?

Andrew and Police Officer 1 both look at her and she looks down.

POLICE OFFICER 1: Did you notice anything different that afternoon?

ANDREW: There was tension, but that wasn't unusual. Naomi seemed different, I suppose.

POLICE OFFICER 2: In what way?

ANDREW: Just not herself.

The police hadn't had access to the lunchtime footage, so they hadn't followed it up, but it lent support to his suspicions. If only he had the CCTV footage of the garden. But he reckoned he had enough to get an idea what had happened. No hug as Ben claimed, that was for sure.

*

I sat back, stretched my arms out over my head, and moved my neck from side to side. The murder kept slipping away from me. Why was I dithering? The DPP needed me to get on with it. The students were impatient. I can't be squeamish.

I'd managed to ignore my aching back, dry eyes, and hunger, but my bladder demanded immediate release. The toilets two doors down were closed for cleaning, so I went up to the next floor. I heard a commotion coming from Percy's office but was too desperate to stop. On the way back, it had got louder. I approached cautiously.

Percy was bashing his keyboard on the desk and shouting.

I knocked on his open door and he threw it open, and stared at me, eyes wild.

'I spent the last two hours – *two hours*,' he shouted as if it were my fault, 'trying to access the fucking learning agreements. I found them in some obscure file, hidden in another file and now I tried too many times, and it logged me out.'

'Oh—'

'Do you know how many of my students have special issues? Twenty-four! And that's out of a class of thirty-five. And me, a senior professor, wasting my time finding out if they need an extra five or ten or thirty minutes per hour to compensate for their dyslexia. This one has fucking dyscalculia.'

Heads were poking out of offices, attracted by the drama.

GG appeared and stood by me, looking worried.

'It's an English exam, for fuck's sake,' he raged. 'I don't care if he can count. Why is this generation such a bunch of snowflakes?'

GG looked around nervously. 'You can't say that kind of stuff.'

'Because they'll get upset? I'm upset!' he thundered.

Marcel joined us.

Percy picked up his keyboard again. 'I knew this would happen. Online fucking exams. I told the admin lot; don't look so smug, I told them. I spend two hours learning to do a job that you could have done in five minutes. But you watch out. They'll get rid of you. No need for admin, they'll say. Then you'll be sorry.'

He stared at us; the keyboard raised above his head. 'Jenna lied,' he declared. 'And Colin. They told us there were no rooms for exams. I walked past the room we used last year – empty as their heads.' He slammed the keyboard back down on his desk. 'They lied to our faces. Now every single sad academic has to learn an entire new system because they can't be fucking arsed and the students are all snowflakes.' He picked the keyboard up again.

I stood there, tapping into the scene. Murderous rage. Just what I needed.

'Look at Chip. You've traumatised her with your wrath.' Marcel stepped forward and removed the keyboard from Percy's hands and replaced it gently on the desk. 'I'll have to tell the Dean, because she may need some time off.'

Percy let out a sudden bark of laughter.

I hurried back, desperate to hold on to the rage long enough to write the murder.

*

Murder in the Citizens' Jury #20: The Murder

Sarah closed the door after them and locked it. Samudrapati led the group around the corner and out a back door into a walled courtyard garden. It had a tiny lawn, a bench by an oak tree, and several chairs scattered around.

Josh collapsed onto a chair, breathing hard. 'Sorry, when it gets hot, I get anxious.'

Sarah sat beside him.

'My—' he gulped, 'my dad. He had a heart attack on holiday. They said it was the heat. Sorry.'

'No need to apologise.' Samudrapati's warm eyes were compassionate. 'All pull up a chair and we'll sit quietly for a while. You too, Sarah.'

Sarah decided to trust him and relaxed into her seat.

'You can close your eyes if you wish or look around you. Let your mind be still. It might help to count your breaths, in... one... out... two.'

Gradually, Josh's breathing slowed.

'Thoughts will come,' intoned Samudrapati, 'but just imagine them like puffs of white clouds across a clear blue sky.'

Josh gazed up into the tree. Glimpses of sky were visible

through the foliage. Sunlight sparkled through the leaves.

'You've had a lot to process, so I'll stop talking and we'll sit quietly for five minutes.'

Sarah breathed a sigh of relief. The sound of birdsong had replaced the click-clack of knitting, and the peace of the garden was working its magic.

Devanika closed her eyes. Breathe in. Today was the day. Breathe out. Stay calm.

Steve's thoughts were less peaceful. One thing stood out for him. If they adopted PCAs, the organic farmer would win. His jaw tightened.

Needles considered the personal carbon allowances. There was hope yet for her grandson if they got these through. Would she get extra for her cats? If not, it would be a small price to pay. She'd try out that insect-based cat food.

Naomi gazed at the oak. She'd never properly looked at a tree before. It was magnificent in its raw beauty. Strong, rooted, branching out in glorious symmetry. Its leaves shimmering green against the vivid blue sky. She thought of the cardboard boxes piling up in her spare room.

Ben was feeling guilty. He'd been irritated at the pride in Josh's voice when he'd talked about his dad showing him how to repair things. He'd thought Josh was having a go at him for not teaching his kids. He'd got it so wrong.

'That's five minutes.' Samudrapati's voice was like liquid honey. 'Would anyone like to share their experience?'

'Hearing nature all around reminded me what we have to lose,' said Devanika.

'Rubbish,' scoffed Steve, 'it made me realise that the world is fine!'

'Listen,' said Sarah. 'What do you hear?'

The soft coo of a wood pigeon, a silence, then the tuneful melody of the garden robin, looking at them sideways from the wall.

'A few years ago, we'd have heard the hum of bees on the honeysuckle,' said Sarah.

The robin drew its song to a close, and the silence seemed

loud.

'I like the idea of a world where we take care of stuff,' Ben murmured.

'It shouldn't be such an alien concept, I suppose,' Devanika agreed.

'We don't want you to take care of stuff,' said Naomi. 'We want you to buy. We don't care what happens to it after that.'

'It's called business, it's the economy. It's a good thing,' Steve said.

'What do you think?' Needles demanded, peering at Naomi.

Naomi reeled under her gaze. The old lady seemed suddenly intense without the knitting.

'It's just marketing.' Naomi thought of the video they'd seen on day one. The horrifying picture of humans marching towards their own destruction like automatons. The image hadn't left her all week. It was too close to home. The unpaid bills, cupboards full of things, boxes everywhere. She'd splashed out on an extra bedroom so her sister could stay, but she could barely squeeze in there now herself. She knew the party was over and it was time to pay the bill. It was a relief to admit it. But she didn't know if she could stop.

She shook her head slowly.

Steve saw it all slipping away from him. 'But didn't you say your customers prefer sustainable products?' he asked desperately.

'We take the same product, put it in a brown cardboard container instead of a shiny plastic box and charge twice as much for half the quantity.'

'That's greenwash!' cried Devanika.

Sarah calmed Devanika with a hand on her sleeve.

Naomi continued her confession in a daze, like she'd just woken up.

'I've made up test results for skin care, saying ninety percent say this or that. Although it's strange, even though I was inventing them, I still kind of believed it.'

'I'd do anything for my grandson,' said Needles, seemingly à propos of nothing.

'If we vote for this, will it really happen?' Naomi asked.

'Yes,' said Sarah.

Naomi's eyes welled up with tears.

'It won't be that bad,' reassured Sarah. 'With everyone on board, it won't be long before you get your Gold Card membership for the library of things. You might even get to borrow a yacht! You can gad about by bus wherever and whenever at little cost and rural economies will be transformed. Life will be cheaper. You'll gain in confidence as you learn to value your stuff, learn how to maintain it. You'll have space in your homes. Picture the roads with no parked cars, no traffic jams. You'll have more time to take slow transport, you'll still have holidays. And you won't need to be resentful of others who aren't doing their bit, or guilty for wanting a beefburger because you'll have your own allotted carbon allowance that's yours to do as you like with. Be green and richer or high-consuming and pay the full cost.'

Naomi gazed up at her through red-rimmed eyes. 'What's the catch?' she whispered.

'It has to be unanimous,' said Sarah.

Everyone looked at Steve.

He shook his head. 'Like I said, it's bureaucratic and costly.'

'So what, if it's necessary?' hissed Ben. Sarah had said he'd be better off under PCAs and he needed a break. The thought of returning to his punishing schedule wore him out just thinking of it.

The others nodded in agreement.

'That's what Churchill said, weren't it? It's not enough to do our best. We must do what's necessary,' said Needles.

'It's always the same,' muttered Ben furiously. His resentment previously aimed at Josh transferred itself to Steve. 'The loud-mouthed rich bastards kick up a stink the moment anything hits their pockets.'

Steve grabbed Naomi's hand. 'You're with me, aren't you?'

'No.' Naomi wrenched her hand from under Steve's grip. She wanted this.

'Global warming, that's more heatwaves, that's what they

said, isn't it?' Josh rounded on Steve. 'A heatwave killed my dad,' he shouted. 'He was only forty-five.'

Steve was forty-six. 'Look around you, we're fine,' he blustered, feeling hot. Then Devanika was in his face.

'My baby died,' she hissed. 'Probably because of nitrates from excessive use of fertilisers from farms like yours.'

Before he could protest the ridiculousness of the statement, Sarah was staring intently into his eyes.

'This citizens' jury is my baby,' she said in an ominously quiet tone.

'Our baby,' Devanika was back in his face.

'And I'll protect it,' Sarah said.

Needles pulled out her knitting. 'This is for my grandson.'

'In the rest of the world, rich, power-hungry leaders might make the decisions,' Devanika jabbed a finger at Steve.

'But in this citizens' jury, with expert input and a calm, reflective environment, people will choose what's best for them,' Sarah shouted.

'Make me,' said Steve.

*

I came to and shifted painfully. I seemed to have got locked into position hunched over the desk. I read back over the scene, my mouth dry with thirst. I wasn't sure if it was enough. Even if we dislike the victim, killing someone is a big deal. We must feel its weight.

The needles ~~went in~~ pierced his flesh, penetrating the ~~liver~~, kidney, ~~bringing instant death. Blood gushed forth.~~ The life drains from his eyes. In his last words, he cries out...

Did she cry out?

The cluttered room crowded in on me. I dashed out, desperate for the reassuring normality of grumbling colleagues. Every room was dark and empty. Lights came on behind me as I walked into the gloom ahead. I saw myself from afar, a lone woman creeping along a deserted corridor, jumping at shadows.

I heard strange sounds. Deep rumbling bass, dissonant, jarring notes. I froze, terrified. The sound continued. I tiptoed on. The notes sounded accusing. They got louder, then softer till they seemed to go. A thunder of drums. Condemning. I stopped dead, and so did the music. The vending machine was at the end of the corridor.

Just because I feel I must atone. It doesn't make me guilty.

I took a few more steps, and music rose to accompany me. Wheedling, pleading, imploring.

'It wasn't my fault,' I mutter. But I don't believe it. Lee wasn't my fault. She was right about that. But Fay. Violin strings. The sound of pure sadness, of grief and loss and guilt. The sweet smell of death, like rotting fruit, suffused the air.

A figure is outlined against the vending machine. It's sensed my presence. It's turning around and looking at me. I'm rooted to the spot. It's walking towards me. I scream and can't stop even when the lights come on and I see it's Colin.

*

I still felt shaky the next day. My office felt dark and oppressive. I made another attempt to tidy it up but was immediately overwhelmed. A quick check of my email revealed over two hundred unread messages. If I got stuck into them, I'd never finish my story. The murder had depleted me, but I couldn't fall over now. I need to bring all the clues together and discern which is *the* clue, the one that counts.

My laptop pinged as more emails came in. Up till now the notifications had barely registered, just the ding, ding, ding, as a kind of musical accompaniment to my fevered writing. Now though, they were a distraction, pulling me back to mundane reality. After several wasted hours of dithering, I turned my laptop off and headed for my bench by the stream. I managed a blissful two minutes of tranquility before a lawn mower started up. I headed away from the harsh noise, mentally compiling an email to estates and facilities suggesting that the University take up wildlife gardening and mow the grass less often. An article I'd read about lambs being brought in to chew the grass came to mind. Some campuses had petting zoos brought in during exams to calm the students – I'd suggest lambs instead. It would be a win-win.

I found myself in a rose garden tucked away behind the teaching block. I sat on a bench, put lamb lawn mowers out of my mind, and tried to concentrate on the next bit of my story. I heard the music again. It was unmistakable and deeply mournful. I stood up and looked around. It was coming from a classroom window. As I approached the building, the music abruptly came to a halt. After a moment, students streamed past, some of them openly weeping. GG appeared, wiping her eyes.

I called her over, and she came to sit beside me on the bench.

'What on earth were you playing them?' I asked.

'Mongolian laments.'

I felt a rush of relief. 'That was your music in the building yesterday?'

'Colin told me off, but I thought everyone had gone home.'

'It was very powerful.'

She nodded sadly.

'Everything OK, GG?'

'You saw the email. No one's taken up the voluntary redundancy option, so now it will be compulsory. Colin will suggest me. He says I upset the students.'

I tried not to notice two stragglers walking past, still weeping.

'Only sad music can transform loss into beauty, pain into joy.'

'Uh-huh.'

'Colin doesn't understand. He turned down my ethics proposal.'

'For your music and pain study?'

She nodded.

'I'm so sorry.'

'That's all right. It's not your fault.'

I said nothing because it probably was. Instead, I cheered her up with my idea for lamb lawn mowers.

'Or rabbits?' she suggested.

'Yes, we could use their droppings to feed the roses.' I checked, and she was almost smiling. I ruined it by adding, 'That's what in the Business School, we'd call a circular economy solution.'

GG was unimpressed. Concepts like the economy had no place in her artist's soul.

*

Murder in the Citizens' Jury #21: Clue

Richard was feeling the pressure. He'd developed a reputation for laser-sharp thinking and now he had to live up to it. He paced up and down his office, soon to be someone else's. Books of law and legal precedents lined the shelves. Pot plants that, after thriving for years, he'd somehow let die in the final few weeks. It had been his home from home, but now it felt like a prison. He was trapped. The closer he came to solving the case, the closer he came to saying goodbye to his chances of grandchildren, because Sarah was right. Once they declared there had been a murder, the Prime Minister and his cronies would use that as an excuse to shut down citizens' juries. The House of Lords, that bastion of privilege and archaic relic of the past, would remain. The promised House of Citizens would be over before it had begun. Nonetheless, he had a job to do.

He left his office abruptly and headed towards the park where he often ate his lunch. He strolled among the roses, processing everything he'd seen and heard. Ben's comment about the hug was the one thing that Richard couldn't explain. Ben said, 'It's always the nice guys that get assassinated.' Was that when the idea took hold? Because Steve wasn't a nice guy. Ben's wife works nights, he works days. They have three young children. I bet it's been a while. Could he be the worm that turned?

Marnie's into worms now. And she's letting the aphids eat the roses – they're part of the food chain apparently. The wildlife gardener told her to avoid pesticides as they kill the natural predators of aphids too. Hoverflies, ladybirds, parasitic wasps will eat the aphids, so you let them be. They're doing you a service. The enemy of your enemy is your friend kind of thing.

Richard paused, gazing at the roses as a thought bubbled up, frustratingly out of reach. It felt important. He didn't chase it but walked on. He'd learned that it would come when he wasn't looking.

It came when he was back at his desk. He picked up the phone. It was time to get them all together.

*

I'm back to writing fast – too fast. I'm nearly at the end of the story, and what will I do then? I'll write my paper up, but it won't be so absorbing or so fun. I asked the students how they liked it, and the feedback was positive, although the mouthy lad at the back said he didn't find it convincing that Josh blamed his dad's heart attack on climate change. I explained Josh was angry and upset and he's been repressing it with drugs and video games. The heat is triggering him. He's probably angry at himself. I got a bit upset, actually. The pressure is getting to me.

The students are desperate to know 'whodunnit' and are having fun with their speculations. I told them the big reveal will be ready by the end of the week. They were amazed I hadn't written it yet. I said that unlike them who make a big deal of having to get a six hundred word assignment in with just two weeks' notice, me, with my full-time job, had to turn out a novella in a few days. They ignored me and instead offered suggestions how to present it. It turns out they're fans of *Murder in Paradise* where the detective implausibly gets all the suspects together, firstly to reveal how clever he has been and then to reveal the murderer. Family tragedies and life sentences are glossed over, and they all go off for a pina colada in the beach bar. I'll grant them their first wish – a fun reveal of who did it in TV drama script form. But their second wish that the consequences will be glossed over will not be granted. Quite the reverse.

Murder in the Citizens' Jury #22: The Big Reveal

The suspects sit in the courtyard garden where the murder took place. Richard paces to and fro looking clever.

RICHARD: It's rare to have sympathy with a murderer. For what it's worth, in this case, I do. We all have skin in the game when it comes to climate change, and the deceased was the only one standing in the way of the policy you all thought would save the world. Besides that, to understand how a man dies, you must understand how he lived. And you all had reason to hate him.

Spotlight on Sarah. She looks back defiantly when he fixes her with a penetrating look.

RICHARD: Sarah. You were an obvious choice. You've given so much to make this jury happen. You've made fixing the climate crisis your life's work. You see the bigger picture. One man standing in the way of better, safer futures for us all. And let's not forget it was you who brought in the knitter. A weapon would have been picked up by security, but knitting needles didn't raise an eyebrow.

Sarah shakes her head but betrays no emotion.
Richard swivels around to face Needles, who continues knitting, unperturbed.

RICHARD: Before the murder took place you said, "this is for my grandson?" What did you mean by that?

Needles lifts her wool.

NEEDLES: I meant the jumper I was knitting, dearie.

RICHARD: You'd do anything for your grandson, you said?

NEEDLES: I know you, don't I? You put Arthur away.

Richard answers stiffly.

RICHARD: I don't make the law.

NEEDLES: He did it for his granddaughter, he said. He were
just doing a bit of chalk spraying. Still, you gotta do your
job, I understand, duck.

She smiles at him kindly, but there's a gleam in her eye.
Discomforted, Richard turns to Andrew.

RICHARD: And Andrew, who isn't really called Andrew. A
Buddhist could be the perfect cover. It was you who led
everyone out into the courtyard – the only place with no
CCTV.

Andrew returns his gaze with a calm expression and says
nothing.

Naomi shrinks back in her chair when he turns to her.

RICHARD: Naomi. Finding out Steve was married must have
been a blow given your last boyfriend cheated on you.
And despite your high salary, your credit rating is poor.
Steve - rich, handsome, interested in you – it gave you a
boost.

Naomi shakes her head.

RICHARD: Except, when something happened, it wasn't how you
imagined it. You realised he was only ever going to use
you, and he did. How badly, I don't know.

Naomi looks down.
Richard paces along the line of suspects and stops in front
of Ben.

RICHARD: And Ben. Life hasn't been fair to you. You and your
wife having to work all the time, barely seeing each
other, struggling to pay the bills. You must have resented
Steve. He has everything you don't. Naomi snubs you but
goes off with him. And maybe you resented him for the
way he manipulated you too, both of you ganging up on
Josh, a young lad who'd just lost his dad.

Ben looks down, ashamed.

RICHARD: Then we have Josh. We discovered that you'd
    moved onto an antidepressant whose side effects have
    been known to cause sudden violence, especially when
    mixed with cannabis. The connection between your dad
    dying in a heat wave and Steve standing in the way of a
    policy that you believed would avert the climate crisis –
    maybe it tipped you over the edge.

Josh listens with interest.

RICHARD: We found a note in the jury room, with Steve's
    name circled. Your name was circled too, Naomi.

Naomi looks up in shock.

RICHARD: We assumed this was done by the killer, and next to
    it we found some cabbage leaves. No one was seen eating
    them, but they weren't food, were they?

Richard spins on his heel to face Devanika.

RICHARD: Cold cabbage leaves are supposed to help women
    with sore breasts after pregnancy, or a late miscarriage.
    How long was it before you lost it?

DEVANIKA: Her. It was our final round of IVF. She was due a
    few days ago.

Needles pats her arm.

RICHARD: The date of the murder, to be exact. I'm truly
    sorry. But I had to consider postpartum psychosis.
    There have been rare cases where hormonal imbalances
    have driven women to murder. We know you blamed
    environmental pollutants like agricultural run-off for
    your failed pregnancies. Steve had taken over an organic
    farm and returned it to less eco-friendly methods.
    He was blocking everything. You blamed him for what
    happened to your baby.

DEVANIKA: I may as well give the baby gear to a Library
    of Things. I couldn't bear selling it to some glowingly

pregnant woman – better just to hand it all over. If it
gets chosen, that is.

SARAH: Oh my God! We haven't chosen!

JOSH: I want the repair bill.

RICHARD: This isn't the time.

SARAH: This will be the last time we're all together.

NAOMI: We did decide. We decided on personal carbon
allowances, didn't we? Otherwise it's all been for nothing!

*Richard looks up sharply. He listens attentively while they
talk.*

SARAH: As Chair, I must acknowledge that Steve wanted on-
demand buses.

DEVANIKA: We don't have to care about him anymore.

Richard notes her comment with interest.

SARAH: He was a plant anyway.

RICHARD: He wasn't.

SARAH: What?

RICHARD: We checked.

*He watches Sarah's face closely as she processes the
information.*

SARAH: I was sure he was.

NAOMI: But we decided on personal carbon allowances. We all
agreed.

BEN: Yes, cos as Andrew said, if we get PCAs, then Libraries of
Things will take off anyway.

ANDREW: That's correct. The effectiveness of Libraries of
Things, Repair Bill and on-demand buses depend upon
their level of take-up – the more people use them,
the better and cheaper the service. Personal carbon
allowances provide the incentive.

JOSH: *(to Naomi)* I thought you didn't like them.

NEEDLES: She changed her mind, didn't you love?

Naomi nods. Josh looks puzzled.

NAOMI: You know, like when there's chocolate everywhere and you're on a diet. It's easier if it's not available, then you don't have to resist it.

DEVANIKA: I don't know how many times I've emerged from the newsagents with a health magazine and a ton of sweets!

Naomi laughs, and there's a moment of bonding.

RICHARD: Here am I, for all you know, about to reveal the murderer, and yet you're not remotely interested. Not one of you. It confirms what I've been thinking. You all know who the murderer is and you don't care.

Richard paces.

RICHARD: And that's why I'm finally, horribly sure. Ben and Josh, you hate each other. Not as much as Devanika and Naomi. But none of you have really gelled together. There's only one person you'd all want to protect. The grandmother of the group. And she took out the one person standing in the way of what you all wanted.

Richard walks over to stand in front of Needles.

RICHARD: You must give your full name this time. I can't list Needles as both the weapon and the name of the culprit.

Naomi looks at Needles, hurt.

NAOMI: You circled my name too.

NEEDLES: I'd do anything for my grandson.

*

I typed "The End" and then whooped and high-fived the empty air. I'd done it. My story was complete. Should I send to Robert? No. I tapped my desk, wondering what to do next. A play maybe.

I remembered the high I'd had when the university theatre group first read through my script for *Jack and the Beanstalk*. They'd loved the beanstalk being a cannabis plant, and I'd made the most of my bit part as the customs officer.

Lee had turned up for the final performance. He'd come backstage afterwards, waited till the mutual congratulations were done, then approached, hands up in mock awe at being in the presence of such an 'actorrr'. I'd basked in the pride in his eyes.

Fay had never seen my creative side. She'd love my story. I'd have printed it out with a cool cover just for her. She'd put on her reading glasses and I'd watch as she laughed at the bits she recognised. She'd like the reference to the wildlife gardener. We'd reminisce about how annoyed I'd got in the early days when she kept going on about how wonderful her wildlife gardener was. She realised I was jealous before I did. It was then she told me she liked women.

She'd enjoy the final reveal. She'd always found it amusing that a highbrow professor had such a love for cosy mysteries. She'd snap the book shut and smile at me and we'd kiss, and it would be bearable that Lee wasn't there anymore. Because I'd still have Fay.

She'd say it would be better if they all did it, so I'd tell her about Robert and the dilemma, but she'd already know because she'd have been there throughout. She'd be alive.

I bent over my desk in my over-full office, darkened by books, and sobbed. I recovered myself and sat up and wiped my eyes and answered a few emails. Another wave took me over and I sobbed again. 'Grief is like labour contractions,' I'd explained to Fay. 'You're perfectly fine one moment, then a minute later, you're overcome with pain.' She'd never had children, and I'd known the analogy would sting. It was the first of my many cruelties to her. But I'd needed to tell her what it was like for me so that she'd stop going on.

I checked the family chat on my phone.

Nothing.

Chapter 20

Not long now until the students get the final assignment and I'd get my answer. My excitement was tinged with nervousness. I'd be less worried about being found out if my conscience was entirely clear. I ran through the arguments again for not telling the students their answers would count. Robert has forbidden it. It would add to their anxiety. What they don't know won't hurt them. On the other hand, it's not my decision to make. An objective onlooker might say I had a stake in the outcome, and this is why we have ethics committees.

I contemplated trying one last time to see if Obi would approve my ethics application. An artist like him would surely pass it without a second thought, and he wouldn't ask questions about whether I was charging a fee. If anyone found out, I'd be berated for sure. Obi too, probably, but the stakes were too high to worry about a bit of telling off. At least it wouldn't be a disciplinary matter.

It was twenty minutes before his lecture finished. I read through what I'd prepared for the final assignment. I'd specified they had to give a definite prosecute or not prosecute – no maybes for this one. Was it good enough? It would do no harm to get a second opinion.

> *Dear GG, Marcel, and Percy*
> *Please could you do me a favour and give me some feedback on the final section of my whodunnit where I ask the students to help the Director of Public Prosecutions to decide whether to prosecute. It's the culmination of the whole thing so I'm keen to get it right. It's only 500 words and I'll buy you a drink tonight as thanks.*

Cheers

Chip

P.S. This scene comes after the big reveal, so we know who the murderer is, and the question is whether to prosecute. Sarah is the chair of the citizens' jury where the murder happened, and Richard is the DPP.

Pps A citizens' jury is basically the same as a citizens' assembly. I thought it would be nicely topical and hopefully encourage them to vote in the referendum.

RICHARD: By rights I could bring you all in on the
    charge of perverting the course of justice.
SARAH: But you won't.
RICHARD: No.
SARAH: Why not?
RICHARD: If pressed, I'd claim 'not in the public interest'.
    But no one will ask because the focus will be on
    Needles.
SARAH: Would it make you an accessory to murder if you
    didn't prosecute?
RICHARD: Of course I'll be prosecuting. It's my job.
SARAH: What about the public interest argument?
RICHARD: A bit woolly - not that I should mention wool.
SARAH: This isn't a joke. There's a lot at stake.
RICHARD: I understand. That's why you got me. Not a
    sergeant or Detective Inspector but Director of Public
    Prosecutions.
SARAH: I wondered about that.
RICHARD: You're not the only one who cares, Sarah. This
    is my last case before retirement and I'd hoped to have
    grandchildren, but now my daughter says she's too
    scared of the future.
SARAH: What would she want you to do?
RICHARD: She'll be furious with me if I prosecute, and
    so will my wife, but... (he stiffens up) I can't let self-
    interest influence my decisions.

*SARAH: This isn't self-interest! For decades we've known
the climate crisis was coming but governments have
done nothing, constrained by electoral cycles and
influenced by vested interests. In just a few weeks this
citizens' jury chose a policy that can save us. We were
here debating climate solutions, but the greatest one
of all is this process. There are many who'd like to see
them fail, and if you prosecute, you'd be playing into
their hands.*

*RICHARD: I'm not stupid, I know that law doesn't always
equal justice. But if you don't prosecute, you have
vigilantism.*

*SARAH: What of those victims that are just statistics?
Not one bereft mother but a ninety percent chance
that this action, or more likely, inaction, will kill this
percentage of people in this many places. We're talking
millions, billions of likely victims of the climate crisis.*

RICHARD: You don't know what you're asking of me.

SARAH: I do.

*RICHARD: Thirty years I've worked in the justice system.
This isn't my first crisis of conscience. The only way
to stay sane is to think of yourself as a cog in a system
that isn't perfect, but still one that's relatively fair and
free from influence.*

*SARAH: It's no longer fit for purpose. You could, given
your standing, get away with saying insufficient
evidence to prosecute. Given everything that's at stake.
Let me spell it out for you. Prosecute and the publicity
will mean the end of citizens' juries. With them goes
our best chance of averting the climate crisis. One old
lady versus humanity.*

Students: This is too much for one person to decide. Please
draw upon the moral philosophies we have covered and your own
independent thinking to decide. You must come to a conclusion
– prosecute or don't prosecute?

*

I waited as students trickled out of the lecture theatre. I poked my head around the door. The lecture had finished, and Obi was holding forth to a group of students clustered around the podium, eagerly hanging on his words. I felt a twinge. I'd never had that many students come up afterwards. He was young and handsome, that was it.

I resisted the urge to leave. If he approved my ethics application before the next lecture, I'd be covered. Although there was still the risk he'd want to pass it through the ethics committee, in which case Colin would say no and I'd have to stop.

I was about to turn away just as Obi emerged from the lecture theatre.

'Hi Iris. Are you teaching next?'

I flashed him a bright smile. 'No, erm. Just wanted to know if you'd do a quick pass on an ethics application?'

'No problem, send it to the ethics portal, and one of us will look at it.'

'It's just...' I paused while the last of the students walked off, then spoke in a quiet murmur. 'Colin hates me, and I need it approved before next week. Sorry it's late notice, but you're an artist – you don't strike me as the bureaucratic type.'

He nodded. 'Yeah, I'll wave it through. It's ridiculous anyway. They have these long forms that cover every department – are you using hazardous chemicals, giving people dangerous drugs, but you're hardly going to philosophise someone to death, are you?'

'No,' I laughed. 'Thanks. I owe you.'

Back in my office, I luxuriated in a wave of relief. Automatically I went to write my story, then realised it was done. I tapped my fingers on my desk. An hour to kill before I met the others down the pub and got their feedback. At the top of my inbox were emails from the marketing team asking me to promote my talk. I copied the blurb from the alumni article and sent it to a mailing list of a hundred or so contacts the Business School had compiled when I'd done a talk for them. Sorted.

I read my final assignment once more and picked at my nails. There were holes in the story if you looked carefully. I could explain them, but do I need to if they don't affect the core dilemma? Would it spoil the narrative flow if I don't, or would it spoil it if I do?

*

I was on my way back from the sandwich bar when Jenna spotted me in the foyer. I wasn't surprised when she waved me over. I suspected the utilitarian essay I'd failed was Emily's, and it was only a matter of time before she complained.

'How was your holiday?' I asked.

'Wonderful. We wanted to go to the Maldives one more time before it sank.' She laughed.

'Er. Ha ha,' I managed.

'How's the talk coming on?' she asked.

'Yes, great.'

'I told Colin to help with marketing, but we'd like a prestigious audience. Can you invite some of your business contacts?'

'Already done.'

'Especially wealthy ones.'

'I know plenty of those.' The Business School had wrung the most publicity possible out of my consultancy work, so I had a healthy network of potential attendees.

'Excellent, we want to make a splash, especially after the last one.' She looked at me conspiratorially. 'Georgina, you know. Made quite the wrong kind of splash.'

I didn't ask out of solidarity to GG, but my curiosity was piqued.

Jenna made to go and then turned back towards me. 'Oh, Colin said our friend Emily has complained again. An accusation about supplying Class A drugs.'

'It's not true, a misunderstanding,' I rushed.

'I'm sure it was. I'm not worried about it at all. You focus on your talk.'

'Of course.' One less thing to worry about. I began to walk on, but there was a final sting in the tail.

'Best to pass her though, to be on the safe side.'

I didn't bother replying. She had no right to ask such a thing, and she knew it. I had more important things to worry about.

*

Down the pub, I bought the first round as promised.

'In this chapter, I set out the stakes,' I babbled as I carried the tray of drinks. 'Basically, if he prosecutes, it has implications for the future of humanity.'

'And animals,' said GG.

'Over there.' Percy saw a free table and veered towards it.

'I also add the DPP's personal stakes, and raise the issue of vigilantism, then I ask the students to decide. What did you think?'

'I didn't read it.' Percy pulled up a seat.

'Me neither.' Marcel sat beside him.

'You should have bought your own drinks then.' I banged down the tray.

'I've been redoing all my module handbooks to the new template.' Marcel filled our glasses.

'What?'

'Don't you read your emails?'

'We must do them by the end of the week,' GG said.

'I've been busy. Jenna dumped a ton of work on me.' Percy sipped the wine and nodded his approval.

'But what could be more important than this?'

Percy raised an eyebrow.

'I…' I took a glug of wine to shut myself up.

'What's Jenna got you doing?' Marcel asked Percy.

'Kate's given up and got a new job.'

'Good for her. Where's that?'

'Stacking shelves at Tesco.'

We did a double take of shock.

'I had a go at Jenna,' Percy continued. 'She said if we'd had the right processes in place back then, they could have done something for Kate. So I said, then get the processes in place. Anyway, she made me diversity sensitivity manager.'

Marcel choked on his drink. 'Diversity sensitivity manager?'

'You?' GG put down her glass.

'So you didn't read my assignment?' I said.

'I got Kate to do it – she has time now.'

'The bastards have driven a respected academic to stack shelves at Tesco?' Marcel looked ready to explode.

'Not Waitrose?' GG inquired.

'She's worried she'd bump into Jenna.'

'She could bump into Emily at Tesco,' Marcel pointed out.

'She doesn't know what she looks like. Or vice versa probably.'

'What did Kate say?' I interrupted Percy. 'About my chapter on the dilemma?'

'She said she wasn't feeling the motivation.'

'But I talked about his personal stakes! If he prosecutes, he won't get grandchildren, and his wife and daughter will hate him.'

'Don't kill the messenger.'

'It's plausible though,' reassured GG.

I nodded. 'They only did the referendum to shut up the critics.'

'Like with Brexit, and you English went and voted for it,' Marcel waved his arms around. 'Brex–'

'That's right,' I said quickly before he went on a Brexit rant. 'So Sarah thinks they put in a plant to disrupt the process. I got that from you actually.' I grinned at them. 'Remember when you thought I was a plant?'

'It's interesting that they're both nature terms,' Percy mused. 'Plant and grass, both meaning similar things.'

Marcel looked at him surprised then turned to me.

'Hang on, Chip. Has there been a murder in the citizens' assembly?'

'For God's sake!' I cried. 'You're not listening to anything I say. I made it up.'

He shrugged, unrepentant. 'You go on about being topical.'

'Anything else?' I turned to Percy.

He put down his drink and pulled out a scrap of paper from his pocket. With a sigh, he rummaged for his glasses and put them on to read.

'Hmm. She said she didn't buy that someone so high up would feel such uncertainty. He'd be used to having the courage of his convictions.'

'I didn't feel it either,' GG said. 'It spoke to the head. Only music can speak to the heart.'

I wanted to shout at them all, but they weren't to know the significance. They just thought I was being precious.

'I can spout statistics about dolphins getting caught in tuna nets,' GG said. 'But it needed a musical to really share the pain.'

Percy and Marcel winced in agreement.

I saw Colin heading towards us.

He stopped behind my chair and leaned in to have a word. I knew exactly what he wanted to say.

'Hi Colin, how are you?' I asked him cheerily.

'Have you read my email?' His tone was grave.

'About Emily?' I hazarded a guess.

'I had to pass the complaint upwards to Jenna. It's a serious matter.'

The others looked puzzled.

'It's OK.' I lounged back in my seat. 'Jenna is fine with it.'

'She is?'

I enjoyed Colin's expression of disbelief.

'She said it was just a misunderstanding. She told me not to worry about it and to concentrate on the talk.'

'Oh.'

'She said to ask you how the marketing is going. Apparently you're helping with that, but she wants a quality audience, so I put word out among my networks too.'

He went to go. I called after him.

'Have a lovely weekend, Colin. Are you up to anything nice?' I gave him my sweetest smile. I was satisfied to see he looked disconcerted.

He muttered something and walked on.

'What was that about?' Marcel asked.

I told them about the incident with the magic mushrooms and Jenna's reaction.

'Don't look too pleased with yourself,' Percy cautioned. 'You may secure some big cheeses, and much is forgiven anyone who brings in the bacon.'

'Croque Monsieur,' Marcel said.

We looked at him.

'Ham and cheese,' he explained.

'But if Emily escalates it, you could find yourself in trouble.' Percy said.

'Yes,' agreed Marcel. 'Colin will be back on your tail.'

'And as for Emily.' Percy's face darkened.

'Maybe she genuinely has mental health issues,' I said.

'Or maybe she's a bitch,' Percy said.

'Says our new Diversity Sensitivity Manager,' Marcel said.

Percy glowered as we cracked up laughing.

*

The next morning, I re-read my final scene and assignment and sent it to the students as it was. I removed the family references and emailed it to Robert as well. The notification button in the bottom of my screen informed me I now had 270 unread emails. With trepidation, I scanned through my inbox. There were outraged emails from colleagues cc'ing everybody in about the decision to axe modules with less than twenty students. I skimmed through several from Jenna, sternly admonishing those who hadn't redone their module handbooks based on the new template, followed by a recent email saying not to worry as the system reformats them automatically.

Among the numerous emails asking me to events were several inviting me to my own talk. They'd booked the smartest room and there would be refreshments, wine, and canapes.

There were five from the admin team marked urgent to complete eight health and safety courses by last week. The final one was heavy lifting. I'd lifted nothing heavier than books for years – how was that urgent? The climate crisis was urgent, yet there was nothing on sustainability. Nothing on how to minimise one's carbon footprint in the cloud, show good housekeeping with file storage, turn lights and PCs off at the end of the day, etc. If I suggested it, I suspected it would be given to me to organise. I'd suggest it anyway. None on diversity yet either. I grinned to myself – that would be Percy's job now.

Two emails appeared from the DPP in quick succession. I'd read them later because I just realised I'd had nothing back from Obi. I couldn't afford to be complacent. My lecture was about to start and once I confirmed the assignment, I was committed. I emailed him a reminder. I turned to the DPP's email, but as I was about to open it, I saw a reply from Obi. That was fast. Too fast. It was an automated reply: *Obi Adebayo is no longer working for the university.*

The email didn't say why, just a list of alternative addresses to contact if you were a student on his modules. I stared at the screen, hand over my mouth. Was it my fault? Maybe he'd passed the ethics assignment and Colin checked it and realised what I'd done. It would be harsh to hold Obi responsible, but they were looking for excuses to get rid of staff. I should fall on my sword and take the blame. I stood up and paced around the small office. Percy and Marcel will find out I could have brought in thousands and chose not to, even while GG was terrified of compulsory redundancy. I could be suspended before I got the answer to the dilemma.

*

Lecture 9 Virtue Theory

Who do you look up to? Who do you think would always do the right thing? This could be someone you know, a famous person, historical figure, or even a fictional character.

Transcription note. I've been teaching this topic for decades. When I began, typical answers were Nelson Mandela, Mother Teresa, Dumbledore or various Star Trek characters – there were always a couple of Trekkies. Some suggestions hadn't changed much over the years: mums and dads were common, as were religious figures such as Jesus, Mohammed, or Confucius. Today, I worried that there were several influencers and YouTubers whose expertise seemed to be pulling off trendy haircuts and holding forth about stuff based on no expertise. They also dished up two mums and a dad, some sports stars and pop singers, and a Greta Thunberg.

So far, the ethical theories we've covered solved moral dilemmas by means of a rule that we can apply in all situations. Kant gives us the categorical imperative – act so that you'd wish everyone to act this way in similar circumstances. Utilitarianism tells us to consider the likely benefits and harms to all affected parties and then choose the option with the greatest ratio of benefit to harm to all concerned, remembering to include the more intangible outcomes too. Rawls theory of justice – what would you choose if you didn't know how you'd be affected by the decision? Next week we'll talk about indigenous theories such as Ubuntu, where the right action is the one that leads to the flourishing of the community and natural world we rely upon for our survival. Religious texts also give us a set of commandments to follow. But as you have discovered for yourself, no rule applies to all situations. Many found the last assignment difficult to answer for that reason. You either weren't happy with the conclusion you came to, or felt dissatisfied with the uncertainty, especially as many of you said that different moral rules of thumb led to different outcomes. Another approach that allows for complexity and variations in context is to ask yourself, what would a virtuous person do in this situation? How would a person of integrity, courage, wisdom, compassion and prudence behave? What would Jesus, my mum, Nelson Mandela do? This is the approach taken by virtue theorists.

Many moral philosophers have adopted a virtue perspective. One of the earliest we know of is the ancient Chinese philosopher, Confucius, who advocated five virtues: benevolence (ren), righteousness/honesty (yi) /honesty, propriety (li), wisdom (zhi) and trustworthiness/integrity (xin). There's much overlap with Plato, who emphasised four cardinal virtues: wisdom, courage, temperance and justice.

Following Plato comes Aristotle. In his best-known work, *Nicomachean Ethics*, he proposes virtues are acquired traits of character that enable a person to live the good life. 'Good' has a double meaning, as he equates moral conduct with a fulfilled life. Aristotle emphasises virtues are acquired in the sense that we're not necessarily born courageous, honest, compassionate, etc. We become this way through habit.

[Ref interdisciplinarity English]

In Hamlet, Shakespeare poetically illustrates this point. Hamlet is unhappy that his mother is marrying his murderous uncle and wants her to be more virtuous:

> *Assume a virtue if you have it not.*
> *That monster, custom, who all sense doth eat,*
> *Of habits, devil, is angel yet in this,*
> *That to the use of actions fair and good*
> *He likewise gives a frock or livery*
> *That aptly is put on. Refrain tonight*
> *And that shall lend a kind of easiness*
> *To the next abstinence, the next more easy.*
> *For use almost can change the stamp of nature.*

He's thus agreeing with Aristotle – we develop temperance by practicing self-control, become honest by developing a habit of honesty. Virtue theory therefore emphasises moral education, since virtuous character traits are developed in childhood. Virtue theorists also advocate we should avoid acquiring vices, such as dishonesty, injustice, and vanity.

Aristotle talked about the 'golden mean', proposing that most virtues are the optimal balance between two extremes. For example, courage is the midpoint between rashness and cowardice.

In the last reading, the Director of Public Prosecutions faces a dilemma – whether to prosecute or not? Your final assignment is to answer the question for him. Imagine this is an actual situation, and the DPP has employed this class as a team of moral consultants to guide his decision. Prosecute the old lady, and risk shutting down citizens' juries and their potential to make climate-friendly policies or go against your legal duty and don't prosecute and let a murderer go free. You're now versed in critical thinking. You have the wisdom and insights of the best philosophers in history to guide you. Take it seriously – your future may depend upon it.

Transcription note. One student raised a hand to ask if there was a right answer.

Your mark does not depend upon what conclusion you come to, but on the thoughtfulness of your answers. If you mean, is there a right answer in a philosophical sense, then perhaps if we had perfect knowledge, then there would be a 'right' answer. However, we never have perfect knowledge. You must commit to a decision on what you believe is the right thing to do. Not necessarily in some absolutist way laid down by God but based on what it is to be human and be part of society, drawing on notions of justice, virtues, and the common good.

Transcription note. Another student asked if they believed in God, should they go by the Bible.

Many religious societies have condoned war despite having commandments against killing. If you believe in God, then one way to avoid getting bogged down in rules and exceptions is to ask yourself what would God do assuming he/she/they loved everyone equally. The best you can do is to cultivate the virtue of wisdom. Do your research so your answer is as well-informed as it can be. Having informed yourself fully, and considered deeply, go forth, my dear class, and be wise.

*

I felt strangely serene walking into the canteen for lunch. It was up to the students now. I tried to hold on to the feeling before it gave way to the usual sense of holding back an oncoming wave. When I joined my colleagues in the lunch queue, they were in full protest.

'I won't have any modules left if they cut the small ones.'

'I did four module handbooks. Two days of my time wasted.' Percy scowled when Colin and Jenna walked past.

'What's up Percy?' I asked as we edged closer to the food.

'I requested training on diversity, and they said no.'

'I didn't know you cared?'

'I want to do it right. My wife works in Tesco's because she got it wrong. Pork chop and mash please,' he barked. 'Maybe she did or maybe she didn't, but they can't just give me a title and it's done.' He scooped up a handful of knives and forks and clattered them onto his tray.

'Has anything happened?' Marcel asked once we were at our table.

Percy looked around and leaned in towards us. 'It's Obi. He may get the sack.'

I tensed, but he wasn't looking at me.

'Why?' GG asked.

'Improper relations with a student.'

I relaxed.

'Oh là là!' Marcel's eyes gleamed at the thought of gossip.

'I knew they'd brought me in just to cover their arses, so I said getting off with students is against the rules for any lecturer, and there's no need to ask me as diversity sensitivity manager just because he's… Then I stopped in case I said the wrong word. Look at that football manager who got hauled across the coals because he used the wrong term, "person of colour" or something. What if the same thing happens to me?'

'It won't,' GG reassured.

'But what if it's Emily? We have history.'

'Don't you know?' GG asked.

'The identity was kept secret.'

'I may have seen her in his office,' I said.

He turned to me. 'What did she look like?'

'All I noticed was the shining look in her eye. Whoever it was, she had a genuine fancy for Obi.'

'It's a hazard of the job,' Marcel said. 'Students falling in love with you.'

'What?'

We looked at Marcel's jowly face, cheerfully red from too much wine.

'Oh yes. It's the aura of power, the French accent. It's knowing what the fuck I'm talking about.' Marcel twirled some pasta expertly on a fork and waved it in the air. 'It's irresistible. And not just to the girls. There's one for you, Percy.'

'Personally, I'd find the thought of someone fantasising about me creepy,' I said.

'I deal with it,' said Marcel.

'You're French,' said Percy. He looked distraught. 'Sorry.'

Marcel looked at him, alarmed. 'What has happened to you, my friend?'

'I'm compromised.'

I put my fork down. 'Go on.'

'The day before I found out about the student, I went to see Obi to get his advice in general, and he said it wasn't his job to teach me how not to be racist, then...'

Percy hung his head.

Marcel caught my eye and shrugged, as puzzled as I was. We'd never seen him like this before.

'What did you do?' GG asked.

'I did an Emily.'

'What?' we gasped.

'I said I was...' he swallowed, '"anxious" about getting it wrong because they'd provided no training.'

Marcel shook his head in disbelief.

'What did he say?' I asked.

'Something about a trope of white fragility.'

Percy did indeed look as fragile as I'd ever seen him.

'They want to get rid of someone. Part of me thought, it is against the rules and if it saves GG... is that wrong?' He looked around to check no one was listening. 'What if someone thinks it's a race thing?'

I pushed my plate away and sat back, ready to dispel wisdom. 'Are you seeking to know what's right or what's best for you?'

Percy attacked his pork chop, carving it into little pieces. 'I don't know. How should I know? No one to ask. You're not born knowing, are you? When my students get things wrong, I don't hector them for being fragile.'

We exchanged looks, remembering Percy bellowing "snowflakes" at the top of his lungs.

'Oh dear.'

'What?' he glared at me.

'I think you're in danger of white male backlash.'

'Don't backlash,' GG pleaded. 'Not for me.'

'I can save you.'

'Let Iris help.'

'They sacked him already.'

'What?'

'I got an automated email saying he'd left the university.'

'So it's not on me?'

'No.'

'Thank God.'

'It means you're safe for a bit,' Marcel said to GG. He picked up the water jug and poured the last few drops.

'I'll get some more,' I said. Once I'd filled it from the water dispenser, I turned with a full jug and bumped into Colin. I stepped back hurriedly.

'Iris?'

'Colin?'

'With reference to our conversation in the pub.' His face distorted into a smile. 'Come and see me in my office.'

My mouth was suddenly dry. Had Obi passed on my application?

'Before the end of the week.' Colin held my gaze as if he could hear my heart hammering. His smile was triumphant. 'We need to take this to the next level.'

GG noticed my white face when I returned to the table. 'What's up?'

'Colin wants to see me.' I sank into my chair.

Percy frowned. 'Emily must have escalated the magic mushrooms.'

My moment of relief was short-lived. This could be just as damaging.

'I might lose my job.' I gulped at my water.

'Only till they find out the truth,' GG said.

'If you're suspended, you won't have to do your marking,' Marcel said enviously.

'Is it too late to pass Emily, after all?'

'You said you'd stand up to her.' Percy lowered his eyebrows at me.

'This is how it happens.' Marcel threw up his arms. 'Next thing you know, Emily will be in charge.'

'I'd feel uncomfortable going against my professional code of conduct, but...' I tailed off, realising there was no way I could explain.

'They won't do anything before your talk,' said Percy. 'Not while there's a chance of donors.'

'He said before the end of the week. My talk is on Friday.'

I had two days.

I pushed my plate away. My stomach was churning too much for me to eat. 'Sorry I have to go.'

I ignored their protests and blundered out. I headed for the stream, chasing the possibilities around in my head. The immediate question was whether to pass Emily and be done. My gut instinct was no. Jenna and Colin may dance to the metric of money, but the colleagues I respected felt bound to a higher code. But if this escalated, the worst-case scenario would be my suspension with immediate effect. They'd get somebody else to mark the assignments and I wouldn't get to know the answer. It would all have been for nothing.

I sank down onto the bench under the willow, my mind still racing. Beyond my suspension, this could have consequences much greater than one student getting higher marks than she deserved. My niggling feelings of discomfort were a self-indulgence when set against such high stakes. There's me asking the students to consider not prosecuting a murderer to avert a climate crisis and I'm dithering over letting off one student. But Marcel was right. This is how we end up with people like Jenna and Colin in charge. Emily, the least competent of the class, is set to follow the path of advancement through manipulation and lies.

What would a virtuous person do? Someone with integrity, courage, compassion, and wisdom? Lee would suggest a Plan B in case the worst happens. Perhaps it was too late to pass Emily anyway. It looked like things had already escalated. Any suspension would be overruled once they knew the truth. Then again, Colin wouldn't be in a hurry. There was still a chance I'd lose access to the students for the rest of the semester. I must act before my meeting with Colin. The students had everything they needed to decide.

*

I toured the student hot spots for hours until I finally spotted Zoe coming out of the library with some others. I made my way over to her and muttered in her ear if she'd have time for a quick chat. Her friends waited, curious about what business I had with her. She waved at them to go on without her and followed me to the bench by the stream.

'Is everything OK?' Zoe asked. 'I'm supposed to meet Emily soon.'

'If I tell you something, you must promise not to tell anyone.'

'Why not?' She looked at me, puzzled.

'Our conversation about magic mushrooms got out. I've been accused of encouraging you to supply Class A drugs.'

Zoe laughed. 'That's ridiculous.' She saw my expression and stopped laughing. 'You don't think I said that do you?'

'No, but you did say you'd tell Emily about our conversation.'

'OMG! But—'

'That isn't why I wanted to talk to you,' I interrupted her.

'It isn't?'

'No, it's just if I get suspended—'

'Oh my God!'

'Listen, there's more at stake than my job.' I watched her expression change from outraged to anxious as I told her the situation. I waited for her questions.

'Will this affect my marks?' she asked.

'What? No. All you need to do is say prosecute or don't

prosecute – two words max. Your essay is separate, and marking is anonymous anyway.'

'I don't know.'

'You'd have ten days.'

She looked uncomfortable, and I began to appreciate how problematic my request was.

'Did you pick me because it's my fault you may get fired?'

'Of course not. I picked you because you always ask relevant questions. I trust you the most.'

Zoe was shaking her head. It hadn't occurred to me she'd say no.

I stared intently into her eyes. 'Zoe, there's too much at stake. I didn't choose you because of the magic mushrooms, but it is the reason I need your help.'

I held her gaze. Oblivious to the babble of students on their way to the bar, I spoke urgently. 'You're just my Plan B, in case I get fired. We oldies can't make such decisions. You have your future ahead; the stakes are higher for you.' She looked frightened. I realised I'd taken her arm and released my grip. 'I can't risk telling all the students. I promised confidentiality. It won't affect your marks, please, Zoe.'

'This is a lot of pressure,' she said.

I put my head in my hands. I should have thought this through first. Laughter reached us from the student bar. The sound was so poignant I wanted to cry.

I sat up and gestured towards the throng; downing drinks as fast as they could.

'We can't escape, Zoe. That submerged dread, a lack of hope for the future, an anxiety that won't go away.'

She stared at me with eyes like a frightened gazelle.

'But they… we… need to face that fear head-on and convert it into courage, into action.'

'You mean there's really been a murder in the citizens' assembly?' she asked. 'The one that's happening right now?'

'No, I made the story up.' I stood up to go. 'It's confidential - all we know is that it will be transformative. It will affect your futures.'

She got to her feet. 'Our futures depend on who makes the decisions and how. That's what you said.'

I gazed back at her, mouth open in shock. I'd said it myself in the assignment. *We were here debating climate solutions, but the greatest one of all is this process.* It wasn't personal carbon allowances; it was citizens' assemblies. That was Robert's dilemma. With the referendum just weeks away, a murder would tip the balance. The media would big it up for all its worth, even without encouragement from those who stood against them.

My phone rang. I saw who it was and let it ring.

'Professor? Are you OK?'

I shook my head. It was the DPP. I'd sent him the assignment. The one I'd sent to forty students.

What had I done?

My mind spun unproductively as I walked back, jumping from reconsidering the dilemma in light of my new understanding to thinking what to say to Robert. And what about Colin? I prayed he wanted to see me about the magic mushrooms. I'd thought being suspended was the worst, but if he knew about the consultancy... I imagined myself pleading with him not to say anything. He wouldn't give a damn about the consequences. He'd just see a chance to land me in it. My fuck-up could have constitutional implications. It would affect the outcome of the referendum. It could literally be the end of the world. I... Robert wouldn't get an answer to the dilemma.

Jenna waved at me as I passed her in the foyer. 'Practicing your talk? Excellent.'

I realised I was muttering to myself and hurried to my office. I shut the door and took deep breaths. Thoughts raced too fast to hold on to. If I could just calm down, maybe I could now solve the dilemma myself. I pulled out my phone, pressed the mic icon and paced up and down, addressing an imaginary class.

'I haven't yet covered Ubuntu so I'll start with that. The focus of Ubuntu philosophy seems to be on what values and behaviours would build the most resilient communities. Perhaps then, the Ubuntu philosopher would advise not to prosecute, on the basis that citizens' assemblies are more closely aligned with the Ubuntu mindset. Our current system is, after all, constructed to be divisive.'

I put on my glasses and checked what it had written. "Ubuntu" was written as "Bluetooth." I corrected it and continued talking slowly, perusing the moral philosophy textbooks on the shelves.

'Kant here is clear one should prosecute. The Utilitarians, though, would say the greater good is served by not prosecuting. Hobbes would urge us to obey the law, as it was devised to keep us safe. But who makes the law?'

I pictured Robert sitting in the front row, considering the question.

'The feminists would say it's mostly privileged white men who've never brought up children or learned to care. Why should their voice prevail when the stakes are humanity itself? Now we come to Machiavelli. You may ask, what is a moral philosopher doing with *The Prince* and *The Art of War* on her shelf? But he understood power. You ignore him at your peril. We don't know for sure that a murder would mean the end of citizens' assemblies, but Machiavelli would caution us that those with vested interests will certainly use that to undermine them. The question is how successful they would be. People are disenchanted with our current system, and excited by this new opportunity for a less divisive approach. The trouble is the media is increasingly in the hands of rich, powerful men who do well out of the status quo. Journalists too love the theatre of politics. Citizens' assemblies – calm, considered, thoughtful. There's no drama in that and drama sells news. It will be front-page headlines and this fragile new alternative will be destroyed before it takes root.

'But it's not just about the process, it's about the outcomes that result. Never have the policies we make and the need for a clear long-sighted approach been so vital. Peaceful environmental protestors are being put away for longer than violent muggers. We're in trouble. The checks and balances have been eroded. Yet not prosecuting would be another nail in the coffin for the system. Once law is compromised for political purposes, we're in even more trouble.

'Really, it is a knotty dilemma. The trade-offs are so finely balanced and on it hangs so much. You think the answer is obvious and then you think again and it's not. It's enough to drive you mad. Should there be a mental health warning for the students? Would they be driven mad? Maybe not if they don't know it's for real. But even hypothetical dilemmas can get you in their grip.

'What if they do find out it's for real? Robert knows now what the final assignment is. He's probably furious, but… maybe it wouldn't be such a bad thing if it gets out because of me. Hear me out Robert. With the amount of misinformation floating around, the fact I wrote a novella about it could work in its favour. We'll just say someone mistook the story for fact.'

I stopped and checked the transcript. Reading it through got me no closer to an answer. I thought my argument to Robert was solid though. I put an out of office on my email account for external contacts and put a block on Robert's number on my phone. Just in case.

*

Colin jumped up when he saw me at the door. 'Ah there you are. Come on in.' His voice was suspiciously genial.

I hesitated.

'Don't be nervous, it's just us.' He looked up and down the corridor to emphasise the point and beckoned me in.

He held the door open for me, and I had to squeeze past him. His hair smelled of mango.

'Sit down,' he gestured to a chair.

I sat.

He hovered by the window. He seemed nervous.

'Ahem,' he said.

'You wanted to see me?'

He went to sit down behind his desk, then changed his mind and pulled up a chair and sat beside me.

'I can't help but notice that you've been very friendly.'

I blinked at him, confused.

'I knew you couldn't be the one to ask.' He stood up again

and went to the window and looked out, his back to me.

'Er…' Was he accusing me of sucking up to get out of trouble?

'You're a moral philosophy lecturer and I'd made that comment about Marcel and Georgina.' A manicured finger tapped the windowsill rapidly. 'You wouldn't want to stick your neck out. Especially while you're in a vulnerable position.' He turned around to face me.

'I am?'

'Class A drugs.'

I sagged with relief.

He returned to sit next to me. 'We don't have that age gap. There's no power differential. I mean, yes, you're higher ranking academically, but I'm Assistant Dean, so that evens out.'

I couldn't help smiling. Thank God he didn't know about the consultancy. And what a palava about a ridiculous idea. Magic mushrooms. Honestly, you couldn't make it up.

'I thought maybe you liked me.'

'What?'

'I didn't respond in kind because, well, one worries about the appropriateness of workplace relationships.' He looked at me, his watery green eyes blinking.

'Huh?'

'But… well, you're not a student and neither am I.' He laughed. 'We are, ahem, both adults.' His face flushed red. He wrung his hands. 'And… I like you too.' He said the last words fast.

I gazed at him dumbstruck as he continued talking.

'You put yourself out there and I wanted to respond in kind. In answer to your question about the weekend. I've always wanted to try out the salsa club.' His hand tentatively placed itself on my knee. 'Maybe you could show me your moves?'

I jumped up. 'Gosh,' I said. It was a strange word, reminiscent of Enid Blyton novels and ginger beer and crumpets, but it was all I could manage.

Colin looked up at me with puppy dog eyes.

'No,' I added, to be clear. I muttered a few words about appropriateness and Colin was saying something about not telling anyone and I was saying I wouldn't, and then I escaped.

*

I reminded myself of my promise when I saw my colleagues in the coffee bar. They were laughing for once. I hastened towards them, already smiling.

'What's funny?'

'Percy's turned woke.' Marcel stepped back to make way for me in the queue.

'He's joined the campaign to change the definition of nature,' GG said.

Percy nodded. 'The dictionary defines nature as "plant and animal life, as distinct from man." Apart from being blatantly sexist…' He ignored Marcel's snort of laughter. 'It overlooks the fact that we ourselves are part of nature.'

'Does this mean you're now integrating sustainability and diversity and critical thinking into your teaching?'

Percy frowned.

'You've spoilt it now,' Marcel reproached me.

'How did it go with Colin?' GG asked.

We'd reached the counter, so I got away with a noncommittal reply.

Once we'd sat down with our coffees, conversation turned to my talk that evening.

'I'm looking forward to it,' GG said. 'Have you written it out, or will you just have notes?'

'Erm…'

'Jenna's hoping it will open a few wallets,' Marcel said.

'She's under fire for bringing you in,' Percy stirred sugar into his coffee. 'She'd promised you'd weave your magic like you did in the Business School to justify the expense.'

'I wonder if Obi will come,' GG said.

'Once you're fired, you're not allowed on campus in case you cause a scene,' said Percy. 'Kate couldn't even empty her own office.'

'That's shocking,' I cried.

'I leave menstrual products in my drawer to deter anyone

going in there,' GG said.

'Quite right,' Percy agreed.

'I feel sorry for Obi,' said GG. 'He's only a couple of years older than the students.'

'Do you think it was just an excuse to get rid of someone?' I asked.

'Yes,' said Percy. 'And there'll be more to come if your talk doesn't deliver.'

'My paper will be groundbreaking,' I promised.

'That will come too late to balance the books, especially now the Vice Chancellor has awarded himself a fifteen percent pay rise.'

'We lost thousands in pay to get a measly two percent,' Marcel cried. 'He already earns five times what I earn, and he wants more?'

'They told me to keep it under wraps, but why should I?' Percy said. 'That will teach them to make me management.'

'This calls for a strike,' said Marcel.

I gulped down the rest of my coffee before they demanded I join them.

'I'll leave you to it,' I said, standing up. 'I'll just work a bit more on my talk.'

*

1. Why moral philosophy is the most important subject in the world
2. My innovative approach 'storytelling for pedagogy'
3. How...

I was interrupted by a tentative knock. I looked up. It was Zoe. I jumped to my feet and opened the door. She looked stressed, her narrow shoulders bowed down by the weight of responsibility.

'Do you have an answer?' I waved her towards the chair.

'Sorry, I haven't done it yet. We have loads of assignments coming up.'

'Don't worry about it.'

'I'm so sorry…'

'It's fine. I don't need…'

'No, about Emily.'

'Emily?' I was immediately alert.

'She promised she wouldn't tell.'

'Tell what?'

'Don't be angry with me,' she pleaded.

I unclenched my teeth and tried to smile. 'What did you tell her?'

'Emily saw us by the stream and apparently it looked like we had something going on.'

'What?'

'She was teasing me about getting off with teacher, so I told her the truth.'

'You did what?'

'I had to. She'd started a rumour about us.' Zoe wrung her hands. She swore blind she wouldn't tell anyone that the dilemma was real, but…'.

My heart hammered in my chest. After fear came a burst of fury at Emily. I took a deep breath and exhaled slowly until I was able to speak. 'Then hopefully she won't.' I glanced at my watch – ten minutes to my talk.

Zoe's eyes welled with tears. 'I'm sorry,' she said again.

'It's fine.' I stood up. 'I have to go.'

She shuffled to her feet, and I followed her to the door. Her shoulders shook as she reached for the handle.

'Are you OK, Zoe?'

She turned around, her eyes wet with tears. 'You're cross,' she whispered.

I noticed how thin she'd become. My anger fell away and was replaced by a stab of shame.

I put a hand on her shoulder. 'Not with you.'

I was angry with myself. I'd been so distracted by Emily's antics, I hadn't seen what was under my nose.

'You're doing such good work,' she sobbed. 'And I got you into trouble and I couldn't even do this one thing.'

My protestations had no effect and all I could do was put

my arms around her as she cried it all out. Pressure to get a first. Being stigmatised for using an outdated term. Emily sneering at her attempts to be green. Guilt about her carbon emissions and fear of the future. Fear of famine, that paradoxically made it hard to eat. Torn apart by the mixed messages she was getting everywhere. A sense that there must be something wrong with her for feeling that way. I made soothing noises and patted her back. Did Emily ever stop to consider the consequences of her actions, I wondered. Her manipulations had cost Kate her job and made a conscientious and caring girl doubt herself. Because of Emily, this whole project was in jeopardy. Citizens' assemblies. My job, my chance to teach the next generation moral philosophy. To finally get my answer. Zoe winced and I realised I'd been patting too fiercely. I took some breaths to calm myself and changed to a gentle stroke.

Out of the corner of my eye, I saw Colin walk past, glancing in as he did so.

I stepped back quickly and held her shoulders.

'I'll refer you to counselling, but because they could help. Not because there's anything wrong with you. Quite the reverse.'

'I sometimes think the world would be better off without people.'

'Not without you, Zoe. You're bright and sensitive. The world needs people who care.'

I was now actively late. I checked her expression.

She wiped her eyes and looked back at me and tried to smile.

'It's alright, I'm OK now.'

'Are you sure?'

She managed a smile this time and nodded.

I ushered us both out of the door. I looked up the corridor. Colin was watching us.

Chapter 21

By the time I got to the hall, there were already people milling about. I headed towards GG and Marcel, who'd taken up position by the wine and canapes.

'Made it then?' said Marcel.

'Sorry, student problem.'

'We heard a rumour you've done an "Obi."'

GG looked at me reproachfully. 'We thought better of you.'

'Still good to know you're human,' said Marcel.

I laughed at the ridiculousness of the idea.

'You have a deep sorrow within.' GG gazed at me intently. 'And you're avoiding it with inappropriate behaviour.'

'For God's sake! I'd have thought you had more faith in me than that,' I protested.

'It's not true?' Marcel looked disappointed.

'No.'

Percy appeared with a woman I didn't recognise. 'This is my wife, Kate.'

'Rumour's not true,' Marcel informed him.

'Never thought it was,' said Percy. 'More of Emily's lies, I expect.'

'Percy says you're taking her on,' Kate said.

'I'm trying.'

'Her accusation was ridiculous. Yes, gender differences research can support discrimination, but we've also won the right for the menopause to be treated more sensitively. This blanket dismissal of research as sexist wasn't genuine. Emily did it to distract attention from the fact she'd learned nothing.'

'Kate made the mistake of trying to defend it rationally.'

'Yes, it was all my fault.' Kate rolled her eyes.

'My point is they're spineless with no academic integrity.' Percy beetled his brows at me. 'I hope that's going in your talk?'

'Um,' GG said. 'Don't forget, we need some donors. I want to keep my job. Oh, sorry, Kate. No offence.'

'No offence taken. When reasoned debate gives way to a slanging match, that's not a world I want to work in.'

'Percy said you work at Tesco's now?' Marcel asked.

'It's relaxing. I know what's expected of me.' Kate turned to me. 'But don't you give up. Don't let the Emilys of this world win.'

'I won't,' I promised.

We shuffled aside to make way for more people who wanted access to the refreshments.

A couple stopped when they saw GG. 'You're the one who put on the musical,' said the man. His tone was accusing.

'Yes, that's me,' said GG.

'It was very upsetting,' the woman said.

'Thank you,' said GG, and shook their hands.

The couple wandered off, looking puzzled.

Percy and Marcel exchanged a grin.

Percy's smile disappeared when we saw Jenna. She was in hostess mode, greeting the guests.

'Come on, let's get some wine.' He took Kate's arm, and they disappeared off before she reached us.

I noticed with concern that Colin was hovering at Jenna's side, trying to get her attention. She saw me, and they headed over.

'What a turnout!' She gestured towards the growing throng. 'Are you ready to blow our socks off with your talk?'

'Er, I think so.' I looked at Colin, who avoided my eyes.

'Wonderful. We have a journalist attending. He said he'll do a piece on it for the local paper.'

Colin muttered something to Jenna.

She glanced towards me, then turned back to him. 'Not before the talk.'

She checked her watch. 'Ready?'

I nodded and followed her towards the stage. My progress was slow as I exchanged pleasantries with ex-colleagues and prominent people from the local community on the way. Jenna was at the podium now, encouraging people to take their seats. She waved at me to join her. Finally, I was on stage, a glass of water next to the lectern. I scanned the audience while she introduced me. I'd hoped that Percy, Marcel, and GG would be at the front, but old habits die hard and I spotted them at the back. They grinned at me and I grinned back. Colin was in the front row, looking like he'd swallowed a lemon. I smiled self-consciously as Jenna completed an inflated list of my accomplishments. She returned to sit next to Colin, and I took my place at the lectern.

'Why moral philosophy is the most important subject in the world,' I began. I paused to acknowledge a few chuckles. 'You think I'm joking, but in my talk, I hope to convince you it's true. People are often surprised by how many students choose my courses. They assume that in today's cynical society, few care about ethics. But we love to make moral judgements. It's in our nature. Look at the popularity of shows such as *Love Island*. Judgements on right and wrong, fair, and unfair, are built into us. It's been shown on neural imaging that humans have parts of the brain that light up when they perceive injustice.'

I smiled at GG. 'Several animals that live cooperatively have also shown responses to unfairness. It's our ability to think in moral terms that lies at the heart of the success of humans as a species.

'And let me tell you something…' I paused for effect. 'I get forty percent attendance in my lectures. And that's all the way through.' Several colleagues gasped, impressed.

'Some are dismissive of philosophy, claiming it's self-indulgent, a load of dusty academics arguing over concepts and definitions. They claim it isn't concrete and important, like science, technology, and business. This is why such subjects receive investment at the expense of the humanities. As a result, economic growth is on a fairly continuous upwards trend, and if it isn't, we panic. Innovation proceeds at breakneck speed. We haven't learned how to operate one system before it's upgraded to another. Data expands exponentially. And it's not stored in some puffy white cloud, but huge data centres, belting out emissions, warming our planet. We run to keep up with the latest new technologies, then we upgrade our hardware to account for the new software and vice versa and on it goes. But what's the point of travelling very fast if we're rushing towards a cliff edge?

'With our intelligence and industry, we have amassed great power. Nuclear weapons, artificial intelligence. Our high levels of production and consumption have changed the atmosphere, and this has led to the climate crisis. Never in the history of humankind has wisdom been a more necessary virtue, and never has our culture been less capable of nurturing it.

'If we look at the history of civilisation, for centuries, morality was at the heart of society. Ancient philosophers debated the nature of right and wrong. Moral education was considered fundamental to creating a flourishing society. Religious institutions were centre stage for much of human history, with congregations expected to attend regularly to be reminded of the importance of ethical conduct. This was reflected in the arts. I shall illustrate this with the shortest and most profound poem ever written. It was just two words, and it was written by the self-proclaimed greatest boxer of all time, Mohammed Ali. It goes: *Me. We.*

'In that brief ode is the plot of every story and the secret of humanity's success and its failures. The tension between self and others lies at the heart of our political parties and our internal conflicts and relationships. Getting the balance right is crucial to our survival. We've aways known this and this is why throughout history, most plays were at heart morality tales. Stories had virtuous heroes and heroines winning out over the bad guys, or their own dark sides.

'Now it's fashionable to do the opposite. We used to teach the virtues. Now our culture promotes the vices. Gluttony, pride, envy, vanity, covetousness, lust. Our heroes are antiheroes – cynical, selfish, often ignorant. Think Homer Simpson and *Family Guy*. Restraint or temperance is seen as a lack of self-esteem. We no longer think it's appropriate to teach morality or values in schools and universities. We pride ourselves on being "objective" and "value free." But amorality, the ignoring of basic human values, isn't a neutral position. Indeed, it's deeply ideological, freeing students from any sense of moral responsibility. Our current economic theories promote self-interest as rational, and greed as good. Countries that have devoted themselves to the spirit of international solidarity are vilified…'

I paused, noticing Colin had put his hand up. 'Do you mean Cuba?' he asked.

'Yes.'

Colin looked meaningfully at the man next to him who muttered something that sounded like 'communist.'

I ignored him and continued. 'Our culture has taken an about-turn. The rapid expansion of information has led to a corresponding increase in misinformation. The profit-based algorithms of news and social media amplify extremist positions and idiocy over reasoned argument.

'Students today tell me they're all about their values. They sense this is wrong but are caught up in the treadmill. But where are we running to? If we don't buy enough, the economy collapses. If we do, we're destroying the planet we depend upon. We suspect we're part of a giant Ponzi scheme and we wonder when it will explode, but it's exploding now. I saw it in the shaking shoulders of a student who is so scared of the future, she can barely eat.

'Nothing in the world is as important as moral philosophy incorporating decoloniality (long overdue), critical thinking (essential), interdisciplinarity (nothing exists in a vacuum), and sustainability. Moral philosophy asks: what's the right thing to do? What are good goals to strive towards? What's best for society? What behaviours will lead to our flourishing and how do we encourage them?'

I paused for effect. I had the audience in the palm of my hand. Jenna was beaming. The big cheeses looked ready to get out their cheque books. I noticed a guy with a camera at the back filming the audience's rapt expressions. Colin looked miserable. I glanced at the clock. Time to move on to point two.

'My fellow lecturers were impressed by my forty percent attendance. I suspect this surprised those who are not in higher education, who no doubt thought that is a dismal figure. But students demand not just to be educated, but to be entertained. In my day, there were fewer distractions. Some swings down the recreation ground, table tennis, space invaders! Now there are computer games designed to be addictive, social media whose algorithms are programmed to keep us checking in, numerous streaming channels. We have a lot to compete with. So when our Dean challenged us to make our courses more entertaining, I went for it. I can't teach the most important subject in the world to an empty room. It's been reported that we're more likely to remember ideas couched in stories than in factual accounts, so I wrote a whodunnit, *Murder in the Citizens' Jury* and used that as a basis to discuss ethical dilemmas and moral philosophies.'

Colin put his hand up.

I laughed nervously. 'It's fiction obviously, but topical considering the upcoming referendum.'

He waved his hand.

'You have a question?'

'What do you say to the charge of tokenism?'

The accusation rang a faint bell.

'You have one gay person. One Asian.'

'That's the whole point of citizens' juries. They're chosen to represent the make-up of the society.'

Jenna frowned and muttered something to him and nodded at me to go on.

I was too experienced to worry about a spot of heckling. Colin had shown his hand and just looked an idiot. Probably no one had mentioned tokenism.

'Citizens' juries, or citizens' assemblies as they're more commonly known, are a great setting for a whodunnit and also provide an opportunity to showcase how we can upgrade our democracy.'

It was me. I'd mentioned tokenism in those research notes I'd posted. Those notes where I'd gone off on a rant. The autosave. I felt cold with dread as I tried to remember what I'd said. Colin must have seen it. The talk. Concentrate on the talk.

This time, Colin didn't bother putting his hand up. 'Is it your job to propose an overturn of our current democratic structures? We're not the politics department.'

'It's interdisciplinarity.' To my dismay, my voice came out as a defensive squeak. 'What would you suggest?' I countered.

'I suggest nothing. You're the one bigging up this module.'

The man next to Colin put his hand up. 'Isn't it naïve to suggest that you can teach moral philosophy and we'll all start playing nicely?'

'Not at all. Our cultural values, whether they reach us via education, the arts, religion, or politics, affect how we behave. Humans are a flexible species capable of heart-stopping bravery and altruism or greed and cruelty, dependent upon our environment. Often leaders appeal to the worst sides of human nature, our fear and our greed to win power, but the longest ever serving political leader Fidel Castro appealed to the best of our humanity. Our sense of solidarity.'

'That's because they couldn't get rid of him. They were brainwashed.'

'And we aren't? Think of the marketing and adverts we're exposed to.'

'That's different.'

'My point is that under such leadership, the Cuban people demonstrated great fortitude, courage, and compassion for the poor. When you talk to businesspeople in the UK about corporate social responsibility, they talk about the tensions between values and profit. But when I did research in Cuba and asked business managers about trade-offs between society and profit, they didn't understand what I meant. For them, the point of business is to serve society, so why would they hurt society through their business practices? They didn't even understand the question. But we're getting off topic.'

Had I mentioned the consultancy? I'd got personal. But how personal? I know it had ended with a fuck everyone. I paused to take a drink of water, trying to pick up the thread of my talk.

'Right,' I began slowly, 'my point is that we're more flexible than we think. Believing we're at heart all greedy and self-interested can become a self-fulfilling prophesy, as can believing we're honest and noble.'

I faltered, noticing Colin checking his phone. He was oblivious to Jenna frowning at him. He looked up at me with a nasty smile, then adopted a censorious expression. I froze. He put his hand up.

'Should we be taking ethical advice from someone who's broken every ethical rule?'

Jenna put her hand on his arm to stop him, but his indignation went beyond his sense of self-preservation.

'You talk to me about inappropriate relations, and you're accused of an improper relationship with a student.'

I exhaled with relief. 'There's a difference between accused and guilty. Check your facts before spreading slander.'

'And...' he looked back down at his phone.

My mouth went dry.

'Asking students to...'

I shouted over him. 'The thing is that the student who complained has learned that one can get ahead more effectively by lies and manipulation, by playing the mental health card than by doing any work.'

Colin tried to speak, but Jenna was shushing him, and Percy was shouting agreement from the back.

I continued quickly. 'That was one of the ethical dilemmas I set in my whodunnit. What responsibility do we have if we have mental health issues? How can we make allowances without at the same time encouraging free riders like Em— certain people to take advantage? I mean, does Emi— the student have anxiety or neurodiversity or is she just a bitch?'

There was a gasp of shock from the audience. That hadn't come out right.

Colin was smiling. I struggled for an out.

'Or is this just a semantic distinction, Wittgenstein would ask? How do we define neurodiversity?' I gulped at my water and blustered. 'I can see you're all looking at me with horror because I've said something inappropriate, and now I'm thinking, could

I claim neurodiversity to get me off? Then I think – hang on – maybe I am neurodiverse. I do, after all, enjoy pointless pedantry and can hold forth for indeterminate length on my pet topics. But by that token, the collective noun for a group of Aspergers would be academics.'

I caught a bark of laughter from the back, but most of the audience were stony-faced. Jenna looked horrified.

'I'm using this to illustrate my point about self-fulfilling prophecies. How do I even know if I'm on a spectrum when it would so clearly get me off the hook to claim that I was?'

A woman I didn't know put her hand up 'Are you saying that mental illness is made up?'

'That's not what I said.'

'It's what I heard you say,' Colin added.

'That's a right-wing trope,' said the woman.

'That's the thing, isn't it? First, I'm a communist, now I'm using Tory tropes. You're not listening to what I'm saying. This isn't considered debate, it's name-calling. This is the problem with our institutions – our political parties, the House of Commons, with two sides opposing each other. The courts, one there to defend the other to attack. They're all designed to exaggerate the differences between us, so we get to the point where we cannot debate the difficulties of developing systems that protect the vulnerable without also disempowering those or incentivising weakness. It's like in Risk, a game I play with my sons. One time I was playing Risk and I was red.'

'Figures,' muttered the man next to Colin.

'And it was suspected that another player had the mission: *Kill all red troops*, so suddenly my weakness protected me as no one attacked me.'

The audience looked puzzled. Colin looked back down at his phone and raised his hand again. I ignored him and carried on desperately.

'No, the thing is, the point is, what you believe about yourself counts. We incentivise people to be snowflakes. I'm not saying young people are all snowflakes, because that's just name-calling. It only makes things worse. It doesn't help us deal with the dilemma—'

Colin stood up. 'I have a question, ethics professor.'

I babbled on, no longer aware of what I was saying.

'My wife didn't like Risk, but she's dead now, so I play all the time just to prove to myself there's an upside. Ridiculous. Maybe it's good to show weakness and not repress your feelings. Look what happens when you do – look at me! Living proof. You go nuts. I'm not nuts.'

'Do you have permission from our ethics committee…'

'Back when things were hard, we taught ourselves to have a stiff upper lip and make the most of what we could do, not dwell on what we couldn't. Weakness is quite a powerful position, although it can backfire—'

'For using your students as unpaid consultants without their knowledge…'

'That's why this is so important. That's why moral philosophy can save the world.'

'On a topic as important as murder?' Colin's words sounded out loudly.

I stopped babbling, frozen like a deer in the headlights.

Colin smiled a victor's smile. Jenna looked ready to throttle him.

She took control and bounded up to the stage, all false jollity, and started clapping with everything she had. Like sheep, the audience began to join in.

Then everything was a blur. I stumbled off the stage. Percy, Kate, Marcel, and GG surrounded me.

'Good on you.' Percy slapped my back.

'What was that about murder?' Marcel asked.

I shook my head helplessly.

'I knew you were harbouring a secret sorrow,' said GG.

Chapter 22

As suspensions go, it was cordial.

'Let me begin,' Jenna said, handing me coffee in the good cup, 'by saying how sorry I am about your wife.'

I put the coffee down on the table without drinking it.

'Also, we must suspend you. Have a biscuit.' She offered me biscuits in a posh tin. I shook my head. 'It's not just you. Colin is suspended from his position as Assistant Dean. I don't know what got into him.'

'What does this mean in practice?' I asked.

'He'll still be in place as head of music, just not Assistant Dean. He was a disappointment anyway.'

'No, for me?'

'After a decent interval, you'd make a suitable replacement.'

'Huh?'

'I'm sure you'd do a great job as Assistant Dean, and you'd still teach a module or two.'

'I'm not interested in that,' I snapped. 'What does suspension mean for me now?'

'Emily will be gone next semester, and she's the only one kicking up, so you can come back then.'

'She failed my module. That means she'll be back for the resit.'

'Oh, we'll pass her, don't worry,' she said airily.

'I refuse to allow that.'

'You're suspended. You're not in a position to refuse.'

I gritted my teeth. Now wasn't the time to lose control. I regarded her office. Papers neatly stacked in the inbox and in files – tidy, unlike mine.

'What will happen to my office?'

'Security will escort you off once we're done, and someone will empty your desk and send anything you need onto you.'

'Escort me off?' My voice came out in a high-pitched squeak.

'Nothing personal.'

'What if I have personal stuff in my drawer?'

'And your email account will be suspended.' The next blow fell casually from Jenna's lipsticked mouth.

'But I won't be able to contact anybody.'

'Just till next term.'

'That's my only email address,' I cried.

'We do say that university facilities are for work only.'

I stood up, desperate to leave, then remembered the moment I did, I'd be escorted off the premises. I sat down again.

'What about my final lecture on cross-cultural ethics?'

'They can read the outline and associated reading online.'

'But they won't,' I cried. 'What about decolonising the curriculum?'

Jenna shrugged. She didn't care. It was on the official module outline and that was enough to tick the box.

'The talk went well.' She assumed a conciliatory tone.

'It did?'

'They liked your stuff about snowflakes. The Tory tropes went down well too… with the ones who had money to give anyway.'

I slumped back in my chair, trying in vain to remember what I'd said. Regardless, it didn't sound good. I felt myself sinking into despair and pulled myself upright. At least there'd been no mention of the citizens' assembly.

'How do I mark the final assignment?'

'Don't worry about the marking. This is good for you; you won't have to do it.' Jenna offered me the biscuits again. 'Go on, they've got chocolate on.'

I waved them away. 'I'm happy to do the marking. No one else could mark them fairly.'

'It's very conscientious, but that's not how suspension works.'

'I insist.' I adopted my firmest professorial voice.

'Tell you what.' She smiled again. 'The advantage of you setting the assignments throughout the course is that they already have eighty percent of their marks in hand. We could round it up to a hundred percent.'

'You can't do that.'

'We did way worse during Covid. This is the best solution.' Her expression was nauseatingly sympathetic. 'Take some time out. Enjoy the break.'

I stared at the congealing coffee helplessly as the implications hit me in stomach-churning waves. My standing up for my principles had achieved nothing. Emily would pass. I'd never find out what the students thought. I'd be denied access to the one thing that had kept me going over the last bleak year, my work. Fay was dead, the world was heating, and my efforts were as irrelevant as the sparks off the grinding wheel of history.

'I'm sorry. I know it's not fair.' Jenna stood up, indicating the meeting was at an end. She walked me to the door. I opened it and two security staff were standing outside. She touched my arm briefly with another sympathetic smile and nodded to them.

Without words, they escorted me off the premises.

*

I was deposited in the staff car park. There was still a chance. I looked around, stiff with the effort of keeping a dignified silence. I made for the coffee bar. Some students might choose this over the student bar, and some would be enough.

The security guards watched me as I took a seat by the door. I stared back and eventually they went. An irrepressible urge to scream gathered force. I pushed it back down. Soon they'd be told that there would be no final assignment. I had a few hours at the most. I'd hail them as they came in. 'What did you decide?' I'd ask cheerily. They'd probably not started it yet, but I find with decisions, the first answer is always the best even if you chop and change it a few times. 'What's your gut reaction?' I'd probe. They'd tell me, hoping to see if I approved or not. I wouldn't bother with following up why. I'd need to let them go and be ready for the next, as they'd all turn up at once when the lecture had finished.

Few attend lectures in the final week, I belatedly realised two hours and three cups of coffee later. I could look for Zoe in the library. I wasn't allowed in there, but would they even know? It would be embarrassing to be thrown out by security guards. But what's a touch of embarrassment against the future of the planet? The DPP needed an answer and I, Professor of Moral Philosophy, had no clue. I drank coffee and kept vigil.

GG, Marcel, and Percy found me still there at closing time.

'We looked for you everywhere.' GG sat down next to me.

'We heard about your suspension,' Percy said.

Marcel clapped his hands. 'Still, at least Colin's been knocked off his perch too.'

'Jenna will probably ask you to take over next term,' Percy said.

'She can forget it,' I growled.

'Maybe you should,' said GG. 'We wouldn't hold it against you.'

'Speak for yourself,' Marcel said.

'You complain about the leadership, but none of you want to do it,' GG said.

'I understand you're upset Emily got away with it.' Percy sat down next to me. 'But you did your best.'

'I can't stick around.' Marcel remained standing. 'I've two hundred assignments to mark in a week. You're lucky, my friend.'

No one understood.

'So, we've been wondering what Colin meant by the murder thing?' Marcel perched on the table. 'What have you been up to?'

'Not now.' Percy frowned at him, then looked at me, eyebrows raised.

The waitress came over and cleared my table with an air of purpose.

'Time to go home,' said GG.

'I can't.'

'Will anyone else be there?' she asked.

I shook my head and peered out of the window, still on the lookout for any of my students.

'Come back with me,' GG said after they'd muttered among themselves.

I remained seated.

'Go on,' GG urged. 'I'll show you the video of my musical.'

The waitress hovered, waiting for us to go.

Curiosity won out over self-preservation. 'Alright,' I croaked, and allowed myself to be led away. I turned back to see Percy and Marcel looking after me with concern.

Chapter 23

On screen, a giant thrashing paper mâché dolphin caught in a net emitted screeching sounds cleverly made, GG told me, by playing dolphins' whistles backwards mixed in with some feedback and a chorus of agonised sopranos. I had no strength to resist. For a while, a long while, I sat immobile, letting the horror unfurl before my eyes and ears. It was over eventually, but I remained sitting there, blankly staring.

So began my nervous breakdown, conducted by GG. I was hazily aware of her scrolling through her music, trying out various songs to 'draw out the grief.' She said, 'I'd kept it in too long.' I remained unresponsive. She uttered terms like 'modern Fado', 'Portuguese Fado *tradicionale* with extra *saudade*.' In the end, the sentimental keening got to me and I shouted at her to turn the bloody racket off.

'You're not ready.' She scribbled something in her notebook. 'We'll try anger.'

I jumped when the room was flooded with dissonant chords overlaid by angry screaming. The lyrics made little sense as they were interrupted at regular intervals by a buzz.

'What the hell is that?' I asked.

'Eminem. It's a lovely mix of raw anger and pain. You can tell he's using one to mask the other.'

'What's all the buzzing?'

'It's the clean version.'

'Right.' I let the music wash over me. Then, when he seemed especially hysterical, there was nothing but a continuous buzz.

A young lad bounced in. 'For God's sake, Mum, play the proper version.'

'I don't want you picking up the language.'

'I'm not going to be influenced by it, for fuck's sake.' He grinned. 'Whoops.'

'Sam, can you disappear for a while?' She cocked her head towards me with a significant look.

He glanced at me, and seeming to understand, sidled out of the room.

I wondered what he'd seen. Haunted eyes. Steel-plated armour with spikes holding in bloodied guts writhing around a hollow pit. I was a long way now from the chipmunk avatar with a mortarboard hat and goofy grin.

'Maybe he's right.' GG fiddled with her phone and the song began again on the speakers.

I was treated to the same anguished chords, this time with a barrage of swear words. It was better actually, and I felt blood returning to my veins. I tapped along with the beat and nodded my head and grimaced with each accusation. His woman had upset him – a lot. And his anger was righteous. I found my legs and stood up and paced. The next track played, with furious energy.

'I'm sorry about your wife,' GG said.

'What?' I stopped and looked at her.

'You said she died.'

'It was her own fault.'

'Really?'

'I didn't even want to go on holiday. She thought it might cheer me up. Cheer me up! As if I've no right to be unhappy. Bloody grief police.'

I paced, fuelled by the grinding bass and angry chords.

'We had a row because I wasn't cheered up enough. She accused me of wanting to save the world, like I had some saviour complex. Then she had the gall to suggest that if I genuinely cared, we wouldn't have got on a flight to this bloody island, which is rich as I never even wanted to go.'

The music was now classical, opera maybe.

'She wanted to postpone getting married when Lee died. Till I was "over it," she said. But I'd never be over it, so we went ahead. I suppose it was our honeymoon. She said, "I'm going for a walk." She was going to look for the ruin that was in some forest up a mountain. And I said, "Don't be bloody stupid, you'll get heatstroke. Look what happened to Lee." She didn't care.'

I spoke louder, struggling to be heard over a choir of sopranos and tenors. They sounded worked up about something.

'Well, she paid the price. She made me pay it too. After I'd just lost my brother.' I had to shout over the chorus, who were heading towards a crescendo. 'Fuck her!' I paced furiously in circles around the tiny living room.

'What you have to realise, GG, is that she went out to spite me. Passive aggressive, that's how I see it. She wanted to punish me.'

I fixed GG with a stare, and she nodded in sympathy.

'I thought I knew her, and I thought she knew me, but it was a mirage. She implied I was arrogant, grandiose, a hypocrite. I was no fun anymore. I thought we had a connection. I thought she was my fucking soulmate, for Christ's sake.'

The next song had a sorrowful air. I slowed my pacing and stood still.

'My first marriage was more we both felt ready for kids, and when they grew up well... With my second marriage, I felt I could be more authentic, not just follow expectations, you know?'

GG nodded.

'The boys liked her. She had this way of seeming to go along with everything but still getting her own way. I overlooked lots of stuff now I think about it. The way she wouldn't let us play games. She'd never say, "I don't fancy it, thank you, but you go ahead without me." No, she'd sabotage them.'

A lone voice soared in sweet melancholy, accompanied by strings.

'You're thinking that I've got this out of proportion, aren't you? You're thinking that if I felt so strongly, why didn't I say something? I don't remember feeling angry at the time. It's just looking back, you know?'

'I know,' GG said. 'I know.'

I slumped back onto the sofa and put my head in my hands.

'When's dinner?' Sam called from upstairs.

GG opened the door. 'Twenty minutes!' She turned back to me. 'Could you eat?'

I stood up. 'You go ahead. I should go home.'

She looked aghast. 'You're not ready. You haven't done grief.'

'GG, you've been great. But there's stuff I have to do.'

'You mustn't go home in the dark. Not if there's no one home.'

I sat back down. I needed to speak to the DPP, but maybe it was best to wait. What would I say anyway?

'I'll be in the kitchen. Are you OK here?'

I nodded.

She left, then a moment later, returned to fiddle with her phone, leaving me with some melancholy jazz. I lay on the sofa, eyes closed, arm hanging down to the floor. Something nuzzled my hand. I yelped and sat up. A white rabbit was checking me out. I'd thought I'd glimpsed it before but had written it off as a hallucination brought on by extreme woe.

Sam appeared. 'There he is.' He picked up the rabbit. 'This is Bun.' He stroked back the floppy ears. 'I wanted to call him Stu – stew geddit?' He grinned at me, and I smiled faintly, 'but Mum wouldn't let me.'

'Sam!' He turned as GG called from the kitchen. 'Here, he might let you stroke him. But you're not allowed to grab.' He placed Bun in my lap. 'Coming!'

I ran my hands over the soft fur. The music and the calm stroking encouraged the thoughts to come.

There's nothing so lonely as being misunderstood.

I understand that all right.

Then she'd left. I'd been in the pool, working off my feelings with a furious front crawl when I'd heard shouting. Smoke was coming from the mountains.

The rabbit squealed and jumped down. I grabbed for him, desperate for a small piece of comfort, but he looked at me reproachfully and hopped away.

My thoughts flailed about and settled on what I'd say to the DPP. I thought of his panicked emails, the trust he'd put in me, the reassurances I'd sent. *Trust me. Everything will be fine. I'll deliver the students' verdict.* If he was going to prosecute, he'd have to do it before the story got out. I must face the music. I unblocked his number. He was going to be furious. Worse than that, he wouldn't know what to do.

I sat up. I could pretend that it had gone OK and send him a fake verdict. For realism, I could say that it had sixty percent of the students behind it. But what would I decide? One discarded the rule of law at one's peril. It's a slippery slope. Then again, people use their power to escape prosecution through fancy lawyers and intimidation all the time. But two wrongs don't make a right. If you use the same tools as the bad guys to win, are you still a good guy? Or is it naïve to think good can ever prevail by playing nice when the rich and powerful have no such scruples?

What would Machiavelli say? Is it a bad sign that I'm turning to him? Perhaps not. He was the most pragmatic of the political philosophers. Aristotle, after all, placed practical wisdom as the highest virtue. One must think of the children. It had been Fay who'd found out that neither of my sons planned to have kids. I hadn't realised they were that worried about the future, but why wouldn't they be?

The mournful jazz was too much to stand. I jumped to my feet to turn the speaker off. The silence was worse. Faint sounds of clearing up came from the kitchen. Soon GG would be back. I grabbed my coat and made my escape.

*

I trembled as I put the key in the lock and let myself into the house. Not a home for months. My office had been my refuge from this space of memories. Now the high of a new job and saving the planet through moral philosophy had fallen through, there was just me.

I sat at my kitchen table and stared at the grubby floor. One more thing to do then I'd have plenty of time to clean up.

I texted the DPP, asking him to call me when ready.

The house was eerily quiet. 'Play Cuban salsa!' I commanded my speaker. The upbeat tempo was enough to get me out of the chair and sweeping. My hips moved of their own volition, and my sweeping became more rhythmic. I managed half the floor before the thoughts crowded in. I had no one to dance with. I'd never know what the students decided. Humanity is in crisis and there's nothing I can do. The music taunted me with its jollity. GG knew what she was doing, after all.

'Music stop!' I let the broom fall to the floor and collapsed at the table, head in hands.

The phone rang, breaking the silence. I picked it up.

'Iris. It's Robert. I'm glad you got in touch.'

'The thing is Robert,' I babbled, sitting up. 'The fact I wrote a murder into a story in a citizens' assembly will just muddy the water if it does get out. Who will even know whether it's true or fiction?' I paused, then continued when there was no reaction. 'Many people aren't even aware of the referendum anyway. If anything, this will put it on their radar, and that has to be a good thing because no one likes the House of Lords.'

'Don't worry,' he said.

'How can you say not to worry when…'

His silence was pointed. I bumbled to a halt, realising at last. Of course, he'd need deniability.

'I'm sorry,' I said.

'I'm the one who should apologise. I had no idea about your wife.'

'Huh?'

'I was at the talk.'

'Oh God.' I felt sick with embarrassment. 'There's so much at stake and I've let you down. I want you to know I feel as deeply about this issue as you do.'

'It's not your job to save the world.' His tone was conciliatory, patronising even.

'I never thought it was.' I got to my feet.

'Have I said something wrong?'

I fired a retaliatory shot. 'Obviously, I'm aware it's not all down to me. We all have a part to play. I'm not arrogant enough to think the fate of the world rests on my shoulders alone. Perhaps that's what you think, though?'

'I don't know what I've said to upset you, but I certainly didn't mean to.' He sounded puzzled.

'I just wondered what you're trying to say.'

'I meant I'd put a lot on you at a time when you're bereaved.'

'Apologies. I misunderstood.'

'No worries.' His voice was kind. 'I shouldn't have put my desperation onto you. It's strange, I couldn't even tell you what answer I was hoping for.'

'Same here.' I sat back down. 'It's good to chat. It's been lonely having all this on my shoulders.'

'I'd love to read your whodunnit.'

I sat up, alert. 'I'm suspended. I can't access my files.'

'Again, I'm so sorry. I feel responsible.'

'To be honest, the distraction was what I needed.'

'But you lost your job.'

'It's just a suspension. The issue is getting access to the students' decision.'

'Don't worry about it. Just look after yourself.'

'I'm nothing in the scheme of things. I'm sure we can think of something,' I insisted.

'It's not your problem. End of discussion.'

After some pleasantries back and forth, the call was over.

'That went well?' My voice sounded loud in the empty kitchen.

'Play Latin music… louder!' I picked up my broom, mamboed side to side with the music and swept it into a low dip.

'Cha cha cha!'

*

I looked at the bedside clock. 3 a.m. Three hours going over what the DPP had said. *It's not fair of me to put the fate of humanity on your shoulders.* That's what he meant. *It's not all on you. You don't have to fix the climate crisis to do right by your brother.* Or had that been Fay? That's what Fay had said.

I managed to text for help before the hot knives of grief stabbed through my armour.

*

In the car, GG selected a track on her phone before pulling off. 'I knew this would happen.'

A forlorn voice soared above a sorrowful chorus. Tears pricked the back of my eyes.

'Hold on till we get home.' She glanced sideways at me and turned down the volume. 'I'm glad you called. I was worried.'

We stopped at the traffic lights, and she wound her dressing gown tighter. 'You can't bypass the grief, but you want to escape.'

'How do you know so much about it?'

'My mum died,' GG said, setting off again.

I stared out of the window. My parents died too. Once you get to a certain age, you expect it. No big deal. It makes you appreciate more those who are alive. I met Fay just after Mum died. Fay's dead now.

'Sorry about your mum,' I squeak, desperate to get out of my head.

I don't know what GG says because I'm back in the nightmare. Fay's hurt face. I grasp at my seat belt, terrified.

'No... no... no...'

'Nearly there,' GG says.

I focus on the streetlights flashing by: one... two... three... four... We're picking up speed. I'm rocking in my chair, hugging myself.

GG hurtles around the corner.

I yelled at her that if she were dead...

I knock the image on its head and then, like the Whack-a Mole game, comes another, and another. The day we met. Fay storming off.

'I can't,' I gasp.

The car screeches to a halt.

A brief burst of night air and then I'm inside, wrapped in a blanket.

I hear GG muttering to herself while scrolling through her phone. 'Start here, maybe skip that bit depending, finish with *Lacrimosa*.' GG writes something in her notepad and presses *play*.

She picks up her baton with an air of reassuring certainty.

She pauses, then points left and bass voices begin, deep and dark.

Fay hadn't stormed off.

She gestures to the right. Sopranos raise their voices in hopeful joy, and a touch of mournful pleading. I picture arms raised in supplication. A soaring soprano sings something and my heart feels uplifted.

GG makes a note on her pad and turns up the volume.

I fall to my knees.

Deep male voices. Female voices mixing it up. They're not sure if they're singing together or in opposition. But they're all agreeing on something now.

I sway on my knees as she waves her baton left, eliciting a firm bass, then right, some agitated sopranos. The voices are building up to some great emotion, but I don't know what. I'm in Mozart's, or is it GG's hands?

I twist and writhe, unwilling to give up my control, but it has been taken.

I submit and listen.

It's got a bit magisterial. So far, so good.

Sinister notes but mostly upbeat in a classical music way. Sweetly beautiful.

GG raises her baton.

They all sing something loudly and wonderfully and agree hugely on the magnificence of it all.

The baton is jaunty, then waves more slowly, up and down, left and right.

There's a conversation going on between the sopranos and the baritones.

I sway unprotected.

Fay, sweet kind, lovely Fay. I'd got her so wrong.

I turn my head sharply away.

The music lulls and retreats.

She was my soulmate. She hadn't been gaslighting me.

I twist and turn as the music builds again.

A jangling burst of angry rap breaks the spell.

'Sorry.' Mortified, GG flaps at her phone and Mozart swiftly resumes control.

The male and female voices sing sweetly in unison, softly, then more insistent.

I turned on her when she was caring for me.

The voices lift and subside and lift once more.

We'd have worked it out in time.

The chorus builds.

She was trying to get away from me.

She was giving me space.

I was being a baby.

My heart fills with each rising note.

She'd waved her water bottle at me. *There'll be shade in the trees.*

The voices subside, a moment of silence, and the chorus rises in calm certainty, agreeing in great volume and then again quietly: 'Requiem.'

Smoke comes from the mountains.

I fall prostrate to the floor and weep.

GG looks down at me and makes a note in her pad.

'Amen,' sings the chorus.

They drag it out a bit, then GG twirls her baton and brings it to a close.

*

GG conducted my exorcism of grief like a grand impresario. I couldn't eat, but she kept me hydrated as I drenched box after box of tissues with my tears. She made regular notes in her pad. I was a challenging case apparently because there were layers of loss, one piled on the other, none of which, she admonished, had been properly processed. Sam popped in now and then with the rabbit for me to stroke when GG had to get on with other things. I met her new boyfriend Phil, who appeared with a cup of tea.

'I'm more of a drum and bass man,' he said to me after interrupting a particularly tortured Mongolian lament.

I recognised one track. Pink Floyd's *Great Gig in the Sky.* When the wailing began, she pointed her baton at me, and I wailed along.

'How did she die?'

'Er…'

The song comes to an end, and a new track begins. GG waits for an answer.

'She went out. I told her not to go out. It's her own fault—'

'We've done anger,' she interrupts.

I glance towards the speaker which is belting out an aggressive riff.

'Oh.' She checks her playlist, and the music abruptly changes to soft classical. She beckons me with her baton to continue.

'I accused her of not wanting me to change jobs because I'd lose money, but I knew that wasn't her issue.'

'Go on…'

'I think I'm done now, GG. I've done Fay, and Mum and Dad and Lee.'

'You were on holiday?' she prompts.

The music slows down. GG looks at me, waving the baton gently to and fro.

'Fay… she… Everything was perfect. Sun, sea, wine on tap. We were working it out. But she didn't understand that I needed to do something. Change my life. She said I didn't need to, as if I had something wrong with me, or it was a problem.'

I'm mesmerised by the baton going back and forth, like the lapping of the waves we'd watched from our balcony.

'She was frustrated more than angry. Or probably sad, because you can't talk someone out of grief.'

GG conducted the chorus which had sprung up.

'You can't sing them out of it either,' I add.

She shrugs and raises her baton and the chorus swells.

'We're on this idyllic island…' I choke and sink into the sofa.

GG lowers her baton.

'Which island?'

I look at her.

The music continues without her help.

She sees the horror in my eyes and I watch understanding dawn on her face. The news footage. Smoke, shouting, people running. Music crashes around us. Cymbals, a rising chorus, drums, cymbals again. Her arms hang limply by her sides.

I heave suddenly, choked with pain, my throat convulsing with sobs. I gaze pleadingly at GG and then towards the baton, and heave with another surge of pain. She picks the baton up.

She waits for a beat and then raises her hand. Cymbals, brass, drums accompany the movie in my head. The music screams its anger and fear and pain. Had Fay screamed? Or fallen silent, consumed by smoke?

GG's eyes are wet with tears. Her arms fly, conducting every crash and bang and sorrowful interlude. Her hair flies around her face as her arms move with precision, in time, trying to contain it all, trying to bring it to a conclusion.

The door opens and Phil bounces in. He stops abruptly, looking from me to GG.

'Gosh,' he says.

'Gosh,' I mimic, and suddenly I'm doubled up. Gasping for breath as my body shudders.

'Are you OK?' GG looks at me uncertainly.

I roar and shudder, belly aching. 'Gosh,' I splutter again.

'Gosh,' she ventures, and I crease up.

She flops on the chair, and I lean back on the sofa and we laugh hysterically, the music raging fruitlessly like an angry sea.

*

Jenna wants to see me. It can't be about the consultancy. That all got sewn up last year. I'd let a dilemma get to me, but we were over that now. No shame – it happens to all philosophers worth their salt. A few get destroyed, but most get over it and go on to live normal lives. Although mine was no hypothetical puzzle. What was the answer after all that? Stop! Don't go down that path. But what actually happened in the real world? Stop it Iris. The relevant question now is what does Jenna want with me? Colin looked delighted when he passed on the message so it must be bad.

'There's been a murder,' Jenna says.

I laugh to show her I'm over all that.

'It was one of your students.'

I feel a stab of pain. *Zoe? The music student. The mouthy lad.*

'The CEO of some fossil fuel company.'

My head swims. One of my early business school students? Perhaps a tutee. A poor reflection on my success as a business ethics lecturer.

I look at Jenna. Her gloss has faded and there's tension in every line of her face.

'It was your student who shot him. Zoe Jones.'

I reel in my seat and try to clear a path through a sea of fog. An image comes into focus. Zoe blowing the smoke out of her gun.

There's something wrong with that picture. The mist swirls and a new one emerges. She's dropping the gun to the floor, her thin shoulders shuddering with exhaustion and terror and grim satisfaction.

It still doesn't make sense.

Not poisoned?

Jenna shakes her head. 'Even so, Iris, a student from this university publicly cited you as the inspiration behind her crime.'

Ooh, this is intriguing. It's a good question in fact. How much responsibility do I bear for this murder? Perhaps I could set it for my students as a dilemma?

Iris you must be careful how this is framed. My counsel for the defence cautions me. I picture him – no make it a her – plump but competent, sitting opposite me in a prison cell. Don't be ridiculous, probably Zoom. But she'd be right. Is it a question of apportioning blame? Or will we end up discussing the morality of the assassination itself? It would depend on whether the jury were Kantians or Utilitarians. Most are one or the other whether they realise it or not. I'm summoning J.S. Mill to my aid when GG appears wagging her finger.

That's not the question you're really asking, is it?

She's right. The question is, am I guilty?

I'm ready now. I roll over onto my back and subject myself to interrogation.

You were being self-indulgent. Yes, you were sad, but you knew you could play the death card and just spew out hurt and anger with not a care where it landed.

Who is speaking? I search the court for Kant. Or is it Socrates?

I see a light glowing with a fierce benignity. God? No, it's not God, it's Good and Good understands and forgives.

I'm still wrong. I run through the sins and tick them off: no, no, no.

What's the greatest sin? The light pulses with the question.

Wrath?

Pride.

I'd never understood why pride was the worst sin before, but suddenly I do. I'm no better than anyone else. I behaved badly and the consequences were unexpectedly tragic. I must not be so fragile that I can't accept my part.

Andrew appears in orange robes and kindness in his eyes. *Your emotions will be as dark clouds scudding against a serene sky. Observe them and let them go. With mindfulness and practice you will become more skilful.*

The light – Good/God – pulses in agreement.

I dance on rapturous feet across a lush meadow towards Lee's shining face and he's so pleased to see me and laughs in his mocking way at my tears of joy, and I look round wanting more and she's there. Fay. Her hands are outstretched, and she understands. Of course she does.

The vision is so enticing but I don't believe it.

I stare out of the apartment window at the rock. The waves line up to wash over it. I'd gazed at it. Standing at the window, ranting under my breath about Fay.

Before going swimming.

Before I knew.

I roll into fetal position and pull the sheet up to my chin.

Regret washes over me. No longer tinged with acid. Just seawater. Clear and relentless and salty. Rhythmic now, lapping, not crashing. Lapping over and over in rhythm with my sobs. I cling to the rock.

I am the rock, and I withstand it.

*

On the third day, GG left me with Bun and some Leonard Cohen while she prepared dinner. Phil came in. 'GG wants to know if you're ready to sit at the table?'

He frowned when he saw the rabbit and muttered something about putting it in a cage. I found myself interested – could there be trouble in paradise? It was the first time I'd thought about anything other than my situation for weeks.

'This will help.' He fiddled with his phone, and a blast of energetic rock streamed from the speakers.

I stumbled to my feet and followed him to the kitchen for bean and sweet potato stew with herby dumplings. The smell of the stew made my mouth water, but for days, grief had tightened my throat too much to swallow anything more than smoothies.

The rabbit hopped into the kitchen and looked at me.

I reached down and scooped him up and held him in my lap, stroking his soft white fur.

'He's a therapy rabbit,' I smiled around at GG, Sam, and Phil. I picked up a spoon with my right hand, while my left stroked Bun, and tried a mouthful. It was delicious. Bun squirmed, but I didn't need him anymore. I set him gently on the floor and finished the stew.

'Marcel and Percy wanted to know if you'd like to go to the pub tonight?' GG said. 'I said you probably wouldn't be up for it—'

'But GG and me are off for a night out ourselves, so we wouldn't be around,' Phil said.

'You don't have to go,' GG said. 'I don't think you're ready.'

'I'll go.' There was something that had been obsessing me, and I needed their input.

Chapter 24

'Why didn't you tell us about your wife?' Percy poured me a large glass of Pinot Noir.

'I didn't want to be pitied, or avoided because people don't know what to say.'

Marcel looked uncomfortable, proving my point.

'How did it go at GGs?' Percy asked.

'We worried about you,' Marcel said.

'I met the boyfriend.'

'Dolphin man?' Marcel grinned. 'What's he like?'

'Smooth and smiley.'

'Doesn't sound like her cup of tea,' Percy said.

'Maybe opposites attract.'

'Enough of the preliminaries.' Marcel topped up my glass. 'What's this about a murder?'

'Hasn't word got out?'

'It's all gone quiet.'

'Hmm,' I mused.

'Colin is back to being Assistant Dean already,' Percy said.

'We suspect a cover-up.' Marcel's eyes gleamed.

'What did they do about my final assignment?'

'I can't believe you're still so conscientious.'

'Think about it, Marcel. The final assignment must be about the murder.'

'Ahh,' Marcel looked at me inquiringly.

I drank deeply from my glass, thinking.

He topped it up immediately.

'Well?' Marcel prompted.

'OK,' I said. 'Answer me this.'

'Go on,' he sat forward. Percy remained leaning back, seemingly indifferent.

'Why was the DPP so nice about not getting a result after harassing me for weeks, saying he needed it pronto?'

'DPP?' Marcel looked puzzled.

'Director of Public Prosecutions.'

'What result?'

'I can't say.'

'I think that boat has sailed now, don't you?' Percy gave up pretending disinterest.

'He said he felt bad about imposing on me when my wife had died, but you don't get to that position by being nicey nice.' I drank some more. 'I don't buy it. There must have been some kind of backroom deal.'

Marcel's eyes lit up. 'I told you. It's a conspiracy.'

'It's time to stop messing about.' Percy poured me some more wine and watched while I drank it. 'Tell us the whole thing and we'll swear to secrecy.'

'I'll probably tell GG,' Marcel said.

'The wine must have loosened your tongue by now.' Percy lowered his eyebrows at me.

'I took on a secret consultancy for the DPP to get student advice on whether he should prosecute a murder. No details. But if he prosecutes, it will have implications for the policies we make to avert the climate crisis and hence the future of humanity.'

'He shouldn't prosecute then,' Marcel said.

'He should do his job,' Percy said at the same time.

'But it's the young people who are most affected. Hence he wanted their input, but it had to be confidential so I couldn't pass it by the ethics committee or get their informed consent.'

'That wasn't so hard, was it?' Percy sat back.

'How smarmy was the boyfriend?' Marcel asked. 'Is it true she lets her rabbit run free?'

'Huh?'

'Are there droppings everywhere?'

'For God's sake Marcel, I just shared a dilemma about

the future of humanity, and you want to know about rabbit droppings.'

'Were there though?'

'No, it went in a tray.'

'Doesn't it nibble on wires?' Percy asked.

'She had them covered. Look, I only broke confidence because I need your advice. Forget it. I'll get off now.' I stood up, swaying slightly.

Marcel pulled me down, and I fell back into my chair. 'Come on Chip. Don't be like that.'

'We gave you our views. But you know, dead wife, and such. Sorry for being…' Percy tailed off, unsure of what he was sorry for.

'I don't want to talk about dead wives. I want to know why the DPP is no longer concerned about the results.'

'He probably decided for himself,' Marcel said.

I shook my head. 'No way. He could have done that at the start. Anyway, what would he decide? I've been going over and over it for weeks and I don't know.'

'Seemed pretty clear to me,' Percy said.

'And me,' Marcel agreed.

Percy nodded. 'Still, one would expect him to be more concerned, I agree.'

'I think he did a private deal with Jenna,' I said.

'Does he know her?'

'He was at the talk, so maybe it was then or shortly after.'

'Was there a consultancy fee involved?' Percy asked.

'Thousands, but I never took it.' I paused for someone to comment.

'The DPP probably offered Jenna the fee to get the students to do the final assignment after all,' Percy said.

'If you got suspended for not getting informed consent from the students for altruistic reasons, how bad is it to do it for private gain?' Marcel cried.

'Exactly. I was being altruistic.'

'We must unearth what went on,' Marcel declared.

'She probably reinstated Colin as Assistant Dean to keep him quiet,' I said.

'And she shut Emily up by giving her a first.' Percy's lips were a thin line.

'I was worried about a pass, and they gave her a first!'

'We can't let this corruption continue,' Marcel slammed down his glass, making me jump. 'We must bring the management down.'

'Hi.' GG appeared.

'I thought you were out with Phil?'

'She wanted to check you were OK.' Phil appeared from behind GG, carrying two pints of beer.

Percy and Marcel checked him out with interest as GG did the introductions.

I escaped to the ladies. We couldn't talk freely anyway now Phil was there. I sat for a while in the cubicle, grateful for the peace, trying to keep my mind blank. The silence quickly got too much, and I returned to the table.

'The question is, why it's gone quiet on the murder,' Phil was saying.

'We've got to break into Jenna's office, hack into her computer and find out what happened.' Marcel emptied the rest of the bottle into his glass.

'I agree,' I said, sitting back down.

'Really?' Marcel was thrilled.

Phil jumped up. 'Right. Let's do this properly. I'll sort the music.' He headed for the jukebox.

'Are you OK?' GG asked me quietly.

'Much better,' I said and downed my wine.

'I'll get the drinks.' Marcel set off for the bar.

Phil reappeared, accompanied by a seventies groove.

GG frowned. 'Is that funky jazz?'

'Yup.' He slid next to me and drew us into a huddle. 'Plan – find out what happened for Chip.'

I nodded.

'Great heist name. Why do they call you Chip?'

'It's because of my toothy grin.' I bared my teeth at him, and he recoiled.

'Right, erm. Step one, access to the office.'

'No one here has a key,' Percy said.

'I'm not even allowed on the campus.'

'And computers are password protected,' GG said.

Phil wasn't fazed. 'It's no fun if it's easy. What resources do we have to hand?' He saw Marcel returning with more wine and formed a square with his hands and peered through it. 'Freeze.' Marcel paused obediently. 'Marcel. Lecturer in history. Brings to the table French perspectives on toppling leaders.'

'Damn right.' Marcel refreshed our glasses and sat down.

'Then Micky here…' Phil pointed to Percy.

'I'm Percy.'

'Can I call you Micky just for this?'

'No.'

'We have Percy. Assets: an intimidating air. Anything else?'

'He's Diversity Sensitivity Manager,' I contributed.

'Really?' Phil looked surprised, then clicked his fingers, 'Right we can use that. What else?'

'The rabbit?' Marcel suggested.

'Love it.' Phil clapped his hands. 'Let's brainstorm, no self-censoring, and we'll come up with a plan.' The music had become especially groovy. He snapped his fingers after the beat. 'I'll start you off. Step one. Someone makes an appointment to see Jenna.' Next. He turned to Percy, who shrugged. 'Any diversity issues to discuss?' Phil prompted. The music continued and on the next beat, Phil clicked at me. I felt the pressure. Inspiration came just in time.

'Percy asks to see Jenna about diversity issues arising from my suspension.'

'Brilliant!'

The beat moved on, and we looked at GG.

'But you have to get Jenna out of the way.'

'My wife works at Tesco's,' Percy said. It wasn't his turn, but we weren't going to quibble.

'Go on.'

'She said one of the delivery drivers got shouted at by Jenna the other day for blocking her drive when he was delivering to her neighbour.'

'Excellent!' Phil went to slap Percy's back, then thought better of it. 'We're getting somewhere. Right. Jenna's blocked in and can't get to the office. Marcel?'

'We let the rabbit loose, and it distracts Jenna.'

'Isn't she stuck at home because of the blocked van?' I asked.

'Her assistant might be there.' GG said.

'She has another assistant?' I asked.

Marcel gave a Gallic shrug. 'She got someone in straight after suspending Colin. Even though he's back already, she keeps her assistant. Two people doing her job for her and there's me working sixty hours a week!'

'She's nice though,' GG said.

'You know her?'

'No, but I recognise the name. She wrote a nice comment about my musical on the feedback sheet. She was the only one who appreciated what I was trying to do.'

This time, I winced along with the others, remembering the tortured musical.

Marcel topped up our glasses, and Phil waited till the next beat then clicked his fingers and the plan came together.

Final plan, accompanied by a funky jazz soundtrack.

THE TEAM

Percy, Professor of English, with a grudge against Jenna. Tall, frightening eyebrows, hawk nose, and air of abstracted impatience. Motivation: to see Jenna brought low in revenge for how she treated his wife. Also properly riled by the fact she gave Emily a first. Resources: an intimidating air and a forensic knowledge of disciplinary rules and regulations. Most importantly, his position of Diversity Sensitivity Manager.

Kate, Percy's wife. The roper. Assets: knows the Tesco delivery driver. Her role: rope in the driver and persuade him to block Jenna in.

Marcel, Associate Professor in modern history. Motivation: to bring down Jenna and Colin and somehow, through indeterminate means, overthrow the system. Brings a revolutionary energy to the table plus ability to gesticulate wildly.

Bun, a floppy-eared white rabbit. Excessively cute. Bun is the bait. We're counting on him to distract Jenna's animal-loving assistant.

Freeze-frame on Phil's eager, handsome face. Phil's role is as chief strategist. He's in it for fun. He also thinks, wrongly, it's getting him in with GG.

GG, rabbit handler. The weakest link. She thinks it's a distraction from me facing my grief. She's also not happy about Bun being involved.

THE PLAN

Percy's shadow looms large, followed by Percy himself. He walks with a purposeful air to the entrance of the humanities block. He flashes his card, and the doors slide open to let him enter.

A Tesco's van pulls up outside Jenna's house. The driver walks away.

Jenna gets in her car, then sees she's blocked in. She walks up to the van. It's empty. She looks up and down the street.

Percy knocks on Jenna's door. The assistant lets him in. Percy uses his intimidating air to demand he see the file relating to my suspension. He tells her there may be dire financial consequences and lawsuit unless he sees it immediately. The assistant looks uncertain. She picks up the phone.

Jenna checks her watch and paces angrily up and down. She hears her phone and answers it.

They converse. Eventually Jenna nods.

The assistant sits at the desk and types in Jenna's password. She's in. She clicks on a file marked confidential. Percy moves to stand behind her so he can see. She isn't happy about it but doesn't dare to challenge him.

Jenna has found the Tesco driver and shouts at him to move. She gets in her car and drives off.

GG appears with Bun, saying she wants to talk to Jenna about using Bun as a therapy rabbit to calm stressed students.

The assistant is smitten and asks to hold him. GG goes to hand Bun over, but Percy shakes his head, and GG lowers Bun to the floor. The assistant crouches down to encourage the rabbit to come to her.

In one fluid movement, Percy takes her place behind the desk and scrolls down the file.

Marcel appears, sporting a black beret. He enters the room with liquid grace. He throws in a bit of Parisienne mime artist. He gesticulates wildly, scaring the rabbit into running off down the corridor.

GG and the assistant chase after Bun, leaving the room empty.

Moving with choreographed precision, Marcel rifles through Jenna's in tray and drawers, taking photos of documents.

Percy pulls out a memory stick and plugs it into the computer. He clicks download.

Jenna parks the car in the staff car park. Scarlet lipstick. Elegant in her Burberry jacket, handbag and shiny hair, she walks with clipped heels towards the humanities building.

Marcel and Percy hear the assistant cry that she's cornered the rabbit. The screen shows the files will take three minutes to download. Percy nods at Marcel. Marcel swivels on his heel and exits to do some more arm-flapping to scare Bun off again.

GG does not look happy.

Two minutes to download.

Jenna swipes her card at the doors, and they open smoothly. She presses the lift button.

Marcel and Percy hear GG and the assistant approach again with the rabbit.

One more minute to download.

The lift dings and Jenna exits.

Percy and Marcel hear Jenna talking with GG and the assistant.

Thirty seconds to go.

Jenna pauses to pet the rabbit.

Done. Percy pockets the memory stick.

Jenna and the assistant enter the room to find Percy sitting calmly in the chair, with no sign of Marcel.

*

1 a.m.

I laid back, closed my eyes and reviewed progress. We'd drunk, we'd plotted, we'd celebrated our brilliance. Then, after all that, no one was up for it. People care, but not as much as you need them to. Fay had cared. The room started spinning, and I threw up into a bowl GG had placed by my side.

2 a.m.

You may try to cheat grief, but she'll lurk, biding her time till she sees a way through. Like a river following its inexorable flow, diverted by boulders, carving gorges. Something blocks its path, creating placid pools, then bubbling up or veering around and ever down. I remembered an image I'd seen of an aerial shot of all the waterways snaking in twists and turns, branching and dividing, then coming together, obeying the laws of gravity anyway they could. Oxbow lakes, tributaries like tree branches, lit up in silver and gold. It was beautiful.

I thought I'd purged it all, but GG was right. You can't expect to get it all out in one go. Grief has its defences. It will seek diversions, put up barriers, but there's no escape.

2.30 a.m.

I'll ask the DPP.

He'll say no.

I'll schmooze him. We made a connection on the phone. Perhaps we could meet in person. I could charm it out of him.

Bit dodgy isn't it, moral philosophy professor?

Is it though?

What would Kant say?

If he knew how badly I need to know, Kant would understand.

He wouldn't.

Dinner, candlelight. Shared confidences. Then, when we're on the second bottle, I ask as if I don't even care. 'Were you pleased with what the students decided, Robert?' I'd sound unconcerned. No, I can't go straight to dinner. Too fast. I'll take him to that salsa club where Fay and I first…

340

Deep breaths.

…met.

I weep.

3 a.m.

Let's work it out. Imagine I'm the mouthy student at the back. Get in the zone. I curl a lip and picture a slight swagger. He'd chat it over with his mates, Socrates style. That's it. He'd pose questions and elicit the answer that lay within them. What is law? he'd begin. His friend would say something like the law is the system of rules and regulations that we as a society agree to because even though it's constraining, it benefits everyone to agree to the same set of rules. It allows business, private property…

Then Socrates/mouthy student would raise a hand to ask. Are you saying then that business and excessive wealth are things we should preserve at all costs?

If the friend had been paying attention to my lectures, he would disallow the question for pushing him into an unnecessarily extreme position and manipulating him into the answer that Socrates was looking for.

This is astute of the student because Socrates wasn't above this kind of manoeuvre.

Socrates would acknowledge the critique and return with an amended question.

'Would you agree at least that profit-driven business and private wealth are not good in themselves, but only deemed to be good things insofar as they contribute towards the wellbeing of both individuals and societies?'

'No one could reasonably disagree with such a claim,' the student would respond.

'What if business and private property only benefitted a minority of the population?'

'That may be true, but you must understand human nature. We like to aspire to these things, even if the system means we're likely to remain without. The dream is half the fun.'

'But that is irrational!' It's Spock from *Star Trek* speaking now.

'People like to dream.'

The music student pops up to say that our dreams are manipulated by marketing people and commercials. Look at the Professor's son's girlfriend, who in her twenties earns more in her marketing job than our beloved professor teaching us this amazing module.

I tip my mortarboard hat to the music student.

Socrates seems to have withdrawn, having got the students debating for themselves.

I struggle to keep control of the argument. It looked like we were getting somewhere but got off the subject of law and on to business and private property.

I look around, hoping Socrates would reappear, but he's gone and so have the mouthy lads at the back and the music student.

Smoke comes from the mountains.

4 a.m.

I don't care whether Jenna kept the money or didn't. I must know what the students said.

I can't get into her computer or password without a lot of prep work, and I need to know now. It's a long shot that a paper trail exists, but it conceivably might. Who knew what answers lay in her office in-tray.

I have no staff card to get in, but there'd be the problem of her locked door too. I'd have to use more physical methods.

*

The Pink Panther theme tune plays in my head as I tiptoe across the campus, darting from shadow to shadow, until I'm under Jenna's window. It's high.

Try the front door first. Just in case it's not locked. I dart across to the recycling area and crouch behind the wall, heart-thumping. I listen. A distant owl hoot, then a returning call. Were they mates? Fay would pick up on my thought immediately. 'Two owls hooting their lerv across the dark sky,' she'd say, and we'd giggle. We'd probably try hooting a bit ourselves, then stop remembering our age. I pause to weep, then pull myself together.

I have a suspiciously large amount of rope swathed around my neck. I hide it by the bins. The Pink Panther tune resumes and I zigzag my way to the front door. I look around, then stride up, willing the door to part before me. I try again. Still no. I picture the height of Jenna's window and try one more time in case it's third time lucky. It isn't. I hasten back to the bins to collect the rope.

Jenna's window is open. I'd have to gain purchase on the window edge in order to cling on and haul my way through. On the other side, I think there's a broad shelf which could take me landing on it. A good chance I'll destroy an in-tray or two. Worry about that later. There's one bit of small pipe stuck out. I swing the rope around my head, lasso style, and hurl it at the pipe. Cowboy music replaces the Pink Panther tune. Even when the rope lands, there's nothing to stop it sliding off. The moment I lean back, it would come off.

I need height. I return to the recycling area and wheel the sturdiest bin over to the window. I wipe off my fingerprints. Still too far off. I need a ladder. I don't have one. I dash back to the recycling area and pull out two more bins and try to wheel them simultaneously to Jenna's window. It doesn't work. I do them separately. I observe the window and the bins before me. I turn the blue one on its side and there's a crashing of glass. I should have checked which was glass first. Never mind. Let's not dwell on past mistakes. I move it forward and push the green bin behind it upright, creating a step. It's now easier to get to the same point I was at before. More height, more bins. Grateful for our recycling policy, I arrange the differently coloured bins before me into two steps.

Now to climb. It might just hold my weight. I'm not as young as I used to be. Then again, I do Pilates. Not for ages, though. Focus on the task. In there, somewhere in that room, probably, will be the answer. Once in that room, I may find out and then everything will be all right.

*

I came to on GG's sofa aching all over. I pushed down on my arm to sit up and yelped with pain.

GG appeared at the door. 'How are you feeling?'

'Why do I hurt everywhere?'

'Security found you in a recycling bin underneath Jenna's window. It looked like you'd fallen from two storeys up.'

'Huh?'

'You confessed your intention to break into her office.'

'Oh.' It was coming back to me now.

'I'm the last person you called on your phone. They have to report it but they didn't want to lock you up, so we came and got you.'

'Thanks. Can I have some water?' I gasped.

GG nodded and left.

I formed a steeple with my hands under my chin and took some deep breaths to get into character.

I called the DPP's number.

He answered.

'Robert, hello.' I gushed, then kept my voice casual. 'I wondered what the students said?'

'Said?'

'I assume you came to a private deal.'

'I can't say.'

'Maybe we should meet?'

'I don't think that would be appropriate.'

'I know a place where they do Latin…' I sighed. 'Right.'

I replaced the phone.

GG returned with some water.

'Have you got any painkillers?' I croaked.

'I've run out, but I need to nip to the shops anyway. Will you be OK till I get back?'

'I'll rest.'

'Good. Shall I put on some music?'

'No.'

'I'll tell Phil and Sam to leave you in peace.'

I nodded. The moment I heard the front door shut, I dialled the DPP again.

'Hello, again.' His voice was wary.

'I want to know what happened.'

'Like I said—'

'No, I'm not having it. How do I know that you and Jenna haven't done some private deal where she pockets the money rather than putting it into faculty funds?'

'Are you accusing me of something?'

'Yes, I am, because secrecy tells its own tale.'

'Look—'

'No, you look. If I don't find out what went on, I'll kick up a fuss.'

'I didn't think you were that kind of person.' He sounded disappointed, but I didn't care.

'It's what I've been driven to.' I slammed my fist down and cried out in agony.

'Are you OK?'

'No, I'm not. I tried to break into Jenna's office. That's how much I need to know.'

'Oh!'

'Oh, indeed… well?'

'Let me think.'

'No. Tell me now.'

'I spoke to Jenna. Your attendance sheets showed twelve students who'd attended all your lectures, so we approached them and asked for their private vote on the decision. It didn't count towards their marks, but we gave them a share of the consultancy fee.'

'That's a good solution. I was worried that concern about marks might distort their answer.'

'Interesting. I was concerned that they could say anything for the cash and not think about it.'

'Don't worry about that, Robert. Once you're trained in moral philosophy, you can't help but think in moral terms.' I sipped some water, and lay back, phone cradled to my ear.

'I'm glad you think so.'

His voice was now warmer.

'What about the confidentiality aspect?' I asked.

'Non-disclosure agreements all round.'

'Right, so you got your decision then?' *Softly, softly, catchee monkey.*

'Thank you for your help.'

'I'm glad if it all came good. Erm, what did they say?'

'I can't tell you.'

'I deserve to know, don't you think?' I kept my voice calm. Nothing.

'OK, cough when I say the right thing. They voted to prosecute?'

'I'm not—'

'They voted not to prosecute?' I waited, but all I got was a heavy sigh. 'Ah! Was it an even split? Cough if yes.'

'Please don't push me. It's not fair.'

'It's messing with my mental health.' These were Emily tactics. But it was justified. 'Look what I've been driven to. Drunk and disorderly, breaking and entering, sleeplessness, obsessive thoughts.'

'I'm sorry.' His voice was firm. 'Please don't call again.' There was a click and my last chance to know went.

Unless I could get back on campus and ask the students. Once I got my job back.

GG returned with painkillers. Marcel, Percy, and Phil trailed in her wake.

Marcel held up a bag of pastries. 'GG made us feel bad for getting you drunk.'

Sam appeared at the door. 'Any for me?'

'There's the rabbit!' Marcel cried as Bun hopped in the room after Sam. 'Here, Bunnybun!'

Percy fell to his knees. 'Come to Daddy,' he crooned, holding out a croissant.

'Not for the rabbit.' GG wagged her finger.

He remembered himself and sat down. 'How are you?' He handed me the croissant.

I waved it away, then winced. I pulled up the sleeve of my black jumper to examine it. 'There'll be a massive bruise soon.'

'They thought you'd broken it to begin with,' GG said. 'They were debating whether to call an ambulance or the police.'

'Bloody stupid thing to do,' Percy said.

'Impressive though.' Marcel perched on the arm of the sofa. 'Did you find anything out?'

'I didn't make it into the office, but there's been no dodgy deal.'

Marcel looked disappointed. 'How do you know?'

'I just spoke to the DPP.'

GG looked at me, surprised.

'I only hope it hasn't cost me my job.' I wriggled painfully so I could sit upright.

'Here you go.' GG handed me some paracetamol.

I swallowed a couple with some water. They watched me, concerned.

'Why are you all quiet?'

'Jenna knows,' Percy said.

'Already?'

'I told her it was our fault, getting you drunk, but...' he shrugged.

'What?'

'You're properly fired this time.'

'No!' I put my hand over my mouth, feeling like I was going to be sick.

'Shall I get you a bucket?' GG asked.

I shook my head and waited. The arguments ran through my head in the familiar order. Why did I always start with Kant? I tried them backwards. It made no difference. The nausea subsided, leaving a dull despair.

'She's gone quiet,' muttered Percy.

Marcel leaned over and poked me.

I put my head in my hands and shook my head. 'I'll never know the answer to the dilemma.'

GG sat down next to me.

'I don't think I can live without knowing.'

'It's not that, though, is it?' she said.

'I've lost everything,' I wept. 'My job, my brother... Fay. Now this.'

Percy stroked his chin.

GG put her arm around me. 'The worst is over now.'

Marcel patted me on the back, and Sam handed me Bun to stroke.

My phone buzzed. I opened it up to see a message.

Tom: check this out

I clicked on a photo of a bodywash label. I zoomed in to see the wording.

Your skin, your bills and our planet all love it when you wash in tepid water. Not too hot and not too long.

I smiled.

'What's that?' asked GG.

I showed her the photo, and she shrugged, bemused.

The phone buzzed again.

Tom: what do you think?

I knew what he was really asking. He'd found his Fay, and he wanted me to love her as much as he did.

Me: Add Martha to the family chat.

Tom: ☺

Me: Come around Sunday, all of you. I'll cook something nice, and we'll take a new photo.

GG moved her arm. I watched nervously as her finger hovered over *play*. She looked at me questioningly. I nodded, and she brought me home with Leonard Cohen, *Dance Me to the End of Love*.

Afterword

Were you unsatisfied with that ending? I was. I couldn't come up with an answer. Readers, I'm desperate. I need your help. I know, let's call it a final twist. Yes, dear readers, *you* can be my citizens' jury. Scan the QR code or see my website to have your say. You can also see how others voted.

Please share your views, because this was a story within a story within a story, and much of it is true. The real me is a professor of sustainable business. Just in case my university takes this act of love the wrong way, I'll not be specific about which one. It's irrelevant - we're all part of the same system and subject to the same pressures.

I love my university. On job satisfaction scores, I give them a full five out of five. Yes, you do provide 'supportive work environments' and I can see you're trying when it comes to sustainability and yes, I'm sucking up, because I'm nervous. My partner warned me against writing this. 'Don't bite the hand that feeds you,' he cautioned. 'What if you're sued or trolled, or sacked?' What he doesn't realise is that when you're scared about climate change, everything else pales into insignificance. My thinking is, even if all of that happens, it's not as scary as the extinction of humanity.

So, I haven't censored myself. But, like many academics, I suffer from imposter syndrome. A good academic is supposed to focus, but I've gone wide, not deep. My first degree was in politics with economics, and later I did an Open University Science Foundation course. I worked for a social enterprise, a medium-sized business, a multinational corporation, and then self-employed. I became a working mother, then a single mother on benefit. Wagging fingers helped me to realise I was the cause of the degeneration of modern youth, and responsible for rising crime, the balance of payments deficit, for cutbacks, for the extinction of the red squirrel and for wasps.

My mental health remained sound, and I returned to university to do a PhD in psychology. I ended up by accident in the Business School and given the job of teaching business ethics and sustainability because I'd nagged them about recycling bins. So, perhaps I'm a bad academic, but who better to have an aerial view of how all the bits of the jigsaw fit together?

It's a big question. What do we do when our systems are leading us to extinction? It's hard to see how to get from where we are now to where we need to be – every bit of the jigsaw needs to be part of a new picture. But we don't have to know everything. All we need to know is the next step and to take it. And just keep going in a different direction. I've suggested some of those steps – the big ones – the ones that are hard for politicians to talk about.

And why the citizens' jury? Because our political parties are like divorced parents offering sweeties to get their children to like them best. But I don't want to be the book equivalent of broccoli (substitute your most hated healthy food as appropriate), but rather pizza on a crispy base with lots of toppings. So, if you liked it, please share your opinion on the ideas and tell others about the book, and rate me with lots of stars!

You may be interested to know that the whodunnit, *Murder in the Citizens' Jury* is available as a standalone play. It is royalty-free for amateur and student theatre companies to stage. Professional theatre companies should go via LazyBee Scripts. It also features as a short story in the anthology *No More Fairytales: Stories to Save*

Our Planet. An extended version of the whodunnit is called *The Assassin*, available in audio, paperback and eBook. Lastly, the wildlife gardener, Needles, and Samudrapati also appear in my first novel, *Habitat Man*. See my website for details: **https://www.dabaden.com/**

Acknowledgements

Thank you to the Thrutopian work-in-progress group, Portswood Writers club and my beta readers for giving me feedback and encouragement throughout. Thanks also to Chris, my lovely partner, who exhibited endless patience with the artistic temperament that presented itself when my writing wasn't going well, and the exuberant (to the point of annoying) ebullience when it was. Thank you also to all those working to make a future we'd be proud to leave our children and grandchildren. And last, but definitely not least, thank you to all those who supported a beta version of this book via Kickstarter. I hope you consider it worthwhile.

www.ingramcontent.com/pod-product-compliance
Lightning Source LLC
Chambersburg PA
CBHW030527190726
48283CB00006B/1798